WHAT THE PRESS SAYS /

"KILLING PLATO is a fast-paced a
through Thailand's spook culture. Needham has forged a powerfully sardonic portrayal of a business professor whose marriage is on the rocks and who is suddenly faced with an impossible series of choices, none of which is attractive." — *Thai Oasis*

"Jake Needham has a knack for bringing intricate plots to life. His stories blur the line between fact and fiction and have a ripped-from-the-headlines feel." — *CNNGo*

"Asia's most stylish and atmospheric writer of crime fiction. In between the lines of his plot, Needham's provocative views about Asian culture jump at you from almost every page." — *The Straits Times* Singapore

"What you will not get is pseudo-intellectual new-wave Asian literature, sappy relationship writing, or Bangkok bargirl sensationalism. This is top-class fiction that happens to be set in an Asian context. As you turn the pages and follow Jack Shepherd in his quest for the truth, you can smell the roadside food stalls and hear the long-tail boats roar up and down the Chao Praya River." — Singapore Airlines *SilverKris* Magazine

"Needham certainly knows where a few bodies are buried." — *Asia Inc.*

"Thrillers written with a wry sense of irony in the mean-streets, fast-car, tough-talk tradition of Elmore Leonard. Needham has found acclaim as one of the best-selling English-language writers in Asia."
— *The Edge* Singapore

BOOKS BY JAKE NEEDHAM

THE BIG MANGO
THE AMBASSADOR'S WIFE

The Jack Shepherd Crime Novels
LAUNDRY MAN
KILLING PLATO
A WORLD OF TROUBLE
(Spring 2012)

KILLING PLATO

KILLING PLATO

JAKE NEEDHAM

Marshall Cavendish Editions

First published in 2003 by Prime Crime Press
Text copyright © 2012 Jake Raymond Needham

Cover art by OpalWorks Co Ltd

This edition published in 2012 by Marshall Cavendish Editions
An imprint of Marshall Cavendish International
1 New Industrial Road, Singapore 536196

All rights reserved

No part of this publication may be reproduced, stored in a retrieval system or transmitted, in any form or by any means, electronic, mechanical, photocopying, recording or otherwise, without the prior permission of the copyright owner. Requests for permission should be addressed to the Publisher, Marshall Cavendish International (Asia) Private Limited, 1 New Industrial Road, Singapore 536196. Tel: (65) 6213 9300, Fax: (65) 6285 4871. E-mail: genref@sg.marshallcavendish.com

The publisher makes no representation or warranties with respect to the contents of this book, and specifically disclaims any implied warranties or merchantability or fitness for any particular purpose, and shall in no events be liable for any loss of profit or any other commercial damage, including but not limited to special, incidental, consequential, or other damages.

Other Marshall Cavendish Offices: Marshall Cavendish International. PO Box 65829, London EC1P 1NY, UK • Marshall Cavendish Corporation. 99 White Plains Road, Tarrytown NY 10591-9001, USA • Marshall Cavendish International (Thailand) Co Ltd. 253 Asoke, 12th Flr, Sukhumvit 21 Road, Klongtoey Nua, Wattana, Bangkok 10110, Thailand • Marshall Cavendish (Malaysia) Sdn Bhd, Times Subang, Lot 46, Subang Hi-Tech Industrial Park, Batu Tiga, 40000 Shah Alam, Selangor Darul Ehsan, Malaysia.

Marshall Cavendish is a trademark of Times Publishing Limited

National Library Board, Singapore Cataloguing-in-Publication Data
Needham, Jake.
Killing Plato / Jake Needham. – Singapore : Marshall Cavendish Editions, c2012.
p. cm.
ISBN : 978-981-4361-26-2 (pbk.)
1. Crime – Fiction. 2. Thailand – Fiction. I. Title.
PS3564.E228
813.6 -- dc22   OCN760050656

Printed in Singapore by Times Printers

For
William Clifford Needham

*Who probably would have insisted
that every word of this is true.*

I miss you, Dad.

THE BEGINNING

PHUKET

"The only player who wins is the one who owns the game."
— Meyer Lansky,
mobster

One

IT STARTED THE way a spy story should start.

On a misty night in Phuket.

In a little bar.

I recognized him the moment I walked in. He was standing by himself holding a tiny stainless steel telephone to his ear. His body was turned slightly away from me, his elbows resting on the polished teakwood of the bar top, and he was gazing out toward the ocean, nodding his head occasionally, listening more than he was talking.

Plato Karsarkis could not be here of all places, casually leaning on a bar in Phuket, a resort island off the eastern coast of Thailand. There was plainly no way in the world that could be.

Yet, just as plainly, there he was.

Anita and I had spent the day exploring. A warm drizzle began to fall late in the afternoon and we decided to call it a day and have an early dinner at a place called the Boathouse that is right on the sand at Kata Beach. I parked the jeep and Anita stopped at the ladies room while I went in to get us a table. The girl at the hostess stand said she would have one free in fifteen or twenty minutes, so I left my name and went into the bar to wait.

The bar was laid out in the shape of a large C. Plato Karsarkis was leaning on the side nearest the ocean and so I took a stool on the opposite side that offered both a striking panorama of the Andaman

Sea and the opportunity to stare at Karsarkis without being too obvious about it. I ordered a Heineken and wondered what Anita's face would look like when she came out of the ladies' room and saw him.

Anita had designated this trip to Phuket as our official honeymoon and she had been obsessive about making every detail of it perfect. We were both well into our forties—I somewhat more so than she—and we had been living together for almost two years before we got married so I really couldn't understand why she was making such a big deal out of having a honeymoon now. Still, Anita had her own ways, and I had absolutely no intention of risking a quarrel by volunteering my thoughts on the subject.

Anita was an artist, a painter whom European art circles had clasped to their bosom as a harbinger of what the critics were calling a new wave of post-feminist revisionism, whatever that meant. Even when her behavior didn't make complete sense to me, I always tried to remember Anita had an ability to see the world in ways that I could not, ways that were continually surprising and frequently illuminating.

I shifted my weight on the stool to cover the turn of my body and glanced back toward Karsarkis.

He seemed taller in person than he had on television, although I had always heard it was supposed to be the other way around. His forehead was quite high, his nose rounded in that way that some people call Roman, and his curly gray hair trimmed closely against his skull. He wore a tight black T-shirt tucked into black chinos cinched with a narrow belt, also black, and although he must have been in his fifties, maybe even older, he looked pretty able-bodied. The whole effect was something like a cross between Giorgio Armani and Richard Nixon.

What he did *not* look like, leaning nonchalantly there on the bar and talking into his shiny little telephone, was the world's most famous fugitive. Which was funny, because that was exactly what he was.

"That was a Heineken," the bartender said, breaking into my reverie. "Right?"

I pulled my eyes away from Karsarkis. "Right," I said.

The bartender placed a tall glass still frosty from the cooler on a blue and white striped square of cotton and poured my beer from the familiar green bottle. When he was done, he rapped the empty bottle smartly on the bar top, nodded, and walked away.

As soon as he did, my eyes flicked right back to Plato Karsarkis.

Karsarkis had put away his mobile phone and now he was just leaning against the bar on his forearms, doing nothing in particular. Oddly, it almost seemed as if he was looking at *me*. So unlikely was that it took several seconds for me to register that he really *was* looking at me. Worse, when Karsarkis saw the realization of it in my eyes, he raised his right index finger and shook it at me in an exaggerated gesture of mock irritation.

I flashed a hasty and very self-conscious smile and, thoroughly embarrassed, looked down at the bar. I was reaching for my glass again just to have something to do when Karsarkis called out to me.

"Are you Jack Shepherd?"

My first thought of course was that I had misunderstood him. Plato Karsarkis could not have been speaking to me or have the slightest idea who I was. So I kept my eyes forward and said nothing.

"Pardon me," Karsarkis called out again. "You're Jack Shepherd, aren't you?"

Christ, I *had* heard him right. Karsarkis *was* speaking to me, and he *did* know who I was. With what I'm certain was a look of utter bafflement, I lifted my eyes back to Karsarkis. He shook his finger at me again, and then he stood up and started around the bar.

Holy shit.

The world's most famous fugitive was not only alive and well and having a drink at the Boathouse in Phuket, right now he was walking straight toward me, his hand thrust out to shake mine.

Two

I TOOK KARSARKIS' hand. What else was I going to do? We shook.

"I'm Plato Karsarkis."

"I know."

Karsarkis nodded quickly and lowered his eyes. The man's brief acknowledgement of his notoriety seemed to me to contain an element of genuine embarrassment and, for a moment, I almost felt sorry for him.

"May I?" Karsarkis pointed to the stool to my right, the one at the end of the bar right up against the wall.

"Of course."

He pulled the stool out and sat down, pushing himself around until his back was to the wall and his face turned toward mine. The bartender had returned when he saw Karsarkis reach for the stool and stood waiting quietly.

"Campari and soda," Karsarkis said without looking at him. "And Mr. Shepherd will have another…"

His eyebrows lifted into a question.

"No thanks," I said. "I'm fine."

Karsarkis nodded slightly at that, but made no comment. After a moment his eyes slid off mine and we sat there together in what was for me an uneasy silence until the bartender returned with his drink. After that, Karsarkis took a deep breath and let it out again and I thanked heaven that it looked like he was finally going to say *something*.

"It's so beautiful here," Karsarkis said very softly. "I could stay in this place forever."

I didn't know exactly what I had been expecting Karsarkis to say, but it certainly wasn't that.

Turning my head, I looked where his eyes were pointing.

The Boathouse was at the edge of the beach in the back of a deep cove on Phuket's west coast. Just on the other side of floor-to-ceiling shutters propped open to the ocean breeze, a wide swath of nearly white sand lay nestled in a U-shaped fringe of spindly palm trees. It was almost dark, but not quite, and a haze of pewter streaked with shards of mango yellow filtered tentatively over the beach like a feeble fog. A lone woman with a black sarong wrapped around her bathing suit—foreign, I thought, but at this distance I couldn't quite tell—ambled along the surf line, kicking her bare feet through the shallow water.

I glanced back at Karsarkis. He didn't seem inclined to say anything else. I should have waited him out, I know, but I didn't.

"Look," I said, taking a deep breath and plunging in, "I'm sure I would remember if we'd met, and I don't think—"

"We've never met. I just recognize you."

"Recognized me?"

"Modesty bores me, and false modesty bores the *shit* out of me. You're well known and I'm sure you realize that. I've even seen pictures of you in magazines and newspapers. That's why I recognized you."

While it was true I had once been associated in various ways with some big players in international finance, I certainly didn't think of myself as well known. I might be recognized here and there by a few people who moved in similar circles, but I really didn't think those circles included the sort of people who breathed the rarified air where Plato Karsarkis flew.

"There aren't many other Americans living out here," Karsarkis went on before I could figure out what to say. "So I just thought I ought to introduce myself."

"There are a lot of foreigners living in Thailand," I said.

I realized how petulant that sounded as soon as the words were out of my mouth, but I couldn't call them back.

Karsarkis didn't seem to notice or, if he did, to care.

"Yeah, but it's mostly Europeans and a few Australians," he said. "Not that many Americans in Thailand. Why do you think that is?"

"I gather most Americans must like it well enough back home."

"Then you still think of the States as your home?"

It was starting to sound like we were going to have one of those expatriate conversations I'd had a thousand times since I'd been living in Thailand. Modesty might be what bored Karsarkis. Expat conversations were what bored me.

"Look," I said, "I live in Thailand now and as far as I know I'm going to keep living here. I really don't know what else to tell you."

"There's something I've always wondered about," Karsarkis continued as if I had not spoken. "When Europeans or Australians live in a country that isn't their own, nobody thinks a thing about it. But when Americans chose to live in another country, people keep asking us why."

"A lot of people seem to think that Americans who live overseas are on the run from something."

As soon as I said it, I went silent and looked away in embarrassment. Karsarkis chuckled at my discomfort.

"Don't worry about it," he said. "You didn't offend me. We Americans need to stick together."

Karsarkis' ethnic brotherhood routine was wearing a little thin. I was pretty sure I'd read once he had been born in London of an Irish mother and a Greek father and had only become an American citizen when his lawyers advised him that it was in his best financial interest. On the other hand, I knew Karsarkis had a pretty compelling reason for not being in the United States right then and I figured it would be indelicate to delve too deeply into the whole issue of nationality and residence so I said nothing.

Karsarkis smiled. At least I think he did.

"Can I call you Jack?" he asked.

"If you like."

"Excellent. Then you should call me Plato."

That'll be the day, I thought to myself, but I just nodded.

Karsarkis took his hand away from the Campari without having drunk a sip and folded his arms across his chest.

"Everybody says you're one of the smart guys, Jack. A first-rate legal mind."

"I don't practice law anymore. I just teach."

"Yeah, I heard that. At Chulalongkorn University up in Bangkok."

"That's right."

"Pretty good place?"

"Pretty good."

"But you don't teach at the law school, do you?"

"No. At the Sasin Institute. I teach international business."

"You speak Thai that well?"

"My Thai's okay, I guess, but the courses at Sasin are all in English so it doesn't really matter."

"You like teaching?"

"Yes, I like it a lot."

What in the world was going on here? Karsarkis sounded like a man interviewing me for a job. I tried to read his eyes, but they had gone flat and in the fading light there at the end of the bar I could see nothing in them at all.

"You ever miss the action?" he asked.

"Action?"

"That stuff you used to do. All the hotshot stuff that made you famous."

I didn't know how to respond to that, so I didn't say anything at all. Karsarkis didn't look like he really cared. Abruptly he stood up and gave the room a quick scan.

"I enjoyed talking to you, Jack, but I've got to go now."

I glanced around to see if something had spooked Karsarkis. There were a few people scattered around the bar, a few others in the dining room, but as far as I could tell there were no SWAT teams storming the place. Maybe Karsarkis just couldn't think of anything else to say to someone he barely knew and was tired of keeping the conversation going. I could certainly understand that.

I stood up, too, and we shook hands again.

"I'll stay in touch," Karsarkis said.

I had no idea what *that* meant so I just nodded mutely.

When Karsarkis turned away and started for the door, a well-built, sandy-haired man of nondescript appearance and indeterminate age stood up from a chair by the wall and fell into step next to him. Almost immediately two other men materialized from somewhere and closed up behind them, covering their backs. I had assumed Karsarkis was alone. Now that I thought about it, I realized how foolish that was of me.

After Karsarkis had gone, I just sat on my stool looking straight ahead, too stupefied by what had happened to do anything else. Then all at once an incredibly vivid memory swept over me.

I had been about seven or eight. My father and I were driving somewhere, although I have long forgotten where, in his green and black Buick, a racy two-door model with a line of chromed ports down each side of the long, narrow hood. I sat on the bench seat next to him as straight and proud as my tiny stature would permit.

We were on a two-lane asphalt highway passing through dense stands of tall pine trees. A short distance ahead, a silver and white Greyhound bus pulled out to pass a tractor-trailer and shifted its whole mass into the lane directly in front of us. My head was half turned toward the road and half turned toward my father and, in the same instant I saw the bus barreling down on us, I also saw my father's face. Although only a child, I somehow sensed that he and I were both sharing the same inexplicable thrill of onrushing menace.

As the bus drew closer and the leaping white dog on its nose grew to a terrifying size, I experienced without really knowing what I was feeling that eerily heightened state of awareness that comes from proximity to something truly dangerous. For just an instant, my father and I were frozen together, bonded to one another by our common helplessness.

Then bus cut back into its own lane, whipped past us, and we were spared. The moment ended. I would never feel that close to my father again.

There at the bar of the Boathouse, looking at the stool where Karsarkis had been sitting and the drink he had abandoned, a feeling came back to me that was just like the one I'd had on that long-ago day: exhilaration intertwined with onrushing ruin. It was a strange reaction, I know, and at the time I dismissed the feeling that flooded over me then as nothing more than a freak misconnection of a few synapses of memory run amuck. It was only later, looking back on everything that happened afterwards, that I could see how wrong I had been.

The feeling that came over me that day in Phuket had not been a memory at all.

It was a premonition.

Three

"YOU LOOK AS if you've seen a ghost, my darling." Anita glanced at the Campari and soda on the bar. "Is that for me?"

"You can have it if you want," I said. "Plato Karsarkis ordered it, but he didn't drink any of it."

I inclined my head in the direction where Karsarkis and his entourage had just disappeared.

"He just left," I added.

Anita sat down on the stool Karsarkis had vacated and crossed her legs at the knee. Arranging her skirt, she pushed the Campari to the back of the bar and studied me closely.

"What happened while I was gone, Jack? You're staring at me like I just turned into Whoopi Goldberg."

I was still trying to decide how to explain what had happened in such a way Anita might actually believe it when she unerringly zeroed in on my uncertainty. But then she jumped to the wrong conclusion.

"Which old girlfriend of yours is here, Jack?" Anita craned her neck theatrically around the room. "Are you going to introduce us?"

Before I could muster a response to that, the hostess walked up carrying two red and gold covered menus.

"I have a table for you now," she smiled.

Then the hostess caught the set of Anita's features and stopped smiling. She glanced from Anita to me and back again.

"Do you still want a table?"

"Of course we do, my dear." Anita patted the girl on her forearm. "My husband is just trying to come up with some kind of a story to explain away his slightly sordid past."

When I stood up, the hostess backed away and shifted her eyes around the room as if she were searching for help, then turned and scurried off toward a table on the far side of the dining room. By the time Anita and I got to it, the hostess had already abandoned two menus and fled back to the safety of her station by the door.

"Nice going," I said as I pulled out Anita's chair for her. "Now that girl probably thinks I'm a pimp on holiday."

Anita said nothing. She turned her full attention to the menu and appeared to lose all interest in whatever might be on my mind. She appeared to, but I knew better. Anita was a master of the technique used by all the best television interviewers. She asked a question, and she waited for the answer. Then after you had answered whatever she had asked, she waited some more in complete silence, which naturally got you to thinking you hadn't given a very good answer or perhaps you had left something out.

That was when you started talking again, usually without thinking very much before you did, and while you were rambling around trying to find something new to say that would satisfy her enough to get her to go on to the next question…BAM!…that was when she got what she needed to kill you.

I knew all that, but I decided to take a chance anyway. What I had to tell Anita was just too good to wait any longer. I pushed my menu to one side and took a deep breath.

"Please listen to me carefully, Anita, because I'm being completely serious here. I did not see an old girlfriend. I saw Plato Karsarkis. I walked into the bar while you were in the bathroom and he was standing there talking on a mobile phone. I sat down and a couple of minutes later he walked over, introduced himself, and took the stool next to me."

Anita didn't react. She didn't even look up from her menu.

"It's true," I said, thinking to myself how pathetic I sounded when I did.

There was a short silence.

"I know I had lobster last night," Anita finally said, "but Phuket lobster is so wonderful. What do you think? Should I have lobster again?"

"Anita, I am telling you exactly what happened when you were in the bathroom. Plato Karsarkis was here."

"And he walked over and introduced himself."

"Yes."

"To you."

"Yes."

"Did he say why?"

"He told me he had heard of me."

Anita finally looked up from her menu, but her expression remained neutral.

"He'd heard of you?"

"Yes. He said he'd heard I had a first-rate legal mind."

Helpless before the male compulsion to brag to an attractive woman, actually to almost any woman, I ventured a bit further down that road before I could stop myself.

"He said I was pretty well known in certain circles."

Anita looked back down again at her menu.

"Then perhaps I *will* have the lobster," she said. "You certainly ought to be able to afford it."

"Anita, I'm telling you I just had a conversation with Plato Karsarkis right over there at that bar."

I gestured pointlessly across the room and I felt suitably foolish as soon as I had done it.

"I thought he was supposed to be dead," Anita said, glancing up again, but only with her eyes.

"Some people think so," I said, "but obviously he isn't."

"And what is Plato Karsarkis doing in Phuket?"

"I don't know. He didn't say."

I had no difficulty at all understanding Anita's conviction that I was pulling her leg. Plato Karsarkis was the most notorious international corporate criminal since Marc Rich had scammed a billion dollars and rented the Prime Minister of Israel to lean on his buddy Bill Clinton to get himself pardoned. What's more, Karsarkis was famously secretive, legendarily elusive, and so stories had it, constantly attended by a squad of Irish bodyguards widely said to be provided by the military wing of the IRA for which Karsarkis did a few favors from time to time in return. Anita knew very well that a few months before, Plato Karsarkis had vanished off the face of the earth and hadn't been seen by anyone since.

Why *wouldn't* Anita think I was joking? Even I was having a little trouble believing this had really happened.

Anita was still studying the menu when I sensed rather than heard someone behind me. I turned my head and sure enough a man was standing there. A moment before he had not been there, and now he was, and since we were sitting all the way across the dining room, a rather long way for anyone to walk unnoticed, I couldn't imagine where he had come from.

He was youngish with a common and forgettable face, and he was dressed in a short-sleeved white shirt with dark trousers and a nondescript blue tie. He made me think of a mid-level bureaucrat at some government agency.

"I'm Mike O'Connell," the man said, not offering his hand. "I work for Mr. Karsarkis."

I shot Anita a triumphant glance, but she took her time looking up and missed it altogether.

Keeping his hands clasped together in front of him, the man went on in a soft voice that carried the hint of an accent I couldn't quite place.

"Mr. Karsarkis would like to invite you to join him for dinner tomorrow night. If you're available, he'll send a car."

Before I had a chance to say anything, Anita did.

"This is utterly ridiculous." She glared at the young man and poked her forefinger in my direction. "He put you up to this and I want you to know right now I'm not going to fall for it."

"No, ma'am, he didn't." Mike O'Connell didn't seem particularly surprised by Anita's skepticism. "Mr. Karsarkis asked me to come in here and invite you to dinner."

"Plato Karsarkis?"

"Yes, ma'am."

"*The* Plato Karsarkis."

"He's the only one I know, ma'am."

"And you seriously expect me to believe Plato Karsarkis is here in Phuket and he sent you to invite us to dinner tomorrow?"

"Yes, ma'am. Mr. Karsarkis just spoke with your husband. Hasn't Mr. Shepherd mentioned it to you yet?"

Anita lowered her menu, closed it with exaggerated care, and put it down on the table.

"I think he might have said something to that effect, now that you mention it."

"Yes, ma'am."

I finally tagged the accent.

"You're an American," I said. "New York? Boston? Around there?"

The young man summoned up something close to half a smile, but I thought he seemed a bit careful about doing it and didn't answer me.

"We'd be delighted to join Mr. Karsarkis for dinner," Anita said all of a sudden.

I turned my face away from Karsarkis' emissary and raised my eyebrows to get Anita's attention. "I'm not sure—"

"I am, Jack."

She flicked her eyes back to the young man.

"What time tomorrow, Mr. O'Connell?"

"Would eight o'clock be convenient? If you'll tell me where you're staying, we'll send a car for you."

"And where are we having dinner exactly?"

"At Mr. Karsarkis' home, Mrs. Shepherd. He is having several people around tomorrow night and thought you and your husband might like to join them."

Anita nodded slowly. "You'll appreciate, of course, I'm still having a little trouble with all this."

"Yes, ma'am. Apparently."

"I hope you'll excuse me saying so, Mr. O'Connell, but it is difficult for me to accept that Plato Karsarkis is quietly living in Phuket and giving dinner parties."

"Yes, ma'am. But that's where he is and that's what he's doing. Where shall I tell the driver to pick you up?"

"Never mind about that," I cut in.

I tried to strike a tone cool enough to leave no doubt at all as to my view of Karsarkis' invitation.

"We're not going," I said. "We have other plans."

"We *are* going, Jack." Anita's voice was low, but her tone was just as cool as mine had been. "I'd like to go."

"Can we talk about this later, Anita?"

"No." Her faced mimed a smile, but I didn't see any humor in it. "We can't."

I looked at O'Connell. He was expressionless. I felt trapped. I gathered I was.

"Okay," I finally said. "But no car. We'll drive ourselves."

"Then may I fax a map to your hotel, sir? That would probably be best."

Not only was Plato Karsarkis living in Phuket and giving dinner parties, he was faxing out maps to his house.

"That's fine," I said. "We're staying at a hotel on Cape Panwa called the Panwaburi. I don't know the fax number, but—"

"You'll have a map by tomorrow morning, sir."

O'Connell took a step back from the table and inclined his head politely.

"Enjoy your dinner," he said. Then he turned and walked away across the dining room.

I looked at Anita without saying anything. She looked back at me with an expression I couldn't read.

"Well," she finally murmured, breaking the silence. Then she retrieved her menu from the table and resumed studying it. "Shall we order?"

Four

THE NEXT MORNING I was sitting on the deck of our cabin drinking coffee and picking at a huge platter of unidentifiable fruit Anita had ordered from room service when I noticed an envelope that had apparently been left at our door sometime during the night. I opened it and found it was the map Karsarkis' emissary had promised, and it made more sense to me than I had really expected it to.

As islands go, Phuket isn't that large. It only takes a little over an hour to drive the length of it from north to south and about half that to cross it east to west. Karsarkis' house was on the far northwestern coast of the island, on the headlands above a place called Nai Thon Beach, maybe a forty-five minute drive from our hotel but no more than a modest jog from Phuket's only airport. I wondered if that was a coincidence. Probably not. Karsarkis no doubt kept a couple of packed bags in the trunk of his car, just in case.

After little more than a quick scan of the map, I saw I wouldn't have any trouble finding the place where Karsarkis was holed up. That, of course, raised a fairly obvious question in my mind. How in the world could everyone *else* on the planet be having so much trouble finding it?

As curious as I might be about that, I wasn't curious enough to let Plato Karsarkis spoil my vacation. After all, the man wasn't *my* problem, was he?

So for the rest of the day, in between moments of laboring earnestly at an arduous regimen of swimming with Anita and napping on the beach, I carefully focused my attention on the young, sarong-clad girls with impossibly shiny black hair who plied us endlessly with sweating goblets of exotic drinks and plates heaped with cold seafood. Then, when the sun began to slide toward the sea, Anita and I showered and changed—what does one wear to dinner at the home of an internationally wanted fugitive?—and just after dusk we left our cabin and began climbing the steep pathway up to the hotel parking lot.

The night smelled of salt water and rotting fish, of neighborhood kitchens and mystifying foods, of diesel fuel and burning charcoal, and of plants and flowers with euphonious but utterly unpronounceable names. I inhaled deeply and wondered exactly what it was about the smell of the night in Thailand that made me feel so utterly alive.

Anita seemed to me uncharacteristically anxious, perhaps even apprehensive in some way, and that wasn't really like her at all.

"Are you worried about this?" I asked.

Anita hesitated before she answered. "I don't know what you mean," she finally said.

"Yes, you do. Have you changed your mind about going to this dinner, Anita? You know I'd be very happy just to bag it."

"Look, Jack. Why *wouldn't* we go? We've been invited to dinner by someone most of the world would kill to have dinner with."

"An unfortunate choice of words."

"Don't be so glib. I want to go. Really. Give me just one reason we shouldn't."

"Gee, I don't know. Maybe because the man's a criminal on the run?"

"Oh, I see. A criminal on the run. You mean like that Japanese guy you play tennis with sometimes, the one the FBI is trying to get its hands on for securities fraud? Or maybe he's more like that Thai banker whose daughter's wedding we went to last week. Surasak? Isn't that his name? They say his bank collapsed because of the hundred million or so he drained out of it and sent to Switzerland, don't they? Or maybe you mean—"

"Now who's being glib?"

"I honestly don't see the difference."

"Look, Anita, Karsarkis is in a whole different league from guys like that. He made his fortune buying massive amounts of smuggled crude oil from Iraq back during the economic embargo before the war. Then he constructed a daisy chain of paper companies in suitably shady places and transformed the Iraqi crude into apparently perfectly legal oil from perfectly legal sources by whipping up a phony paper trail for it. He funneled money to the Iraqis when he knew they would end up using it to kill Americans."

"I thought he had a rather interesting explanation for all that," Anita said.

Interesting was the right word for it, although whether Karsarkis' tale actually amounted to a defense was another question altogether. Still, after Karsarkis' lawyers had artfully arranged for his story to leak to the press, it was what had made of the whole case such a public sensation.

Karsarkis' lawyers were prepared to admit he had done what the government claimed, more or less, but they insisted he had been secretly functioning as an American agent when he did, and acting under the direct instructions of the White House, no less.

"You don't really believe any of that spy crap, do you, Anita?"

"Then what about that woman? What was her name?"

"Cynthia Kim."

"Yeah, her," Anita nodded. "She was going to testify it was true, wasn't she? That the president himself had told her it was?"

Although Karsarkis' defense attorneys had always remained

properly mute in public, his numerous apologists had been everywhere claiming Cynthia Kim was going to be the defense's star witness. According to the pro-Karsarkis people, who seemed to have more than a passing linkage with the anti-White House people, Miss Kim would testify she knew Karsarkis' dealings had been authorized by the White House. She knew this, they said, because she herself was secretly placed inside Plato Karsarkis' business operations by the White House in the first place. She had been put there to monitor Karsarkis' activities and report back regularly to somebody, although precisely who was a bit unclear.

That would probably have been more than enough to mesmerize the public right there, but of course there was more.

During the time Miss Kim was supposedly spying on Karsarkis for the White House, it was widely and enthusiastically speculated—without the slightest supporting evidence, as far as I was aware—that she had been delivering her reports directly to the president. Perhaps, some claimed, she had even been giving the president something along with her deliveries that the FedEx man seldom if ever offers.

No one would ever know for sure.

Three days before Karsarkis' trial was to have begun, Cynthia Kim's body had been found in a suite at the Hay Adams, a terrifyingly expensive hotel a stone's throw from the White House. She had been stabbed to death, first reports said, but when the full text of the medical examiner's report inevitably leaked out, the whole truth turned out to be considerably more sordid.

The District of Columbia Medical Examiner reported that Cynthia Kim had been killed with a wide-bladed knife that was serrated along about an eighth of its length, one that was probably about the size and weight of a US military-issue K-bar knife. Miss Kim had been killed by a single slash that had severed her neck from ear to ear. So deep was the cut that her head had been nearly hacked off her body. The medical examiner also concluded that Miss

Kim had been on her knees when the fatal wound was inflicted. Speculation as to exactly what she had been doing on her knees ran rampant, although not in family newspapers.

Cynthia Kim's brutal murder naturally enough sent the press baying in search of Plato Karsarkis, and that was when everything *really* hit the fan.

Because Plato Karsarkis was nowhere to be found. He had vanished, utterly and completely, as absolutely as any human being could disappear from the earth.

The spinners of conspiracy theories went berserk. Had Karsarkis been killed as well? Or was he Miss Kim's killer and now on the run? Was Karsarkis the mastermind behind some great crime? Or was someone methodically silencing the witnesses to an even greater crime?

Since the day he vanished, Plato Karsarkis sightings had been reported almost daily. Companies controlled by his financial empire operated dozens of businesses in half a hundred countries. None of them showed any signs of curtailing their usual activities, so there was plenty of potential for the dedicated Karsarkis-spotter to exploit.

The whole thing inevitably became, as they say, a carnival. It was Jimmy Hoffa, Robert Maxwell, and O. J. Simpson all rolled up in one. It was Lord Lucan and the dead nanny. It was Robert Blake and what's-her-name. It was even more than that. Somehow the mysterious disappearance of Plato Karsarkis became nothing less than the Kennedy assassination of the twenty-first century.

"I'm not going to argue with you any more, Anita. Plato Karsarkis thinks he is a law all to himself. He doesn't care how he makes money as long as he makes it. And as for what happened to Cynthia Kim, I bet you she was really going to send him down instead of backing up that bullshit story about him working for American intelligence. And he probably had her killed, too. You can take that to the goddamned bank."

"And this you know exactly *how*, counselor?"

I hated Anita calling me that, and of course she knew it, which was exactly why she did it.

THE RED SUZUKI jeep we had rented at the airport was parked about halfway around the hotel's circular driveway, sitting by itself under a clump of spindly coconut palms. The night was steamy, but I didn't feel any rain in the air and since the Suzuki's top was already down I left it that way. We got in and I put the key into the ignition and twisted it, hard.

"Okay, Jack, you've made your point. Now calm down and don't go all batty on me here. I think most of the people you know are criminals of one kind or another. What's one more to you?"

"If you really think there's any comparison between the other people I know and a man like Plato Karsarkis, Anita, then I *haven't* made my point at all. Karsarkis is a fugitive from the United States," I said. "He jumped bail and fled the country."

"Like you fled the country, Jack?"

"That is a ridiculous thing to say."

"Is it?"

Without waiting for Anita to say anything else, I started the Suzuki and put it in gear, then I drove out through the hotel's gates and turned right toward the main road.

Several minutes passed before anyone spoke again.

"Is all that out of your system now, Jack?" Anita eventually asked in a quiet voice.

"Yes, I think it is, Anita. Thank you for asking."

I shot a quick glance across at her, but she was looking straight ahead and I couldn't see her face clearly enough to read anything in it. There was a period in my life when I'd understood women—I must have been about six or seven at the time—but since then, almost everything about them has been a complete mystery to me.

The road to Phuket Town was lined with street vendors, their metal cooking carts strung with fluorescent tubes and their charcoal fires painting the air with a streaky haze. A barefoot boy in dark shorts and a T-shirt who looked to be not much more than ten sat on a rock near the edge of the road eating some kind of meat off a wooden stick and following our jeep with his eyes. When he saw me looking at him he broke into a grin and waved. I waved back and glanced over at Anita, but she seemed not to have noticed.

We followed the highway through the edge of Phuket Town and then turned north toward the airport. As the road rose over the spine of the island, hills punctured the lush jungle here and there, black clouds drifting over their faces like puffs of smoke. Off to the left two streamers of cloud twirled in circles around the crest of a steep, forest-covered rise, and at its peak a forest of microwave towers threw spidery silhouettes onto the darkening sky.

Anita and I continued to ride in silence. At first I thought of it as a companionable silence, but the longer it went on the less certain of that I became.

"What are you thinking?" I finally asked Anita.

The moment I spoke I was sorry I had, partly because the question sounded so desperate and adolescent and partly because I wasn't absolutely certain I actually wanted to know what Anita was thinking.

"That he must have liked you."

"Who?"

"Plato Karsarkis. If he invited you to dinner, he must have liked you."

"Maybe. Why does it matter?"

"It probably doesn't," she said. And then after a moment added, "What do you think his wife is like?"

"How do you know he has a wife?"

"Well…if he did have a wife, what do you think she would be like?"

"Probably a blonde with big hooters."

We came to a tiny village. Doll-sized houses built mostly of concrete stood open to the night. Wide porches sheltered motorbikes propped against front walls, but there were no driveways and no cars. Occasionally the blue-white glow of a television flickered from a window, and you could feel rather than see people moving in the darkness.

I turned my head as we passed and saw one house that had been converted into a barbershop. A television set played soundlessly, and a pink sheet covered a little boy sitting in an ancient chair. A couple of dozen people, mostly other kids, sat silently in the darkness of the front porch, watching the little boy and the television set through the open windows.

I found the big grove of rubber trees about three miles past the village, right where the map said it was. White-splotched trunks in hundreds of perfectly parallel rows marched into the distance until they were lost in the darkness. Another two miles to the west I spotted the dirt track I was looking for. It led off to the left, running toward the coast through a thick grove of palms.

I slowed down and turned off the highway.

Five

"*PAI NAI, KRAAP?*"

The man at the gate had a voice that was flat, neither rude nor polite. He sounded young although I couldn't see his face very well. As he approached the driver's side of our rented Suzuki jeep there was only enough light to tell that he was a Thai with short-cropped hair wearing a uniform that looked military: camouflage fatigues, boots, and a webbed belt with a holster on one side and a flashlight on the other. In his left hand was a small walkie-talkie, and his right rested on the flap covering his side arm.

"We were invited for dinner. By Mr. Karsarkis."

When the man gave no sign he understood English, I tried it in Thai.

"*Tan kao yen, kraap.*" We are here for dinner.

"*Kor chue duay, kraap?*" the guard asked. What is your name?

"Mr. and Mrs. Shepherd."

The man considered my reply for a moment, as if comparing it in his mind with a list of correct answers. Then he exchanged the walkie-talkie for his flashlight, snapped it on, and stepped back, playing the beam over our Suzuki.

"*Rod jeep kong khun rue plan, kraap?*" Is this your jeep?

"*Mai chai, kraap, kong Mister Avis.*" No, it belongs to Mr. Avis.

"*Krai Khun Avis, kraap?*" Who is Mr. Avis?

"Mai pen rai." It's not important.

The man nodded thoughtfully and made his way methodically around the jeep, inspecting it with his flashlight. Except for the jerking beam, the darkness was nearly complete. We sat still and said nothing.

When the man reached Anita's side of the jeep, he leaned over and played the beam into the tiny back seat and over the floor behind the front seats. When he was done, he lifted it up and scanned forward inside the jeep, the beam of light bouncing through the rear-view mirror and into my eyes.

At last, apparently satisfied, he clicked off the flashlight and walked to the front of the Suzuki. He waved to someone who must have been standing just out of sight somewhere in the darkness. The gate squeaked loudly on its tracks as it was pushed open from the inside.

The first man stepped back, came to attention, and snapped us a salute, which I took to mean we could pass. I turned my headlights back on and, when I did, I could see the second man was almost a twin to the man standing next to our jeep, right down to the camouflage fatigues and the sidearm on his belt. I put the jeep in gear and we rolled forward. I felt the gate's track bump past underneath us.

When we were inside, I looked across at Anita. "Well, that was interesting."

"Yes, it was," she murmured in a low voice. "I suppose."

The driveway beyond the gate was asphalt and it climbed steeply into a dense, very green rain forest with scatterings of cashew and rubber trees among the otherwise impenetrable stands of mangroves and coconut palms. What seemed to be about a mile on, it twisted suddenly to the right and the forest disappeared. Directly in front of us, although still a good distance away, was a small rise and at the top of it we saw the house. Taking my foot off the gas, I let the jeep coast to a stop.

Bathed in floodlights and so white and colorless it hurt my eyes to stare directly at it, Karsarkis' house looked like a cross between a movie set and a flying saucer crash. It was composed basically of four towers connected into a rectangle with long glass corridors. From the tops of each of the towers, glass pyramids rose some twenty feet further, each of them emitting a yellow glow suggestive of imminent levitation. At the foot of the rise there was a grass and stone surfaced courtyard with a low rectangular fountain in its center from which three nozzles burped rings of water into the night air. Just past the fountain, wide pebbled-concrete steps led from the courtyard up to a pair of glass doors flanked on both sides by a garden of what looked like lava rocks.

"You may park up there, sir."

The sound of the voice from the shadows startled me, but not nearly as much as did the submachine gun I saw in the blond man's hands when he stepped into the glow cast by our headlights. Although his voice was firm and commanding, the soft Irish lilt in his tones was impossible to miss.

"Up there with the others now, sir, please."

Never much inclined to engage in dialogue with a man holding a submachine gun, I stepped on the gas and rolled on into the courtyard.

There was another Suzuki parked next to the fountain, a white one with the top up, and a dark Mercedes sedan just past it. There was also a big four-wheel drive of some kind, although I couldn't immediately identify the make.

When we pulled to a stop behind the other Suzuki, I saw two drivers in gray safari suits sitting on the edge of the fountain, waiting and smoking cigarettes, silently watching. I assumed one went with the Mercedes and the other with four-wheel. It was pretty hard to imagine anyone being driven around in the backseat of a Suzuki.

When we got to the top of the steps that led up to the front doors, I stopped and turned around. The elevation of the rise gave onto a view out over the dense mangrove forests and across most of the sleeping island. The moon had risen and it cast a dim glow over the landscape. I could see a highway far away and for a moment I tracked a single pair of distant headlights creeping along its length. I thought I could almost see a pale glimmer of moonlight on the sea out on the eastern horizon, but probably it was just my imagination.

"Not bad," I said to Anita.

I glanced over and saw her looking at me strangely.

"No, really. It's not bad at all. Sort of like living in Big Sur, I guess. That is if you can imagine living in Big Sur with the Thai army guarding your outer perimeter and IRA patrols roaming around inside your fence line."

Then I lifted my right arm over my head and waved it back and forth a couple of times.

"Who are you waving to?" Anita asked.

"I just wanted to be sure we haven't missed anyone," I told her.

Anita was silent for a moment.

"Are you ready now, Jack?"

"Yes," I said, "I think I am."

I said I was ready, but I wasn't. And not being able to find the goddamned doorbell didn't do much to help either.

THE PAIR OF glass doors at the top of the short flight of steps was positioned in a glass wall. I had to admit the effect was spectacular, but if it was an intelligence test to see who could figure out where the freaking doorbell was, I flunked.

So what did Karsarkis expect us to do? Knock on the glass like a couple of ninnies?

I could see right through the doors, across the corridor, and out the other side, straight into an interior courtyard where there was a huge rectangular swimming pool with water so Tidy-Bowl blue it looked like it had been dyed. Arranged in groupings around the pool were a dozen or more teak lounge chairs with white canvas cushions, most of them shaded by large beach umbrellas. Several groves of strategically placed palm trees set off the whole tableau.

"Wouldn't you think he could afford a doorbell?"

I addressed the question to Anita. I didn't really expect her to answer, and of course she didn't.

I was just giving consideration to reaching for a rock when a maid in an ankle-length black skirt and white blouse silently materialized and swung open both doors. She stepped back as we entered, inclining her head and bringing her palms together in front of her face, the tips of her fingers reaching just to the bridge of her nose.

It was a traditional gesture Thais call a *wai* and I have always thought it a uniquely warm and elegant form of greeting that makes the western handshake seem hopelessly gawky by comparison. Of course, the *wai* is also a profoundly nuanced signal of relative social standing, and the way Thais wield it frequently leaves me a little bewildered. The inferior *wais* the superior, and the younger *wais* the older. That much I understand, but I still screw up my response most of the time because I am never entirely certain how to deal with the subtleties inherent in that equation. For instance, how to respond to a *wai* from a waiter who is really old? What carries the greater weight, the age or the station?

Since I'm just a foreigner, of course, no Thai ever expects me to get it right anyway so it isn't really that big a problem. Nevertheless, Anita always seems to manage a lot better than I do, and I frequently find myself admiring the cool sense of standing and entitlement that she seems to bring to every new encounter.

We followed the maid as she led us down the wide glass corridor that defined the front of Karsarkis' house. Lining it were a succession of small sculptures displayed on tall pedestals, and I paused briefly to examine one that turned out to be a likeness of a very fat woman bending forward and displaying her formidable rear end. The piece was made of something that looked like terracotta, and the material and the soft lighting of the corridor combined to cause the woman's imposing posterior to glow with a bright pink sheen.

"I've heard that having a huge pink bottom helps females attract males," I whispered to Anita.

She shifted her eyes toward me, but said nothing.

"Of course, the bad news is it only works if you're a baboon."

Naturally Anita pretended she hadn't heard me.

The maid gestured us between two large fig trees that seemed to sprout straight out of the corridor's marble floor and toward the pool outside in the courtyard. It wasn't until we had taken half a dozen steps that I realized we weren't outside at all. There was an unobtrusive glass dome that sealed over the whole courtyard, which was as comprehensively air-conditioned as the rest of the house.

I nudged Anita, rolling my eyes up at the dome. "I wonder if it's bulletproof."

"Cut it out, Jack," she hissed.

Karsarkis was standing near the opposite end of the swimming pool with a distinguished-looking, somewhat elderly man who appeared to be Thai and wore a beautifully cut dark suit. It had to be the only beautifully cut dark suit on the whole island of Phuket where in most circles even the donning of long pants was considered hopelessly pompous. Karsarkis himself was plainly dressed in jeans, loafers without socks, and a long-sleeved white shirt with the sleeves rolled up to his elbows. He seemed to be listening intently to whatever the man in the suit was saying and he nodded slowly as the older man tapped the air with his fingers.

I took a deep breath and followed Anita as she walked toward him.

Six

WHEN KARSARKIS GLANCED up and saw us, he apparently excused himself from the man with whom he was talking because soon he was giving my hand the kind of vigorous, two-fisted pump that left the impression we were the oldest of friends.

"So happy you could come, Jack. Or should I call you Professor?"

"It was nice of you to ask us," I said, ignoring Karsarkis' question.

"Mrs. Shepherd, I'm Plato Karsarkis."

"Of course you are."

Anita shook Karsarkis' hand as well, although I noticed that with her he restricted himself to a one-hander.

Another uniformed maid appeared beside us so silently I wondered if she had grown out of the marble like the two fig trees. She carried a silver tray with a half-dozen champagne flutes and Karsarkis distributed glasses to both of us. Then he took one for himself.

"This is quite a house," I said to Karsarkis, mostly just to be saying something.

Naturally the real question on my mind was how a notorious international fugitive had gone about acquiring such an extravagant house in a world-famous resort like Phuket, and more to the point, how he had done it without anyone apparently noticing. Karsarkis obviously realized what I was thinking because he benevolently offered an explanation without forcing me to make my curiosity explicit.

"One of our local companies built this place about five years ago. It was supposed to be for entertaining or to loan to clients. I never stayed here myself until now, but…" Karsarkis trailed off with a shrug that looked genuinely rueful. "I'm sure you understand."

I smiled tightly without saying anything. I also drank some of the champagne, which I wasn't surprised to discover was pretty good stuff.

Karsarkis watched me, his face a mask.

"Maybe I'm wrong, Jack, but my guess is you're not too happy to be here tonight. Am I right about that?"

I responded quickly, too quickly for my better judgment to have any chance to grab my elbow and warn me to keep my big mouth shut.

"The only reason we're here tonight is because Anita wanted to come," I said, "and I didn't think it was worth arguing about. I don't know how much of what they say about you is true and how much is made up, but I think enough of it probably *is* true to make me certain I wouldn't be in your house tonight if Anita hadn't insisted. I'm sorry if you think I'm rude, but you did ask."

Karsarkis lowered his head and something resembling a repentant smile slid over his face.

"You are married to a very straightforward man, Mrs. Shepherd."

"That's one of the things I've heard Jack called," Anita said. I noticed she didn't look at me when she spoke. "But most of the other things are considerably more colorful."

Karsarkis laughed, but somewhat automatically, I thought. Then he lifted his eyes to mine again. "What is it you don't like about me, Professor?"

"I don't know you," I said. "It's what I've heard about you that I don't like."

The abrupt change in the way Karsarkis had addressed me caught my attention. At least calling me professor was less pally than calling me Jack, and less pally was just fine with me. Maybe our relationship was moving in the right direction after all.

"Jack," Anita murmured, obviously more than a little uncomfortable, "I don't think—"

"No, let me finish. I'm sure Mr. Karsarkis would prefer it if I spoke my mind."

Karsarkis tilted his head slightly and gave a little wave with his champagne glass, a gesture I took to be an invitation for me to continue. So I did.

"Coming here has put me in an impossible position. What am I supposed to do now? You're a fugitive, Mr. Karsarkis. You jumped bail and fled the US."

"Are you done, Jack?" Anita's voice was crisp now.

"No, Anita, thank you for asking, I'm not done. I am a lawyer, as you may recall, a member in good standing of the Bar of the Supreme Court of the United States, and although I admit my personal connection with the concept of justice may sometimes be a touch tenuous, I still have at least a degree of concern for the ideal. So what do I do now? Have dinner at this man's home and then turn him in? And what if I do nothing? Am I helping to harbor a fugitive? Shouldn't I just call Bangkok right now and tell the American Embassy where they can find this guy?"

"They know where they can find me," Karsarkis said. He spoke so softly I wasn't absolutely sure I had heard him right.

"Pardon me?"

"I said the American Embassy knows where they can find me," Karsarkis repeated. "A lot of people have known about this house since the day it was built, and anybody who has the slightest interest in me knows I'm here now."

"Then why don't they send somebody down here and arrest you?"

"This is Thailand, Professor. The United States government has no jurisdiction to arrest anyone here."

That was true, of course, but Thai authorities could certainly arrest Karsarkis if the American Embassy requested it. I wasn't an expert on such things, but I was pretty certain there was an extradition treaty in effect between the United States and Thailand. I knew I'd heard of people being extradited in drug cases to face American courts, at least a few, and if the embassy requested Karsarkis' arrest and extradition, I couldn't imagine why he wouldn't get the same treatment.

Again, Karsarkis seemed to sense the question that was in my mind before I asked it.

"The Thais' view of my presence here is rather different from the American view," he said. "Nothing I have been charged with is a crime under Thai law, my lawyers tell me, so happily I am not subject to the terms of the extradition treaty. The Thais are pleased to have me in their country."

I'll bet, I thought to myself. *And I wonder exactly how much that is costing him.*

"Please excuse my husband, Mr. Karsarkis." Anita tossed a hard look in my direction. "He's a terrible bore sometimes."

"Please, Anita. It's Plato."

Anita fidgeted. She shot me another hard look and I thought I saw unease in her eyes.

"Fine. Plato then."

"I don't mind the professor here saying whatever he wants to, Anita. He's a smart guy. Smart guys think a lot."

Karsarkis shifted his eyes back to mine and reached out and tapped me on the forearm with one finger.

"But don't believe everything you've heard about me, Professor. You just keep asking questions and listening to the answers and maybe you'll learn some things that will surprise you."

After that Karsarkis led us around and introduced us to the rest of his guests as if we'd just had a brief conversation no more awkward than a chat about the weather. The man had self-confidence out the butt, I'd give him that.

The distinguished Thai in the dark suit turned out to be a former prime minister, a man named Sakda who had resigned suddenly a few years back under somewhat cloudy circumstances. He was now married to a blonde Australian at least six inches taller than he was, a woman who looked to me like she must have played the trombone in her high school band. I wondered if she was part of the punishment meted out to Sakda for whatever he was supposed to have done. Regardless, I figured him for the dark Mercedes.

Next there was a short, middle-aged Englishman with bad teeth and a bad complexion who was accompanied by an attractive Thai woman with good everything. She didn't appear to like him all that much, it seemed to me, but perhaps that was just my imagination. I made the Englishman for the four-wheel drive.

And then there was a bland, pear-shaped man who I thought looked generically European. He was wearing a rumpled suit without a tie and had a Russian-sounding nickname. Karsarkis called him Yuri, which seemed about right when I looked at him closely, but he also had an American accent, which didn't. Like the Englishman he was accompanied by an Asian woman, although after a brief inspection I decided Yuri's companion was probably Chinese rather than Thai. That left them as the white Suzuki.

"And this is my wife," Karsarkis finally said, leading us over to a tall woman with long, dark hair. She had her back to us and was talking animatedly with Mike O'Connell, the man Karsarkis had sent into the Boathouse the night before to invite us to dinner.

"Baby," he said putting his hand on her shoulder. "I'd like you to meet Jack and Anita Shepherd."

The woman turned with a smile that startled me with its

unexpected warmth. While she may not have been a blonde, other than that I had nailed her cold. I tried to catch Anita's eye, but she wouldn't look at me.

"I'm Mia," Karsarkis' wife said, shaking hands with Anita first, and then me. "We're so glad you could come. It's nice to see some other Americans for a change."

"Actually, I'm not American." Anita said.

"You're not?" Mia looked a little puzzled.

"No, I'm Italian."

"You don't look Italian," Karsarkis observed, although I wasn't absolutely sure what he meant by that. Maybe he thought if Anita was really Italian that she ought to be wearing a long black dress with a white apron over it, black stockings, and a pair of little black shoes.

"My mother was Italian," Anita said. "My father was English, but *mi considero Italiano*."

"Most people who marry Americans seem to want to become American citizens," Mia said.

She was replying to Anita, but I noticed she was looking at me when she spoke, almost as if it was somehow my fault Anita was still Italian.

"Not me," Anita said cheerfully. *"Sono fiero di essere Italiano!"*

"È bello essere fiere di ciò che si è," Karsarkis responded.

Anita inclined her head appreciatively at his apparent fluency in the language.

"È meglio di essere Francese," she said.

"Could we get back to a language I speak?" I asked.

"Why?" Anita asked. "Is there someone here you haven't insulted yet?"

Karsarkis laughed loudly, but Mia sensed something unpleasant might be happening and quickly changed the subject.

Turning toward me and conjuring up a pleasantly inconsequential tone of voice, she asked, "Are all those things I've been hearing about you true, Mr. Shepherd?"

"I wouldn't doubt it a bit," I replied, looking straight at Anita.

I knew it was an ungracious response to a woman who was only trying to keep the conversation light, but I was still smarting from Anita's dig and Karsarkis' appreciative response to it so to hell with them all.

Showing the reflexes of a battle-hardened hostess, Mia realized she needed to do something to defuse whatever that burning smell in the air might be.

"Now that everyone is here," she asked the room at large, "shall we go in to dinner?" She phrased it as a question, but her tone said it wasn't a question at all.

Then, just to make sure than no one had missed her point, Mia started walking toward the dining room without bothering to wait for anyone to answer her.

Seven

THE DINING ROOM was high ceilinged and windowless except for the wall that faced the courtyard, which was all glass. A thick clump of banana trees and several pieces of modern sculpture were set in a rock garden just outside the glass and the deep blue light from the swimming pool was a glowing presence in the room. At the center was a long, narrow table with a black marble top. It was covered in candles and set for ten.

Mia took a seat at one end of the table and directed the former prime minister to sit on one side of her and me on the other. Karsarkis sat at the opposite end between Anita and the prime minister's Australian wife.

Everyone stuck largely to murmuring about the weather and such while a small army of servants came and went, pouring wine and serving food. The first course was a local dish I didn't recognize, but no one else asked what it was and I didn't want to make an ass of myself so I didn't ask either. The second course put me onto safer ground. I knew it was a mango salad of some kind, and it was pretty good.

The Englishman prattled on and on while the rest of us ate, but I hardly registered anything he said, tuning him out in favor of studying the other guests more closely.

Yuri didn't appear to have much to say for himself, which disappointed me since I was hugely curious about him and was hoping he would drop a hint or two as to who he really was and what his connection with Karsarkis might be. Neither Yuri's companion nor the Englishman's companion said anything at all. I thought the Chinese-looking girl with Yuri seemed genuinely puzzled as to who all these people were and what they were talking about. She appeared so uncomfortably out of place I felt a little sorry for her.

The Thai woman who was with the Englishman, however, was quite another matter. A tortoiseshell band pinned back her long black hair, there was just a touch of a suntan on her face, and whatever make-up she wore was imperceptible. If the woman had been English, I would have described her as horsy, but as she was manifestly Thai the term just didn't seem to sit right on her. Still, it was hard to come up with a better one. She had a high forehead and a bit of rosy flush that looked healthy and seemed to speak of outdoor living and riding mannishly. The only things about her that didn't fit were the obviously very fine and very expensive diamond ear clips she wore.

The conversation drifted around to the usual cannon fodder of such dinner parties: money and sex. Money in the form of speculation over the reasons for the recent wild swings in the world's stock markets; sex in the form of conjecture as to the orientation of the newly appointed American Secretary of State. The man had an extremely attractive wife, at least for an American Secretary of State he did, and I had never heard before that there was any doubt at all as to his sexual persuasion. From the conversation around me, however, I judged there were a goodly number of such things I had never heard before.

Then, out of nowhere, the Englishman leaned down the table and put a question to Karsarkis in a loud voice, one that stopped all the idle conversation cold.

"Plato, does all this talk about American politics make you miss the United States?"

I cut my eyes at Mia while waiting to hear what Karsarkis had to say to that and I was pretty sure I saw her wince slightly.

Karsarkis seemed to think for a moment, although I figured that was mostly stagecraft on his part, and then he exhaled slowly. "I love Thailand and I may well live here for the rest of my life. Nevertheless I would like to visit America from time to time…so yes, I guess that must mean I do miss it, in a way."

"You're up to something, Plato," the Englishman blundered on, apparently heedless of the consternation he had caused at the table. "I know it. I can feel it."

"I'm not sure what will happen from here," Karsarkis responded very slowly. "I'd like to work things out, but I don't really feel very sure of anything anymore."

Suddenly Yuri spoke up, back from the dead.

"There must be something that can be done, Plato," he said. "I have many friends. All you must do is say the word."

I wasn't sure what *that* was supposed to mean, but I didn't much like the sound of it.

"Well…" Karsarkis seemed to think, but again the gesture struck me as affected, although to impress whom I had no idea. "There are one or two people standing in my way."

Everyone laughed merrily at that while a few obvious solutions to the problem danced through my mind, such as Karsarkis having all those people's throats slashed exactly like Cynthia Kim's had been. Not to appear disagreeable, I kept my thoughts on the subject to myself and mimed a chuckle or two of my own.

The former prime minister, who had been almost completely silent throughout the entire meal thus far, rumbled to life. His voice was smooth and cultured, and the sound of it suggested the man's formative years had probably been spent at an expensive English boarding school, certainly not in Thailand.

"The Kingdom of Thailand is proud to have Plato here," he said.

"And we hope he will stay with us for many years to come."

"Thank you, Prime Minister." Karsarkis bobbed his head in acknowledgment of the man's endorsement and tried—without any success, I thought—to look modest and self-effacing at the same time. "You are too kind."

"Not at all, Plato. Not at all. You are one of the giants. It is our honor to have you in our country."

Sakda looked as if he had more to say—and Karsarkis looked as if he hoped he didn't—but the old man started talking again before Karsarkis could head him off.

"You are a true friend of the Thai people, Plato, and the Thai people are your friends. Your work on our behalf has guaranteed a supply of competitively-priced petroleum far into the future and given us a secure basis for rapid industrial expansion."

With that, the old man went back to his lobster.

Ah ha, I thought. *So that's it.*

Translation: Plato Karsarkis was selling Thailand some of the embargoed Iraqi oil he was accused of smuggling, naturally at cut-rate prices.

Most Asian countries lacked any domestic sources of oil at all and were almost wholly dependent on a steady stream coming in from the Middle East to keep their cars going and their electrical generators turning. High oil prices and tight supply meant economic stagnation, or a good deal worse. Low oil prices and loose supply meant prosperity, particularly for the people who controlled the oil and took a cut as it flowed by.

And that was no doubt the second part of the equation here.

Karsarkis' supplies of Iraqi oil were obviously being delivered through Sakda and his cronies, which explained where Karsarkis' protection was coming from. That was a vastly more effective arrangement for Karsarkis than straight bribery. When you bought a politician, your problem was the same in any country—to make sure he *stayed* bought. If the buying was done through a continuing drip feed of Iraqi oil at below-market prices, then you had the problem pretty well licked. Shrewd of Karsarkis, I had to admit to myself. Very shrewd indeed.

The former prime minister's sudden wakefulness seemed to energize his Australian wife as well. All of a sudden the woman pitched forward in her seat, banging the base of her wine glass against her plate. The noise caused me to glance over at her and I noticed for the first time she had a bracelet tattooed around her right wrist. It was purple and appeared to be a likeness of intertwined grape leaves and barbed wire. What would ever possess a woman to do that, I wondered as I looked at her? Why would any woman get up one morning and say to herself, *I think today I will have a bracelet of grape leaves and barbed wire tattooed in purple around my right wrist because no doubt it will make me look indescribably beautiful and eerily desirable.* I had to admit that there were some things about life that just eluded me entirely.

"This is boring," the Australian woman announced in a voice that invited no discussion of the point. "Let's talk about something real sexy instead."

"Oh, good," I spoke up. "I like to talk about me."

"Behave yourself, counselor," Anita murmured from the other end of the table as several people tittered.

"Here's something I've always wanted to know," the woman went on without cracking a smile. "What is it with you men and Asian women? I mean, what the hell is it?"

I stole a quick glance at the two women around the table who were obviously Asian. The Thai was regarding the prime minister's wife as she might eye a muddy sheepdog that was about to walk right across her new snow-white living room carpet, but the Chinese-looking woman who was with Yuri had the look of a startled raccoon suddenly caught in the headlights of a car.

Karsarkis seemed to appreciate the diversion, or maybe he just felt a bit of blood sport coming on, but regardless of which it was, he pushed the door wide open.

"I don't understand, Karla," he said, although it was obvious that he understood very well. "What are you talking about?"

"Ah, you know, Plato."

I wondered if the woman had had too much to drink because she seemed to have difficulty speaking and was slurring her words. On the other hand, maybe it was just her Australian accent. It was difficult to tell for sure.

"You men go all gaga over these little girls here and I got a theory about that. I think men who run after Asian women are really all bloody pedophiles at heart. That's what I think."

"Yes, it's very possible you're right," Anita joined in, and I nearly choked.

She smiled warmly at both of the Asian women sitting around the table, but went on quickly.

"My own observation is that western men who come to Asia are generally unsuccessful with western women and they are looking for harmless playthings who will feed their egos and make no demands. Essentially, they're looking for children."

Anita smiled again at the two Asian women sitting at the table as if to say that of course she didn't consider either of them to be any such thing.

"That doesn't mean that's what they find," Anita finished, "but it's still what they're looking for."

"Have you been into the cooking sherry again, my dear?" I inquired in what I thought was an arch enough tone to make my message unmistakable.

Too late. The Australian chick was in full flight now. I looked at Karsarkis, who had pushed back in his chair and had an enormous grin spread across his face.

"Doesn't it just make you sick?" she was saying to Anita who was bobbing her head in earnest agreement. "Sometimes I think these halfwits go around screwing these tiny girls just because it makes their pathetic little peckers look bigger."

Karsarkis was about to bust a gut, but then I noticed that the other men around the table had gone unnaturally quiet, even the Englishman, who before this had looked as if he might never shut up. I glanced at the former prime minister. The old man had his head down diligently examining the texture of his carrot mousse. I got the distinct impression that he had probably heard all this before.

"You see all these fat, smelly wankers strutting around dragging these poor little girls behind them or riding a motorbike with one propped up on the back. Jesus, they treat those little girls like they were no better than pets who give blow jobs. What's worse, the silly cows don't even seem to mind it."

The Australian woman tossed her head and pushed her hair back. There was something about her face that made me think of a badly drawn cartoon.

"Of course, they're just doing it for the money." She looked around the table and drained the rest of her wine. "The silly buggers run out of money and they're out on their dirty arses before they know what hit them."

"Serves them right," Anita nodded, looking straight at me as she did.

Suddenly a mobile phone started to ring and for a moment nobody said anything.

"Excuse me," I spoke up after the sound had gone on for a while. "That's probably my Thai girlfriend calling."

Everyone laughed, particularly Karsarkis, who looked as if he might have a stroke.

The Englishman eventually pulled out his telephone and flipped it open. He glanced at the screen, and then he closed it again without answering.

Eight

AFTER DINNER MIA invited the other women to see the rest of the house while the men took their coffee and went out by the pool. In Thailand people still did that kind of thing. The mere thought of an arrangement like that in California these days would get you five to ten in San Quentin.

A houseboy wearing a white jacket and black bow tie offered cigars from a Dunhill humidor. The cigars were Davidoffs so naturally I took one, as did Karsarkis, but the others waved the houseboy away with varying degrees of courtesy.

The old prime minister stretched out on a lounge chair and within a few minutes was either dozing or dead. Meanwhile the Englishman and Yuri made vague excuses about telephone calls they had to make and headed off for other parts of the house. In short order I found myself alone with Karsarkis by the pool and I wondered if that was entirely coincidental.

We busied ourselves in silence for a while cutting and lighting our cigars. When Karsarkis eventually spoke, he kept his eyes on his cigar rather than looking at me.

"May I make a personal observation, Jack?"

I waved my cigar in what I figured was a suitably magnanimous gesture.

"Sure," I said, "go ahead."

"You seem to be pretty hostile tonight."

"Good Lord," I snorted, flipping my spent match in the direction of an ashtray. "I never would have guessed you watched Oprah."

Karsarkis chuckled slightly at that, but then he lifted his eyes, cocked his head to one side, and stared at me until I looked away.

"You really don't like me, do you, Jack?"

"Well…" I sorted through a number of possible responses to that and finally went with the one I thought was most honest. "No."

Karsarkis shifted his cigar from the left side of his mouth to the right and smiled slightly. "You want to tell me exactly why?"

"Sure. You're one of the people who get away with it. I don't like people who get away with it."

"With what?"

"With whatever you want. You make ridiculous amounts of money any way you like. You brush off any inconvenient laws that happen to get in your way. You let the suckers do the productive work and pay the taxes. You ruin people when they threaten you, maybe you even have a few of them killed every now and then if they get to be real nuisances. And what happens to you?" I raised my arms and gestured around me at Karsarkis' extraordinary house. "Not a fucking thing. You live like the king of the world, laughing at all the idiots who can't do a damn thing about it."

To my surprise, Karsarkis just stood and listened to me, nodding his head slightly as if he were in full agreement.

Then, taking another long pull on his cigar, he exhaled and watched the smoke drift away. "You see me laughing, Jack?" he asked.

"You know what I mean."

"I know this: I can't go back to the United States now and I have a daughter there who needs me. Did you know *that*?"

I said nothing at first, but then I saw Karsarkis was staring at me as if he actually expected me to answer him so I did.

"No," I said. "I didn't know that."

"She's nine years old. Living in New York with my first wife. She has leukemia, Jack, and she's too sick to come here. If I can't straighten all this out, she'll die before I see her again. What do you think it feels like to be in exile halfway around the world, living in a country where you can't read the signs and aren't sure who you can trust, when you have a nine-year-old daughter back home who's dying of leukemia?" Karsarkis pushed one of the lounge chairs around with his foot, sat down on the side of it, and looked up at me. "What do you think that feels like, you self-righteous son of a bitch?"

I didn't know what to say to that, so I said nothing.

"I think you at least owe me an honest answer to my question, Jack. Do you see me laughing?"

I wanted to say if Karsarkis cared so much about his daughter maybe he should have thought about her back before he started peddling smuggled Iraqi oil to the highest bidder and pissing off the FBI, the IRS, the CIA, and God-only-knew who else. But I didn't say any of that.

"What's your daughter's name?" I asked him instead.

"Zoe. After my mother."

"Do you talk to her often?"

The silence went on for what felt like several minutes before Karsarkis spoke again.

"No, not often. It's hard for both of us. She always ends up crying. I don't deal with it very well."

Drawing deeply on his cigar Karsarkis stood up and walked slowly over to the edge of the pool and peered down. For a moment I had visions of Robert Maxwell and wondered if I ought to take off my watch and shoes just in case he was about to jump in.

"You have any kids, Jack?" he asked all of a sudden.

"No, but…" I trailed off when I realized I wasn't at all certain what I had started to say, so I didn't say anything.

Karsarkis looked back over his shoulder at me with a kind of half smile on his face.

"You were going to say that you and Anita were talking about it, weren't you?"

"No. I wasn't."

But, of course, I was.

"I've got a son as well as a daughter," Karsarkis carried on, letting me off the hook. "Did I tell you that?"

I shook my head.

"Yeah, Frank's at Columbia. I'm proud as hell of that boy, but I worry about him, too. Sometimes I think we've all lost our way. The kind of world we're leaving for him and the rest of our kids is a less decent place than the one our parents left for us. I'm not sure he's ready to deal with that." Karsarkis smiled again, but in a minor key. "Anyway, he got into Columbia. That's about as good a start as he could get. Maybe he'll be okay."

I had to admit I had never really thought of Karsarkis before as a guy who worried about his children's future. Maybe I had judged him too harshly. On the other hand, maybe this was all just a load of crap he was shoveling out to make him sound like a decent guy and I hadn't judged him harshly enough. Either way, I was growing somewhat curious about this man now and decided it wouldn't hurt anything to keep the conversation going.

"Did you go to Columbia yourself?" I asked him.

"No. Georgetown."

"Really? So did I. Georgetown Law."

"Those Jesuits were tough little bastards, weren't they?" Karsarkis smiled. "I learned a lot from them."

"Like what for instance?"

Karsarkis seemed to be taken mildly off balance by the question, which was my whole reason for having asked it, of course. To his credit, however, he paused before he answered and I sensed he was thinking seriously about it.

"A sense of good grace," he said after a moment, "and a perspective on life. You know: this too shall pass."

I was pretty sure if Karsarkis was applying that lesson to his present circumstances, he was dreaming.

"What year did you graduate from Georgetown?" I asked.

"1969."

I did the math as subtly as I could. That would make Karsarkis about sixty.

"The law school?" I asked.

"No, undergraduate. I had no interest in law school. I figured I could always rent all the lawyers I needed, so why bother going to law school myself?"

The image of a *For Rent* sign hanging around my neck wasn't particularly appealing, but I let Karsarkis' observation pass without starting a pointless argument over it. Instead I walked over to a lounge chair, sat down, and watched Karsarkis out of the corner of my eye while I smoked my cigar and wondered exactly what in the hell was going on. Here I was sitting around chewing the fat with the world's most famous fugitive and what were we talking about? His children and the good old days back when we were both Georgetown Hoyas.

I had the feeling none of this was just idle chatter. Karsarkis was trying too hard to sound congenial. He was working up to something and I wondered what it would turn out to be.

Then I found out.

"Before I forget, Jack, there's something I wanted to ask you," Karsarkis said, breaking the silence. "One of our local companies is thinking about making a bid for a broken-down hotel chain they think they can do something with. I was wondering if you could look at the deal for me, just tell me what you think about it before they go any further."

"I don't have a private practice anymore, Mr. Karsarkis. I just teach. I already told you that."

"Yeah, you did, but…" Karsarkis took another pull on his cigar. "I was hoping perhaps you would do this as a favor for a friend."

"I already told you that, too. We're not friends."

"I don't expect anybody to work for free, Jack. Whether they're a friend or not. Nothing for nothing. I've always believed that."

"Look, I really don't—"

"I had in mind a fee of $100,000."

"I'm sorry?"

"$100,000. To look over the deal and give me your opinion."

I wasn't sure what Karsarkis expected me to say to that—it was too silly an offer for me to take it seriously—but he was standing there looking at me and obviously expected me to say something so eventually I did.

"That's ridiculous," I said. "Surely it wouldn't take more than a few hours to go over whatever you have. Nobody pays that kind of money for a few hours' work."

"I'm not proposing to pay you for your time, Jack. I'm proposing to pay you for your opinion. I could make a hell of a lot of money from this or I could lose a hell of a lot. You're a smart guy and you know the territory out here. What you think about the deal and the way it's structured is easily worth $100,000 to me."

"Look, I'm very flattered, but—"

"Just think about it, will you?"

"I don't need to think about it, Mr. Karsarkis. Even if I wanted to do it, I couldn't. The school wouldn't be happy about it."

"Meaning what?"

"Meaning they don't mind me doing some consulting work on the side, but they want me to keep it low profile."

"We could keep this low profile. That's no problem."

"It's not that easy."

"Yes, it is. I won't tell anyone if you won't."

"That's not what I meant. Look, what I'm trying to say is the school…"

I trailed off. I was trying to be polite and I didn't want to flat-out insult the man, but I decided there was nothing wrong with telling Karsarkis the simple truth.

"Let me put it this way. What I'm saying here is this: I really do not want to work for you, Mr. Karsarkis. Not even if you're willing to pay me $100,000 for a few hours work. And I'm sure you understand exactly why that is."

THE HIGHWAY WAS nearly empty when Anita and I drove back to the hotel from Karsarkis' house. The heavy wetness of the night was so dense the air felt almost like fog. We crossed the hills at the central core of the island in silence, both of us watching our headlights as the bobbing beams splintered in the moisture and made the thick vegetation lining the road glitter as if it were covered with fireflies.

"Be careful, Jack."

I looked around, but didn't immediately see what Anita was concerned about.

"I'm sorry?"

"I said be careful," Anita repeated.

"Of what?"

"Of this man."

I grunted. "Greeks bearing gifts? Something like that?"

"Be serious, Jack, and listen to me. Are you listening to me?"

I glanced quickly across at Anita. When I saw the set of her jaw, I knew there was only one possible answer to her question.

"Yes, Anita. I'm listening to you."

"I am only going to say this once."

"Okay."

"People who live in the darkness are very seductive to you, Jack. So whatever you think you're doing with this man, be very, very careful."

"Oh, for God's sake, Anita, I not doing anything with him."

"You're about to take a huge chance here. I can feel it. You're walking straight into something horrible, and you don't even have the sense to be afraid."

I didn't reply.

It was a gorgeous night, quiet and very dark. The road was a divided four-lane arched here and there by concrete pedestrian bridges with a rank of tall aluminum streetlights marching down the grassy divider in the middle. The streetlights glowed a sulfurous yellow and the water vapor hanging in the air caught the butter-colored radiance and shaped it into luminous globes. It made me think of a line of huge yellow snow cones impaled on stainless steel sticks.

We drove in silence for a while and it was a few minutes before I realized Anita had slipped off to sleep, her head tilted against the back of the seat with her face turned away from me. I watched jack-o'-lantern houses drifting past the windows of our Suzuki, their waxy lights flicking through tiny openings. I smiled as a Buddhist temple loomed up briefly out of a grove of rubber trees, its fanciful, brightly painted towers sparkling fiercely, even in the darkness.

Moving into the left lane I passed a slow-moving Isuzu pickup. It had been converted into a primitive bus with rough wooden benches rigged down both sides of the bed, but that night it was empty. The stillness of the night in Thailand is always an illusion. It is never really empty. There is always something moving out there in the darkness: a car, a bus, a motorbike, a truck. Once I got myself lost near the airport in Bangkok very late at night, rounded a curve, and found myself face-to-face with an elephant somebody was riding right down the middle of the highway.

It took another half hour to get back to the hotel. Anita slept the whole way. I thought several times of waking her, maybe asking her again exactly what she was trying to tell me and what it was that I should do, but I didn't.

I should have.

Later, looking back, I realized that if I had listened to Anita right then I might have had some kind of a chance to stop everything.

But, of course, I hadn't listened to her, I hadn't paid any attention to her at all. And after that, it was too late.

Nine

THE NEXT MORNING Anita and I had breakfast on the desk outside our cabin and then lounged around for a while reading yesterday's newspapers from Bangkok. That had always been one of the charms of Phuket for me. You could read yesterday's papers instead of today's and it didn't make a damned bit of difference. Back in Bangkok I felt I had to be the informed man and every day I dutifully plowed through both of the local English-language newspapers and two or three international papers as well. In Phuket, I could never think of a single thing I really wanted to be informed *about*.

"Let's drive over to Patong later, Jack. Want to?"

I was half dozing when Anita spoke. I didn't respond immediately since I wasn't absolutely sure I had heard her right. Had she really said she wanted to go to Patong?

Patong had once been a sleepy little fishing village on the west coast of Phuket, one that lay at the back of a deep bay with what had probably been one of the world's most beautiful beaches. But now it was something else altogether. In less than a decade, the international glitterati, the famously beautiful, the notoriously stylish, and the just plain stinking rich may have seized the once drowsy tropical island of Phuket and made it their own, but they left Patong behind.

Patong had instead become ground zero for the hordes of

package tourists shipped to Phuket by mass-market tour operators all over Europe, the Middle East, and Australia. The sleepy little fishing village was now mostly a jumble of travel agencies, cheesy souvenir shops, Indian tailors, all-night discos, and open-air girlie bars. Once Patong may have been the kind of gentle, palm-fringed South Seas paradise they wrote musicals about, but now it was just another nasty little hole.

"You want to go to Patong?" I asked. "Jesus, Anita, that place is a shit hole."

"Don't so snobby, Jack. It's just a tourist town. There's nothing wrong with that."

"I hate tourists."

"Oh, I see. Then, just out of interest, how do you think the Thais see you, white boy?"

That hurt. Boy, did that hurt.

THE USUAL ROUTE from Cape Panwa followed the southern coast of the island for several miles and then abruptly swung inland and climbed through the rain forest in a series of steep switchbacks before descending again to the western beaches through another equally steep set of switchbacks. The road was slick from a light misting by a clutch of rain clouds still huddled over the center of the island and the traffic was light, but just as we crested the road's highest point everything on the road in front of us abruptly stopped moving altogether.

We crept along for a half-mile, moving slowly through a double switchback, and then we saw the accident. A motorbike had gone down on a curve and the rider had skidded right into the path of a bus coming the other way. The mob of Taiwanese tourists from the bus was now huddled on the road's shoulder snapping pictures of each other in front of the crumpled motorcycle. They were wearing

Bermuda shorts and brightly colored golf hats and looked as if they thought the whole business might have been concocted just for their amusement.

The middle-aged Thai woman who had been riding the bike was sitting in the road just in front of where the tour bus had come to a halt. She had her legs stretched straight out in front of her and there was blood on her grease-streaked face. She held a grubby piece of cloth to the side of her head and stared off into the middle distance as one by one the Taiwanese stood in front of her and snapped pictures.

Anita shuddered and turned away. "Oh, Christ. I can't look at that."

"She seems to be okay. Probably more scared than hurt."

"That's easy for you to say, Jack."

It was indeed, so I shut up and edged our jeep past the accident scene. Twenty minutes later we were rolling slowly through Patong searching for a parking place.

Since the whole village of Patong consists of essentially just two long streets, finding a place to park is pretty much a matter of cruising north along the ocean on Beach Road then turning around and coming back in the opposite direction on the parallel road that is about a hundred yards inland. It was barely past mid-day and we had no problem finding a spot almost immediately.

The west side of Beach Road is mercifully devoid of development and a broad concrete walkway runs along the sand for well over a mile. The beach itself isn't all that great—the strip of sand is more khaki-colored than golden and a good deal of it is invisible under the ranks of canvas lounge chairs set out for rent by beachfront entrepreneurs—but the ocean is another matter altogether. Maybe, I grudgingly admitted to myself as we locked the Suzuki and set out walking, this hadn't been such a bad idea after all.

The surf was rolling in as we walked, a low shore break that was useless for anyone hauling a board but otherwise suitably picturesque, and a warm breeze washed our faces with heavy salt air. The wind carried a jumble of pungent smells from which I could swear I could pick out the sharp spices of Madagascar and the moist veldt of Tanzania. Of course, I hadn't the slightest idea what either of those things actually smelled like, but I was still pretty sure they were in there somewhere.

"You hungry, cowboy?"

I was just about to remind Anita we'd eaten breakfast pretty late and it was probably still too soon for lunch when I realized the salt air was already working its customary magic on my appetite.

"I could eat," I said. "Where do you want to go?"

"I don't know. What do you feel like?"

"Seafood."

Anita laughed and the sound of it tinkled in the warm breeze like wind chimes.

"Now there's a surprise," she said.

We crossed Beach Road and turned north. Open-air seafood restaurants lined the sidewalk, all of them displaying the day's inventory on beds of ice spread out in big metal tubs. Offered for inspection were local lobsters, giant prawns, mussels, calamari, oysters, and an array of whole fish that were largely unidentifiable, at least to me. Most of the restaurants also sported huge outdoor grills where the seafood was cooked after it had been selected. The cloying smell of burning coconut shells mixed with the meatier odor of charcoal tugged at the river of tourists that flowed up and down the sidewalks of Beach Road.

Young women dressed in traditional sarongs of dazzlingly colored Thai silk greeted passers-by in front of most of the restaurants. Some offered diffident *wai*s, while others bowed and held out menus. A few cut straight to the chase with smiling shouts of "Come inside, please, sir and madam!"

Anita and I wandered past a dozen or more such places without stopping. I had never been very good at this sort of thing. The technique of picking a restaurant or a place to stay in a town I didn't know very well was always a puzzle to me. How could I be sure a better choice didn't lurk just a little way up the road?

Anita and I walked past something called the Pizzadelic Internet Pizzeria, which seemed pleasant enough in spite of its name. It offered a blue and white tiled outdoor bar and functional tables set up near the sidewalk underneath a mural that looked like it had been ripped off from a Grateful Dead concert.

"Want to go in here?" I asked, but Anita kept walking without bothering to reply.

A few moments later I spotted a McDonalds. It was pretty nice looking, too. The brick patio out front had some white plastic tables scattered around under a red and yellow striped awning and the place was jammed with an assortment of tourists and locals knocking back the Big Macs, reading newspapers, and generally engaged in what appeared to be some pretty vigorous hanging out.

I half turned toward Anita, but she spoke before I could manage to say anything.

"Don't even think about it," she said.

"Hey, okay, maybe it's not all that great a place to eat, but at least you got to admit the fries have a lot going for them."

Anita shot me a look.

"It's not the food," she said. "And you know it."

"Know what?"

"You don't see anything wrong with it, do you?'

"Wrong with *what*, Anita?"

"Those people." She gestured with her head at the crowd lounging around in front of McDonalds. "Look at them."

I looked.

"What are you talking about?" I asked. "It's mostly just tourists hanging out with their girlfriends."

"*Girlfriends*?" Anita snorted. "Those women are whores, Jack."

Ah-ha, so that was it.

"Young Thai girls hanging around with scruffy middle-aged westerners who are probably twice their age? What do you think those women are, Jack? Schoolteachers on holiday?"

"What is it that bothers you so much, Anita? Is it that those men give the girls some money while they're here? Or is it that the men are middle-aged and the girls are young."

Anita didn't bother to answer, but I wasn't ready to let her off the hook yet. I was still harboring some resentment from the dinner table conversation at Karsarkis' party.

"Or maybe," I pressed on, "it's mostly that the men are white and the girls aren't."

"I don't make judgments based on skin color," Anita snapped.

"Excuse me," I pointed out, "but you just did. Western women usually do when it comes to Thai women. You see a Thai woman with a white man and you assume the white man is there because he's getting sex and the Thai woman is there because she's being paid for it. And the worst part is you're not even ashamed of assuming that."

"It's not that easy."

"Oh yes, it is. It's *exactly* that easy. I made a deal with guys like those over there a long time ago, Anita. They don't judge me. I don't judge them. I figure it's a pretty fair arrangement all around."

Anita let the subject drop, which I took to be a pretty good sign, and we walked on for a while after that in a silence.

Eventually we came to a waist-high stone wall behind which black iron tables were scattered across a brick courtyard shaded by a thick canopy of palm trees. The tables were dressed with white linen and folded pink napkins and the whole thing made an undeniably pretty picture. When we stopped to take it in a very young woman of uncommon beauty approached with a shy smile, bobbed her head in a diffident greeting, and proffered a menu. I took it and pretended to study its offerings, but mostly I sneaked surreptitious glances at the girl.

She was wearing a traditional Thai sarong made out of green and gold silk that encased her slim figure from head to toe in a sheath of shimmering color. Her long hair was tar black and glowed with a sheen that held its own even against the vivid luminescence of her dress. She had the wide, unblinking eyes of a cat—a Siamese cat, I thought, but quickly dismissed the comparison as far too obvious—and her face formed a warm yet slightly shy smile that for the life of me I could not imagine to be purely commercial.

"That looks good, Jack. Don't you think?"

"Yes indeed, I do."

Anita was considerate enough not to require me to acknowledge we were referring to different things altogether.

The young woman showed us to a table positioned between two thick palms, one which had a fine view of the ocean just across the road. I ordered a bottle of some no-name white wine and we sipped it as we studied the menus. The wind rattled the palm fronds above us, the surf rolled with a basso drumming in the background, and the smells of grilling lobster drifted on the warm, salty air.

It was a nice moment, I had to admit, but not nice enough to make me stop wondering why Anita had wanted us to drive to Patong in the first place. Anita had just made it unmistakably clear that Patong was hardly her kind of place and I knew there was something on her mind other than lunch and a walk through town. I just didn't know what it was yet.

That was the very moment Anita chose to close her menu, put it down, and tell me what was really going on.

Ten

"I THOUGHT MAYBE after lunch we could have a look in some of the real estate offices, Jack. I've been thinking it might be nice to buy a house down here. Someplace I could get out of Bangkok to paint."

I examined Anita carefully. She seemed to be completely serious.

Anita's career as an artist had recently taken off. Her London agent was a genius at PR and he had hyped Anita as an Italian woman living and painting in exotic Thailand at exactly the right time to make her sound like the next great hot find. Of course, she had a lot of talent, too, and that was probably the biggest reason for her success, but great PR never hurt anybody. Everything she painted was selling and the prices she was getting were jumping, so I had no reason to doubt the guy's sales pitch that Anita was hot. Of course, that had always been exactly my own point of view.

Regardless, none of that led me to conclude we ought to be buying a house in Phuket.

"No way, Anita. Absolutely no way. We have a perfectly nice apartment in Bangkok, and don't forget that I'm just a poor business school professor. I can't afford a vacation house in Phuket."

"I didn't ask you to buy a vacation house in Phuket, Jack. I said *I* was thinking of buying a place here to paint. It won't be your money and it won't be your decision."

Uh-oh.

"I'd like your help and your support, Jack. But it's not absolutely necessary."

"Okay, Anita. Calm down. I'm sorry if I was a little harsh. I was just surprised, that's all. We've never talked about anything like this before."

"Well we're talking about it now."

We were indeed, and something about it was already making me uncomfortable as hell. The subject had only just come up, but already I had the distinct feeling we weren't just talking about a house here. Worse, I couldn't see exactly what it was we actually *were* talking about.

The rest of lunch went quietly without either of us mentioning real estate again. The palm fronds continued to rattle, the surf continued to roll, and the smell of lobster continued to drift, but everything was different all of a sudden. It felt to me like Anita had just taken several giant steps back into a place where I was not invited.

When our plates had been cleared and we had both declined coffee, Anita scooted her chair back slightly by way of preface. I had no trouble guessing what was coming next, and of course I was right.

"I'm going to walk around to a couple of the real estate offices and see what they have listed. Are you coming?"

"I'd rather not, if you don't mind."

"That's fine. I won't be long."

Anita's voice was matter-of-fact as she stood up.

"Where will you be?" she asked.

I looked around, but nowhere particularly interesting came to mind, so I shrugged. "I guess I'll just have another glass of wine here," I said. "I'll meet you back at the jeep in…what? An hour?"

"Fine. The jeep then, in an hour."

"You remember where it is?"

"Yes, Jack." Anita pitched her voice in that particular way that always made me uneasy. "I can find the jeep without you holding my hand."

"You're sure you don't mind me not going with you?"

"Of course not, Jack. Why would I mind?"

Why, indeed?

Anita had been gone only a few minutes when a fresh glass of wine arrived, closely followed by a busload of tourists. As the gaggle of extended families unloaded and began piling into the restaurant, the sound of their heavily accented Cantonese clearly marked them to me as Hong Kong Chinese. I decided my peaceful afternoon was probably at an end. Cantonese isn't a spoken language, it's a screamed language.

I looked around, sizing up possible escape routes, and noticed a middle-aged westerner sitting by himself at a table not far away from me. He had a straw Stetson tipped back on his head and was gazing at the invading horde of Chinese tourists with obvious bemusement. When he caught my eye, he nodded a friendly greeting.

"How you doing?" he hollered over the clamor.

"I'm doing fine," I called back noncommittally, although of course I wasn't.

When the man stood up, collected his beer bottle, and started toward me, I was less than thrilled. Companionship was the last thing I wanted right at that moment, much less the companionship of some yahoo sex tourist wearing a cowboy hat.

"I'll bet you're a Yank," the man beamed as soon as he walked up to the table.

"You got me."

"Well, hot damn," he said sticking out his hand. "Me, too. My friends call me CW."

"Jack Shepherd," I said, shaking the man's hand.

He eyed the chair Anita had abandoned. "Mind if I set a spell?"

I didn't know what else to say and I didn't want to be rude to the guy, so I shook my head. "Go ahead," I said.

The man sank heavily into the chair, removed his hat, and wiped his forehead with the back of his hand.

"I'm from Dallas myself, but I don't mind telling you, this heat here is knocking me for a goddamned loop."

"I guess I must be used to it."

"Where you from?"

"I was born in the States, but I live in Bangkok now."

"You live in *Bangkok*? No shit?"

"No shit."

"What do you do there, if you don't mind me asking."

"I teach at Chulalongkorn University."

"Really?" The guy bobbed his head in interest. "What do you teach?"

"International business, corporate planning. That kind of stuff."

"Wow! Ain't that something?" The man bobbed his head around as if he could hardly grasp such a thing, then he slyly shook his finger at me. "Something tells me that you're a lawyer."

"Yes," I said. "That's right."

"I knew it," he nodded. "I knew it."

Tex took a moment to look pleased with himself for his perspicacity.

"Well, hey," he said after a moment of awkward silence, "you being a local and all, how about answering a question for a fellow countryman?"

"Sure. What do you want to know?"

"Oh, I was just wondering…"

The cowboy leaned back in his chair and chewed at his lip for a moment, presumably demonstrating all the wondering he was doing, before he spoke. "Exactly how long have you known Plato Karsarkis?"

At first, of course, I thought I had misunderstood him.

"I'm sorry?" I said.

"I asked how long you've known Plato Karsarkis. Actually, Jack, I suppose I ought to ask you this first. Are you representing him? Are you one of Karsarkis' lawyers now?"

"No, I don't represent him," I responded automatically.

Then I recovered enough from my astonishment to start working up a royal mad-on over this rube's ambush.

"But, just out of curiosity, who the fuck are you to be asking me something like that, Tex?"

The man reached into a back pocket and took out a black leather folder that looked like a wallet. For a moment I thought the man was about to show me his driver's license, but then he put the folder on the table between us and flipped it open and of course it wasn't a driver's license at all.

There was a big silver star inside. It was pinned to one side of the wallet and an identification card inside a plastic-covered pocket was on the other.

"I'm Deputy United States Marshal Clovis Ward and I'm assigned to the Special Operations Group of the United States Marshals Service. We're responsible for transporting high-profile prisoners and apprehending fugitives."

"I don't believe it." I sat there shaking my head. "You have got to be shitting me."

The cowboy used his forefinger to slip a business card out from under his ID and then pushed it across the table to me.

"Call the marshals service in Washington, Mr. Shepherd. They'll vouch for me."

I pushed back from the table without picking up the card and folded my arms.

The fellow looked ex-military, like a noncom who had put in his twenty, retired to Florida, and let himself go slightly to seed; but he still looked a little dangerous, too, mostly around his eyes, which were hard and black and weren't smiling even though the rest of his face was. His hair was close-cropped and badly cut above his receding forehead, and while his upper body appeared fit and muscular his khaki shirt stretched where it buttoned over his belly. I thought I glimpsed the thin purple ghost of a tattoo on the back of his left hand, but he kept it turned slightly away from me and I couldn't be certain. He had a smoker's face, heavily lined and with a pattern of sharp ridges and clefts that looked like a topographical map of the Grand Canyon, and his leather-toned skin suggested exposure to a lot of sunlight without the use of FDA-approved creams.

The man sat there saying nothing while I studied him, smiling unblinkingly at me and twirling a pair of aviator-style sunglasses between his thumb and forefinger.

"What do you want?" I asked.

"To talk to you."

"About what?"

"Oh, I think you know."

"Just in case I have the wrong idea, why don't you spell it out for me?"

The man unbuttoned the flap on one of his shirt pockets, reached in with two fingers, and pulled out something that looked like a thin stack of photographs. He put them on the table on top of his business card, but the pictures, if that's what they were, were face down. When I reached to turn them over, he covered them with a big hand that was hard and callused.

"You know where the Paradise Bar is?"

"The one here in Patong?" I asked, puzzled, not seeing why he wanted to know.

The man nodded.

"Sure," I said. "It's just up the road from here, but—"

"Nine o'clock tonight. Be there or be square."

"*Be there or be square?* Jesus, pal, where do you get your dialogue? Old Cheech and Chong movies?"

The man pushed himself out of his chair. He picked up his Stetson and when he put it on he carefully adjusted the angle of the brim, bending it slightly between his fingers until he seemed to be satisfied it was sitting exactly right on his head.

"Well, Slick, if I was you I wouldn't worry about it none. You've got a whole shit load of better things than that to think about right now."

Then the man slipped on his sunglasses, tossed me a little salute, and walked away. As I watched him thread his way among the tables crowded with Chinese tourists wolfing down their set-price lunches, I reached over and picked up the small stack of photographs he had left on the table.

There were three of them. The images were blurred and grainy as if they had been taken from a great distance and they had an odd green cast to them. My guess was that they had been taken through some kind of high-powered night vision equipment, although I was certainly no expert in such things and couldn't be sure. Nevertheless, the contents of the photos were unmistakable.

In the first, I was getting out of our rented jeep in front of Karsarkis' house. In the second, Anita and I were standing at the front door waiting for someone to open it. In the third, I was standing at the top of the steps to Karsarkis' house waving idiotically into the night. When I had done that on the night of Karsarkis' dinner party and Anita had asked me why, I told her something about wanting to be certain I hadn't missed anybody who might be out there watching us. At the time I thought I was joking. Apparently I wasn't.

I glanced up just in time to see Deputy United States Marshal Clovis Ward reach the sidewalk. I followed him with my eyes as he turned left down Beach Road and walked toward the Holiday Inn. Even when I could no longer distinguish him in the crowd of tourists that filled the sidewalk, I could still see that damned Stetson bobbing just above the flowing mass of bodies. Then I lost sight of it, too, and the man was gone.

Eleven

I DIDN'T INTEND to tell Anita about this guy bracing me after she had left the restaurant, and I sure as hell wasn't going to tell her about the photographs. I thought the idea of being watched and photographed by the United States Marshals Service might frighten her, particularly since it scared the crap out of me.

Still, not telling her might be a problem, too. Driving back to the hotel in the jeep, we would be together in awfully close quarters and Anita had eerie radar. I wasn't absolutely sure I could get away with keeping it from her.

I needn't have worried. Anita had made arrangements with some real estate agent she had found in Patong to look at a house on our way back to the hotel and she talked on and on about the place while we drove. I let her, because it kept me off the hook.

"And guess the best part," she concluded breathlessly. "Go ahead. Guess."

"They're going to give the house to you for nothing."

"Be serious."

"I was."

"Jack, it has a tennis court."

That gave me pause. I'd always wanted a house with a tennis court and Anita knew it.

"What kind of court?" I asked, trying to keep my voice as disinterested as possible.

"I don't know. The usual kind, I guess. You know, with a net."

"I meant what kind of surface does it have, Anita? Hard court? Clay? Grass?"

"I know what you meant. I was just joking. The woman didn't say."

"Woman?"

"The agent," Anita said and gave me a big wink. "I think you're going to like her as much as you'll like the tennis court."

That naturally enough tickled my curiosity and shut me up for a while, exactly as Anita had probably intended it to. The woman had given Anita a map and was going to meet us at the house. I could hardly wait.

Following the route marked on the map in yellow ink, we went south from Patong past the Le Meridien Hotel complex to Karon Beach and then further south to Kata Beach. Just beyond a huge Club Med complex that bore a remarkable resemblance to an abandoned POW camp, the main road turned east, tracing a route over the coastal hills and back to Phuket Town.

According to the map, instead of turning there we were supposed to go straight ahead and follow a smaller road that continued south until we saw a sign just beyond Little Kata Beach that read No DRIVE BEYOND THIS POINT BY POLICE ORDER. At that sign, according to the instructions the woman had given Anita, we were to drive straight on. Naturally. Welcome to Thailand.

We located the sign without difficulty and then, about a quarter mile beyond it, we found ourselves on a winding asphalt road that climbed steeply up from the coast into a lush, tropical jungle. It was not long before we were completely engulfed in a jungle of giant ferns, banana trees, oversize cattails, and coconut palms. Everywhere bougainvillea grew wild, etching red and white veins in the tangle of the rain forest. The temperature dropped so abruptly it felt like someone had turned on a huge air conditioner.

The house we were looking for was at the end of a driveway off the road to the right. The entry was marked with twin rows of rubber trees, their white-splotched trunks glowing like runway lights in the deeply saturated green of the forest. The two rows were so perfect, every tree so flawlessly aligned and utterly identical in height and growth, they looked like a cartoon. I half expected to see Jiminy Cricket skipping along just ahead of us, whistling happily as he showed the way.

The agent's silver Range Rover was parked at the end of the driveway, right in front of the house. As we pulled up the woman got out and stood waiting, smiling in that particularly servile yet obviously artificial way real estate agents seem to smile the world over. Anita introduced us, but I was too busy looking the woman over to get her name straight. I thought it was Sanilee, or Saralee, or some kind of Lee, but at least I got her nickname. It was Nok.

Nok was tall for a Thai, nearly six feet, and she had the slim figure and bouncing strut of a runway model rather than the more generally compact and inconspicuous way of walking most Thai women employed. She wore a white blouse and a long yellow skirt with a wide belt and high-heeled sandals that taken together were perhaps just a touch too elegant for the occasion. Her long hair was slightly teased up and then swept straight back from her high forehead and her eyes were invisible behind huge tortoiseshell sunglasses. She looked vaguely familiar, although I was sure I'd never met her before. Then in a moment it came to me. She looked as if she had stepped straight out a seventies photograph of Jackie Kennedy and her friends.

"The house was built about three years ago," she was saying as I eventually tuned into the conversation, "but no one has ever lived in it. We're selling it for the bank that provided the financing."

The woman's right hand held a mobile phone and she was gesturing toward the house with it, using its little antenna as a pointer. I followed it with my eyes and for the first time took a close look at the house.

I had to admit it wasn't bad. Not up to the standard of Plato Karsarkis' house, of course, but still very nice. The style was something you would probably call early Hollywood Hills, hardly the sort of thing you'd expect to find in Phuket. Still, I had to admit the whitewashed walls and plain lines went surprisingly well with the green of the rain forest and the streaky blue of the sea beyond.

"What do you think, Jack?" Anita asked.

I mumbled something suitably vague that seemed to satisfy her and then trailed along behind the two women as they started their tour.

As it turned out, the house was impressive and Nok was thorough and professional in her presentation. For twenty minutes or so we paced the huge living room with a stone fireplace that looked somewhat out of place on a tropical island, examined the teak-floored bedrooms, peered at the designer-perfect kitchen, and took in the sweeping views from the hillside westward over the Andaman Sea. The thing that really grabbed me of course was the tennis court, a green-tinted Har-Tru surface carefully laid out along a north-south axis just as it should have been. It, too, enjoyed a spectacular sea view.

When the tour was done, we regrouped by the cars and Nok handed us both business cards and little booklets about the house. I flipped through my copy of the brochure while she was talking, but nothing really caught my eye until I got to the last page and saw the asking price. It was eighty-five million Thai baht, nearly three million United States dollars. If this Hollywood Hills house had actually been in the Hollywood Hills, at least on one of the better streets, that probably would have been just about right. But it was in

Phuket, and I couldn't imagine there was any house in Phuket that had ever sold for that much money.

I held the little pamphlet up and looked at Anita.

"Have you seen the price?" I asked her.

"Yes, it's pretty ridiculous," Nok spoke up before Anita had to say anything. "But Thai banks are completely unrealistic about the value of property. They'd probably take a lot less if you offered cash."

"It does seem high," Anita mumbled, but she didn't look at me.

"Well, my husband and I bought a house from the same bank," Nok said, still pitching hard. "We offered about half of what they were asking and stuck to it and eventually they took it."

"That's still may be a little more than I wanted to spend," Anita admitted.

"It's a *lot* more than I wanted to spend," I added.

"Did you have a figure in mind?" Nok asked politely, looking at me rather than Anita.

"Yes," I smiled. "Zero."

Nok looked puzzled, as she should have.

"I would be buying the property," Anita explained. "Jack's not sure it's a good idea. That what he means."

Nok started talking to me again, although I wasn't sure why.

"Phuket is a great place to have a second house, I can tell you that," she said. "My husband and I have a penthouse in Bangkok and a farm up north of Chiang Mai as well as our place here, but we spend as much time in Phuket as we can."

That was a lot of real estate, even in Thailand. Now that I thought about it, I realized it would have taken at least a month of my university salary to pay for the simple, but elegant clothing in which Nok was dressed and another six months or so to cover the elaborate, but refined jewelry she wore with it. Now it was my turn to look puzzled. I had never guessed there was so much money to be made selling houses in Phuket.

"Oh, I'm not really a real estate agent," Nok quickly volunteered, sensing my curiosity. "I just do this sometimes to help out a friend. And for the gossip, of course. Phuket's just loaded with gossip. When you deal with real estate, you get to hear every bit of it."

"I'm sure you do," I nodded.

"Neither my husband nor I really work," she shrugged.

"You don't?"

"My husband is an American," she said, as if that explained everything.

"I'm an American," I said. "I work."

"Oh, I didn't mean it *that* way. My husband sold a business in the United States. I don't really know what kind of business. He doesn't like to talk about it. Anyway, he's retired here now."

"What's his name? Bill Gates?"

"No," she said, not getting the joke, which was okay with me since it wasn't a very good joke. "It's Edward Dare. Most of his friends call him Eddie. Do you know him?"

I shook my head.

"You should. You'd like him, and he doesn't know that many other Americans out here. Maybe we could all have dinner somewhere one night soon."

"That would be nice." Anita jumped in to rescue me before the ethnic solidarity routine spiraled completely out of hand. "But I'm afraid we're going back to Bangkok tomorrow."

"Well, maybe another time." Nok seemed genuinely disappointed. "I'm sure he'd really enjoy meeting a couple from back home."

"I'm Italian," Anita said. "Jack's the American."

"And I live in Bangkok," I added. "That's where 'back home' is for me."

"Oh…" Nok briefly looked disappointed again, but then she abruptly brightened. "Anyway, I hope you'll think about the house. Phuket is a wonderful place to live and there're so many prominent people here. It's just that you never hear about them because everyone is so discreet."

I rolled my eyes and said nothing, but Anita couldn't resist.

"Prominent people?" she asked, her voice dripping innocence.

"I don't like to gossip," Nok said, "but I hear…"

She bent toward us and lowered her voice, although I had the impression the house was sufficiently isolated we could have set off a low-yield nuclear device without anyone hearing it.

"A cousin of the British royal family secretly owns a beautiful house at Karon Beach through a Cayman Islands company, and there is a *very* prominent American actor who owns a beautiful villa above Cape Panwa which is in his manager's name. I'm not permitted to tell you who it is, but…well, I can promise you've seen a *lot* of his movies."

I struggled to look impressed, but I just couldn't pull it off.

"And of course our most prominent resident of all has a stunning house up on one of the northern beaches you probably haven't seen. It's very private and very isolated."

I glanced smugly at Anita and then back at Nok.

"Now who would that be?" I asked.

"Ah…" Nok glanced from side to side and lowered her voice even more. "No one knows for sure if he's here now, but there are these people all over the island. They're trying to be low-profile, but you can't do much around here without somebody noticing."

"Who's all over the island?"

"You know," Nok winked at me. "You Americans. The Secret Service, the FBI, the military. Probably even the CIA."

"So why are they here?" I asked as naively as I could manage.

"I'll bet you know already."

"No, I don't. Really."

"You're going to make me say it, aren't you?"

"Yep."

"Okay."

Nok raised her chin slightly and shifted her eyes first to Anita and then back to me. I could have sworn I actually saw them glitter, possibly with dollar signs.

"They're getting the house ready for Barack Obama. It's going to be his secret retreat."

I burst out laughing. I couldn't help it. Anita looked embarrassed and a suspicious look crept over Nok's face.

"Say…you're not one of *them*, are you?"

For one wild moment I thought about confessing I was actually the Director of the CIA and then telling Nok I would have to kill her now that she knew, but I let it slide.

Twelve

IN THE CAR on the way back to the hotel Anita floated the topic of the house a couple of times, but I absolutely refused to bite. My guess was she was working up to a suggestion we put in equal amounts and buy the house together in spite of its cost, but there was no way in hell that was going to fly with me. Tennis court or not, a three-million-dollar house in Phuket was a long way out of my league.

Still, Anita's radar must have been at full power, or maybe she just saw something in my face that I hadn't realized was there, but it wasn't very long before I realized I was getting the hard eye from her. That was when she dropped the subject of the house and focused her full attention on wheedling out of me what was really on my mind.

I didn't even try to resist. It would have been useless.

Taking a deep breath, I told Anita about Marshal Ward and how he had accosted me back in Patong when she was off exploring real estate offices. I omitted only the part about the pictures Ward had left on the table. Somehow announcing to my wife that people were following us around and clandestinely taking pictures seemed to me to be unduly alarmist. Of course, that one photograph of me waving like a madman in front of Karsarkis' front door would probably have made me look like a real asshole to her, too, but I told myself that had nothing to do with why I was keeping quiet about the pictures. Nothing at all. Really.

"And he wants you to go back to Patong and meet him tonight?" she asked.

"I don't have to go."

"But you *are* going, aren't you?"

"Well...I guess I'm curious."

That was embarrassingly lame, of course, but there it was.

"Are you at least going to call somebody and check on him before you go?" Anita asked after she had thought about that for a moment. "Maybe he's not who he says he is."

"Oh, I think he is."

"And this you know exactly how, Sherlock?"

I thought back to the way the man had examined me appraisingly with his flat, cop's eyes.

"I've had a lot of experience with guys like this, Anita. I know a Fed when I see one."

Anita looked at me and raised her eyebrows.

"You were a corporate lawyer in Washington, Jack. Your idea of life on the streets was walking to the garage to get your Mercedes instead of calling somebody to deliver it to you. Don't let your romantic fantasies get the better of you."

That brought on a few minutes of silence, as I suspected Anita intended for it to.

"What do you suppose this man wants with you?" she resumed, ignoring the third-degree burns she had just inflicted.

"I think he just wants to be certain I'm not one of Karsarkis' lawyers."

"Why would he care if you were?"

Anita had a very good point there, it seemed to me. Why indeed?

The only role the marshals would have in a matter like this would be to transport Karsarkis back if the State Department could convince the Thai government to agree to his extradition. Who Karsarkis' lawyers were, or who they weren't, didn't offhand seem to me to have much to do with that.

"Maybe he wants you to spy for him," Anita said.

"Oh, come on," I snorted. "Now who's having romantic fantasies?"

"No, Jack, really. Maybe he wants to ask you what the inside of Plato's house looks like, how many guards he has, things like that."

"And why would he want to know about any of that?"

"Well…maybe he's planning a snatch."

"A *what*?" I shook my head. "Look, Anita, the marshals service doesn't go around kidnapping people. They're just a bunch of glorified security guards."

"I don't know. You heard what that real estate woman said. What would the Secret Service, the military, the FBI, and the CIA be doing here on Phuket all at the same time if there wasn't something big planned?"

"Getting a secret hideaway ready for Barack Obama?"

"Be serious, Jack. There's something going on here, and if this man wants anything from you, he's part of whatever it is."

Now I knew I was the poor guy who had been handicapped for life by three years of legal education and Anita was the freethinking artist here, but sometimes it seemed to me she was still the one of us more likely to view the world from deep inside a bunker of suspicion. I was generally the one who took what I saw pretty much at face value unless there was some obvious reason not to. Maybe, I thought to myself, having the soul of an artist wasn't all it was cracked up to be.

"You want my advice?" she asked.

Anita didn't wait for me to tell her whether I did or not, but I wasn't about to point that out.

"Stay out of this, Jack."

"Look, Anita—"

"This isn't the kind of stuff you're used to. I know you flushed out a money launderer or two and exposed a couple of banking scams, but don't start thinking you're Indiana Jones. These are big guys. Stay out of it, Jack."

"All the fellow wants to do is talk to me, Anita. I think you're making way too much out of this."

"Do you?"

Anita examined the nails of her right hand as if they had just become inordinately interesting.

"You had a taste of something dangerous with that Asia Bank of Commerce thing, didn't you, Jack? And, as much as I hate to say it, I can see that life won't ever be the same for you again."

Off toward the east a thick line of black cloud etched the sky along the horizon. Above the line everything was serene. The sky was clear and puffs of white cloud drifted peacefully across it. Below the line, however, it was another story altogether. The sky first went light gray and then purplish-black, and then just at the horizon it turned into a malevolent greenish-black hole that looked like a deep, ugly bruise. It was as if a window into the abyss was slowly opening in front of us and we were driving straight into it. Those puffy little billows didn't have the slightest idea what was coming at them, I mused, and I knew exactly how they felt.

Anita and I made the rest of the drive back to the hotel in silence. I was thinking about what she had just said to me. I couldn't even imagine what she was thinking about. We spent the rest of the day on the beach ignoring the subject of my approaching get-together that night in Patong with Marshal Ward. Then we had an early dinner at the hotel and ignored it some more.

Anita's instincts were usually pretty good, particularly the more dire ones, and her suspicions made me uneasy even if I didn't want to admit it. The whole time I was driving back to Patong after dinner, Anita's stern warnings about where this all could lead were bouncing around my head. Just this once, I really did hope she had it wrong.

Thirteen

THE PARADISE BAR is a Phuket landmark, one of the first and probably still the most famous of what are now dozens of rundown bars along Patong beach. I parked at the Holiday Inn, cut through the garden past the darkened swimming pool, then emerged from their back gate into the nighttime hubbub of Beach Road. Turning north, I walked the fifty or so yards to a little shack on the beach.

The Paradise was more of a sunset watering hole than a nighttime hangout. By now, just after nine, most people had moved on to livelier haunts and the place was pretty calm. Those few patrons who remained were drinking quietly, either at a long counter that faced the ocean or further back inside at the scarred wooden bar with a big-screen television above it.

Clovis Ward was on a stool in a far back corner with his Stetson cocked back on his head, which made him a hard man to miss. I noticed he had chosen a seat that had a clear field of vision across the entire bar and all the way out to the street. It could have been just a coincidence, but somehow I doubted it. He didn't look at me when I walked in. He was leaning on his forearms against the bar, and he appeared to be completely absorbed in a golf tournament on the television set up over his head. Somehow I doubted that, too.

"You play golf?" I asked as I pulled out the stool next to him and sat down.

"You gotta be joking. I don't get paid enough to afford clubs. It's you rich people who play golf. Not guys like me."

"Is that why we're meeting here in this dump, Marshal? To demonstrate what a working-class guy you are?"

Now he looked at me.

"I like this place," he said.

"Figures."

"Besides it's handy. I'm at the Holiday Inn next door."

"That figures, too."

A golfer I didn't recognize, which was to be expected since I didn't recognize any golfer who wasn't Tiger Woods, belted his drive into a lake and Ward chuckled in enjoyment.

"Look, Marshal," I said after a moment, "I gather—"

"You can drop that cutesy bullshit," he interrupted. "People call me CW."

"Okay, fine. CW it is. But only if you take off that stupid-looking hat."

CW made a snorting noise. I hoped it was a laugh, but I couldn't be sure. Whatever it had been, he took off his hat and laid it on the bar.

"Happy now?"

I gave CW a very small smile, but I didn't say anything.

"Okay, Jack. Now, I'm buying, so what's your poison?"

"Mekong and soda," I said to the middle-aged woman waiting behind the bar.

"Mekong?" he asked as she walked away to make my drink. "What's that?"

"It's Thai whiskey."

"Pretty good?"

"No. Actually, it's awful."

"Then why are you drinking it?"

"It's refreshing on a hot night, if you put enough soda and ice in it."

"Maybe I ought to try it," CW muttered. "This beer tastes like dog piss."

CW raised one hand and caught the bartender's eye. Then he pointed to me, made a drinking gesture, and held up two fingers. The woman nodded and took down a second glass.

"Okay," I said. "Enough of this happy horseshit."

I pulled the three pictures he'd given me out of my shirt pocket and dealt them out onto the bar one by one like playing cards.

"You going to tell me what this is all about?" I asked.

CW waited in silence for the bartender to serve our drinks. The woman glanced at the pictures while she was setting out the glasses, but apparently didn't see anything of interest to her. CW picked up his drink, sniffed suspiciously at the amber liquid, and tried a sip.

"You were right," he said. "Not bad at all."

"How wonderful for you. So can we get to it now?"

CW seemed to consider that for a moment. "You sure you're not one of his lawyers?"

"I already told you this morning that I wasn't."

"Yeah, but you got to appreciate my position here, Jack, me being an officer of the law and all. If you're one of Karsarkis' lawyers, then that's one thing. But if you're just a guy who's hanging around with him, then that's something else."

"I'm not one of Karsarkis' lawyers and I'm not a guy who's hanging around with him either. I've laid eyes on Plato Karsarkis exactly twice in my entire life."

"Okay." CW didn't seem very interested in the last part of what I said. "But you're *not* one of his lawyers. That's right, isn't it?"

"Just out of curiosity, what is it that makes you think I *might* be a lawyer for Plato Karsarkis?

"Because you look like one slippery son of a bitch to me, Slick. You're just the kind of shyster a piece of shit like Karsarkis would want to keep around."

I wasn't really sure what to say to that, so I kept my response as neutral as possible.

"I do not represent Plato Karsarkis in any capacity whatsoever. Is that clear enough for you, CW, or would you like it in writing."

"Yeah, I would, but I don't have a pen."

"I was kidding."

"So was I."

"No, you weren't."

"Well, mostly."

CW took another sip of his Mekong and soda, but he didn't say anything else.

"So do I get an answer now?" I asked after I had waited a while.

The photographs were still lying on the bar and I rapped on one with my forefinger.

"Why in Christ's name have you been following me around taking pictures?"

"We're not following *you*, Slick. We don't really give a shit about you. But we have Plato Karsarkis under surveillance around the clock and you just happen to get in the way."

"I don't see why that gives you any particular right to tell me who I can associate with."

"Don't go all prissy on me here, Slick."

I collected the photographs off the bar and held them out to CW. He shook his head. "Keep 'em. I got plenty more."

I tapped the three photographs into a neat pile and then ripped them in half. For good measure, I stacked the six halves together and ripped them again. Then I piled all the pieces into an ashtray and wiped my hands.

CW nodded absently a couple of times, then looked over at me and cocked his head as if he was trying to size something up.

"How do you feel about Plato Karsarkis?" he asked.

"We're not having an affair, if that's what you mean."

CW returned his gaze to the golf tournament still flickering soundlessly on the big Sony above our heads.

"You know what I'm talking about, Slick."

"Actually, I don't."

"I mean, do you like him? Are you sympathetic with him?"

"He's okay," I said. "But I wouldn't call myself sympathetic. He's a bail jumper and a fugitive, for God's sake."

"Do you think he's guilty?"

"Of what?"

"Of selling stolen oil smuggled out of Iraq. Of killing that girl."

"I don't know." I rubbed my forefinger in the condensation on the side of my glass and tried to find a way to get off the subject of how I felt about Plato Karsarkis. "He could be guilty of one and not the other. Or of both. Or neither. What do you think?"

"Me?" CW seemed startled at the question. "I'm just shoveling shit from a sitting position here, Slick. I bag 'em and tag 'em whether they're guilty or not. What happens to them after that is somebody else's problem, not mine."

I pushed myself around on my stool until I was facing out toward the sidewalk and watched the passing tourists for a while. There were an awful lot of them and they came in all shapes and sizes. Still, I figured that most of them at least knew why they were there, and whether it was to have a meal, or get drunk, or chase girls, being somebody who knew what he was doing there looked pretty good to me right about then.

"You didn't ask me here tonight to seek my counsel on whether Plato Karsarkis is guilty as charged, did you, CW?"

"Nope." He shook his head and turned around on his stool as he stifled a yawn. "That I didn't."

The sidewalk in front of the Paradise Bar was running high with a river of people heading for the center of Patong. They were a decidedly mixed bag: Scandinavian families with matching hair;

Japanese couples who might have been on their honeymoons; sweaty, rotund Germans holding hands with tiny Thai girls; mustachioed Arabic-looking men wearing tank tops and trailed by women in black chadors covering them from head to toe; a clutch of tattooed young Brits with several pounds of metal stuck through various parts of their bodies; a pair of hairy, middle-aged women in dirty T-shirts and baggy shorts who brayed nonstop at each other in broad Australian accents; and hundreds of other unidentifiable but equally uninspiring folks sweating out their cheap packaged holidays in paradise.

"I've been here almost three weeks now," CW said. "And I haven't done a fucking thing that's been useful to anybody. It's all been just a lot of hurry-up-and-wait bullshit. Son of a bitch, I am so damned tired."

I nodded sympathetically, not having any idea what else to do.

"I got two boys back in Dallas with my ex-wife and I miss 'em. I want to pop this bastard and go home, but I don't feel any closer to doing that now than I did the day I arrived."

"So you're still waiting for Karsarkis' extradition to be approved by the Thais? Is that it?"

"Yep. You got it, Slick."

CW's eyes flicked at me and then away. For a moment he seemed like he was going to say something else, but he didn't.

"So then tell me, what's your relationship with Karsarkis?" he asked instead.

"Dinner guest."

"Nothing professional?"

"For Christ's sake, CW, you're not going to start that again, are you?"

"I asked you before if you were one of his lawyers, Slick. You said you weren't and I believe you."

"How nice."

"Now I'm asking you if you have any other professional connection with him. Maybe a business arrangement of some kind."

The question surprised me, but I struggled to keep my eyes still so CW wouldn't see it. Did he somehow know about the conversation Karsarkis and I had had about his hotel deal? From the photographs it was clear CW wasn't operating alone, and he obviously had some pretty good technology going for him so I supposed it was at least possible. But even if he had somehow eavesdropped on the conversation at Karsarkis' house, what was I worried about? I'd told Karsarkis clearly that I wanted nothing to do with his business, hadn't I? Why was I feeling vaguely guilty now about nothing more than having the conversation with Karsarkis?

"Should I take your silence to mean you *do* have some kind of arrangement with him?" CW prompted before I had finished my musings.

"No. You should take my silence to mean I'm searching for a polite way to say it's none of your goddamned business. So far I haven't come up with one."

"You'd best tell me the truth right now, Slick. Things will go a lot better for you that way."

I wanted to tell him to fuck off. I really did. But I didn't really see what that would accomplish and what I wanted even more than that was to put an end to the whole damned conversation so I could go back to the hotel and Anita.

"I have no relationship at all with Plato Karsarkis. Neither business nor social. I met him by coincidence in a restaurant here."

"The Boathouse. Yeah, we know. How come Karsarkis recognized you?"

"I have no idea. He said he'd heard of me and seen pictures of me."

"And you believed him?"

"Why wouldn't I believe him? Why would the most famous man in the world walk up to me and lie about knowing me?"

"I can't put my finger on it, Slick, but something just don't sound right." CW shrugged slightly and rubbed at his face again. "Okay. Go on. How have you been involved with Karsarkis since then?"

"I haven't been. Anita and I went to his house for dinner because…well, because he asked us and my wife was curious about him. I didn't even want to go. That was the only time I've ever seen the man, other than at the Boathouse."

"So you have no commercial relationship with him."

I threw up my hands and rolled my eyes.

"Lordy, Mr. Marshal, don't hit me again with your big stick. I'll confess everything."

"Stop being such a smart ass, Slick. Just answer the fucking question."

"I have no commercial relationship whatsoever with Plato Karsarkis. Clear enough for you?"

"If you're lying to me, I'm gonna use your butt for a broom, boy."

"Don't you think you're laying on all that cornpone bullshit a little thick?"

CW smiled. "Yeah. Maybe I am at that."

He dug some bills out of his pocket, twisted around, and dropped them on the bar. Then he stood up and started to put on his hat, but perhaps remembering his promise to me he tucked it under his arm instead and jammed his hands into his pockets.

"There's somebody I want you to meet. You want to go someplace else with me?"

"Where do you have in mind?" I asked.

"There's a bar a couple of my boys like to hang out in. Up where the action is. I've never been there before, but they said it's called the Blue Lotus and it's right at the beginning of a street called Soi Crocodile. You know where that is?"

Soi Crocodile, huh? Indeed I did know where that was.

Maybe my evening was about to get interesting after all.

Fourteen

IF PATONG IS the rat's ass of Phuket, which it is, I don't know what you can call Soi Crocodile.

Objectively speaking, Soi Crocodile is one of a half-dozen tiny streets near the center of Patong, all of which are lined with open-air bars where hordes of foreigners hang out every day and every night drinking an awful lot of beer. Pretty much Patong's only real attraction is that thousands of young Thai girls, most of them fresh from tiny villages and poor farms far upcountry, constantly throng those same streets and bars.

The girls are prostitutes, of course, but on the whole and in a different context, you might be hard-pressed to tell. Instead of the makeup-caked, crack-addled hustlers most western men can spot easily enough back home, these girls are mostly casually dressed and pleasant looking; they are friendly in a way that seems genuine; they laugh and joke easily among themselves; and they respond to even the stupidest comments from the tourists with smiles that appear unfeigned.

When there are no customers to entertain, the girls eat the food they buy from the street vendors, drink cokes, watch television, listen to music, and gossip among themselves. Occasionally, in a modest effort to improve business one of them might call out, "Hello, handsome man!" or "Come talk me!" to any unattached males who wander into range, but mostly they appear unconcerned with commercial promotion and seem content to let fate shape their prospects.

Soi Crocodile is one of the little lanes right in the heart of it all, and it is every bit as much a part of the action as are the other little streets in the area. But there is one way in which it is just a tiny bit different.

The street is known locally as Soi Katoey, the Thai word for the men turned women for which Thailand is, in some circles at least, justly famous. Thailand has achieved international recognition for precious little in its history, but Thai doctors have become universally celebrated for at least one thing: their ability, with a few judicious snips here and there, to alter biological men into women indistinguishable from real ones, except of course that they frequently look a whole lot better.

Thai *katoeys* are as distant from the lumpy, clumsy transvestites who lurk in the western sexual shadows as doves are from crows. On the whole, they are tall, slim, tanned, and toned. They generally wear stylish dresses and chic, take-me-tonight slingback heels, and they often sport refined jewelry and expensive handbags. They look, almost to a man, like elegant and sophisticated women.

If CW was going to a bar on Soi Crocodile, I figured he had a huge surprise coming. I really wanted to be around to see him unwrap it, so to speak.

WALKING TOWARD THE center of Patong we jostled through the evening crowds along Beach Road. On the whole, these were mostly people I wouldn't have wanted to invite back to meet Anita.

"Jesus, Slick," CW muttered, reading my mind, "is this the parade of the fucking mutant tourists, or what?"

A man who looked either Indian or Pakistani abruptly

materialized out of the crowd right in front of CW, grabbed his hand before he could pull it away, and began pumping energetically.

"Nice suit for you, sir? Welcome! Welcome! Yes, sir. Yes, sir."

CW tried to extract his hand, but the little man wouldn't turn it loose.

"Best price for you, sir. Very best price."

"No thanks."

"But, sir, I am waiting for you. Welcome! Here is my card."

When the tailor held out a business card, CW feinted with his left hand as if suddenly seized with enthusiasm to accept it and then snatched his right hand away as the man loosed his grip in delight at apparently having latched onto a live one. Without another word, the man turned away and scanned the crowd for a better prospect.

"Nice move," I said.

"Yeah, well, I see the little fellow takes rejection well."

"I imagine he's had a lot of practice."

A small boy held out a black cloth duffle bag with large plastic wheels. An old woman unfurled a piece of cloth with a red and green pattern that might have been the flag of some country I didn't immediately recognize. A young girl, a plastic tray of cigarettes hanging from a strap around her neck, gripped half a dozen packs in one hand and waved them back and forth as if she were semaphoring. At the edge of the sidewalk a man was selling hammocks woven from thick blue and white cord. Every time he spied a group of likely looking prospects, he would slip out of one of his sandals and use his bare foot to stretch the hammock out by way of demonstrating its size and potential for comfort. When too many tourists walked by at the same time, the guy looked as if he was doing an impression of a pissed-off stork.

The Blue Lotus Pub sits right at the beginning of Soi Katoey. Like the Paradise Bar, it's open to the street and offers a panoramic view of the exotic delights of the neighborhood. CW nodded at two men sitting on stools that had an unobstructed view of it all and led me to an empty pair of stools right next to them. After ordering us each another Mekong and soda, CW made the introductions.

The one CW introduced as Chuck Parker looked exactly like somebody who ought to have a name like Chuck Parker. He was in his late thirties and had the thick, fleshy neck, light brown crew cut, and slightly heavy frame of a college athlete sliding into middle age.

The other man CW introduced as Marcus York. He was a slim black man of medium height and he wore round, gold-framed glasses that stood out memorably against a thick shock of prematurely gray hair. York looked like a character from a David Mamet play: black jeans, black shirt, and a two-day growth of very black beard. If Chuck Parker had been on the college football team, Marcus York had been in the drama club.

CW said both men were Deputy United States Marshals, but I wasn't so sure. Parker, yeah. He vibed street cop all the way. But York was another matter altogether. I'd bet my last dollar York was FBI, or maybe even something creepier.

"I wanted the boys to meet you," CW said as we shook hands all around.

"Why?"

"Well shit, Slick, they might bump into you somewhere out there on a dark night and I wouldn't want them to shoot your candy ass clean off."

Parker heehawed at that, wiggling his thick neck up and down, but York didn't move. He didn't even smile.

I got the feeling CW and his sidekicks were waiting for me to say something, but I couldn't figure out what it was supposed to be so we all just sat for a while in silence and watched the comings and goings across the street on Soi Crocodile.

"God *damn*," CW gasped a few minutes later. "Look at *that*."

The *katoey* CW was watching had just climbed up onto a round platform at the entrance to the *soi* and had begun to sway languidly to music blaring from speakers in one of the bars. At least six feet tall with long, glistening black hair tied away from her face in a ponytail, she wore a black silk sheath that ended less than halfway down her smooth brown thighs and she balanced gracefully on red platform slingbacks with six-inch heels. After a few minutes, a second *katoey* joined her on the platform—this one slightly shorter and heavier, but with a chest on her that would freeze a moose—and they began to dance together.

"Ah, *shit*," Parker chimed in. "I'm gonna have me a fuckin' *stroke*."

York, I noticed, said nothing.

As more and more of the *katoeys* gathered across Soi Bangla, I watched the three men out of the corner of my eye. Parker and CW, at least, couldn't get enough. Parker moaned and groaned and CW licked nervously at his lips.

Then CW noticed the two *katoeys* wearing giant rhinestone tiaras and ballgowns who were posing for pictures with tourists. He shot me a quick side-glance, but I kept a straight face and he couldn't be sure. It wasn't until he spotted the one in the hoop-skirted Scarlet O'Hara dress bringing a bottle of beer to the one who was dressed like Pocahontas that he got it.

"Fuck," he moaned, and I admit I had never heard the word used more movingly.

"Gotcha," I said.

"What?" Parker looked genuinely confused.

"They're men, you fuckwit," York finally spoke up.

"You're shittin' me," Parker mumbled, but from the way he climbed back into his drink you knew he saw it now, too.

We sat silently for a bit after that, gazing across the street. The whole scene was almost abnormally good-natured. The *katoeys* chattered among themselves, ate and drank, waved to passing tourists, posed for pictures, and took turns boogieing on the little round platform in the heavy night air.

"They don't sweat, man," CW said to me after watching three of them dance together for a while. "It ain't natural."

I gave him a long look.

"Okay," he nodded. "I see your point."

York smiled slightly at that, but he didn't say anything.

Another silence fell and I started to feel a little sorry for Parker and CW in spite of myself. CW in particular seemed almost embarrassed.

"Everybody here's been fooled at least once, CW," I finally said. "Don't let it get you down."

"That's not it, Slick," CW shook his head sadly. "It's just if I have to spend another week or two on this fuckin' island, I may have to think about turning queer."

"Keep it zipped, CW," I said. "It's tough to be a stranger in a strange land when your pants are down."

CW shook his head again and made a noise I couldn't quite put a name to. He waved for two more drinks, then stood up and beckoned me toward an empty table at the back of the bar.

Fifteen

PARKER AND YORK watched as I followed CW to the back of the bar, but neither said anything. A tall girl with bad skin had brought our drinks and then drifted away out of earshot.

"We got to get serious here," CW said.

"I can hardly wait."

"It's my job to see that Plato Karsarkis is returned to the US."

"That's got nothing to do with me."

"Yeah, it does."

I gave CW a look, but I didn't say anything.

"Look, Jack, I need your help here."

"I thought you told me you were just waiting for the Thai government to approve Karsarkis' extradition."

"Well…" CW appeared to think for a moment. "It's a little bit more complicated than that."

I waited.

"Look, Jack, I'm not really allowed to give you the whole thing—"

"Wait a minute." I held up my hand like a traffic cop. "Are you telling me the Thais aren't going to support extradition."

"Not exactly."

"Not exactly?"

"Well…not at all, really."

"I see."

"I doubt that."

I recalled Anita's prediction and shook my head a little at the memory of it.

Damn. How could she always be so dead on about stuff like this?

"So you and your little elves over there are here to kidnap the poor bastard and drag him back to the US no matter what the Thais have to say about it. Is that about the size of it, CW?"

"This is an evil man, Jack. He's a criminal. He has people killed. He's a traitor to his country."

"What movie is that speech from?" I asked, raising my eyebrows. "I forget."

"Then tell me what you think we should do about Plato Karsarkis, Jack. Just forget about him? Just forget about everything he's done and leave him alone to live out his life on the beautiful tropical island of Phuket?"

"Look, this isn't my problem."

"Well, shit," CW leaned toward me, "then maybe I'll just *make* it your problem."

I took a pull from my drink, trying to take the edge off my anger before I said anything I might regret. It didn't work.

"Well, fuck you, too, Marshal Asshole."

"Look, Jack—"

"Who the hell do you think you are? Do you threaten everybody, or am I something special to you?"

"I'm sorry," CW said and he did seem genuinely discomfited. "I was way out of line there and I apologize."

The man sounded so completely contrite I wasn't sure what to say, so I didn't say anything.

"Look, Jack. I really *am* sorry. I had no right to say that. I need your help here. Hell, I'm begging for your help."

"What are you talking about?"

"I need intelligence on Karsarkis. How he lives, what his house is like inside, how many guards he has, stuff like that. You've been in there. You can tell me all those things."

I raised my glass in a silent toast to Anita.

"What does that mean?" CW asked me.

"Never mind," I said. "Forget it."

CW looked puzzled, but he let it go. "So. Can you help me pop Karsarkis or not?"

"I could, probably. But I'm not."

"Plato Karsarkis is a fugitive from the United States, Jack. You don't mean to tell me you're unwilling to help the United States Marshals Service apprehend a dangerous fugitive, do you?" CW tilted his head and widened his eyes in a gesture so corny and theatrical I almost laughed out loud. "I thought you lawyers were supposed to be officers of the court, supporters of the law. That's right, isn't it, Jack?"

"Let me see if I understand this, CW. You're planning to kidnap a man who I gather is legally in Thailand and smuggle him out of the country and back to the United States. Do I have that right?"

"We're going to do what we have to do to—"

"You're running a kidnapping operation in violation of both local and international law and you're lecturing *me* about being an officer of the court?" I just shook my head. "Man, now I've heard it all."

"You're still an American, Jack. Have you forgotten where your loyalties lie?"

"No, CW, I think I've got all my loyalties in pretty good order, and fuck you for asking. By the way, you're not on my list."

"Then you're not going to help?"

"I will not be a party to a kidnapping in Thailand or anywhere else. Not by you, not by the fucking President of the fucking United States. Is that clear enough for you?"

CW tapped on his glass with his forefinger and let the silence run for a while before he spoke again.

"You're making a big mistake here, Slick."

"And exactly why is that?"

"Well..." CW sighed and shifted his weight on the barstool. "You saw those photographs. We could—"

"Whoa," I said, raising both hands, palms out. "Is it time for the part of the program where you threaten me? Because, if it is, you need to understand this: I don't deal with threats very well. Particularly threats from cops and other government types. I start thinking about testifying to Congressional committees about government corruption. Just can't help it."

"Hear me good, Slick. I'm going to take Plato Karsarkis down. If you get in the way, I'm going to take you down, too. I'm telling you that as a favor, not as a threat."

"I'm not part of this, CW."

"Well, Slick, you ever heard that line that goes, 'If you're not part of the solution, you're part of the problem?'"

"Listen very carefully to me. I am only going to say this one time. I am not part of your problem. I am not part of your solution. I have a nice life here in Thailand and I am not going to screw it up. Not for Plato Karsarkis, not for you, not for anyone."

"You really think it's going to be that easy? You think you can just walk away from all this and that will be the end of it?"

"Yep, I do. From now on, just think of me as Switzerland."

"He's reeling you in just like a big, dumb old fish, Slick," CW shook his head, "and you don't even know it."

"You've been a cop too long, CW. You smell shit everywhere."

"He's settin' you up, boy."

"Look, this may come as a real shock to you, pal, but I'm a grown man and I make all my own choices these days. Only people who're greedy or stupid get set up, and I'm neither."

"Whatever you say, Slick," CW shook his head slowly again. "Whatever you say."

There wasn't much more of any consequence left to talk about after that and CW seemed to lose interest in me once I had made it clear I wasn't going to be any part of whatever he was planning. York and Parker had left while CW and I were trading insults in the back of the bar and it wasn't very long before I wished CW a nice life and left, too.

I walked out of the Blue Lotus and back to the Holiday Inn, then I drove all the way to the hotel with the top of the jeep down. A breeze had come up from somewhere and I thought the wet night air slapping against my face might clear my head by the time I got back, but it didn't even make a decent start. I parked the jeep in the hotel lot and walked down the hillside toward our cabin.

About the time I passed the swimming pool, still and empty in the darkness, I started wondering if maybe CW did have a point after all. There might be something sticking to my shoe that wasn't going to be nearly as easy to scrape off as I thought.

Perhaps Switzerland was a little too much to hope for.

THE MIDDLE

BANGKOK

"Living in a foreign country is like being on a football team without a home field. You're always playing away."
— Desmond O'Grady,
journalist

Sixteen

IT WAS MONDAY afternoon and Anita and I had been back in Bangkok for less than a week. If there was ever a vacation glow at all, it was already pretty much gone. Something was clearly out of rhythm with Anita. I had no idea at all what it might be and I couldn't imagine that just flat out asking her would get me very far toward finding out. Still, I had students to see and courses to teach so I wasn't worrying a lot about it. Instead I was smoking an afternoon Montecristo in my office, feet up on my desk, reviewing my notes for the next day's lecture in my tax havens course.

The subject of tax havens was surprisingly popular with the kids. I have always thought it was probably because the sorts of places we talked about absolutely reeked with international intrigue and distant romance: places like the Cayman Islands, Liechtenstein, Hong Kong, Luxembourg, and Monte Carlo. Any discussion of tax havens immediately conjures up riveting stories of a world awash with drug barons tucking away narco money, terrorists laundering arms money, and third-world ministers hiding bribe money. And the idea of all those naughty people whooping it up in Monte Carlo while giving the rest of us the finger is absolute catnip to a room full of business students casting about for the quickest possible road to undreamed-of riches.

In spite of the strange vibrations Anita had been emitting ever since we got back, on the whole I felt pretty good. A few days of hanging out at the beach had left me with a nice tan and a clear head. Best of all, I had successfully evaded all further conversation with Anita about buying a vacation house in Phuket. I figured I just might be on a roll.

At least I figured that until my telephone rang about six. Bun, my secretary, had already gone home for the evening so I answered it myself. Looking back, I should have let it ring.

"Hello."

"Professor Shepherd?"

"Yes."

"This is Sanilee Dare."

The woman's voice was on the breathy side, but pleasant. She spoke American-sounding English and, like her name, her accent struck me as about halfway between Thai and American. Still, I had no idea at all who she was.

"I'm sorry, but are you a student?"

The woman laughed and it was a nice laugh.

"I showed you and your wife a house in Phuket last week. I'm Nok, remember?"

She laughed again before I could say anything. "I'm devastated. Thank God most men remember me a lot better than you do."

I apologized to the woman for not recognizing her name, but I finessed her flirty approach to reminding me who she was. That could go nowhere good.

"I have some really good news for you, Jack."

Nok may have been Thai, but she had apparently embraced the annoying American habit of jumping right into addressing everyone by their first name at the earliest possible opportunity. I guess it didn't really matter one way or another, but I'd always hated that and it put me in the wrong frame of mind to hear the rest of whatever she had to say.

"I'm calling about that house you and your wife were interested in," she said. "Remember?"

Somehow I didn't recall expressing the slightest interest in the house Nok had shown us, but I didn't say anything. She was a real estate agent and it wouldn't really matter to her whether I did or not.

"Well, someone called from BankThai this morning," she continued, "and guess what? They're willing to drop the price to fifteen million baht."

For a moment I wasn't sure I had heard her correctly.

"To what?" I asked. "Fifty million baht?"

"No, *fifteen*."

From eight-five million baht, nearly three million dollars, to fifteen million baht, more like four hundred and fifty thousand dollars. Jeez, I was a hell of a negotiator, wasn't I? God only knows how low the price might have gone if I'd actually opened my mouth.

"That doesn't make any sense to me," I said.

"Well..." Nok hesitated. "Actually, it doesn't to me either. I never talked to anyone over there. I don't even know how they knew you had looked at the house. A man from BankThai just called me this morning and said he had been told you were interested in the property and his instructions were to reduce the price for you. He even said the bank would be willing to loan you the full amount if you wished."

"Did he?"

"Oh, yes. He said the bank had absolutely the highest regard for you and he wanted to do anything he could to help you acquire the property. I had no idea you were such an important man."

"Neither did I."

There was a long silence. Nok apparently expected me to fill it. I didn't.

"Ah…" Nok sounded tentative. Under the circumstances, I could hardly blame her. "Shall I tell them you're interested?"

"No."

"But your wife…" Nok abruptly stopped talking and slid into an uncertain silence.

"What about her?" I asked.

"When I called her she said you would definitely be interested and that was why she gave me your number. She asked me to call you."

"Well, she was wrong. Please tell BankThai we are not going to buy that house at any price. Thank you for calling."

I hung up before Nok could say anything else and tilted back in my chair, folding my arms over my chest.

This was turning into a fine mess, wasn't it? The last thing I needed was to have my name bandied about in connection with an offer by a Thai bank of an under-the-table deal to buy an expensive vacation house in Phuket. The implications were legion, and none of them were good.

After stewing over Nok's call for a while longer, I picked the telephone up again and dialed Anita at home. She answered on the third ring and I skipped right past the usual pleasantries.

"What do you know about this house business, Anita?"

"Well, hello, darling. And thank you for calling. I love you, too."

"I'm sorry to be so abrupt, Anita, but I'm working up a real mad-on here. Did you talk to BankThai about that house in Phuket without telling me?"

"No, Jack, I didn't."

Anita's tone had turned icy, which I probably deserved, but I plowed ahead anyway.

"You talked to no one at that bank?"

"No one."

"Did you talk to anyone else?"

"No."

"Then why in Christ's name would someone at BankThai suddenly call this real estate agent and…"

I trailed off, turning the woman's story around in my mind looking for some kind of an explanation.

"Look, Jack. Sometimes nice things do—"

"Oh shit," I interrupted.

I could almost hear Anita's bewilderment in the silence that followed.

"What in the world is wrong with you, Jack? This is wonderful news and you're treating it like some kind of calamity. The bank has offered to—"

"You don't get it do you, Anita?" I interrupted again before she could get wound up.

"No," her voice faltered. "I guess I don't."

"Just stop and think a moment."

There was a brief silence.

"What am I supposed to be thinking about, Jack?"

"Anita, I didn't talk to anyone about this house. You didn't talk to anyone about this house. Even the real estate agent didn't talk to anyone about this house. So why do you suppose the bank just rang up all of a sudden and offered to reduce the price by eighty percent and loan us the full amount?"

"I don't know."

"Don't you think somebody must have told them we looked at the property, then gave them a pretty good push to help us out?"

"You're saying that somebody's trying to do us a favor?"

"That's right."

"Oh, I see. You think somebody wants to do us a favor and then ask you for something in return."

"Right again," I said. "Now who would that somebody most likely be?"

"I can't imagine who… oh, shit."

"Bingo. A big cigar for the little lady."

This time the silence was longer and I let it stretch on until Anita eventually broke it.

"How do you suppose that US marshal guy found out about the house, Jack?"

"Give me back the cigar."

"What?"

"You've got it wrong, Anita. It's not the marshals."

"Then who is it?"

"Come on, Anita. Don't be ridiculous. Think. Who could possibly have the clout to be behind something like this? Mr. Plato Karsarkis himself, I'd wager."

"Oh, Jack, I don't think so. Plato wouldn't be so sneaky. If he wanted something, I think he'd just come out and ask you for it."

"He *has* asked me, Anita. And I said no. Remember?" I struggled to keep the testiness out of my voice. "I told you all that business about the hotel deal and the big fee he offered me for doing very little, and I told you I turned him down. I gather Karsarkis isn't a man who likes to be told no."

"Don't you think you're being just a little egocentric, Jack?"

"A little *what*?"

"I'm just saying, I'm sure there are plenty of people Plato can call on if he needs help. He hardly has to sit up nights thinking up ways to lure you into his debt."

I sighed. It was obvious Anita liked Plato Karsarkis regardless of the dire warnings she had given me about him. In fact, even if she decided I was right and Karsarkis was indeed behind the sudden and unexplained generosity of BankThai, I'd bet she was more likely to say it was just a friendly gesture from a nice man than to see it as the cynical dangle which I was absolutely certain it was.

"We are not going to buy that house, Anita."

"Maybe Plato has nothing to do with this."

"And maybe I just saw a flock of pigs flap by outside my window. I will not buy that house, Anita, and you can't either. You can't put me in that position."

I could feel waves of bad vibrations coming down the telephone line at me.

"I'm sorry you feel that way, Jack, but I don't take orders from you."

"I'm not giving you orders, Anita, I'm trying to get you to understand that—"

"You will not tell me what to do, Jack. I'm very angry with you and I am going to hang up now. Good-bye."

And with that Anita put down the telephone.

I hung up, too. Then I sat quietly for a while trying to calm the loud buzzing sound that had started up somewhere in my head.

Eventually I retrieved my Montecristo from the ashtray where I had abandoned it when Nok called and relit it. I took a long pull, filling my mouth with the bittersweet smoke and exhaling in a long, protracted stream. That helped, at least a little.

I stood up and walked over to the windows. The heavy particles of chemical crud that made up a good part of Bangkok's air occasionally captured and diffused the last light of day in a way which caused a soft, mango-colored fog to creep over the city right before sunset. When that happened, it made the city seem almost unbearably if only fleetingly romantic.

I stood at the window and watched the sun sink out of sight behind the mirrored office towers that lined Silom Road. I waited for the mango fog, but it never came.

Seventeen

I TRY TO rustle up a tennis match every now and then to fight the good fight against onrushing decrepitude, but it's usually difficult to find anyone in Bangkok who wants to play tennis. Men in Thailand mostly play golf. That generally means lolling around a course for half a day drinking beer with your pals while one eighteen-year-old girl scurries around holding an umbrella over you and another drags your heavy golf bag. Breaking a sweat isn't part of the deal.

Finding a place to play tennis in Bangkok is a challenge, too. Other than the courts at a couple of snobby private clubs where you have to pay a generous bribe to the membership committee to get in, the few tennis courts in the city are pretty crummy. They're usually not much more than cracked and buckled slabs of concrete wedged between high-rise buildings, not so much athletic facilities as parking lots with nets that generate income for the landowners until they get some financing together to build yet another apartment tower.

So as an alternative form of exercise I try to run a few miles every now and then. The big problem there is that places to run in the city are at almost as much of a premium as tennis courts. That is, unless you have a particular affection for climbing in and out of potholes while playing tag with thirty-year-old Chinese buses driven by teenagers zonked out of their mind on uppers.

Queen's Park isn't very big, but it is one of the better places in Bangkok to run. It's quiet and pleasant, at least it is if you measure it by the standard of the few other public parks in Bangkok, which is pretty modest. Sandwiched between the Emporium, the city's ritziest shopping complex, and some nondescript commercial buildings including a walled compound belonging to the Iranian Embassy, it amounts to a couple of acres of concrete pathways, a little grass, some trees, and a few fountains with a small lake in the middle of it all. The place actually feels pretty much like a real park, if you don't think about it too much.

I parked on the street and walked into Queen's Park from the Sukhumvit Road side, looking around for my usual jogging companion. Near the back of the park, I spotted Jello bouncing impatiently on the balls of his feet while he watched some kids playing an energetic if not particularly skillful game of basketball.

Technically Jello was just another Thai police captain and the Thai police had a lot of captains, but as long as I had known him he had also been a senior member of the Economic Crimes Investigation Division. It was a position that gave him a considerable amount of personal clout since ECID was primarily an intelligence operation. Most cops concerned themselves with who was doing what to whom, and occasionally even why. Jello focused more on how much they were getting paid for it and what they did with the money. Since money in Thailand was more important than life, it made him a key player in almost everything of any consequence that went down anywhere in the entire country.

I had never been entirely certain what the source of Jello's colorful nickname was. For a while I had assumed his rotund physique had something to do with it, the image of his belly quivering like a bowl of jello coming easily to mind whenever we ran together. However lately I had gotten the impression the name might have gone all the way back to his childhood when he had been sent away to a boarding school in Connecticut. I wondered if hidden within it was one of those scarring cruelties most of us could recall from our childhood but would rather not. If there was, he never mentioned it.

Jello must have seen me coming out of the corner of his eye. He glanced back over his shoulder when I was a good fifty feet away and gave me a wave. I tossed out a little salute and broke into a jog toward him.

"You're late," he said when I got there.

"I am," I agreed, jogging in place next to him.

"Aren't you at least going to say you're sorry."

"I am not. Any other preliminaries?"

"Guess not."

"Then you're ready for a few miles?"

"Let's do it."

"What you think? Five today? Maybe ten?"

"Whatever, old man."

I knew perfectly well some kind of warm-up routine before running was almost mandatory now that I wasn't a young hot shot anymore, but most of the time I couldn't be bothered so I just ran slowly for the first half a mile or so and hoped after that everything would take care of itself.

A pebbled concrete walkway circled the small lake in the middle of the park and we jogged slowly through the first circuit without conversation. Jello was a man of few words, which to my way of thinking made him the perfect companion for a run, maybe the perfect companion for every occasion. On the other hand our sporadic runs together were also a good time to talk about things that needed talking about. Sometimes he had questions for me. Sometimes I had questions for him. The lifeblood of Thailand was favors done and debits accumulated. Jello and I had kept our personal accounts pretty much in balance, but this afternoon it was my turn to apply for a little withdrawal.

We picked up our pace on the second circuit and were moving pretty well before I finally broke the silence.

"Want to play word association?" I asked.

Jello turned his head slowly and looked at me, but he didn't say anything.

"It works this way—"

"I know how it works," he said.

"Okay, good. Then I'll say a word, and you tell me the first word that comes into your mind."

Another slow back and forth swivel of Jello's head. Another silence.

"Here we go," I said, undaunted.

A nanny in a white uniform was pushing a baby carriage down the middle of the walkway and I dodged around her, glancing quickly at Jello to see if he had noticed my phenomenally graceful sidestep. If he had, he was concealing it nicely.

"Ready?" I asked.

"Stop asking if I'm ready."

"Okay, then, here's the word," I said. "Plato Karsarkis."

"That's two words."

"Think of it as one and you'll be okay."

"Still two words."

"Don't be a fucking pedant, Jello. Just tell me the first thing that comes into you mind when you hear the words Plato Karsarkis."

We ran on for several minutes after that without either of us saying anything else, which was pretty much exactly what I thought would happen. Flocks of pigeons had taken up residence on the walkway ahead of us and as we bore down on them they rose into the air and dispersed like puffs of brown-gray smoke, their cooing and flapping barely audible in the rumble of the city around us.

"So," Jello eventually said, "I gather you've heard."

"You're supposed to give me the *one* word that comes into your mind, man. That's five words."

"Fuck you."

"That's two—"

"Just lay it out," Jello interrupted. "You've got something to tell me about the guy or you wouldn't have brought him up."

A heavy woman with an appalling blonde dye job walked straight into us swinging her elbows so wildly she nearly pushed us off the pavement. I gathered she was a tourist since she was wearing a conical-shaped straw hat she had apparently bought in some street market along with a red hill-tribe vest. No local would ever wear a get-up like that.

"I hear Karsarkis is in Phuket," I said.

"Bullshit, Professor. You're fishing."

"That's what I heard."

"From who."

"From Plato Karsarkis," I said, keeping my voice as empty as I could. "When Anita and I went to his house for dinner."

Jello ran on after that as if I hadn't said anything worth commenting on. I used two slowly moving girls in high school uniforms to screen off a group of boys who were kicking a soccer ball and then slipped back into stride alongside him again.

"You don't believe me," I said.

"How'd you work that out?"

"I've got finely honed instincts for subtle human responses."

"Uh-huh," he said. "You do."

We passed the fountain and started around the lake again.

"So," I said, "know what's going to happen next?"

"Nope."

"I do. I've got finely honed instincts for predicting the future, too."

"Is that right?"

"It is. We're going to do one more mile after this one, then we're going to walk across the street to the Bull's Head. When we get there, you're going to buy me a large Carlsberg draft, and when I've had about half of it you're going to turn to me and you're going to say, 'So, Professor, what the fuck you talking about?'"

"That's what's going to happen next?"

"That's it."

"Huh," Jello said. "Imagine that."

THE BULL'S HEAD was unusually quiet when we got there and Jello and I took a table in the back where there was no one else within earshot. After we had each drunk about half of our Carlsberg drafts in silence, Jello wiped his mouth with the back of his hand and leaned toward me.

"So, Professor" he said, "what the fuck you talking about?"

I took my time about it, but I told Jello more or less everything about my encounter with Plato Karsarkis in Phuket, including the dinner at his house. I even told Jello about the dangle from Karsarkis to do some work for one of his companies.

"Did you know Plato Karsarkis was in Phuket?" I asked when I had finished.

"I think I heard something like that."

"So what are you guys going to do?"

"Do?" Jello sipped at his beer. "About what?"

"About Karsarkis."

"Why should we do anything?"

"You're not going to arrest him?" I asked.

"What for?"

"What *for*? To turn him over to the Americans, of course."

"They haven't asked us to do that."

"Oh, come on. Karsarkis has got to be on the Interpol watch list."

"Yeah, he is. There's a red notice out."

An Interpol red notice was a request to any country that found Karsarkis to detain him.

"Thailand isn't going to pay any attention to it?"

Jello looked at me over the rim of his glass for a long moment, but he didn't say anything.

"Oh, it's like that," I said.

Jello gave a little shrug with his eyebrows, but he stayed silent.

"What if the American Embassy files a formal request for Karsarkis' arrest?"

"We don't have to think about that until they do it."

"How very Thai of you."

"Thank you."

Jello slugged down the last of his beer and waved to one of the waitresses. She came over and gave him a smile that would have melted the McMurdo Ice Shelf.

"One more?" she asked.

"Two more. One for me and…" he poked a thumb in my direction, "one for my dad."

The girl suppressed a giggle and flashed him another thousand-watt smile before she moved away.

"How come you get the big-eye, goo-goo routine and she ignores me completely?" I asked Jello.

"Women radar stuff. They know when you're already hooked up and aren't available."

"I'm willing to lie."

"Wouldn't do you any good," he said. "They *know*."

We sat in silence until the waitress had replaced our empty glasses with freshly drawn drafts, during the course of which I had to endure another round of her flirting with Jello and ignoring me.

When she had gone I cleared my throat and told Jello about meeting Marshal Clovis Ward. Then for good measure I described our night out together in Patong and repeated CW's appeal for intelligence on Karsarkis' security.

"You have a funny habit of ending right in the middle of all kinds of shit, don't you, Professor?"

"It's a talent."

"That's one way to look at it, I guess."

"So…did you know the US Marshals were in Phuket?" I asked.

"Uh-huh."

"And it doesn't bother you they're there without the embassy having filed an official request to detain Karsarkis?"

"What bothers me isn't the point," Jello said.

I shoved my beer glass around in a circle on the tabletop and it left a thin trail of water on the heavily lacquered wood. I reached out and traced the water with my forefinger.

"So what are you going to do?" I asked after a while. "Let the marshals kidnap Karsarkis and hustle him out of the country?"

"It's not going to come to that."

"Are you sure?" I asked.

"Look, Professor, whenever your guys think the time is right, I'm sure they'll make a request for extradition to the prime minister."

"If they do, what will the prime minister say?"

"No idea."

"Right."

"Really. I have absolutely no idea."

I reached out and tapped my forefinger on the table in front of Jello. "You and I both know Karsarkis didn't get where he is by being stupid," I said.

Jello glanced at me, but his eyes bounced off without sticking. Still, there had been a flash of embarrassment there and I had caught it full on.

"Karsarkis isn't just rolling the dice," I said. "He wouldn't be here if he weren't absolutely certain he has the Thai government in his pocket."

"Doesn't really matter," Jello said, without looking at me. "If your guys really want him, you'll get him."

"Watch that, would you? It's the second time you've said it. They're not *my* guys. I'm not in involved in any of this."

"Then just keep it that way, Jack. There's a lot going on here you don't understand."

"That's what you always say."

"That's because it's always true."

"Maybe I know more than you think."

"Doesn't look that way to me."

Jello was right, of course. I knew damned near nothing about the intrigues that were no doubt churning like a tornado around Plato Karsarkis' presence in Thailand, which was exactly why I was sitting with Jello right then trying to bait him into telling me something.

"A United States Marshal trying to recruit me as a spy makes me uneasy," I said. "I don't want to find myself in the middle of an international incident."

"Your guys will come to their senses before they do anything stupid."

"And if they don't?"

"We're not going to fight a gun battle with them at the airport, Professor, if that's what you're asking me."

That wasn't what I had been asking, of course. All the same, it was good to know.

Eighteen

THE SASIN SCHOOL of Business occupies two buildings on the far northern edge of the Chulalongkorn University campus, a hodgepodge of early Thai and late Stalinist architecture right in the heart of central Bangkok. The first building is pretty good looking. It has a sheltered garden at its entrance and students often gather there at tables scattered in the shade of big oak trees to grab a smoke or drink a coffee. The second building is ugly. Its utilitarian bulk sprouts straight out of a barren concrete pan that soaks up heat and roasts the feet of anyone foolish enough to try to cross it. My office is in the second building, on the sixth floor.

I was still there late the next afternoon, working on a Montecristo and trying to think of something brilliant yet witty to say to the following day's International Securities Regulation class, when Tommy opened the door without knocking.

"Your secretary's gone home," he said. "There wasn't anyone to announce me."

"So naturally you just barged right in."

"Naturally. Occupational habit."

I had known Tommy for several years. His real name was Tommerat something or another, but everyone I knew just called him Tommy. In the face of all provocation he stuck cheerfully to the story that he held some position in the Ministry of Foreign Affairs.

Regardless, if there was anyone in Bangkok who didn't know that Tommy actually worked for the National Intelligence Agency, I had never met him.

The first time I had introduced Tommy to Anita, she had been terribly amused at the idea of meeting a Thai spy and had tossed out a couple of pretty snappy one-liners on the subject. I tried to explain to her later that there was absolutely nothing amusing about Tommy, and certainly nothing to laugh about, but I don't think she really believed me.

Tommy settled into one of the guest chairs in front of my desk without being invited.

"You got any more of those?" he asked, pointing to the cigar I was smoking.

I waved vaguely at the humidor on my desk. "Help yourself."

Tommy leaned forward and with his index finger carefully lifted the lid of the Dunhill humidor Anita had given me as a wedding present.

"Just these crappy Montecristos?" he asked, inspecting its contents suspiciously. "No Cohibas?"

"Hey, you don't like 'em, don't smoke 'em."

Tommy looked genuinely annoyed with me, but he took one of the Montecristos anyway. "It's all you got, Jack. What choice do I have?"

My heart wasn't in it, but we made polite chit-chat while Tommy cut the cigar, lit it, and puffed it into life.

"You don't look so good, Jack," he said after he was done. "Everything okay?"

"Fine, Tommy. Never better."

"Good," he said. "Good."

Tommy nodded and drew on his cigar. I nodded back and drew on mine. My office was fast filling up with nods and smoke.

"Why are you here, Tommy?" I asked when it became apparent

he wasn't in any hurry to tell me. "Is there something specific on your mind, or are you just trolling for gossip?"

"Well…look, Jack, you want to go out? Maybe get some dinner or something?"

"No thanks."

"There's a new steakhouse at the Marriott that everyone says is great. All imported American beef, not that Australian shit."

"I'll take a rain check."

Tommy fiddled with his cigar and then abruptly stood up.

"I'm afraid I'm going to have to insist, Jack."

I took the cigar out of my mouth and leaned forward. "I'm sorry?"

"Hey, if I were you I wouldn't want to come with me either, but there's somewhere you need to be. I'm here to deliver you."

"Whoa." I dumped the remains of my cigar in the ashtray and put both hands flat on my desk. "What the hell are you talking about?"

Tommy looked grave. "You need to see somebody, Jack, and he can't come here. You've got to go to him."

"Who is it?"

"Just come with me, Jack."

Tommy pointed to the ceiling with his right forefinger and cupped his left hand around his ear in a listening gesture.

"Trust me a little here," he added in the most inane stage whisper I had ever heard a grown man use.

I leaned back in my chair and rolled my eyes. "You're out of your goddamned mind, Tommy. Do you seriously expect me to believe that my office is bugged?"

"Who knows? Anyway, better safe than sorry, I always say."

I segued from rolling my eyes into shaking my head. My personal experience with guys in the intelligence business was that most of them eventually went around the bend in one way or another. It looked like it might be time to wave bye-bye to Tommy.

"What have you got to lose, Jack?" he went on before I could say anything else. "Are you in such a big a hurry to get home tonight that you can't spare an old friend an hour?"

Not surprisingly, Anita had resurrected the issue of the house in Phuket and for the past couple of days had been expressing her unhappiness over my rejection of BankThai's cream-puff deal in quite colorful terms. I shot Tommy a look to see if his reference to my home life was just a coincidence. His expression gave nothing away so I couldn't tell. Regardless, he had a point. I certainly wasn't in all that big a hurry to get home tonight.

"Okay, I surrender." I raised both my hands, palms out. "I'll go quietly, officer."

"Good, good," Tommy nodded.

I collected some books and papers, mostly at random, and jammed them into my briefcase. Then I shut off my office lights and followed Tommy out into the hall.

"Give me the address and I'll meet you there," I said as I locked the door behind us.

"It would be better if you rode with me. I'll bring you back to get your car when we're done."

I gave another shrug and followed Tommy down the hall to the elevator. Why not? After what has already happened in the last week, how many surprises could be left in one man's lifetime?

Later that night, looking back on what happened next, I made a mental note never to ask myself a question like that again.

Nineteen

A BLACK MERCEDES was waiting in the circular driveway when we emerged from the building. The driver jumped out and opened the back door for Tommy. While he was getting in, I walked around to the other side of the car and joined him in the back seat. I accomplished that by opening and closing my own door. It really wasn't all that hard.

"You know, Tommy," I said as we pulled away, "I've never been absolutely clear just what a Thai spy actually does."

"I'm shocked, Jack. Shocked. I'm not a spy. I'm merely the deputy to the spokesman for the Ministry of Foreign Affairs."

The Mercedes had pearl-gray curtains on its side windows and I pushed the one on my side of the car back and forth on its chrome rails a few times, trying it out. The car's windows were already so dark I probably could have fired off a flare gun inside without anyone seeing it, so the curtains seemed a bit much. Still, when they were closed I had to admit that the whole effect was very pleasant. The Mercedes became a dim, cool submarine sliding silently through the debris of the Bangkok streets.

"So anyway, Tommy, what does a Thai spy really do?"

Tommy sighed and seemed momentarily absorbed in studying something outside his window; then he sighed again and jerked his curtain closed.

"Thailand is in an unusual position as nations go, Jack. We are small and unimportant in the great scheme of world politics, and yet not entirely a joke. Much of what matters in the world seems to pass through us in one way or another. You should think of Thailand this way: we are like a hallway."

"A *hallway*?"

"No one really cares about a hallway. It's not a significant room in any building. It's just a way to get back and forth between the places where the important things happen. But you know, if you stand quietly in a hallway, sometimes you can hear and see extraordinary things. Sometimes you can learn more standing in the hallway than if you're invited right into the rooms."

I didn't quite know how to respond to Tommy's moving tribute to the importance of hallways, so I just sat and watched his soft, almost pink face in the glow of the lights from outside the car.

Tommy wasn't very tall. He was slightly overweight and he wore a conservative gray suit with a white shirt and a dark tie. He could be anybody, I thought to myself. If someone told me Tommy was really a Canadian grocery store owner or a Portuguese real estate developer, I would have had no reason at all to doubt them. That was exactly what made Tommy such an effective spy.

The big Mercedes left the campus and turned north on Phayathai Road. It edged steadily through the heavy traffic between Siam Square and the imposing bulk of the Mah Boonkrong Center, an eight-story concrete bunker with a huge shopping mall inside it through which thousands of people poured every day of the year searching for cheap mobile phones, pirated software, and knock-off designer clothing.

"You going to tell me where we're headed?" I asked Tommy, but he didn't answer. Instead he pushed the curtain on his side open again and sat quietly examining a crowd of university girls who were gathered around a bus shelter.

The driver punched the accelerator to make the light and I saw we were going east toward the Sukhumvit residential district, the area where most of the foreigners in Bangkok lived in a forest of luxury high-rises that had sprouted over the last few years from what had not so long before been only rice fields. Those Thais who had the extraordinary good fortune to be the heirs of the farmers who had owned those rice fields had grown wealthy beyond most people's understanding of the word. Those Thais whose ancestors had owned fields that were just a few hundred yards away in one direction or another had grown envious beyond most people's understanding of the word.

"What have you been doing with yourself, Jack?" Tommy abruptly asked. "I mean recently."

"Teaching my classes. Hanging out with Anita. The usual."

"No adventures?"

"Not so as you'd notice."

Tommy smiled.

"Miss the action?" he asked.

"No."

Tommy chuckled, crossed his legs at the knee, and turned his head back toward the window. "You're full of shit."

"Possibly," I allowed. "But not about that."

Tommy chuckled again.

"Believe me or not, little man," I said. "It is so."

"Don't give me that crap, Jack. You were a player. And now you're just…well, what? You teach a little? You do some consulting? And you're happy? Don't try to shit a shitter, man. You miss the action. I know you do. I'll bet sometimes you even wonder if you could still cut it in a big game, don't you?"

That was a little close to the nerve, so I glanced away from Tommy and concentrated on the back of the driver's head.

"Shit," Tommy snorted. "I knew it. Once a player, always a player."

I took a deep breath and turned toward Tommy, staring at him until he stopped fidgeting and held my eyes.

"Listen very closely, my friend, and make notes if you want to, because I'm going to tell you something you ought to remember."

I imagine I sounded a bit testy and I didn't particularly care.

"I have a nice life and a woman who loves me, and I will fight you or anyone who threatens to screw it up for me to the death. You hear me, Tommy? To the very fucking death."

The Mercedes slowed and moved over to the middle lane. It edged past a handcart loaded with straw brooms that a stooped old woman was pushing along next to the curb. Tommy didn't answer me, but I hadn't really expected him to. Instead he tilted his head back against the seat and shut his eyes.

Since Tommy didn't seem much inclined to continue the conversation, I pushed open the curtain on my side and looked out at the street. We were in a residential neighborhood I vaguely recognized, one somewhere between New Petchburi Road and Sukhumvit Road. I hated driving in that area since I always got turned around in the bewildering warren of tiny streets. The problem was that the street signs were all in Thai, which no westerner I knew could read, and there were no other real landmarks to navigate by. The high concrete walls that enclosed the small apartment buildings and huge, unseen estates all looked more or less alike, and the broken glass and sharpened iron spikes that lined the top of most of them gave the whole area an air of secret and no doubt illicit doings.

After a while I gave up on trying to make sense of our route. We were going where we were going and I wasn't about to give Tommy the satisfaction of showing too much interest.

At one point the street we were traveling on made a right-angle bend between two high walls and the Mercedes came to a complete stop while a green truck with sheets of dark canvas strapped over it slipped past us in the opposite direction. The space between the walls was narrow and the truck came so close to the Mercedes that a bulge in the canvas hit the driver's mirror. The *creak* of the mirror folding inward and then the *thump* of it snapping back into place caused me to flinch, but neither the driver nor Tommy seemed to take any notice.

As we sat there waiting for the truck to pass, my eyes drifted to a black metal gate in the wall at my side of the car. The gate was open a crack and in the gap I could see a tiny girl in a blue and white school uniform who couldn't have been more than five or six. She was looking out at us, and her huge, deep brown eyes stared at me without expression. I wondered if the proximity of the big car and my white face looking out of it frightened the girl or just tickled her curiosity, but I could read nothing at all in those big wet eyes, not even whether she could actually see me through the dark glass of the windows. I smiled and wiggled my eyebrows stupidly at the little girl just to see what would happen, but I got no response. Then, after a moment, the truck passed by, the Mercedes began to edge forward again, and the little girl was gone.

Less than five minutes later the car stopped at a pair of gates built of close-set green metal bars with gold curlicues on the top. A guard wearing a uniform of some sort walked up to the driver's window and bent down, and the driver opened the window a crack and said something in a low voice I didn't quite catch. It must have been the right thing, because the guard whipped out a crisp salute then stepped around in front of the car and pushed open the gates. The Mercedes rolled forward and I saw we were in the courtyard of what appeared to be a small apartment building.

"Okay, Big Jack. We're here."

I glanced at Tommy. His head was still tilted back against the seat, but now his eyes were open.

"So does this mean you're going to cut the crap and tell me what's going on?"

"Yeah." Tommy stretched and yawned. "Plato Karsarkis wants to talk to you about something. This place is…"

All of a sudden Tommy's eyes began to dart around wildly. I knew he had just realized he was about to say the wrong thing, but was stuck for a quick alternative.

I let him off the hook. "One of Plato's fuck pads?" I asked.

The corners of Tommy's mouth flicked up and down a couple of times. "Something like that," he said.

"So, tell me, Tommy. I don't really figure I'm this guy's type. Why am I here?"

"Just shut the hell up for once in your life and have a little patience, would you, Jack?" Tommy looked to me like a man who very much wished he were somewhere else right then. "Let's go upstairs."

We got out of the car and I followed Tommy toward the lobby of the building. A man wearing a white jacket and a black bow tie pulled open the glass door and then jumped over and pushed the elevator button. The doors slid back immediately. After we were inside, he leaned in and pushed a button marked PH, which I assumed stood for penthouse, then he pulled his arm back out and bowed slightly as the doors closed again. It was a pretty snappy move, but Tommy was staring hard at the floor and didn't appear to appreciate it as much as I did.

Neither of us spoke as the elevator hummed upward. When the doors opened I followed Tommy out into a small, marble-floored foyer. English hunting prints decorated the walls and there were two dark green upholstered chairs with a lamp table between them. It might have been the waiting room of a prosperous, but badly underemployed, dentist.

Almost immediately a door swung open. Mike O'Connell stood

there smiling and holding his hand out toward me like a man with something to sell.

"Thank you for coming, Mr. Shepherd."

"Your invitation was so gracious, I didn't see how I could refuse."

"Come on, Jack," Tommy grumbled. "Cut the shit."

Then he glared at Mike O'Connell and pointed a perfectly manicured forefinger at him. O'Connell stepped aside and I followed Tommy into the room.

Twenty

THE EXPENSIVELY DECORATED apartment had a distinctly masculine air about it, but it was somehow impersonal. It might have been the living room of a suite at a Four Seasons hotel in almost any city anywhere in the world.

Plato Karsarkis was sitting in a red leather chair with his legs propped up on an ottoman and crossed at the ankle. He was facing away from me, looking out a large window and contemplating with apparent interest whatever it was he saw out there.

"Can I offer you coffee, Professor Shepherd?"

It was Mike O'Connell who spoke, not Karsarkis.

"Or perhaps something stronger?" O'Connell went on when I didn't respond immediately.

"Am I going to need it?" I asked.

Karsarkis laughed at that and turned his head toward me.

"Not really, but the least I can do after dragging you all the way out here is to buy you a drink," he said. "Scotch for me, Mike, and…"

Karsarkis raised his eyebrows at me.

"Same." I said. "Water, no ice."

"No ice? That surprises me, Jack. Very European. Americans always seem to want ice. Lots of ice."

"I'm full of surprises."

Karsarkis nodded slowly several times as if I had just told him something important. Then, in a kind of afterthought, he glanced at Tommy.

"You want anything?" he asked him in a tone that made his lack of interest unmistakable.

"Vodka," Tommy mumbled quietly. "Neat."

O'Connell disappeared, I assumed to get our drinks, and Karsarkis gestured at a pair of couches.

"Sit down, gentlemen. Mike is going to have to play waiter since we've sent the staff home. It's just the four of us today."

Tommy seemed uncomfortable, although I couldn't see why. Then it occurred to me I was probably about to find out.

"So, Jack." Karsarkis had gone back to looking out the window. "That house in Phuket you wanted. You must be pretty happy about the deal the bank offered you."

"I rather thought that was your hand at work there."

"Does it matter?" he asked.

"It does to me."

"You wanted the house," Karsarkis shrugged. "I just thought I'd help you out."

"I didn't want the house. Anita did."

Karsarkis glanced at me and lifted one eyebrow as if he didn't see why that mattered. Little did he know.

"How did you find out about it?" I asked him.

"The agent who showed you the place said something to her husband. Tommy here knows the guy from somewhere. He heard it from him. Thailand's really a small place, Jack. At least it is for foreigners. Everybody knows everybody else's business."

"Then you must already know I'm not buying the house." I thought a moment and added, "And neither is Anita."

Karsarkis shifted his eyes to me, his interest caught. "I thought the bank offered a pretty good deal."

"For who?" I asked.

"For you and Anita," he said. "Who else?"

"Oh...I thought you meant it seemed like a good deal for you. Making a call or two, getting BankThai to sell me the house at a fraction of its real value, leaving me owing you a big favor. Like that."

Karsarkis chuckled and shook his head. "You're a real pistol, Jack. A friend tries to do something for you and you act like he's just pissed all over you."

"We're not friends. I already told you that. And if I want a favor, I'll ask you for it. But don't hold your breath."

"So basically the house..."

Karsarkis let the phrase hang in the air like a question, but without a question mark.

"Basically," I said, "that's none of your business."

Just then O'Connell reappeared carrying a wooden tray with three drinks.

"What?" I asked as he set my whiskey and Tommy's vodka on the low table in front of the couch. "No pretzels?"

O'Connell acted as if he hadn't heard me. He walked over and put Karsarkis' whiskey on a small table next to him; then he took another chair across the room, put the tray down on the floor next to it, leaned back, and folded his arms. He watched me without expression and I found myself wondering for some reason if he was armed. I examined the lines of his blue suit jacket searching for bulges. I didn't see any, but I didn't stop wondering.

Tommy picked up his drink and sipped tentatively at it, then put it down again. Karsarkis left his drink on the table without touching it.

"Oh, hey," Karsarkis suddenly said. "Where are my manners? You want a cigar, Jack?"

"No, I don't want a goddamned cigar."

"A simple no would have covered it. You don't have to be so antagonistic."

"*Antagonistic?* Look, Karsarkis, I was about to go home to my wife when this little asshole kidnapped me and dragged me halfway across town to this apartment, and you say *I'm* being antagonistic?"

"Now, Jack," Tommy said, "calm down." He pushed himself around on the couch until he was facing me. "I don't particularly like being called an asshole and I think claiming you were kidnapped is a bit of an exaggeration, but you should—"

"Yes, I apologize for all that, Jack," Karsarkis cut Tommy off, looking at me, not him.

Tommy made no protest at the interruption and went back to sipping at his vodka.

"It was unseemly," Karsarkis continued. "On the other hand, it was impossible for me to come and see you, and I was afraid if I just asked you to come here, then well…"

Karsarkis gave a rueful shrug and trailed off.

"You're right," I said. "I wouldn't have come."

"So there you are, Jack," Karsarkis nodded. "You see my dilemma. That's why I had to ask Tommy to prevail on you like this."

I sighed heavily and slumped back into the couch.

"Okay," I said. "So now I'm here. Tell me what you want and let's get this over with so I can go home."

Karsarkis cleared his throat unnecessarily and stood up. He walked to the window and looked out for a moment, his back to me, and then he folded his arms across his body and turned around.

"I want you to represent me, Jack."

"We already talked about that. I told you I wasn't interested in being involved in your hotel deal."

A flash of genuine annoyance crossed Karsarkis' face and he waved a hand as if brushing it away.

"Forget the goddamned hotels, Jack," he snapped. "That was all just bullshit anyway and you know it."

Karsarkis unfolded his arms, took a couple of steps toward me, then refolded them and sat back down in the red leather chair. He seemed to me to be a little nervous and I wondered why. I sensed we were getting close now to whatever Karsarkis had really brought me there to say, so I folded my arms too and waited.

I didn't have to wait long.

Twenty One

"I WANT YOU to file an application for a presidential pardon for me, Jack."

"A pardon for what? You haven't been convicted of anything yet. You only get pardoned after you're convicted, not before."

"My lawyers have looked into that. The presidential power to pardon is absolute. Ford pardoned Nixon before he was even charged with anything. This president can do the same thing for me."

Karsarkis might have been technically right, I knew, but I didn't really feel like getting into a debate with him on the finer points of constitutional law. Instead I stuck to the obvious practical problem.

"You know there's no way that would ever happen," I said. "No way in hell."

"Oh, I think there may really be a pretty good chance," he smiled, looking like a man who knew something I didn't. "All I need is the right person to explain some facts to the White House. Those facts are very much in my favor."

"What facts?"

"That's not the point right now," Karsarkis said.

"Then what *is* the point?"

"You, Jack. You're the point right now. You have both access and credibility at the White House. You can reach people there and they will listen to you. That's why you're the guy I need."

Okay, so I knew someone at the White House. To tell the truth, I knew someone there pretty well; and it wasn't just someone, it was really *someone*. William Henry Harrison Redwine and I had even been roommates for two years when we went to law school together at Georgetown, and ever since this president had moved into the West Wing, Billy had been White House counsel. No one outside of the innermost circles of the White House ever knew for sure how the power was distributed or who really had the president's ear on what matter, but whenever commentators speculated as to who the most powerful people in Washington were, whenever lists of the influential were made up and torn apart, inevitably Billy Redwine's name was right at the top. In Washington, that was the ultimate definition of *someone*.

Karsarkis said nothing else, but he watched me closely. He was clearly less nervous now that everything was on the table and his careful examination of my reaction seemed composed of equal parts curiosity and expectation. Still, I tried to give him very little reaction to examine.

"In compensation for your efforts on my behalf," Karsarkis went on when I said nothing, "I am prepared to pay you a fee of one million dollars."

I tried to remain expressionless, but I'm sure I gaped at that regardless. Karsarkis was back on familiar ground, not asking for help, but controlling a proposition by drowning it in money. His face once again displayed the self-assured look of a man in control.

"Let me make this very clear, Jack. If you will agree to represent me in seeking a pardon from the President of the United States, I will pay you a fee of one million dollars right now, tonight. I will arrange for it to be wired in full to any bank account you designate anywhere in the world within the hour. That money is yours to keep whether you succeed or fail."

Karsarkis smiled slightly, but he didn't seem to mean anything in particular by it. I waited. He waited. I waited longer.

"If you do succeed, however, I will pay you a further fee of four million dollars."

Tommy leaned forward, his knees banging into the low table so hard he sloshed some of the vodka out of his glass.

"That's five million—"

"I can add, Tommy," I cut him off. "So for Christ's sake shut up."

Tommy opened and closed his mouth, but then he leaned back on the sofa again and said nothing else.

Ever since I began practicing law, I had dealt with vast, mostly unreal sums of money—ten million here, a hundred million there—so the mention of five million dollars hardly caused me to fall out of my chair. Still, all those enormous sums were just numbers on pieces of paper, nothing like real money, and certainly nothing like *my* real money. This was altogether different.

"So what do you say, Jack? Are you with me here or not?"

I stared at Karsarkis in complete silence for a good thirty seconds. He just sat there and stared back.

"You've got the wrong guy," I finally said. "You really have."

"Do I?" Karsarkis looked annoyed. "Don't shit me, Jack. You have a private line straight into the White House and we both know it. You are well respected and well connected and you have significant credibility with someone who has the ear of the President of the United States."

"Look, Mr. Karsarkis, I—"

"So will you do it, Jack? Will you go to the White House and put my case for me?"

After that everyone, including me, sank into silence. I assumed they were waiting for me to say something, but I had absolutely no idea *what* to say.

Eventually Karsarkis leaned forward and fixed me with the kind of sincere gaze I figured they probably taught you at the Dale Carnegie School. "Can you do it?" he asked in a near whisper.

"Sure," I said. "I can also eat a box of rat poison and stick my finger in a wall socket, but on the whole, I'd rather not."

Karsarkis didn't even smile at that. Instead, he just looked at me, then leaned back and waited some more.

"I really don't know what to tell you," I said after a long time had passed in silence.

"Just think about it. Mike will call you tomorrow. If you accept my proposal, he will wire your money immediately."

I nodded slowly, not trusting myself to do much of anything else right then.

"Oh, yes. I almost forgot, Jack," Karsarkis added, "there is one other thing."

Karsarkis put a hand on the back of his neck and left it there as if he was trying to recall all the details about whatever it might be.

"It has come to my attention you may be in some danger."

"Danger from whom?"

"There are several possibilities. Our association is rather well-known already and people who are associated with me attract a certain amount of attention."

"We're not associated."

"I suppose it depends on how you look at it."

Karsarkis let his eyes linger on me.

"You're sitting here in my apartment right now, drinking my liquor, aren't you? I just made you a business proposition, and no matter what you might say, we both know you're considering it."

I didn't respond for a bit, which Karsarkis plainly expected because he just sat there and smiled at me.

Eventually I cleared my throat. "What kind of danger?"

"I've got a lot of enemies, Jack. Powerful enemies. People who want to do me harm. I really don't understand why that is."

Because you're a lowlife scum-sucking bastard who sold out his country and then had a woman killed to cover his ass and keep his wallet dry?

"If the perception gets around that you know things about me," Karsarkis continued, "there are people who would go to considerable lengths to find out what they are."

"What people?"

"People," Karsarkis shrugged. "I doubt you want to know anymore than that. I wouldn't if I were you."

I started to say something, but then thought better of it.

"There are those who will stop at nothing to get to me." Karsarkis looked genuinely puzzled as to why that might be. "And my friends and associates occasionally get rather rough treatment."

"We're not friends and we're not associates, so I guess I'm okay."

"These are serious people," Karsarkis continued as if I had never spoken. "You need serious people on your side, too, Jack."

Without moving his head, Karsarkis shifted his eyes to Mike O'Connell who was still sitting silently across the room. O'Connell folded his arms and fixed me with what I take it was his hard-guy stare. I almost laughed out loud.

"We could help out with the problem, Jack," he said. "If you let us, that is."

Tommy slurped the last of his vodka and the sound startled me. I'd all but forgotten he was there.

"Listen to him, Jack," he said. "A man needs his friends."

I glanced at Tommy without saying anything.

Encouraged, he leaned toward me and spoke in a confidential whisper. "You really ought to—"

"Shut the fuck up, Tommy," I snapped.

There was a long silence after that. Again, Karsarkis seemed to have anticipated it and was prepared to wait me out. This time I let him win the staring match.

"You may recall," I said, "it didn't impress me when you tried to get me involved in that hotel deal and offered me a lot of money for doing very little."

Karsarkis watched me without responding.

"And it didn't impress me when you tried to hook me in by leaning on BankThai to give me that house."

Karsarkis nodded, but only very slightly.

"And I'm a lot less impressed than you may think by you waving a few million dollars around."

Karsarkis was impassive.

"So now maybe you think you can impress me by trying to scare the crap out of me?"

"May I freshen anyone's drink?" O'Connell was standing in front of me when he spoke, but I swear to God I have no memory of how he got there. I guess something was distracting me.

I stood up. "No, I don't want another goddamned drink. I'm ready to go."

Karsarkis was smart enough to know he had already made his best play so he made no effort to prolong the conversation. I had already turned toward the door when something occurred to me. I stopped and looked back over my shoulder at Karsarkis.

"Did you kill her?" I asked.

"You mean Cynthia?" Karsarkis seemed genuinely surprised at my question. "The Korean woman?"

"Is there more than one dead woman to ask about?"

Karsarkis gave a little shake of his head and looked away.

"No," he said after a moment. "I didn't kill her."

"But you know who did."

"I think so."

"Who?" I asked.

Karsarkis blinked at that and let his eyes slide back to mine. I could see him thinking about it for a second, maybe two.

Then he gave another quick shake of his head and looked away again, saying nothing.

Twenty Two

TOMMY AND I took the elevator downstairs. Neither one of us spoke.

When we got back into the Mercedes, the driver headed south, winding through the neighborhood's backstreets until he reached Sukhumvit Road, where he turned west. Sukhumvit was like a long neon tunnel. Streaks of colored light danced on the night and the roadway shimmered with rainbows of grease and gasoline. I felt like I could have been anywhere, but I wasn't anywhere. I was in Bangkok, in the back of a darkened Mercedes, with a slightly tubby Thai spy, having just met secretly with the world's most notorious fugitive who had offered me millions of dollars to seek a pardon for him from the President of the United States.

Damn. Looking at it that way, even *I* was impressed.

Traffic was heavy past Queen's Park and the car crawled along until we reached Soi Asoke. I passed the time watching the lights rolling down the lenses of Tommy's glasses and it wasn't until we were abreast of the Sheraton that I finally posed the question I'd been silently turning over in my mind ever since we had left Karsarkis' apartment.

"What's your angle in all this, Tommy?" I asked. "Exactly why are you here?"

Tommy turned his head and looked at me, and when he did I

saw he had been waiting for me to ask.

"I'm here because we need your help, Jack."

"*We?* Is that the royal we, Tommy? Or are you trying to tell me this is something official?"

"I guess," he said after a pause, "that depends on what you think of as official."

I raised an eyebrow. "What the hell does *that* mean?"

"I have instructions to tell you there are people in the Thai government who would consider it a great service to our country if you would render Mr. Karsarkis whatever assistance he may require while he is our guest here."

"Those sound like very cautiously chosen words, my little friend. Very cautiously chosen indeed."

"Look, Jack, stop giving me shit, will you? I'm only the messenger here. I'm just doing my job."

"I'm not giving you shit, Tommy," I said. "I'm just listening to you carefully, and I was particularly interested in one word you used."

"What word?"

"Guest. You called Karsarkis a guest."

"Ah, Jack, drop the cutesy crap, would you?"

"No, wait a minute here, Tommy. I think that's important. I'd like to know exactly how you draw the distinction between a fugitive and a guest. It wouldn't have anything to do with being stinking rich and selling Thailand cut-rate oil while kicking back part of the deal to some heavy-hitting politicians, would it?"

"Look, Jack, I don't need one of your wiseass lectures on honesty in government tonight. I really don't." Tommy twisted toward me and folded his arms. "Just tell me what I have to do to get you to help Plato Karsarkis get his fucking pardon and I'm out of here."

"I want to be absolutely clear I'm hearing you right here, Tommy. Absolutely and completely clear."

I pinned him with my best tough guy stare. I thought he flinched slightly, but perhaps I was only being hopeful.

"You are telling me the Thai government wants me to help Plato Karsarkis obtain a pardon from the President of the United States. That's what I hear you saying here. Have I got that right?"

"Not the entire government," Tommy said, turning away. "Don't be a goddamned idiot."

"Then I guess I don't understand," I said.

"Jack, do I have to fucking spell it out for you?"

"Yeah, fucking spell it out for me."

Tommy looked completely exasperated and for a moment I didn't know if he was going to say any more or not, but then he started talking again.

"Everybody in the government here isn't on the take, Jack, regardless of what you might think."

"Jesus, you mean a few people have eaten so much already they've left the table?"

Tommy ignored me, as he probably should have.

"There are some very senior people in the Thai government who think Plato Karsarkis is a danger to us," he said. "They want him to go away. But they want that to happen without Thailand's direct involvement."

"Ah, I get it now," I said. "The famously neutral Thais who, lest we forget, somehow managed to finesse World War II."

Tommy made a sound like air rushing out of a tire. Then he sat back and folded his arms. I looked out at the street as the big Mercedes kept right on plowing through traffic like the Queen Elizabeth through a fleet of dinghies.

"These people I am referring to would owe you if you help Karsarkis, Jack, and take it from me these are people who you would *like* to owe you. You do this and you can just about write your own ticket around here."

I didn't say anything, although Tommy's announcement certainly put a different light on all this, didn't it? If at least part of the Thai government was pulling for Karsarkis to get his pardon, that gave the undertaking a certain sense of legitimacy it had lacked before. And then, too, some pretty impressive compensation had been laid on the table here. First Karsarkis counted out five million bucks and then Tommy made it sound like the Thai government would give me Phuket or something.

Karsarkis is going to pay *somebody* a shit load of money to represent him, I told myself. It wasn't as if I would be serving truth and justice by refusing. If I said no, he'd just get someone else. So why not me? Why throw all that money and the everlasting gratitude of the Thai government away for…well, what? Besides, it might even be fun to show up at the White House as Plato Karsarkis' lawyer. Billy Redwine would get a real hoot out of that, and everyone's entitled to a lawyer, right?

After I had completed my personal orgy of self-justification, I flipped my bad-boy stare back on and gave Tommy a long look.

"Before I decide anything, I need to see all your intelligence files on Karsarkis. The raw files, Tommy. Not the edited crap."

"I don't see what good that would do you. Most of the stuff is from local sources so it's in Thai anyway. You don't read Thai as I recall, do you, Jack?"

"Not too well."

"Well, there you go."

"You got wiretaps on Karsarkis, don't you?"

Tommy coughed and looked out the window.

"Yeah, I figured," I said. "As far as I know Karsarkis doesn't speak a word of Thai so whatever you've got has to be in English."

Tommy cleared his throat and tried for a pacifying tone. "Look, Jack, I'd like to help you out, but—"

"You're not helping me out. You're helping yourself out. No

files, no Jack Shepherd doing a single goddamned thing for Plato Karsarkis. That's my deal."

"Ah, man, I just can't do it, Jack."

Tommy sighed heavily and rubbed at his face. I said nothing. I figured if I kept quiet for a while, Tommy was bound to fold. I figured right.

"Look, Jack, I'll talk to my boss," he said, breaking the silence. "But that's the best I can do."

"Who's your boss?"

Tommy suddenly grinned and winked at me. "I can't tell you that."

"Well, *fuck*, Tommy…"

"That's all you're getting from me, Jack. I'll ask my boss about the files."

"Okay, you do that."

"But if we *do* give the files to you, does that mean you'll represent Karsarkis? That you'll try to get a pardon for him?"

I twisted around until I was facing Tommy full on. He looked alarmed and tilted his head back as if he thought I might be about to haul off and smack the crap out of him.

I leaned in close, my face right up against his, and I held it there until he flinched.

Then I winked.

"I can't tell you that," I said.

Twenty Three

AFTER TOMMY DROPPED me off at the university I went straight to the garage and retrieved my car without bothering to go back upstairs to my office. It was almost nine and I was hungry and a little pissed off and all I wanted to do was go home, open a beer, make a grilled-cheese sandwich, and kiss my wife. Although not necessarily in that exact order.

When I caught a traffic light on New Petchburi Road, I just sat and stared out at the city trying not to think about much of anything. The red tile façade of Chidlom Place was up ahead, and I counted the windows up from the bottom looking for the lights of our apartment on the eleventh floor. The windows I figured for ours were dark and I knew Anita was at home, so I tried again. I ended up at the same dark windows for a second time and I decided I must be miscounting somehow and gave up.

Chidlom Place is quite a nice building by local standards, medium-sized with no more than two apartments on each of its twenty floors, and Anita and I had lived there ever since we've been together. There were hardly any Thais at all in the building for some reason. Foreigners with no visible means of support seemed to occupy most of the apartments. Anita had long ago christened it the eurotrash building.

The traffic light was still red when my cellphone started vibrating frantically in my trouser pocket. It goosed me so badly that my foot shot out and punched the accelerator, which caused my car to lurch into the intersection. Although I hadn't come close to hitting anything, a cop directing traffic saw me and gave me a long look to appraise my cash value. When the cop saw I was a foreigner that pretty much sealed the deal since all foreigners are assumed by Thais to be rich. He was just starting to stroll over when a truck made an illegal turn right in front of him and he became distracted.

Spared for a moment, I fished the phone out of my pocket and flipped it open.

"Hello?"

"*Sawadee krap*, Professor," Jello's voice rumbled out of the tiny earpiece.

"Hey, man," I said. "You caught me in the car. I'm on my way home."

"I figured. I just tried you there but nobody answered."

I tilted my head and searched again for our apartment windows. That was odd. I thought for sure Anita was home.

"So what's up?" I asked.

"I need a favor."

"Sure."

"Don't speak too quickly. I'm about to ask you if I can bust in on your happy home life tonight, maybe get you to look at something for me."

"What is it?"

"I've got some incorporation papers here for a company that turned up in an investigation and something doesn't look right to me. I'd like to run them by you."

"I'm not sure how much I could tell you from looking at Thai incorporation papers."

"It's not a Thai company. It's a BVI."

The British Virgin Islands is a fairly respectable place to organize holding companies that are perfectly legal but still exist as nothing more than a few pieces of paper in some lawyer's filing cabinet. There are hundreds of thousands of such companies in use around the world for all sorts of purposes, most of them perfectly ordinary, although no doubt some of those purposes are less ordinary than others. Still, you seldom encounter a BVI company in Thailand and Jello's call tickled my curiosity.

"I guess Anita's not home so my hopes of a romantic dinner for two are pretty much in the crapper anyway. What time were you thinking of?"

"A half hour from now?"

"No problem," I said. "Come on around."

"Thanks, Jack. I appreciate this."

As I closed the telephone, the traffic light changed to green, and the cop swiveled back toward me. I tossed the phone on the passenger seat, gave him a cheery wave, and drove away before he could hit me up for a contribution to his favorite charity.

THE ELEVATOR OPENED on the eleventh floor of our apartment building and I crossed the small foyer and unlocked my front door. The only light inside was coming through the big windows in the living room and I had to turn on the lamps in the entrance hall as I walked through it. Wondering if Anita had gone to bed already, I stuck my head into the master bedroom, but it was empty.

I went into the kitchen and fished around in the refrigerator until I found a cold bottle of Corona and popped the top. Then I wandered into my study, turned on the lamps there, too, and flopped down in the big chair behind my desk.

After taking a long hit on the Corona, I pulled out my telephone and punched the speed dial for Anita's studio. I listened to the number ringing for a while, then pushed the disconnect button and tried the speed dial for Anita's cell phone. After two rings her voice mail kicked in and I hung up without leaving a message.

That was odd. Anita hadn't said anything about going anywhere tonight, at least not that I could remember. And even if she had gone somewhere, I couldn't imagine why her telephone would be off.

On top of that, something else was making me uneasy. I couldn't put my finger on it, but it wasn't the surprise of Anita's unexpected absence or even the residual effects of my meeting with Karsarkis that I was feeling. It was something completely different, something like a disturbance in the air around me.

I mulled it over while I sat there drinking my Corona, but I couldn't grab onto anything solid. Finally, I put the bottle down, reached for my laptop, and swung my feet up onto the desk. After I lifted the lid to wake it from standby, I waited the usual couple of seconds for the screen to spring back to life, but it didn't.

Wonderful, I thought to myself. *Now my laptop is screwed up. What the hell else can happen today?*

After the obligatory muttered curses, I took a closer look and almost immediately discovered the problem.

The laptop was shut down rather than in standby the way I usually left it. I pushed the power button and immediately heard the reassuring whir of the hard disk spinning up. I almost never shut the thing down and I couldn't remember doing it when I last used it, but I supposed I must have. God, I sighed to myself as I watched the Windows logo flash up and then disappear again, I must be getting forgetful in my old age.

When the log-on screen came up, I had to stop and think for a moment since I'd just changed my password a few days before, but then I typed in the new password and waited for the desktop to appear. It didn't. Instead of the usual display of colorful icons against a restful blue background, I found myself contemplating a dialog box with an angry-looking red border around it.

WARNING, it said in big letters across the top. Then below that, in somewhat more restrained type, it announced:

> THERE HAS BEEN AN ATTEMPT TO ACCESS THIS COMPUTER WITHOUT PASSWORD AUTHORIZATION. FOR FURTHER INFORMATION PLEASE CLICK INFO BELOW.

What the hell?
I clicked the button with INFO on it.

> AT 1937H ON 23 APRIL AN UNSUCCESSFUL ATTEMPT WAS MADE TO ACCESS THIS COMPUTER. AFTER THREE INCORRECT PASSWORD ENTRIES, IT WAS SHUT DOWN AND LOCKED. PRESS OK TO CONTINUE.

At least that explained why the laptop was shut down rather than in standby, but the explanation paled into insignificance next to the new question it raised.

Just who the hell had been trying to get into my laptop?

I glanced at my watch. It was twenty minutes after nine. 1937h was 7:37pm in actual people time. At 7:37pm I had been with Tommy at Plato Karsarkis' hideaway off Sukhumvit Road.

Had Anita been fiddling with my laptop? That seemed unlikely since she wasn't in the apartment now. Would she have been here a couple of hours ago, tried to use my laptop, and then left again? Surely that couldn't be right. Besides, Anita wasn't very fond of computers and seldom even used her own. She had never touched mine at all as far as I knew. Why would she to start now?

On the other hand, if not Anita, then who? The maid was a sixty-four-year-old woman from a tiny village up on the Laotian border who left promptly at six every evening to go back to her daughter's house across town. Even if she had still been here at 7:30, she wouldn't have thought of trying to use a laptop computer anymore than she would have taken a whack at piloting the space shuttle.

I hit OK and the familiar Windows desktop filled my screen just as it always did.

I glanced through the files on my hard drive. Everything looked just as I had left it. Of course, that was the way it ought to look. The laptop had locked up when the password wasn't entered correctly and no one could have accessed the hard drive anyway. Or could they?

What was going on here? Had someone been poking around in my study while I was out at Karsarkis' hideaway? As improbable as that seemed, there didn't appear to be any other explanation unless of course my security software had all of a sudden gone around the bend on its own, which I suppose was possible. The feeling of unease I'd had before, the sense of a disturbance in the air, was becoming distinctly more tangible.

Still, I asked myself, why would anyone have wanted to look at the files on my laptop? There really wasn't much in them. I had the usual stuff most people did—some personal correspondence, a lot of pointless emails, a list of credit card numbers, some old tax returns, spreadsheets for my brokerage accounts, and a few other bits of personal information. It was hardly the sort of thing that would have held much interest for a cat burglar.

I looked closely at the surface of my desk, but nothing appeared to have been disturbed. Then I got up slowly and walked over to the lateral file cabinet on the opposite wall. I stood there a moment contemplating it warily.

When I pulled open the top drawer I guess I half expected to find a dead body inside. What I actually found, of course, were my files, and they looked pretty much the way they always looked. I ran my hand over the forest of manila tabs that stuck out above the dark green suspension folders. Then I pulled a couple out and glanced at their contents. Nothing struck me as out of the ordinary, so I put them back and closed the drawer again.

I was still standing there wondering if I ought to check out the other drawers and closets around the house—and exactly how far I would get before sheer embarrassment at my own foolishness would cause me to abandon the effort—when the doorbell buzzed.

My state of mind at that moment being what it was, the sound of it scared the unholy crap out of me.

Twenty Four

SO ABSORBED WAS I in my outbreak of paranoia, I had forgotten for a moment that Jello was coming around. Opening the door I saw he had dressed for the occasion. He was wearing a lemon-yellow Hawaiian shirt with a chorus line of topless hula dancers strung out across the considerable width of his chest. The shirt hung out over a pair of baggy khakis and the cuffs of the khakis flopped onto a shiny pair of silver Air Jordans with black laces. For Jello, this was dressing.

I led him into the study and he paused next to the straight chair in front of my desk, examining it as if he wasn't quite sure what it was. I had to admit it looked a little dainty next to him. A lot of people doubted Jello was a Thai since he was so big. Rather than possessing the wiry, whippet-like physique usually associated with Thais, Jello was build more like a sumo wrestler. A *big* sumo wrestler.

"You got something I won't break?" he asked, pointing at the chair.

I sat back down behind my desk and waved him into the chair without saying anything. He settled gingerly onto it. Remarkably, it held.

"You get some bad sushi for dinner or something, Professor?" Jello studied my face as he laid the red accordion file he was carrying in his ample lap. "You don't look too good."

I tapped my fingers on the desk and avoided Jello's eyes. How much should I tell him?

The last conversation I had with Jello had ended with ominous warnings from him not to have anything to do with Plato Karsarkis. If I told him I had just been hanging out with Karsarkis while somebody was breaking into my apartment and checking out my laptop, he would have looked at me pretty strangely. I could hardly blame him. Shoot, *I* was looking at me pretty strangely.

"Well…" I paused, but Jello didn't say anything to help me out, so I made a snap decision to stick strictly to the mystery of the moment and leave Plato Karsarkis out of it. "It looks like somebody's been messing with my laptop, but there's nobody here who could have."

"Anita?"

"No, she's out and it happened just a couple of hours ago."

Jello leaned forward and tossed the file he'd brought me onto the desk, then he folded his arms and looked at me.

"Go on," he said.

I told him what I knew about what had happened, which wasn't much, so it didn't take long.

"Is there anything on the laptop anybody might want?" he asked when I was done.

"Not really. My class preparation stuff, a little personal financial data. Like that."

"No client files?"

"No…well, nothing important. Certainly nothing anybody would want to break into my apartment for."

"You think this was a break-in?"

"I don't know what I think. Maybe the damned software is all fucked up. You asked me why I looked a little strange and I told you. Now lay off. Don't grill me about it."

I looked at Jello for ten or fifteen seconds and he looked back, but he never said a word. Then abruptly he stood up and began to wander around the study, apparently aimlessly, examining the framed memorabilia hung on the walls.

"Any signs of forced entry?" he asked.

"No," I said.

"Anything missing?"

"I don't think so. Somebody just tried to get into my laptop, that's all."

"So you've checked everything?"

"No," I admitted. " I've looked around in here. Not in the other rooms."

Jello nodded very slowly as if I had somehow just confirmed all his deepest suspicions.

"You piss anybody off recently, Professor?"

"Not that I know of."

"How about the stuff you're working on now. You involved in any flaky shit I ought to know about?"

I apparently took a beat too long to respond because Jello shot me a dead-eyed look over his shoulder and then went back to examining the hangings on my walls with considerably more care than I thought they merited.

"Look, could we just drop this?" I asked as Jello scrutinized the elaborately engraved certificate attesting to my good standing with the United States Supreme Court. "It's probably nothing. You're making me wish I hadn't told you."

Jello worked his way around the wall to the low filing cabinet. All of a sudden he hopped on top of it with such astonishing agility for a big man that I just sat and stared, too dumbstruck to do much else.

Jello reached up and ran the fingertips of his left hand lightly back and forth over the wide molding that joined the wall and the ceiling. Then a small penknife materialized in his right hand and, after feeling around a bit more with his left, he pressed the point into the soft wood and twisted it into the molding with a corkscrewing motion.

"Jello, what in Christ's name—"

He waved me into silence without turning around. Digging something out of the molding with the blade, he closed the knife and cradled whatever it was in his palm, examining it, but his body blocked my view and I couldn't tell what it was. Jello's body was so big he could have been holding a small automobile and I wouldn't have been able to tell what it was.

"Look, man, what the hell are you doing?" I asked. "What's that?"

Jello turned around and hopped off the filing cabinet, then walked over and gently placed what looked like a nail on my desk blotter. I stared at it for a moment and then looked up.

"Okay, it's a nail," I said. "So what?"

"Not a nail."

Jello picked up the thing that still looked to me like a nail and held it right in front of my face, rotating it between his thumb and forefinger. Then he cupped it in his hand and closed his fingers around it, burying the head in his palm.

"It's a wireless transmitter," he said. "Short range, maybe three hundred yards, but pretty reliable over that distance. The main drawback to this model is its internal power only lasts for about seventy-two hours. After that you have to replace it."

"You've got to be shitting me."

"I shit you not, Professor. I shit you not one little bit."

I stared at Jello's closed fist and tried to envision the device he had cupped inside it.

"Oh, come on," I shook my head at him again. "Surely it's not really..."

"Very sophisticated stuff, too. Almost looks like one of ours, although it isn't."

"You mean somebody's listening to us right now?" I asked.

"Not as long as I've got the business end blocked like this." Jello wiggled his fist at me. "But somebody *has* been listening to everything that's been said in this room."

"For how long? Three days?"

I began frantically trying to remember what might have been said in this room during the last three days.

Jello shook his head. "Not necessarily."

He carefully reseated himself on the fragile looking chair in front of my desk, keeping the listening device closed up inside his big hand.

"I said this thing was good for about three days," he said. "That doesn't mean it's been here three days. Maybe whoever was looking at your laptop put it in. Maybe it wasn't here until tonight. On the other hand, maybe they were replacing one they had put in before and its battery was gone. No way to tell."

"Why would anyone want to stick a bug in my study?"

Jello shrugged. "Why would anyone want to look at whatever you have on your laptop?"

"I don't know," I said.

Jello looked unconvinced.

"Look, Jack, you're going to have to tell me what you're into here. Otherwise, I don't see what help I can be."

I was still trying to make up my mind whether to tell Jello about Tommy and the meeting at Karsarkis' apartment when he leaned forward, used his free hand to pick a pen out of the cup on my desk, and began to write on a legal pad lying next to it.

"Anyway," he said as he continued to write, "your bug is dead now."

Then abruptly he rotated the yellow pad and pushed it toward me.

On it Jello had scrawled *it may not be the only one*.

I held Jello's eyes across the desk until I was sure he wasn't joking around.

Then I took the pen and wrote *what do I do?*

"Look, Jack, you can tell me what you've got yourself into here or not." The whole time Jello was talking, he was writing again. "I don't really give much of a damn either way."

Walk across the street to McDonalds, he wrote, then he looked at me and raised his eyebrows.

I nodded.

Take your phone into the upstairs toilet.

I would have laughed right out loud, but it hardly seemed the thing to do under the circumstances.

"Look, Jello," I said instead, over-enunciating like a bad actor, "I don't really know what to tell you here."

Then call me, he finished writing. Then he popped the pen back into the cup and pushed the pad over to me.

"Okay, Jack, suit yourself. I just came to drop off these incorporation papers." Jello stood up and pocketed the bug. "But I can see this isn't a good time. If you change your mind about telling me what's going on, let me know. I'll try to help."

I picked my phone up off my desk and pushed it into my pocket.

"Okay, Jello. I understand. I'll do that."

We walked to the front door together in silence.

"Maybe I'll go downstairs with you," I said as I opened it for him. "I might go out and get something to eat."

"Suit yourself," he shrugged.

Neither of us spoke again until the elevator had come and we were inside.

"Look, Jello—" I started to say, but he shook his head before I got any further than that.

"Not yet."

We stepped into the lobby and walked outside. Jello turned toward the visitors parking area without the slightest indication that he even remembered the notes we had traded upstairs.

"Night, Jack," he said, and gave a little wave over his shoulder.

"Night, man."

I turned the other way and walked through the building's main gate and out to Soi Chidlom. There was a huge two-story McDonalds on the other side of the street, and its red, yellow, and green neon outlines looked incongruously cheerful among the other buildings in the neighborhood that were mostly dark at that hour.

A nearly unbroken river of cars, trucks, buses, and motorbikes still flowed south along Soi Chidlom toward Ploenchit Road about half a mile away. While I stood there waiting for enough of an opening to dart across without ending up as a hood ornament on a Mercedes Benz, Jello's nondescript white Toyota pulled out of Chidlom Place and turned right into traffic.

He drove right past me. If he even noticed me standing there on the curb, he didn't let on.

Twenty Five

"WHY EXACTLY AM I sitting on a toilet in McDonalds talking to you on my cell phone, Jello?"

I looked around. The inside of a bathroom stall didn't have a great deal to recommend it as a place to carry on a telephone conversation, but then I could probably have guessed that if I had ever thought about it before, which I hadn't.

"I was hoping you'd tell me," he said. "What have you gotten yourself into this time?"

"I'm not into anything, man."

"Oh, I see. Then I guess that little bug I found in your apartment must have been put there by mistake. You figure?"

"Why didn't we just have this conversation outside the apartment?" I asked.

"Shotgun mikes are pretty effective. Your friends could have had one on us from a hundred different places and we'd never know it."

"So why don't you come on back here and I'll buy you a Big Mac. Then we can sit at one of those nice red plastic tables downstairs and talk this whole thing through. If there are any people in here tonight with shotgun mikes, I'm sure we'll spot them right away."

"Not a good idea. A laser anywhere outside could pick up the conversation right off the windows. We'd never even know it was there."

"You're scaring me, Jello."

"Good. That's my intention."

"But then why the hell are we talking on a telephone? Isn't there a risk in that, too?"

"You're using a GSM phone, aren't you?"

"Yeah."

"Those things are real bastards to intercept here even if you've got the right cap code and can tell which signal you're looking for. Once the transmission gets to the first tower the whole signal stream goes digital and a mess of different conversations are scrambled together. GSM phones are secure enough we don't even bother to send encrypted radios with our guys when they're out on an operation anymore. They just use their phones to talk to each other."

I wasn't sure whether that made me feel better or not.

"Anyway," Jello continued while I tried to make up my mind. "Now you're in an enclosed space where no one could possibly have expected you to be and talking on a GSM cell phone. That's about as secure as you're going to get."

"Wonderful," I said. "So what do we do now?"

"Either you tell me what's happening here or you don't. Right now I don't know jack shit."

"Well, I don't know jack shit either, pal."

"Horse manure. Somebody pretty sophisticated has got you in their sights and my guess is you know exactly who it is."

"Then your guess would be wrong," I snapped.

A long silence fell after that. I wouldn't have blamed Jello if he had just hung up, but he didn't.

"Let me ask you something," I finally said, breaking the silence. "Who around here has the capacity to do something as sophisticated as this?"

"We do," Jello said, referring to ECID. "But it's not us."

"Well, that's a relief."

"And the National Intelligence Agency could do it, of course."

Jello paused, apparently considering the other possibilities, and while he did I pictured my ride with Tommy earlier than evening and wondered if his NIA buddies might have been responsible for doing the deed while he kept me out of the apartment.

"Then there are all the foreign embassy intelligence operations. There are twenty or so that we know about and a lot of them are pretty good. Could be almost any of them."

Suddenly an image jumped into my mind of CW sitting on a bar stool in Phuket. Was it possible that the US Marshals could be bugging the apartment of a US citizen in Thailand?

"The equipment isn't really all that hard to get," Jello continued before I decided. "You can buy stuff pretty much like that over the internet these days. Quite a few local police and military guys freelance and pick up a few baht on the side, although generally those people only work for wives who are setting their husbands up for a ride into the sunset. You haven't pissed Anita off recently, have you, Jack?"

"Very funny."

My butt was going to sleep sitting on the hard lid of the toilet, so I stood up. I pulled the stall door open and stepped outside. I leaned back against the sink.

"Don't be so quick to shrug off that possibility, Jack. You know what they say. The husband is always the last to know."

"Cut it out, Jello. That's not funny."

"I wasn't trying to be funny."

I let that hang there a moment, then changed tack.

"So you're telling me there are a lot of people around here who could have done this," I said.

"Yep. Hundreds. Maybe more."

Jello had a note of cheerfulness in his voice I found annoying.

"Unless, of course, you can narrow it down for me, Jack. Maybe by giving me a hint about who you've been fucking around with lately."

I had just about decided to float Jello a heavily edited version of my recent tête-à-tête with Plato Karsarkis when the door opened and a woman walked into the toilet. She was probably in her late twenties, tall, wasp-waisted, and wearing a white shirt with tight jeans that had lines of silver studs running down both legs. She didn't seem in the least embarrassed to be in the men's room and gave me a smile that could have blown out light bulbs. Then she went into the stall I had just vacated and closed the door.

"So what's it going to be, Jack?" he pressed, not knowing of course that I was now sharing the men's room with a startlingly beautiful woman.

"Ah…" My eyes flicked to the stall door, but I heard nothing from the other side. "That's a little hard for me to say right now."

Jello caught the change in my voice.

"Has some guy just come in?"

"You're half right."

Jello considered that in silence, trying to read between the lines.

"I don't understand," he finally said.

There was still no sound or movement behind the stall door, but my discomfort had increased to the point where I thought it might be better just to get the hell out of there and take my chances with the lasers and shotgun mikes. At least that seemed preferable to standing in the men's room trying to carry on a telephone conversation while a beautiful young woman relieved herself.

"Never mind," I told him. "I've had it for tonight. I'm going home."

"You want me to get somebody to sweep your apartment tomorrow?"

"Yeah, that would be good."

"Okay," he said. "I'll work something out," he said, "but Jack…"

Jello took a deep breath and let it out again. "Until I get that taken care of, be careful what you say."

"Oh, golly," I said. "That never crossed my mind."

"Good night, Professor."

"Night, Jello."

I punched off my phone and stuck it back in my pocket. Then I pushed out through the door and shot a quick glance back over my shoulder just to make certain the woman wasn't following me. When I did, something caught my eye, and it caused me to stop walking and turn around very slowly.

That was the first time I clearly registered the black scrollwork painted on the door to the toilet I had just come out of. It read... LADIES.

I HAD BEEN back in the apartment for a nearly an hour sitting at my desk with my feet up and trying unsuccessfully to make some sense out of the evening's festivities when I heard the front door open and close. A few seconds later Anita walked into the study.

All at once it occurred to me I had no idea at all what to say to Anita about any of this. If I started pointing at the walls with one finger while holding another over my lips, she wouldn't know what to think. On the other hand, blurting out something like, *Darling, it appears our apartment has been bugged by a sophisticated intelligence operation that wants to know everything we are saying,* didn't quite seem the way to go either.

Anita stopped in the doorway instead of coming over to the desk to give me a little peck as she usually did.

"Hello, Jack."

There was a brittle edge to her voice and I was left with no doubt Anita was unhappy with me for some reason. That was just great. Here I was under surveillance by persons unknown for reasons unknown and now my wife was apparently mad at me and I didn't know what the reason for *that* was either.

"What's wrong, Anita?"

"Nothing's wrong. Why would you ask?"

Uh-oh.

Whatever it was, it had to be serious. When a woman says something like, *Nothing's wrong and why would you ask,* my own personal rule of thumb is that you're pretty well fucked right there.

"We have to talk, Jack."

Stee-rike one!

"But not now. I'm very tired and I'm going straight to bed."

Stee-rike two!

"Good night, Jack." And with that Anita turned her back on me and walked toward the bedroom.

Stee-rike three and you're outta there!

So far I was having a heck of an evening, wasn't I? And hell, it was barely ten-thirty. The night was young. There was still *plenty* of time for a few more tons of shit to fall on me before the day was officially over.

Twenty Six

ANITA MUST HAVE taken a sleeping pill because when I woke the next morning she hardly seemed to have moved all night. I showered and dressed, trying to do it quietly, and she never stirred.

I went into the study to pick up my briefcase and then, remembering I hadn't brought it home with me, all at once I also remembered everything else from the night before as well. Since I hadn't yet had even a drop of coffee, that wasn't too swell.

The maid didn't come in until eight and I briefly considered making some breakfast for myself, but with the apartment wired for sound and Anita apparently ready to rip into me about something as soon as she woke up, getting out of there as quickly as possible was far more appealing. I left by the front door, got into the car, and drove to the Starbucks in Amarin Plaza. Forty-five minutes later, thoroughly buzzed on the caffeine from a double-shot latte and riding a sugar high from ingesting a couple of blueberry muffins, I parked in the garage on campus, collected my notes from my office, and made it to my nine-o'clock class more or less on time.

I had planned to give a lecture that morning on the development of international tax avoidance legislation, but I knew under the circumstances I'd never make it through something that tedious. Instead I fell back on the traditional refuge of every distracted academic who didn't feel like lecturing and who'd had at least some practical experience in the subject at hand. I soft-shoed through a hastily improvised routine composed of my greatest and wittiest war stories.

I imagine former surgeons tell their students about patients whose lives they saved through their quick thinking, and no doubt every trial lawyer has a fund of anecdotes about criminals he freed with his clever tactics. But if you've been a corporate deal guy like me, what you talk about when all else fails is money. Largely how you scored unholy piles of it for some client by being really sneaky. In Asia at least, those kinds of stories are always guaranteed to keep the kids absolutely riveted. Forget about life and liberty, you can almost hear the little bastards chanting, let's get right down to all that pursuit-of-happiness stuff.

I ended the day's entertainment with a flourish—always leave them laughing, somebody said—and speed-walked back to my office before a student could ambush me either with a genuine question or, more likely, a transparent attempt to suck up a little. My secretary wasn't at her desk, but then Bun was seldom at her desk so I grabbed myself some coffee from the kitchen down at the end of the hall and then went straight into my office. After hanging out a *Do Not Disturb* sign I kept at the ready, I locked the door.

I flopped down into my desk chair and made myself comfortable. Then I propped my feet up on the side of a half-open drawer and sipped at my coffee. The time had clearly come to do some serious pondering.

But where to start? The last completely normal moment I could remember for weeks was when Anita and I had decided to go to the Boathouse for dinner. It had been a placid, soft-toned evening on the western beaches of Phuket and we were looking for nothing anymore exciting than a romantic dinner for two, which can be exciting enough all by itself if you get it right.

But where had that led?

The world's most wanted fugitive was trying to become my new best pal and at the same time an undercover team of US Marshals was trying to recruit me as a spy. Two powerful groups were tugging me in exactly opposite directions, and that was just if I was lucky. Maybe there were *more* than two groups who had me in their sights. If neither Karsarkis nor the US marshals were responsible for wiring my apartment, that meant I had somebody else on my tail, too, somebody who hadn't shown himself yet.

I felt like a man who had started out skiing down a gentle slope only to discover he was really on Mount Everest. And he wasn't wearing skis.

Everything was becoming clearer and fuzzier all at the same time. Perhaps if I told Jello the truth about what was going on, particularly the part about Karsarkis offering me a huge sum of money to try and get him a presidential pardon, maybe he would at least point me in the right direction. There were some pretty strict limitations as to how much Jello could tell me, of course, even if he *did* know something I probably ought to, but at worst he would probably tell me there was nothing he could say and I was on my own. I was *already* on my own, so what did I have to lose by asking?

I had just about talked myself into telling Jello the whole story when my cell phone rang. I scooped it up and glanced at the number on the screen. I thought I recognized it as Jello's so I answered.

"Hey, man, I was just thinking of you."

"Ah, Jack, that's so sweet. I didn't know you cared."

I looked at the telephone. It wasn't Jello.

"Who is this?" I asked.

"I thought you said you were just thinking of me. Now you ask who this is? You're a fickle motherfucker, Big Jack. Just when I was feeling all warm and loved, you jerk the rug right out from under me."

"Tommy?"

"At your service, my friend. At your fucking service."

"I'm sorry," I said. "I was expecting someone else."

"So I gather."

There was an awkward silence after that. I was waiting for Tommy to tell me why he was calling, but he apparently was waiting for me to ask, so eventually I obliged him.

"What do you want, Tommy?"

"You asked to see some files, didn't you, Jack?"

In all the upheaval since last night I had completely forgotten the conversation Tommy and I had about the NIA's intelligence files on Karsarkis.

"So your boss said you could give them to me?"

"Not exactly."

"Not exactly? What does that mean?"

"It means my boss is going to give them to you."

"Fine."

"Okay. Here's what you do, Jack. Go downstairs and—"

"Whoa, Tommy. I'm not in the mood this morning for a goddamned scavenger hunt. If your boss has got some files for me, tell him just send them on over."

"No can do, Big Jack. Here are the ground rules. You talk directly to my boss. Maybe you get some stuff to look at and maybe you don't. And even if you do, no notes and no copies. That's it. Take it or leave it."

I sighed and studied a point on my office wall that had nothing in particular to recommend it.

"Okay, Tommy," I finally said. "Whatever."

"Good call."

"I'm so glad you approve."

"Downstairs then," he said. "Now."

And with that he hung up.

I closed my phone and sat looking at it for a moment. Tommy worked hard at being obscure. I gathered he thought spies were supposed to be obscure. Generally, the effect was comic, but occasionally it was irritating. I put today down in the irritating column.

By the time I got downstairs I was wound up enough to give Tommy a boot in the ass for jerking me around, but the building lobby was empty and I found myself deprived of an immediate target. I stood there for a moment looking around, but it was a very small lobby so that was a pretty pointless exercise. Empty was empty.

Not having any better idea what I was supposed to do I walked outside and stood at the top of the steps. That was when I saw the black Mercedes parked in the circular drive with the engine running. It looked like the same car in which Tommy and I had ridden out to Karsarkis' hideaway. At least I thought it was the same car because it had the same kind of darkened windows and sliding curtains, but it might have been a different one. I couldn't tell, and when I thought about it for a moment, I also realized I really didn't give a damn.

April is the heart of the hot season in Thailand. Although it wasn't even eleven yet, the sun was already brutal. I could feel the heat in the concrete through the soles of my loafers. As I walked toward the Mercedes, it was like taking a stroll on a warming tray.

When I was still fifty feet from the car both front doors opened in near perfect synchronization and two men I'd never seen before got out. They were athletic-looking locals wearing nearly identical white shirts, black pants, and dark neckties, and they were both expressionless behind their opaque sunglasses. I recognized government security when I saw it no matter what country I was in and either that's what these guys were or they had seen *Men in Black* way too many times. The driver stepped away from the car and moved back a few strides, his head swiveling slowly back and forth. Then the man who had emerged from the other side went to the rear passenger door and held it open without taking his eyes off me. It was a silent yet unmistakable command for me to get into the car.

Taking my own sweet time about it, I sauntered over and got in. When I did I discovered the car was already pretty crowded. There were two people in the back seat, and neither one of them was Tommy. The two passengers were a man and a woman. I recognized both of their faces immediately, but I couldn't remember where I had seen them before.

The woman in the middle of the back seat appeared to be in her late thirties, although I could never really tell with Thai women. She was stylishly dressed in a cream silk suit with matching heels. Sitting straight, her bare legs crossed at the knee, she dangled a shoe off the toes of one foot which caused her straight skirt to ride up well above her knees and leave her smooth brown thighs very agreeably displayed. When the white-shirt-and-tie muscle outside closed the door behind me, he shoved me up tightly against the woman, which I had to admit I didn't really mind at all.

The man, on the other hand, was short and sallow and middle-aged. He wore a dark suit that appeared expensive, although it also looked like it hadn't been pressed since the day he had bought it. I assumed he had to be an Englishman, mostly because of his bad teeth and worse complexion and the puckered look on his face that suggested a terminal case of constipation.

"Good morning, Mr. Shepherd," he said without looking directly at me. "Thank you very much for coming."

His voice sounded familiar, too, but I still couldn't place him. Regardless, the accent was unquestionably English public school, so I gathered my first impression had been right.

"Well, gee," I said, not offering to shake hands. "How could I refuse?"

The Englishman said nothing in response, but with my arm still pressed against the woman's side I thought I felt a little ripple of amusement roll through her body. Then perhaps I was mistaken about that. Around beautiful women all men tend to be irrationally hopeful that they are being regarded as witty and charming. It's pure genetic programming.

The driver and the guy who was riding shotgun had resumed their places in the front of the car. The Englishman leaned forward slightly and spoke to the driver.

"*Okay, pai gun teu,*" he said. "*Bork duay ta mee krai tam ma.*"

The man spoke Thai so colloquially I almost missed what he was saying, but his accent left me with little doubt he was completely fluent.

Let's go, he had said, *and let me know if you pick up anybody tailing us.*

The driver put the car into gear and we rolled slowly around the driveway and out into one of the many small streets that ran through the campus. I assumed the driver would turn right toward busy Phayathai Road, the main artery that bisected the campus north to south, but he didn't. Instead he turned left, drove behind the National Stadium, and then turned left again on a quiet residential street that led in the general direction of the Chao Phraya River.

Neither the man nor the woman said anything else and I certainly had no intention of giving them the satisfaction of asking what the hell was going on. I concentrated instead on trying to figure out where I knew these two from. I had seen them both recently, I was reasonably sure, but where? And had I seen them together or had I seen them separately?

I was still trying to work that out when the man twisted his body around until he was half facing me and laced his fingers around one knee.

Twenty Seven

"MY NAME IS Smith."

"Really?" I said. "What an unusual name."

"I could give you a lot of rubbish, but you probably wouldn't believe it anyway, so let's just jump right to it. I am with the British Embassy and I work there in an intelligence capacity."

That stopped me for a moment.

"You're Tommy's boss?" I asked the man. "You're telling me Tommy works for *British* intelligence?"

The woman spoke for the first time. "No, Mr. Shepherd," she said.

Her voice was so soft I had to bend toward her slightly to hear her words. Her rounded tones and deliberate intonation were an even more obvious if less blatant sign of a childhood spent in English public schools than the man's overly plummy accent had been.

"I'm Tommy's boss," she continued. "I am the Director General of the National Intelligence Agency."

I examined the woman's face for some sign she was joking. I saw none.

"I'm speechless," I finally said.

"Somehow I doubt that."

The woman smiled slightly when she spoke. I noticed it was a very nice smile, particularly for a spook.

"Okay," I admitted, "maybe not. But I had no idea the head of the NIA was a woman."

"Really? And now that you know, why are you so surprised?"

"Well…" I tried to think of a diplomatic way to put it. "On the whole Thailand is something of a man's world, and generally one thinks of Thai women as—"

"Maids and whores, Mr. Shepherd?"

I glanced at the woman. When I saw she was still smiling, I was greatly relieved.

"Seventy-five percent of the university graduates in Thailand are women," she continued. "We probably run more major companies and are responsible for more meaningful decisions here than in any nation on earth. My personal belief is that in another decade most Thai men will be driving motorcycle taxis and this will be the world's foremost matriarchal society."

"That's a little difficult to imagine," I muttered, stalling for time while I tried to figure out where this was going.

"Why?" the woman asked.

"Well, for one thing, almost every government minister and the permanent secretary of every department is a man."

"That is because government counts for very little in Thailand, Mr. Shepherd, at least when it comes to the exercise of real power. We will continue to let the old dinosaurs preen their egos, line their pockets, and run after schoolgirls for so long as they do nothing else. But then you no doubt already know that is all politicians do here anyway. I'm sure you are just too polite to say it."

I kept my mouth shut. That was something I didn't do very often, but this seemed to me to be a good time to test out the concept.

"Look, old boy," Mr. Smith cut in. "This is all absolutely fascinating, I'm sure, but could we get back to the important point here?"

All at once the penny dropped. I placed both of them.

These two had been at Plato Karsarkis' dinner party in Phuket. And they had been there together. *Oh my, oh my.* British intelligence and the Director General of the NIA keeping company? The mind boggled as to whom exactly was fucking whom.

"I just realized where we met before," I said.

"That doesn't matter," Smith said. He shook his head and looked away.

"It matters to me."

"I'm not really concerned with what may or may not matter to you," Smith continued. "I will say only that the British government does have a certain interest in your friend Plato—"

"Karsarkis isn't my friend," I interrupted.

"Whatever you say," Smith shrugged. "Still, we have an interest in keeping Mr. Karsarkis both alive and reasonably happy, and I'm not so sure your own government shares that interest."

"What is that supposed to mean?"

"That's not for me to say," Smith shrugged again, a gesture he seemed to have practiced a lot. "I'm just along for the ride. This is Kathleeya's show."

It was the first time I could recall hearing the woman's name. Certainly, she hadn't introduced herself today and I couldn't remember how she had been introduced to me at Karsarkis' dinner party either. I wondered if that was her real name. Regardless, Kathleeya—or whatever her name actually was—spoke up before I could ask.

"How much do you really know about Plato Karsarkis?" she asked me.

"Not much. Mostly what they tell me on CNN."

"You should watch the BBC," Smith put in. "CNN is nothing but a load of self-conscious twaddle. Americans trying to pretend they're citizens of the world instead of just Americans. Bloody joke, if you ask me."

I glanced at him to see if he was smiling. He wasn't. Nevertheless, when I looked back at Kathleeya she was, and I thought that was nicer anyway.

"You told Tommy you would be willing to help us if we gave you Plato Karsarkis' files," she said to me.

"No, I didn't."

"Then, Mr. Shepherd, before we go any further perhaps you had better tell me exactly what you did say to Tommy."

"Karsarkis asked me to try to get him a presidential pardon, and Tommy said the Thai government wanted me to help Karsarkis. I told Tommy I needed to look at whatever the NIA had on Karsarkis before I decided what I was going to do."

"Yes, I see."

"By the way, is there any particular direction in which you'd like me to speak so you can get a clear recording of this conversation?"

"Not really. You're pretty well covered from every direction."

"Yes, well, your own car is one thing, but bugging my apartment seems to me to extend your coverage area a bit beyond what I would view as fair."

Kathleeya and the Englishman exchanged a look.

"What makes you think your apartment has been bugged?" she asked.

I realized immediately that I should never have said anything about the bug in my apartment. Men always talk too much in front of beautiful women. It's an incurable male disease, frequently fatal.

I had jumped too quickly to the conclusion that NIA had something to do with placing the bug, but it looked like I was probably wrong about that. I had given up something that could be important and gotten absolutely nothing in return and, to keep myself from sounding like a paranoid lunatic, I would to have to bring up Jello's name; but I had absolutely no intention of doing that so I tried a modest finesse.

"Look, I know about the break-in attempt on my laptop and I found your cute little bug in my study. I know there are probably more bugs, too, of course, so some friends at the American Embassy are sweeping my apartment regularly now."

A clumsy piece of embroidery maybe, but close enough for government work.

"The NIA has nothing to do with whatever you may have found in your apartment, Mr. Shepherd."

"Of course you don't."

Kathleeya turned her head and leaned slightly toward me. She remained silent until I was looking directly into her eyes, which I was more than willing to do.

"It is important that you believe me. I did not know your apartment was under surveillance or your computer had been compromised. I would never have authorized such a thing."

"My computer wasn't compromised. I said someone *tried* to break in. They didn't succeed. And I think I got the bugs almost immediately after they went in, so I doubt they produced anything of value for anyone either."

"Well there you are then. If it had been our operation, it would have succeeded."

I wasn't sure what to say to that so I pushed away the curtain and looked out the car window while I thought about it. The driver had taken Rama IV to the expressway and was heading north. The airport was just off to the east and I followed a departing United 747 with my eyes until it disappeared behind a bank of clouds.

This was probably all just bullshit, I told myself. Of course it was the NIA who had fiddled with my computer and planted the bugs. Who the hell else could it be? Whatever Jello said, I had a little difficulty buying into the idea that all kinds of foreign intelligence services were running amuck in Thailand bugging apartments and breaking into computers.

Still, this woman had looked me right in the eye and denied the NIA had anything to do with it and I wanted to believe her. Would I have tried nearly as hard to believe her if she'd been short, fat, old, and ugly? I knew what the answer to that was, regardless of how embarrassing it might be to admit it.

"What about Karsarkis' files?" I asked when I turned back from the window. "Do I get them or not?"

The woman opened her dark green leather purse and took out a clear plastic case containing a DVD.

"This is everything we have that is relevant."

"I asked for the raw files, not what you chose to edit for me," I said.

"Regardless of what you asked for, this is what you're getting."

She held the case toward me. She seemed to assume I would accept it without raising any further objections. She was right, of course.

"I think you'll find enough there to keep you interested," she said. "By the way, you should know that when you open the file on the disk, a clock will start."

"A clock?"

"Exactly one hour from the time you open the file, everything on the disk will be scrambled in such a way as to make it entirely unrecoverable. The same thing will happen immediately if you attempt to print, email, or copy any part of the file. Do I make myself clear?"

"You do indeed. But why all the melodrama?"

"I wouldn't be very happy to find copies of NIA documents in the New York Times next week."

"You could have just asked for my word that I wouldn't give them to anyone."

Smith snorted audibly, but I thought I saw a flash of something like embarrassment slide across Kathleeya's face.

"I'm sorry, Mr. Shepherd. We felt this was the appropriate security to impose under the circumstances. Please don't take it personally."

"So it's not personal, it's just business."

"You will also find a text file on the disk which contains nothing but a nine-digit number," she continued without looking at me. "That is my private cell phone number. After you have read the materials on the disk, I would appreciate it if you would call me and tell me whether you have decided to help us."

"You mean help Plato Karsarkis, don't you?"

Kathleeya smiled and I allowed myself to enjoy it this time.

"Interests frequently have a way of getting tangled up in odd ways, Mr. Shepherd. You have heard the saying, "The friend of my friend is also my friend.""

"As is the enemy of my enemy," I said.

"Something like that." She smiled again.

Smith leaned forward and spoke to the driver and the big Mercedes swung off the Expressway and made a U-turn. No one said much while we were driving back to the city, but as I juggled the DVD case in my fingers I couldn't help but think about what I might find on that disk.

Her personal cell phone number, huh?

Maybe later when I told Anita about all this I'd skip over that part.

Twenty Eight

AFTER THE BLACK Mercedes dropped me off I went straight upstairs to my office, locked the door, and picked up the telephone. I dialed a number, let it ring once, and hung up. That might not be the usual way to reach someone by telephone, but then I was calling Darcy Rice and there was absolutely nothing usual about her either.

Darcy had retired to Bangkok following a career with the US government doing things about which she was now professionally vague. A lot of people figured Darcy for CIA, certainly back when she was an active government employee and maybe even still, but I doubted that was true. I was pretty sure Darcy had spent her career with the National Security Agency. The NSA monitors and intercepts all sorts of communications, breaks encryption, tasks spy satellites, and engages in a whole range of technology-driven black arts that most people would dismiss as science fiction even if they somehow found out about them, which they wouldn't anyway. That was exactly the sort of stuff Darcy seemed to know everything about, which was why I had made her for NSA right from our earliest conversations.

These days Darcy was like so many retired government types who had learned their trades in the Cold War. Now that peace had broken out, or at least the game had changed into something nobody understood anymore, she had taken her considerable experience and talents into private enterprise. Darcy ran a small company that operated out of a stylish if aging mansion in the oldest part of Bangkok, a place she had remodeled from dilapidated elegance into a high-tech marvel. She described her business as an information gathering and analysis consultancy, which was vague enough to cover most anything. What it actually was, of course, was a private intelligence agency.

At first I had been amazed an operation of such technological sophistication existed in a backwater like Bangkok, but the more Darcy and I had become friends and the more I learned about what she was doing, the more I understood Bangkok was a perfect place for her. Bangkok was where international criminals, law enforcement personnel, intelligence agencies, terrorists, drug runners, arms peddlers, and the inevitable collection of scam artists, hangers-on and wannabes mingled in teeming streets and grimy bars under an unspoken understanding. They could let down their guard in Bangkok. They could just hang around or even party a little without taking all the usual precautions since it was understood they would all leave each other alone while they were here. Even the Thai government didn't much care what anyone did in Bangkok, as long as it didn't involve them. The cantina in Star Wars was a run-of-the-mill saloon compared to the bars of Bangkok.

The moment I heard the warnings about the traps the NIA had supposedly built into the disk I had been given, I decided there was no way in hell I was going to touch the thing without talking to Darcy first. I gave her a little help with her projects from time to time and she paid me back by doing me favors when I needed them. I figured I needed one now.

Darcy was very careful about her own security, probably because she had so little difficulty shredding everyone else's. The only way to reach her was by calling and hanging up. The call went to a computer somewhere and I didn't have a clue what happened then although I figured it was something really cool. But Darcy always called me back right away so I didn't really care.

After hearing the one ring and hanging up, I surveyed my desk and briefly examined the pile of mail Bun had left stacked on top of *The Wall Street Journal*. If I hadn't had to move it off the newspaper, I probably wouldn't have bothered. No one in Thailand was foolish enough to use the postal service for anything that actually matters. Tossing the mail in the garbage, I swung my feet up on my desk and unfolded the *Journal*. I hadn't even made it past page one before my direct line rang.

"Jack, baby," Darcy purred when I answered. "You called?"

"You have my mobile number, don't you?"

Darcy cut the connection without another word and a few seconds later my mobile beeped.

"Okay, baby," Darcy said when I answered, "so what kind of shit are you in this time?"

"The usual, I guess. The brown kind."

"You figure your phone is monitored?"

"Maybe. I don't know."

"Just because you're talking on a GSM cell now, you're not invulnerable."

"I thought it was pretty solid," I said.

"Depends on who you're up against."

"Everything always does, Darcy."

"Uh-huh," she said. "So, baby, enough of the happy talk, huh? Let's have it."

I told her about the disk Kathleeya had given me and about the security measures she claimed it contained. Darcy didn't ask for any details of why I was riding around town chatting with the head of the National Intelligence Agency, nor did she ask me what was on the disk. Her standards of professional discretion ruled out both questions.

"So what do you think?" I asked. "About the disk."

"Everybody underestimates the Thais when it comes to technology," Darcy said. "Besides, stuff like that is pretty common now. You can buy off-the-shelf software that will prevent copying, printing, and emailing of any file just by pasting a transparent image over it. The part about the disk corrupting itself after a set period would be a little harder to do, but it's probably a variation on the built-in detonation a lot of corporate users are putting into their email now."

"You lost me."

"It doesn't really matter. If Kate told you your disk was rigged to corrupt itself, my guess is it's true."

"You call her Kate?" I asked. "So you know here pretty well?"

Darcy ignored my question.

"Just in general," she asked me instead, "do you have any idea what type of files are on the disk?"

"Some text files, I think, or maybe PDFs. Nothing fancy that I know of. I asked the NIA for some stuff and they decided to give it to me, at least with all this security attached."

"And you want to know if I can beat their security measures."

"Yeah," I said. "Something like that."

"Why do you care, Jack? Why not just read whatever is on the disk and let it go at that? Why do you need to copy it?"

"If there's something that I end up relying on, Darcy, I don't want them to claim later that it never existed."

"You think they'd do that?"

"Sure. Particularly if they have some purpose I don't see right now for giving me this stuff in the first place."

Darcy made some little clucking noises with her tongue. "I imagine I can get past whatever they've put on your disk without too much trouble."

"I thought you said they were good."

"They are, baby," she murmured. "But I'm better."

I summoned up the required chuckle right on cue.

"You want me to bring the disk out to you?" I asked.

"Why don't I send one of the boys over to pick it up now?" Darcy said. "Then come out for dinner tonight and I'll tell you what we've got. How about that? Nata would love to see you, baby."

Darcy didn't have to dangle Nata as an incentive to me to come out to her place for dinner, although I guess it didn't hurt. Nata was a stunningly beautiful Thai woman in her forties whose ex-husband had been a powerful and well-connected general until he ended up on the wrong side of some long-forgotten military coup. These days the former general was living in Copenhagen, and Nata was living in Bangkok, with Darcy. The two had been companions longer than I had known Darcy and I'd always assumed Nata had as much to do with Darcy's choice of Bangkok for her retirement as did the relatively cheap real estate and nice people. Darcy would hardly be the first person I'd met who had upped stakes and moved to Bangkok for a woman.

"Don't know why not," I said. "Let me call Anita and see if she's planned anything yet."

There was an unmistakable beat of silence.

"Sure," Darcy said, "bring her along if you like."

I knew Darcy had never particularly cared for Anita. I wasn't certain why that was and I had often wondered about it. I got a vague feeling Darcy was suspicious of Anita in some way, as if her radar had picked up something about Anita she didn't like but didn't think it appropriate to mention to me. Maybe it was more than that, or maybe it was less, but I hadn't flat out asked Darcy about it and probably never would.

"Nah, probably not a good idea," I said. "Anita would just get pissed off watching me flirt with you."

Darcy gave a throaty chuckle and didn't even offer the pretense of an argument.

"Okay, baby. I'll have somebody in your office for the disk within a half hour. Why don't you get here about seven. That okay with you?"

"Done deal," I said.

After Darcy had hung up, I punched the speed dial for Chidlom Place, but Anita wasn't home and the maid didn't know where she was. I tried the speed dial for Anita's cell phone, too, and ended up listening to her voice mail the way I had been doing a lot lately. I hung up without leaving a message.

I was a little annoyed I couldn't reach Anita and then I was immediately annoyed with myself for being annoyed. I swore not to think about it anymore, picked up the *Journal* again, and kicked back to finish it while I waited for Darcy's messenger.

I was never exactly sure how Darcy put people almost anywhere in Bangkok in such a short time since the local traffic was so awful it had attained legendary status. I had visions of dozens of nondescript-looking boys on motorcycles orbiting slowly in various parts of the city just waiting for Darcy to ask them to do something. Actually, maybe that *was* how it worked.

Less than fifteen minutes later there was a soft tapping on my office door. A polite young man in his early twenties wearing a dark and completely forgettable gray shirt and equally gray pants entered and *wai*ed deeply. I gave him the floppy disk in a padded envelope and he slipped it into a leather dispatch bag slung over his shoulder, *wai*ed again, and disappeared without having spoken a word.

Twenty Nine

WHEN THE BOY had gone I glanced at my watch. It was only twelve-fifteen, but I was hungry and figured I probably deserved an early lunch anyway. Some comfort food seemed very much in order, which to an American abroad generally meant a cheeseburger, so I headed out Sukhumvit to a local joint called Bourbon Street popular with American expats.

The origins of Bourbon Street have been lost in the mists of Bangkok expatriate history, meaning they go back more than five years. There is a rumor that the place was originally opened by a retiring CIA station chief who loved his hometown of New Orleans but wasn't all that anxious to move back to it since his wife lived there and he had found far more congenial companionship in Bangkok. Regardless, if Bangkok had a cop bar, it wasn't the smoky little go-go joint down in Nana Plaza most people would imagine, it was Bourbon Street. On any given night, you could find enough heavily armed DEA, FBI, CIA, Secret Service, and Diplomatic Security guys there to strike fear into a small country.

I turned off Sukhumvit into Washington Square and circled around an old-time movie theater that had found new life hosting a transvestite review for Japanese tourists. A snappily uniformed parking guard whistled me into a vacant space and ushered me out of my car with a salute so crisp it would have brought tears to the eyes of General Patton.

Inside, Bourbon Street was a cool, dim haven from the midday sun. One of the girls behind the bar started making a glass of iced tea as soon as she saw me come through the door and I grabbed an *International Herald Tribune* off the rack at the door and made my way to a table in the back. When a waitress brought me the iced tea, I ordered my cheeseburger with a side of onion rings. I was just opening the *IHT* when Bourbon Street's owner wandered over and plunked himself down across from me.

"Hey, man," he said as we shook hands. "How yawl doin'?"

Doug's southern accent had remained so strong during the couple of decades he had lived in Thailand that I half suspected he practiced with tapes just to keep it sharp.

"Doing fine, pal," I answered. "How's business?"

"Business is great. Real great. A lot of new Yanks in town for some reason."

"Really?"

I wasn't particularly interested, but Doug was a convivial fellow and shooting the breeze with him for a few minutes was one of the attractions of hanging around Bourbon Street.

"Come to think of it, one of them was asking about you the other day," he said.

Now I was interested.

"Somebody was asking about me? Asking what?"

"Aw…nothing really. Just if I knew you. If you came in much. That kind of thing."

"And that was it?"

"Yeah, pretty much," Doug nodded. "Well…actually he did ask one other thing that I thought was a little weird."

"Weird?"

"Yeah, he asked if you came in alone or if you were with Anita most of the time."

"Huh," I said, not being able to think of anything else.

"He even asked if you ever came in with women. I mean other women. Other than Anita."

"Who was this guy doing all this asking about me?'

"I don't know," Doug said. "Just a guy."

"Did he know you?"

"No. Well...now that you mention it, I guess he did. He came over and shook my hand and said he really enjoyed the jambalaya. You know I've got my own crayfish farm now and—"

I interrupted Doug before he could get too far into his commercial.

"Did he tell you his name?" I asked

"He must have, Jack, but I just can't remember. I hear so many names in this place."

A woman who looked tired and didn't smile much put a cheeseburger down in front of me along with a plate filled with onion rings. She took my nearly empty tea glass away and handed it over the bar where another woman refilled it.

"What did this guy look like?" I asked.

"Oh, hell..." Doug twisted his eyes toward the ceiling and seemed to think about it. "American, I guess. Average size. Wore glasses. Shoot, man, I don't know how to describe people."

The woman walked around from behind the bar and put the fresh glass of tea next to my cheeseburger. Then Doug stood up and stuck out his hand.

"Hey, enjoy your burger," he said. "I gotta go. Playing golf this afternoon."

"In this heat?" I asked as we shook hands again.

"Yeah, well, we got all them little girls to carry umbrellas and keep us in the shade while we're walking around," he winked. "Some of them's not half bad."

Doug took a couple of steps away and then stopped. He looked back over his shoulder and pointed his forefinger at me.

"There was one thing," he said. "This guy who was asking about you was a black guy, and he was dressed all in black, too. Looked pretty weird if you ask me, man."

"A black guy dressed all in black?"

"Yeah, I almost pissed myself laughing after he got out the door." Doug gave me a little wave. "See you, man."

I reached for the mustard, lifted the top of my burger bun, and shook out a generous dollop. I piled on some onions, a slice of tomato, a couple of pieces of lettuce, sprinkled salt and pepper over the whole mess, and closed it back up. I pushed down and crunched the burger together until it was about the right size for my hands, then I lifted it and paused as I always did to savor its profoundly American aroma.

Well, damn, I thought to myself as I took a big whiff. *That sounds an awful lot like Marcus York, doesn't it?*

I wondered if it really had been York and, if it was, if he had been snooping around about me entirely on his own or if CW had put him up to it for some reason. And regardless of whose idea it was to start asking around about me, what the hell was the reason for it?

I skimmed through the sports section of the *IHT* while I ate and I thought some more about what Marcus York might have been up to, but nothing obvious came to me. Then when my plate had been cleared away and I had a cup of coffee in front of me I turned to the front page to read the real news. The white ceramic mug was up to my lips and I was just about to take my first sip when I spotted the story.

Plato Karsarkis Associate Killed in Bangkok Shoot-Out, the headline read.

Just below the headline was a picture of Mike O'Connell. The photo had obviously been taken when he was younger, and he was ducking away from the camera as if he wasn't particularly enthusiastic about being photographed, but it was the Mike O'Connell I knew. No doubt about it.

I put my coffee down and spread the paper out on the table. Taking it slowly, I read the story through once and then I went back and read it again.

According to a wire service report from the *Agence France-Presse*, about eight on the previous evening O'Connell had been leaving an apartment building in the Sukhumvit Road section of Bangkok. He was walking from the door of the building to a waiting car when a shot from a sniper rifle entered his left eye and exploded in his skull killing him instantly.

No one had heard the shot, which suggested strongly that the rifle from which it was fired was silenced, and it appeared likely that the shooter had been several floors up in a neighboring apartment building since that was the only place from which anyone would have had a clear field of fire down into the courtyard where O'Connell's car was waiting. A Thai security guard had drawn a weapon, apparently a handgun, although the story was vague on the point, and he had gotten off three shots in the general direction of the building, although apparently he hadn't hit anybody and it wasn't even entirely clear what he might have been aiming at.

The rest of the story was sketchy and provided no other useful details about the shooting. It consisted mainly of speculation as to what O'Connell might have been doing at an apartment in Bangkok with an armed security guard, and whether that meant Plato Karsarkis himself was in Bangkok, perhaps close by or even in the building O'Connell had been coming out of when he was shot.

It was hardly necessary for me to speculate, of course. Tommy and I had left that same building only a few minutes before Mike O'Connell was murdered.

If a sniper lying in wait in the building next door really had shot O'Connell, he would certainly have already been there when

Tommy and I had come out of the building ourselves. No doubt he must have been watching us, too. He would have been checking us out, tracking us with the crosshairs of his telescopic sight as we got into Tommy's Mercedes.

I rubbed a hand across my face. Good Lord, a silenced sniper rifle was tracking me when I walked across that courtyard outside Plato Karsarkis' apartment?

I took a deep breath, let it out, and read the newspaper story a third time. Not surprisingly, nothing in it had changed. When I finished, Mike O'Connell was still dead, the Thai police still had no clue as to who the shooter was, and the taste of burger in my mouth had been replaced with something sour and metallic.

Thirty

THE FIRST THING I did when I got back to my office was get a Montecristo out of my humidor and light up. I took a long, full draw, rolled the sweet smoke around in my mouth, and exhaled slowly as I tilted back in my chair and swung my feet up on the desk. Perhaps a cigar struck most people as a peculiar choice of tranquilizer, but it always worked just fine for me.

After a half hour or so of nicely anesthetized reflection, I was no closer to deciding whether Mike O'Connell's murder had anything to do with me than I had been the first moment I saw the headline in the *IHT*. I glanced at my watch, then dumped the remains of my cigar in an ashtray, collected my notes, and headed for the elevator. Murder or no murder, I had a three-o'clock class to teach.

My lecture was uneventful, as much for my students as for me, then afterwards I had a string of conference appointments and I manfully slogged through every one. Very few of my appointments had anything to do with wheedling a better grade out of me, which is the way I figured they would usually go back in the States. Instead, the most popular topic with my students by far was how I could help them score a place in a prestigious American MBA program. Since I really didn't have a clue, those conversations were mercifully short.

By a little after five-thirty the procession ended and I tried again to call Anita to tell her I was going to Darcy's for dinner. Now there was no answer at all at the apartment and Anita's mobile number continued to connect me directly to her voice mail. I couldn't figure out where she was and I was starting to worry a bit. I wasn't sure why or what I could do about it, but there it was anyway. It was after six by then so I let it go, locked up the office, and headed for Darcy's house.

Darcy and Nata lived in the oldest part of Bangkok, an area not far from the King's palace, but there was nothing particularly stylish nor fashionable about the neighborhood so few foreigners ever ventured out there, which I thought was a pity. Around dusk, along the grassy banks of the canals that still crisscrossed the area, food vendors lit their charcoal cooking fires, the cicadas began to rumble in the trees, and a soft purple haze filled the air. In the mid-city financial district, the part of Bangkok where most of the foreign community lived, everything seemed somehow forced. The breakneck conversion of rice fields into a forest of high-rise apartments and acres of glitzy shopping malls felt temporary and superficial, as if it could all be swept aside in an instant and no one would really care. But the old city seemed *real* somehow, substantial and resistant to time. The colors were brighter, the smells were richer, and the sounds were warmer. As the lights came on in the late twilight of a moist tropical evening, everything about it felt whole and sweet and true.

To get to Darcy's house, you headed west from the university, crossed the Padung Krung Kasem Canal, and took Wisut Kasat Road toward the river. Then you turned off behind an Esso station and followed a narrow *soi* between two beat-to-hell shophouses that were once probably white. At the very end of the *soi* was a green metal gate set in a high ginger-colored wall overgrown with stands of bamboo. I pulled up in front of the gate, waved toward the security camera, and almost immediately the gate split into two panels and swung inward.

As I parked in the circular driveway, Darcy stepped out onto the house's wide front porch. She was a small woman, trim and crisp in a green silk blouse and white sarong, and her silver hair was cut in a tight and vaguely masculine crop. I would have placed her somewhere in her sixties, but that was just a guess. Darcy had looked exactly the same ever since I had known her and I really had no idea how old she was.

"Hey, baby," she called out, giving me a wave.

I waved back as I got out of the car and when I got up on the porch I gave her a hug as well.

"Nata's not here tonight," she said before I could ask. "Some kind of family thing."

"I hope that doesn't mean you're cooking."

Darcy balled up her fist and popped me on the shoulder, then looped her arm through mine.

"I've arranged for dinner to be served by the pool. Not too hot outside for you tonight, is it, baby?"

Without waiting for an answer, Darcy led me off the porch and along a graveled walkway that circled around the house. Geraniums outlined the path on both sides, their bright red blossoms so perfectly formed that they might have been made of plastic.

"You have any luck with that disk?" I asked, unable to contain my curiosity any longer.

"It's like I told you before, baby. People underestimate the Thais. They seem stupid and lazy and corrupt, but generally they're not that bad." Darcy seemed to reconsider for a moment. "Well, some of them are, but mostly they're in the government where we can keep an eye on them"

I laughed. Darcy didn't.

We rounded the house until we came to a courtyard paved with red brick laid in a herringbone pattern. At its center was a rectangular swimming pool. The underwater lights were on, which caused the pool to glow and pulse as if possessed by some otherworldly source of energy. Two places had been set at a round glass table next to a grove of banana trees and the candles on the table flickered in rhythm with the wind.

"You realize, of course, I read what was on the disk, Jack. Can I ask what interest you have in Plato Karsarkis?"

It was a good question, of course, maybe even a better one than Darcy imagined. A girl who looked about eighteen and was dressed in sharply creased dark trousers and a white shirt helped us with our chairs and poured white wine while I thought about what a good answer to Darcy's good question might be.

"Did you copy the disk," I asked after the girl had left us alone again, "or just read it?"

Darcy gave me a long look.

"I'm sorry," I said. "That came out wrong."

"Uh-huh. It did."

"Obviously you read the file, Darcy. I meant for you to. I'm just asking if you were able to get a hard copy, too."

Darcy picked up her glass and tried her wine. Apparently it met with her approval because she drank some more of it before she put the glass down and cleared her throat.

"Avoiding the copy restrictions was child's play," she said. "I already told you that's just off-the-shelf stuff. The timer was a little harder. The NIA put a routine on the disk that works like an email destruct timer. You trigger it by opening the file, then you have an hour to read everything before the destruct routine goes active. After it does a simple algorithmic will run and corrupt all the files on the disk by changing the data into random characters. It's really very clever, very thorough. They wanted to make sure everything disappeared after you read it."

"But you beat it."

"Sure, I beat it, darling. You know I did."

"You get a hard copy?" I asked. "Or just a clean copy on another disk?"

"Got both."

"Damn you're good."

"Tell me something I don't already know."

I chuckled appropriately. "Well, Darcy, let me at least tell you I appreciate it."

"I want you to tell me a lot more than that."

"I'm sorry?" I asked.

"What I said, darling, is that I want you to tell me more than that you appreciate it. I want you to tell me why the hell the NIA is giving you files about Plato Karsarkis."

I thought about that briefly.

"Are you just generally curious, Darcy?" I asked carefully when I was through thinking. "Or do you have some specific reason for wanting to know."

"I don't think you realize what you're getting into here, Jack."

"I'm not getting into anything."

"The hell you're not. I read the newspapers. There's a copy of today's *International Herald Tribune* right inside on my desk."

I played with my wine glass and wondered how much I ought to tell Darcy. She wouldn't usually ask questions like this, but I suppose I should have been prepared. Plato Karsarkis was hardly a usual subject.

"Look, Darcy, the NIA asked me to do something for them. I told them I wanted to see some of their internal files before I made up my mind whether I would do it or not. They gave me that disk, and frankly I have no idea what's on it."

"But you do know it concerns Plato Karsarkis."

It was a statement, not a question, so I didn't say anything. I just sat quietly and watched Darcy nod slowly as if she was putting some things together.

"They know where Karsarkis is," she said after a moment, "but I guess you already realize that."

"Yeah. I do."

"Do *you* know where he is?"

"Uh-huh."

There was a pause and in the silence I listen to the low hum of the pool pump in the distance and the rhythmic buzzing of the cicadas in the trees.

"I'm worried about you, baby," Darcy said very quietly after a minute or two had passed. "You're playing in the big leagues with stuff like this. I'd like to watch your back, but I can't if you won't trust me."

"It's not a matter of trust, Darcy. I wouldn't have given you that disk if I didn't trust you. I just don't want you to get involved. It can't be a good thing."

"Then why are *you* involved?"

I had no answer for that so we both sat in silence while the young girl returned and served us both from a large wooden salad bowl heaped with greens and slices of chicken topped with croutons and smothered in Caesar dressing. As I cut a sliver of chicken and rolled it through the dressing, Darcy selected a bread stick from a basket on the table.

When Darcy snapped the breadstick, the sound of it cracked in the silence like a shot.

Thirty One

"LET'S DO IT like this, Jack. I'll give you the printout of the file that was on the disk. After you read it, you can decide how much more you want to tell me."

"Okay," I agreed, popping some chicken into my mouth. "Sounds fair enough."

"You want to read it now?"

"How long is it?"

"Thirty, thirty-five pages. Not long."

"Now's good then," I said.

Without another word Darcy pushed back her chair and walked past me into the house. When she came back she placed at my elbow an unmarked manila file folder. I flipped it open and eyed the neat stack of pages stapled together inside it.

Darcy picked up her wine glass and tipped it in my direction. "Take your time, baby," she said.

I worked my way methodically through the first twenty pages or so while I ate my salad and drank white wine. Normally salads weren't my kind of dinner, but this one was extraordinary and the deep sweetness of the chicken's richly charcoaled flavor more than made up for the piles of rabbit food I had to negotiate in order to get at it.

Darcy didn't say a word while I read and ate, but I wouldn't really have minded if she had. There wasn't much in what I was reading and conversation wouldn't have been any real distraction. The first ten pages could have been a transcription of some broadcast on CNN. It was nothing but a routine biography, a summary of Karsarkis' indictment, and a few notes on his subsequent disappearance. I had read deeper stuff in People Magazine.

The second ten pages were a little more interesting, but not much. They consisted of excerpts from something that looked like a transcript of a pretrial deposition, but since the preparations for Karsarkis' trial had taken place several months before and been extremely well publicized, it contained nothing explosive. The excerpts were all from the testimony of Cynthia Kim, Karsarkis' personal assistant who was later murdered in Washington, and they concerned various technical details about the organization of Karsarkis' corporate empire. What's more, I saw nothing in any of them that seemed to bear one way or another on Karsarkis' claim he had been acting at the personal request of the President of the United States when he sold embargoed oil for the Iraqis.

I finished reading the transcripts, pushed my salad bowl away, and wiped my mouth with my napkin.

"Seems like a bunch of useless garbage," I said, speaking for the first time since I had begun to read.

Darcy finished her wine and looked past me, nodding almost imperceptibly to someone. The young girl immediately reappeared and began to clear the table.

"How far have you gotten?" Darcy asked.

"To the end of the deposition transcripts. Does it get any better?"

Darcy ignored my question. "We've got some pretty good double chocolate cake from the Oriental Hotel," she said instead. "Can I tempt you?"

I shook my head.

"Nope. With the summer heat and everything else, I haven't been running very much. I can feel the flab already. Just coffee for me."

"*Gafair dam song*," Darcy said to the girl. Two black coffees.

The girl bobbed her head without raising her eyes and slipped away with such gliding grace that I watched her until she disappeared into the house.

"They get younger all the time, don't they, Darcy?"

"Or we get older, baby," she murmured. "Or we get older."

Darcy looked away and drifted off into some private reverie, and I went back to reading the file while the girl returned and served coffee. I skimmed the printout as I finished my first cup, but after only a few pages I was lost.

"What the hell is this stuff?" I asked, glancing up at Darcy. "It looks like some kind of email, but it doesn't have anything to do with Karsarkis."

"It's email all right. At first I thought it was Carnivore product they had been collecting on Karsarkis, but now—"

"What's Carnivore product?" I interrupted.

"Carnivore is a program developed by the FBI to monitor email. It's like a wiretap placed on an email account. The problem with it is the software has to be physically installed on the servers of the provider that has the email account you want to tap. It's so easy for the target to shift providers that the process only works if the operation is entirely covert and the target has no reason to suspect he might be tapped. That would obviously be a problem in monitoring Karsarkis."

"I guess I'll start being more careful what I put in my email."

"You should. In God we trust. All others we monitor."

I chuckled. "You just make that up?"

"Nah. It's an old Cryptocity line."

Cryptocity was the way people in the know referred to the NSA headquarters complex at Ft. Mead in Maryland, just north of Washington. It was the closest I had ever heard Darcy come to admitting she had indeed been an NSA spook, but I didn't comment.

"So what is this stuff?" I asked instead, tapping my forefinger on the printouts Darcy had made from the disk.

"Well…"

Darcy hesitated and I watched her carefully. She seemed to be weighing up something, but I had no idea what it was.

"I think this *is* Carnivore product, but not from surveillance of Karsarkis, and certainly not by the FBI."

"I'm sorry, Darcy. You lost me."

"Let me ask you something before I say any more, Jack."

Darcy pursed her lips and looked out across her pool. She took her time and I didn't rush her.

"Karsarkis is here in Thailand, isn't he?"

"Yes," I said. "He is."

"And the feds know it and they're after him?"

"Uh-huh."

"What brand?"

"What do you mean?"

"What brand of feds. Is it the FBI? The Secret Service? Who's out here after Karsarkis?"

I hesitated briefly, then I decided there was no reason not to tell her, so I did.

"The US Marshals."

Darcy nodded slowly as if I had just confirmed her worst suspicions.

"They don't intend to bother with extradition." She made a statement out of it, not a question.

"I don't know that," I said. "Not for sure."

"But you think you do. You think they're here to kidnap Karsarkis, don't you?"

"Maybe," I answered carefully.

Darcy nodded again and for a moment she studied a grove of banana trees over my shoulder.

"What you've got there," Darcy said after a moment, inclining her head at the sheets of paper stacked on the table, "is the product NIA obtained from intercepting email between somebody who is out here and somebody who is back in Washington."

"You mean the Thais have the FBI's software and they're using it to tap the marshals' email?" I laughed out loud. "Damn."

"I told you not to underestimate them, Jack."

"So then they know all about the kidnapping plan."

I thought I was beginning to see why the NIA was trying so hard to enlist me in bailing out Karsarkis' sorry ass. If the marshals kidnapped the world's most wanted fugitive from right under the Thais' noses and spirited him back to Washington, the loss of face would be almost unthinkable; and if there is one thing the tolerant Thais absolutely cannot tolerate, it is loss of face. On the other hand, if Karsarkis were pardoned, then there would no longer be any need for a kidnapping and the whole problem would just go away. Neat.

"Now that you know what you're looking at, read it again, Jack." Darcy seemed to think for a time, then her expression hardened and she exhaled audibly. "Read it all again and tell me what you think it really says."

The girl returned and refilled out coffee cups and I read the last dozen pages of the file again in silence.

This time I started to get a queasy feeling about halfway through. I glanced up at Darcy but she was looking away, apparently consulting the banana trees again. Then I went back and read it all a third time. I shifted in my chair, stretching my legs first one way and then another, but I couldn't seem to make myself comfortable.

There was nothing explicit in the emails, of course. Whoever had written them had been very careful. There wasn't a single sentence there I could quote to prove anything, certainly nothing that made it clear in so many words; but now I had no doubt at all what it was that I was really reading.

After the third time through I gathered all of the pages into a stack, squared them up at the edges, and put them back into the manila file. Then I moved my coffee cup to one side, clasped my hands together, and placed them on top of the file.

"You read this stuff the same way I do, don't you, Darcy?"

"Yeah, baby, I do."

I studied Darcy's face, but it gave nothing away.

"Maybe this is a fake," I said. "Maybe the NIA put it all together just for my benefit."

"Maybe."

"But you don't think so."

"No, I don't," Darcy said. "What motive would they have for that?"

"Well, for starters…" I trailed off and thought about it.

"I don't know," I finally said.

Darcy smiled without humor. "Neither do I."

"So you think this is all the real stuff."

"I'd say so."

I could tell Darcy was weighing her words carefully.

"The form looks right," she said, "and the text feels right. But there's no way to be absolutely certain, Jack. There's just no way."

I nodded and we sat together in silence for a while as I considered what I knew now that I hadn't known a few minutes before.

"Even if the email is genuine, isn't there the possibility of some other interpretation?"

"Sure," Darcy nodded. "I guess there's always that possibility."

"But you think we've got it right, don't you?"

"Yeah," Darcy spoke as if from behind a mask, "I do."

I nodded slowly and looked away.

The intercepted emails left everything clearly understood without making it explicit. Whoever sent the emails and whoever received them were both operating on exactly the same understanding. They both knew there was only one possible outcome to the manhunt for Plato Karsarkis.

None of this was about arresting and extraditing Karsarkis anymore. It wasn't even about kidnapping him. Washington didn't have the stomach any longer for trying to lock him up. Karsarkis had already shown them how pointless that was.

No, this time it was different.

This time when they got him, they were going to kill him.

Thirty Two

DRIVING HOME THAT night I kept the air conditioner on high and the windows rolled up tight. A hot breeze was blowing in from the south and warm tropical evenings ripe with possibilities were generally a perfect time to cruise the city with the wind in your face. On this particular warm tropical night, however, there was something I liked a whole lot about the feeling of security I got from traveling in a closed-up car.

Someone had coolly laid in wait with a sniper rifle right in the middle of Bangkok and put a bullet in Mike O'Connell's head, and I knew from Doug at Bourbon Street that Marcus York had been in town the night O'Connell died. From what I had just learned about the real reason the US Marshals were in Thailand it was all too easy now to add that up; and I didn't like the answer I got when I did.

What the hell was going on here? Was I really ready to believe that the cornpone Texan I met in Phuket was actually leading a band of stone killers stalking Karsarkis and all the people around him? Surely not.

But *somebody* killed Mike O'Connell; and if it wasn't CW and his United States Marshals, who in God's name was it?

Darcy and I had stayed out by the pool until just after ten. We sipped coffee and Darcy sat silently over a brandy while I smoked a Montecristo and told her the whole story of my entanglement with

Plato Karsarkis. When I finished, she hadn't said much. She only warned me again to be careful and promised to keep her ears open and let me know what she heard. From some people, of course, that would have been nothing but a kiss off, but from Darcy, it was a pledge of support solemn enough to put in the bank.

I took the expressway home. Gliding along on its elevated structure always made me feel like a ghost skimming over the sprawling yellow glow of the city. Part of the place, yet at the same time separate and invisible. It was a feeling I liked a lot.

I wanted nothing to do with Plato Karsarkis, nothing at all; yet I had to wonder if he had any idea what was really out there waiting for him. I wondered, too, who it was in Washington who wanted Karsarkis dead, and who commanded the power needed to turn the United States Marshals Service into a personal hit squad. But most of all I wondered what it was Karsarkis knew that frightened someone so much they were willing to run the risks involved in killing him; and I wondered what Karsarkis might do with that knowledge before they got to him.

By the time I pulled up to the gates of our apartment building it was nearly eleven. The guard poked his head out of the shelter and I lowered the driver's window and gave him a thumbs up. He jumped to his feet, hauled the gate open, and snapped off a salute. I returned it as I passed inside and I listened to the gate clang shut behind me.

The garage was deserted. I locked the car and took the elevator up to the eleventh floor without seeing anyone. I knew Anita would be wondering where I had been. As I unlocked our front door, it occurred to me that I probably should have left a message on her voice mail, but with all the distractions of the evening I had forgotten.

I entered the dark apartment quietly, not wanting to wake Anita if she had already gone to sleep. Pushing the door closed behind me and muffling the click of the lock with my body, I bent down and flipped on a lamp.

I stared in puzzlement at the two suitcases. They were large bags, and they looked very much like the ones Anita packed for herself when she and I went on long trips together.

Had Anita told me she was going somewhere tonight and I had completely forgotten? God, if I had she'd kill me.

I frantically searched my memory. No, I was certain she hadn't said anything like that, but then what were the bags doing there? If some emergency had come up, surely she would have called me.

I pulled my telephone out of my pocket and looked at the screen. The date and time glowed back at me as always. No missed calls.

Still trying to work out what Anita's bags were doing in the hallway, I walked into the living room and switched on the lights.

Anita was sitting in one of the two brown leather chairs facing the windows. She was waiting there in the dark, looking out at the city, her body turned slightly away from me and her hands folded in her lap. She didn't move when the light came on. She didn't even blink. She hardly seemed to know I was there. Although I had seen her sit in that same chair many times, it suddenly struck me how small she looked in it, as if either she had shrunk or the chair itself had become mysteriously enlarged.

My first thought was that something had happened, that perhaps she was ill and waiting for me to take her to the hospital. Then she turned her head very slowly and looked at me with an expression I had never seen on her face before, one I couldn't even begin to put a name to. I knew then that she wasn't ill. Something must have happened to someone we knew. Something terrible.

"Anita, what—"

"Please don't say anything for a moment, Jack. Just come in and sit down."

I walked the length of the living room, growing more bewildered by the step, but I settled into the second of the pair of leather chairs facing the windows and waited for Anita to tell me what was going on. They were big chairs, deep and cushy, and Anita and I had often sat there in the evenings just like this, drinking after-dinner coffees, listening to music, and talking about our days. I looked at Anita, waiting for her to say something, but she didn't seem to be in any hurry. She had turned her face back to the windows and I couldn't see her eyes.

"For God's sake, Anita, has something—"

"Can't you do just one thing I ask, Jack?" she snapped before I could finish. "I asked you not to say anything for a moment and the first thing you do is start talking. Why can't you do just one thing I ask? Just *one* fucking thing."

I couldn't have been any more stunned if Anita had reached over and slapped me, which in a way I guess she just had. Her tone didn't suggest there was a great deal of room for argument, so I sat in silence and offered no response.

Later, looking back, I couldn't remember how long it was before Anita spoke again. It was probably less than a minute, but at the time it felt like hours passed as my mind churned through every conceivable way to account for Anita's obvious distress. I discarded each possibility in turn and wound up back again exactly where I had started: utterly and completely mystified.

Evidently something absolutely awful had happened, but I was going to have to wait until Anita was ready to tell me about it, and to do it entirely in her own way.

Thirty Three

AFTER A WHILE Anita turned her head away from the windows and looked at me, then she folded her arms across her body as if she had suddenly become cold. I studied her face, but could read nothing in it.

"I'm going to London for a while, Jack."

All at once I was aware of the sound of the air conditioning humming in the background. It sounded somehow unnaturally loud.

"When? *Tonight*?"

Anita shifted her body in the chair, turning further away from me.

"Things aren't right," she said. "With us. Just not right."

"What are you talking about, Anita?"

She went on as if I hadn't spoken.

"I hoped getting the house in Phuket might help. Maybe even give us some kind of a fresh start. But obviously that's not going to happen."

I leaned back and exhaled loudly, not even trying to hide my irritation. Anita seemed so upset she had scared me half to death and all the time it was just about that goddamned house again.

"Okay, now I get it—" I began, but that was as far as I got.

"No, you don't," Anita snapped. "You do *not* get it, Jack, and you never will."

Anita stood up and took several quick steps as if she were leaving the room. Then she stopped and turned back, her arms still folded tightly across her body. I remained sitting in the chair watching her, tilting my head in puzzlement and rubbing at the back of my neck.

"I'm sorry," I finally said. "I don't understand."

"Yes, you do. But you're dealing with it just as you do everything else. You acknowledge only what you want to know. You shut everything else out."

And just like that, I saw.

I realized then exactly what was happening, and even though the massive shock of it nearly paralyzed me, some part of my consciousness still marveled at how I could have missed it up until then. The telephone turned off, the bags in the hall, the sitting in the darkness waiting for me to come home. Now it was all so obvious.

Anita was leaving me.

"Something has changed since we were married, Jack. Something's changed, and I don't like it."

"What do you mean?"

"It's all too much."

"Too much *what*?"

"Too much like little boys playing spy games, hiding in the woods until people end up dead. Then you come out just as if nothing happened and go on just as you were before. You have no idea of danger, no concept of risk. Maybe you'll be the next body to turn up somewhere, Jack. Did you ever think of that?"

"I'm just a teacher, Anita. I'm not playing spy games and I'm not in any danger."

"Oh, bullshit, Jack. Everybody you know is a spook, a criminal, or a cop. And if you're not up to your neck in one thing, it's another."

The words were tough, but the look on her face was tougher.

"Look, if this is about Plato Karsarkis," I stammered, "last week you were saying you thought I ought to help him, and now you're saying—"

"I'm not talking about Plato. I'm talking about *you*."

"About me?"

"Not you, I guess. Not really," she said. "About what you do."

"Same thing."

Anita shook her head very slowly.

"I knew you'd say something like that," she said.

"Look, Anita," I started, "think about—"

"I've done so much thinking these last few days that I can't think straight about anything anymore. But I do know this, Jack. We have to be apart for a while. We have to sort things out."

"I don't."

"Well, I do. And if I have to sort it out for us both, then I'll do that. I need some time to decide, and believe me I'm thinking of you, too. I'm not sure I'm the right one for you."

"I'm sure, Anita. I'm absolutely sure."

"Please, don't say that. Don't make this any worse than it already is."

"I don't want to live without you, Anita. I won't go back to the way I was before."

"I have never asked you to change for me, Jack. I know you and I don't think you could even if you wanted to. I'm not saying…oh, *fuck*, I don't know what I *am* saying, let alone what I'm not."

Anita was crying now. I could see the tears in her eyes and I watched as they rolled down her cheeks, first from one eye and then from the other. I wanted to stand up and walk over and put my arms around her, but I knew absolutely that would be exactly the wrong thing to do. Instead I looked out the window and followed the blinking white lights on the wingtips of an airliner as it climbed out over the city and disappeared to the south. I wondered where it was going and who was on it, and I wondered whether I might like to be on it, too.

"Look," I finally said, "it's after midnight and you can't go out there alone tonight. You take the bedroom and I'll sleep on the couch in here and tomorrow we'll decide what to do."

"No," she said, "my flight is tonight. I have a car waiting downstairs."

There was a long silence as we both groped through our pain, looking for purchase or maybe just a place to hide. I glanced away, not able to bear the sight of Anita's tears any longer, but there was nothing at all I could do right then to make them stop.

"I'll do whatever you want, Anita."

"I want you to go into your study," she said in a voice that was suddenly clear and strong. "I want you to wait there and let me leave without making things any worse than they already are."

"Yeah," I nodded as if in a daze. "Okay."

"Just give me some time, Jack."

"Time to decide?"

"Yes," she said. "Time to decide."

Anita walked over and collected her purse from the chair where she had been waiting for me. I stood up, but she turned away without looking at me. I put out my arm to stop her and she brushed by it. When she reached the doorway, she stood for a moment with her back to me.

"Please do what I asked. Go into your study and let me leave, Jack."

Then she went into the bathroom and closed the door. I could hear her crying.

I didn't say anything. I just left the living room, walked into my study, and closed the door. I was sick at heart and I didn't know whether I felt hopeful or hopeless or what I felt, but it was Anita's move now and whatever feelings I might have or not have weren't going to change that.

I settled behind my desk and spread my hands on top of it,

palms down. The room seemed to move around me and I sat as still as I could, holding onto the desk until it stopped. When it felt safe to turn loose, I lifted one hand cautiously and poked with my forefinger at a glass heart that lay on top of a stack of papers. It was crystal and Anita had given it to me for my last birthday, a beautiful pebbled glass heart with a ribbon of red winding through it. I hadn't been sure what else to do with it so I had kept in on my desk and used it as a paperweight.

Don't break it, was what Anita had said to me when I unwrapped it. *Don't break it, Jack.*

I examined the crystal heart now and wondered about it. It looked intact, the same as it had always looked; but maybe there were fault lines there I had never noticed before, cracks and imperfections that even the best, most loving eyes could never find. Maybe it had already been broken when she gave it to me and I had never even noticed.

I sat there for a while in absolute stillness staring at the little glass heart. For a time I teetered on the edge of hope that any moment Anita would walk in and tell me she hadn't meant any of it, she had had a bad day and that was all there was to it; but then I heard the front door open and close again, and I knew Anita wouldn't be coming in after all.

Some time after that, I have no idea how long, I swiveled around in my chair and stared out the window. The city was very dark and seemed utterly still. I wondered what time it was, but something stopped me from looking at my watch. Instead I just sat and stared, focusing on nothing, seeing nothing.

As blanked out as I was, at some level that was less than conscious I could feel my mind's instinctive protective devices beginning to react. A part of my brain, entirely unbidden, began shuffling the cards, slowly dealing out new hands, examining each for possibilities, then collecting the cards and dealing more hands. I could not bear to look at any of them.

All at once a feeling possessed me as if it was only my body sitting there in that chair looking out the window, that my conscious self had stepped outside my body and even then was doing a reconnaissance of the dark apartment like one of those mechanical devices bomb squads use to examine unknown packages, warily probing the gloom for hidden dangers.

It found none, but it found no hope either.

When eventually my consciousness returned and resumed its accustomed place within my body, the first thing I noticed was that I had been crying. I wondered about that because I couldn't remember crying since I had been a child and I wasn't absolutely certain I had ever cried even then. I stuck out my tongue and cautiously tasted the tears running down my cheeks. I did not find the taste to be one I could recommend.

How long I sat like that I have no way of knowing. Eventually I realized the sky outside was no longer black, but had turned a sort of feeble gray. I gathered dawn was not far off so I pushed myself out of the chair, shut off the light, and walked into the kitchen. I took a bottle of water out of the refrigerator, unscrewed the cap, and drained half of it. I hadn't known how thirsty I was until the moment the cold water touched my tongue. But then I doubted I had ever been so thirsty, and I was absolutely certain water had never tasted so good.

I walked into the bedroom and stood in the doorway for a while. Everything was just as it should have been, except of course that the bed was empty and neatly made. I went across to the windows and pulled a drape aside. The new day was beginning, creeping in as quietly as a mouse.

I looked off beyond the brick wall that surrounded our building and saw a man on the sidewalk. He had a dog with him and followed it lazily, apparently unconcerned about where it was going. The pallid half-light of dawn rendered both figures in shadowy halftones, all gray and white and black. I watched the man and his dog slipping in and out of focus, first there and then not, and then suddenly there again, unearthly apparitions on the stroll, the air bit by bit coloring around them.

It was all so beautiful that I could hardly breathe.

Thirty Four

IT HAD BEEN three days since Anita had taken her bags and left for God only knew where. She had told me she was going to London, of course, but I didn't really believe that anymore and I don't think Anita expected me to.

That morning I gave my last corporate finance lecture for the year and then went back to my office. A good many of my colleagues had already begun their end-of-term holidays so the building was unusually quiet. I had a few last papers to read and grade, but I really didn't really feel much like it. Mostly I felt like sitting there just staring at the wall and feeling sorry for myself. When the telephone rang, I considered ignoring it, but eventually I snatched up the receiver mostly to shut the damned thing up.

"Yes," I snapped.

There was a short pause as whoever was calling processed my curt answer.

"Perhaps this is a bad time for me to call you, Mr. Shepherd." It was a woman's voice, a very nice voice, mellow and warm with an unmistakably upper-class accent.

"Yes, it is," I said. "Who is this?"

"This is Kathleeya Srisophon."

It took me a minute to connect the name with a face, but then I did. *Oh, Christ.*

"I'm so sorry," I mumbled quickly. "I apologize. The damned telephone just caught me by surprise."

"You don't usually receive telephone calls?"

"Yes, I receive telephone calls, but…"

I stopped talking before I sounded like a complete idiot, or maybe it was already too late to prevent that.

"I will not disturb you further then, Professor," she said. "I merely telephoned to express my hope that the death of Mr. Karsarkis' assistant will not affect your decision in any way."

"My decision?"

"As to whether or not to help us. To help Mr. Karsarkis."

I shifted uneasily in my chair. In the shock of Anita leaving, I hadn't given much thought to anything else, certainly not to the disk or my promise to call after seeing its contents.

"Have you read the files yet?" Kathleeya asked.

"Yes, I have. But there's been…" I was fumbling, so I tried again. "I've had…"

What was I going to tell her? I felt like a jerk.

"Something personal came up," I finished quickly.

"Yes," she said.

It was just one word and she spoke it without any particular inflection, but it left me with no doubt at all she already knew everything.

"In any case, Mr. Shepherd, that's not what I called about. I was actually wondering if you would have lunch with me."

I sat back, surprised.

"Ah…okay," I said. "When did you have in mind?"

"Are you free today?"

I waited for Kathleeya to fill in the rest, and I sensed there *was* a rest although I didn't have a clue what it could possibly be. But she remained silent and against all odds the silence actually felt comfortable.

"I'd like that," I said after a moment.

"Good, twelve noon then?"

"Fine. Where shall we meet?"

"I'll pick you up."

"Am I allowed to ask where we're going?"

"Of course. It's a nice day, so I thought we might drive to Pattaya."

That seemed a little strange. Pattaya was what passed for Bangkok's local beach resort, a smallish town of dubious reputation nearly a two-hour trip east along the Gulf of Thailand.

"That's rather a long way to drive for lunch," I said, "isn't it?"

"Not the way I do it, Mr. Shepherd."

THE BIG BLACK Mercedes had barely cleared the entrance ramp to the expressway before it was hitting a hundred miles an hour. We were passing other vehicles as if they were parked and the sound of the speed warning strips beneath our tires blurred into a single, drawn-out note, a raspy buzzing sound that seemed to be coming from everywhere and nowhere at the same time.

Contained as we were in the cool, quiet womb of the big car, the outside world seemed far away. Kathleeya was wearing a silk suit just as she had been the first time we met, but the color was a vibrant shade of purple rather than the more conservative cream she had chosen then; and while it may only have been my imagination, I could have sworn her skirt was a bit shorter, too. We sank back on the soft leather of the backseat and made small talk while the driver continued his low-level flight to Pattaya. There was a second person in the front passenger seat, but he neither turned nor spoke so I assumed he was security rather than another luncheon guest.

I had no doubt the murder of Mike O'Connell was very much on Kathleeya's mind right then, but she didn't mention it. Instead she asked questions about my classes and she showed an apparently genuine curiosity as to the subjects in which university students now had the most interest. From there the conversation rambled effortlessly into slightly more personal territory. I told her some of my stories and she told me some of hers.

We made the two-hour drive from Bangkok to Pattaya in one hour flat. When the driver left the expressway and slowed down to make his way into town, it felt as if the car had come to a sudden stop. He took South Pattaya Road toward the beach and, passing the Marriott on the left, cut across to Pattaya Beach Road and turned south when we reached the water.

To our left was an unbroken strip of tacky cafés, open-air shopping areas, tourist hotels, go-go joints, beer bars, and shabby souvenir stands. To our right, across a narrow strip of coarse, hard-packed sand was Pattaya Bay, flat and brown in the afternoon light. Pattaya may have been world famous for a great many things, but glamorous buildings, great beaches, and sparkling water were not three of them.

After a few hundred yards we came to the entrance to Walking Street, a narrow road running right along the water. After dark, when it was completely closed to all traffic, Walking Street turned into a mile or so of uninterrupted debauchery, but during daylight hours the area was a bit more benign. The car stopped in front of one of the street's vast seafood restaurants, one that was built on a large but rickety pier extending out into the bay. It was the sort of place popular in Thailand where glass tanks displayed live fish, shrimp, crab, and lobster to prospective customers. You inspect the day's selections, pick what you want from the tanks, and describe to a hovering attendant exactly how you want it cooked. Normally places like that aren't really among my favorites. Looking a fish in the eye, pointing to it, and saying, "Kill that one," had never struck me as a particularly appealing way to begin a meal.

The tables out on the pier were covered in pink fabric of some uncertain type and the chairs were green and looked like lawn furniture. Plastic palm trees lined the railings, although with so many real palm trees around I wasn't sure why they were really necessary. After Kathleeya and I had ordered the deaths of several species of seafood, a woman who looked Chinese led us past the kitchen and all the way across the pier to a table by the rail, one that was well away from the entrance. I asked her for a Heineken and looked around while Kathleeya examined the wine list.

The sky was overcast and the breeze from Pattaya Bay blew in gentle ripples over the pier, which made the hot afternoon almost comfortable. The oily waters of the gulf sloshed rhythmically against the pier's pilings and from somewhere I heard a boat engine start up. It knocked badly with a throaty rasp that reminded me of a smoker too many packs gone. After a while the engine caught and settled into a steady rhythm and I listened to the hypnotic putt-putt sound, counting the beats to myself as I watched Kathleeya's driver and security man cross the pier and select a table positioned on a direct line between us and the entrance.

Kathleeya consulted with the Chinese woman and ordered a bottle of some Australian chardonnay I had never heard of. Then my Heineken arrived and the sound of the boat engine faded into the distance.

"You're not a wine drinker, Mr. Shepherd?"

"I'm not really much of a lunchtime drinker at all," I said. "One drink in the middle of the day and I'm ready to go straight to bed."

Kathleeya smiled and looked away.

"I think," I said, "that may have come out wrong."

That kind of conversation could go nowhere good, so I changed tacks as quickly as I could.

"Every time you call me Mr. Shepherd I feel about a hundred years old. Would you mind just calling me Jack from now on?"

"I wouldn't mind at all, Jack. And, please, call me Kate. Not Khun Kate. Just Kate."

Khun is a polite form of address used by Thais, mostly among each other. It is prefixed as a gesture of courtesy to the first names of both men and women alike, indicating that the person being addressed is roughly equal in stature. Like most indicators of status used by Thais, and there are a great many of them, the basic rules sound simple enough, but the concepts are nuanced in so many ways that westerners are usually helpless to grasp anything but the simplest variations. Asking me to abandon the use of Khun altogether was Kate's way of telling me we were about to have a western conversation, not a Thai one. I was both pleased and relieved at that, but now even more curious what the subject of our little chat would turn out to be.

"Thank you for coming today," Kate said. "I know this isn't a particularly good time for you."

I didn't ask her how she knew that, and I certainly didn't ask her exactly what it was she thought she knew.

"I'm glad you called me," I said instead, leaving it at that.

Then I went straight to the subject that so far we had both been circling like two airport guards around an abandoned suitcase.

"What do you know about Mike O'Connell's murder?" I asked her.

"You do get to the point, don't you, Jack?"

"I try to."

"Did you read the files on the disk I gave you?" Kate asked.

"Yes."

"What do you think?"

"Probably what you want me to think."

"Which is?"

"That the marshals aren't here to arrange for Karsarkis' extradition, or even to kidnap him. They're here to kill him."

Kate nodded slowly. I wondered fleetingly if she was agreeing I was right, or just agreeing I was indeed thinking what she wanted me to think.

"Is that why O'Connell was murdered?" I asked when I got bored with her nodding. "Are they starting with Karsarkis' people and working up to him? Or did somebody mistake O'Connell for Karsarkis and just screw up?"

Before Kate could answer, a young boy materialized beside us carrying a metal tray as big as he was. A woman in a rumpled blue sarong and a white blouse rushed over and began transferring pink plastic plates from his tray to our table. There were half a dozen of them and they all seemed to contain either fish or prawns in some form. I assumed these must be the dishes we had ordered when we had run the gauntlet of fish tanks on our way in, although to tell the truth I wasn't absolutely sure. The woman completed her task by placing a plate of rice in front of each of us, and then she and the boy withdrew as quietly as they had come.

Kate reached across, took my plate, and spooned small portions of each of the dishes around my rice. Then she set the plate back in front of me, lifted her own plate, and served herself. The gesture really meant nothing in particular—Thai women frequently did that sort of thing whether they were dining with men or even with other women—but the sheer gracefulness of it still charmed me every time I experienced it.

"We don't know exactly what happened, Jack. Mike O'Connell could have been killed by mistake, or it might have been intentional."

"Do you think the marshals shot him?"

While she considered the prospect, Kate chewed thoughtfully on a bite of something that was unidentifiable, at least to me.

"Possibly," she said after a moment. "But it's hard for me to see a US marshal coldly murdering someone with a silenced sniper rifle."

Kate glanced at me as if she was asking me to confirm her

impression of what United States government agents might or might not do. I kept my features neutral. If she wanted to presume the essential morality of the kind of guys I had known back in Washington, that was okay with me, but she was on her own.

"Then who?" I asked.

"How much do you know about Plato Karsarkis' business operations, Jack?"

"Not very much." I thought a moment. "Not anything really, except for what I read in the newspapers."

"And what is that?"

"That Karsarkis was indicted by a federal grand jury for doing deals with the Iraqis back before the war. He used one of his trading companies to barter embargoed oil or something like that."

Kate leaned forward, lifted one of the serving spoons, and pushed at a fat prawn on one of the plastic plates.

"What do you know about the structure of his operations?"

"Nothing."

"That surprises me. I thought the transcript I gave you would be quite enlightening to a man with your background."

So that's why the excerpts from Cynthia Kim's deposition had been on the disk, to illustrate the company structures through which Karsarkis had worked. I had skimmed over all that at the time without appreciating its significance.

"Never mind," Kate continued. "You want the high points now?"

"Sure."

Kate put the spoon down and left the prawn where it was.

"Plato Karsarkis controls a web of companies with operations in forty-seven countries. We have identified sixty-one of those companies so far, and we know there are a number of others we haven't yet traced. A company called Icon Holdings seems to be at the center of everything. It was registered in Luxembourg in 1987, and it has since taken over control of most of Plato's operating companies."

"Does Karsarkis personally control Icon?" I asked.

"We think so, but of course it's not straightforward. Icon's stock is actually registered to seven different trusts located in the Cayman Islands, Monte Carlo, the British Virgin Islands, and the Netherlands Antilles, and each of those trusts has a different bank as its trustee, most of those banks registered in Hong Kong and Panama. Tracing the real ownership of Icon would be almost impossible, which is of course the whole point of establishing that sort of structure in the first place."

"What do these companies controlled by Icon actually do?"

"A fairly usual range of things: oil trading, commodity brokerage, real estate, banking, pharmaceuticals, mining, air transportation, shipping. The sort of diversified commercial operations typical of large multinational companies, at least on the surface."

I said nothing.

"Those are also the sorts of businesses frequently used to conceal a whole range of other activities, Jack. Arms dealing, money laundering, bribery. Sometimes worse."

"That's a pretty big stretch, Kate. By that logic General Electric could be the world's largest terrorist organization."

"Plato Karsarkis' companies started dealing smuggled Iraqi oil around the time the United Nations embargo was imposed on Iraq before the first Gulf War. As far as we can tell, Icon controls a Panamanian oil trading company called Sedco that was the primary vehicle for those sales. We also have reason to believe Sedco had close links with Iraqi intelligence. It may even have been a major source of barter funding for the Iraqi weapons procurement program."

"I guess I'm not following you. Why does the Thai National Intelligence Agency have any interest in a Panamanian oil trading company even if it actually did have some kind of link to Iraqi intelligence at one time? That's old news. There *is* no Iraqi intelligence service anymore."

"Back then Iraqi Intelligence also had a lot of operations here, Jack."

"Where?" Now I was sure I had lost her. "Surely you don't mean in Thailand?"

"Yes, here in Thailand. Also in the Philippines, Indonesia, and Malaysia. The same countries where Karsarkis sold most of the embargoed oil."

A mobile telephone began to ring and Kate retrieved her purse from beneath her feet and took out her phone.

"I'm sorry," she said, glancing at its screen. "I have to take this." She stood up and moved off until she was out of earshot, then lifted the phone and turned her back.

I noticed her driver and security man both stand at the same time and spread apart slightly. They kept a professional distance while she talked, but they stayed directly between Kate and the restaurant's entrance. They looked as if they thought a terrorist hit squad might charge into the restaurant at any moment.

I could only hope they were wrong about that.

Thirty Five

THE WOMAN IN the rumpled sarong returned and refilled Kate's wine glass.

"One more beer?" she asked, pointing to my empty Heineken bottle.

I nodded. Why not?

I didn't really have anything important to do for the rest of the afternoon so getting a little sleepy from the beer wouldn't be a complete disaster. Besides, I figured having a beautiful master spy whispering exotic tales of shadowy international intelligence operations into my ear justified at least a modicum of flexibility.

Out over the Gulf of Thailand thunderheads were building and the afternoon light had turned thin and watery. I watched as lightning danced among towers of gunmetal-colored cloud somewhere very far away. The breeze kicked up a notch and brought with it distant smells of dead and dying fish. It rippled the plastic palm trees lining the railings and they made a sound like tape being ripped from a box.

A young boy brought me a fresh Heineken. At almost the same moment, Kate returned to the table.

"Does the name Ramzi Yousef mean anything to you?" she asked, sitting down and watching the boy until he had gone.

"Didn't he have something to do with the first World Trade

Center attack? The one back in..." I hesitated, searching my memory for the right year. "Was it 1993?"

"That's right. In 1992, Yousef entered the United States on a fake passport supplied by Iraqi intelligence and made contact with a group of Iraqi immigrants who had grandiose plans for attacking Americans on their own soil. Yousef organized those people into the operation that eventually became the first attack on the World Trade Center in 1993."

"Okay," I nodded.

I had absolutely no idea where Kate was going with any of this, but it was a nice afternoon and I was on my second Heineken so I was willing to listen to her pretty much as long as she wanted to talk.

"The Americans didn't get Yousef until 1995," she continued. "During the two years following the first World Trade Center attack, Yousef spent most of his time here in Southeast Asia mounting elaborate operations to kill westerners."

I scooped up a spoonful of rice with a spiral of garlic calamari in it and chewed unhurriedly, waiting for Kate to get to whatever point she wanted to make.

"Do you remember a couple of months after the attack on the World Trade Center there was an attempt to assassinate George Bush with a car bomb in Kuwait?"

"Vaguely."

"Two hundred pounds of Portuguese PE-4A was packed into the door panels of a Toyota Landcruiser, but the Kuwaitis got wind of the plot and grabbed the Landcruiser before it made it anywhere near Bush. They also arrested seventeen people who were connected in one way or another with the plan. The two ringleaders eventually admitted to your FBI that they were acting under the instructions of the Iraqi intelligence and they named Yousef as their contact. The batch of plastic explosives they used was identified as having come from Malaysia."

"That doesn't mean much," I said as I sipped at my Heineken. "The stuff could have passed through dozens of hands before it ended up in that Landcruiser."

"It could have, but it didn't. Do you remember the attempted bombing of the Israeli Embassy in Bangkok?"

"No."

"That was in 1994. A stolen water truck packed with explosives was in a traffic accident very close to the Israeli Embassy and the Arab-looking man who was driving it abandoned the truck in the street and ran away. The police towed it off and never bothered to look inside, at least they didn't until it began to smell. When they finally opened the back, they found the decomposing body of the truck's owner and enough explosives to take a square kilometer out of the middle of Bangkok. We can put Yousef in the room in the Nana Hotel where the detonator was built and the bomb assembled."

All of a sudden Kate was hitting a little close to home. The Nana Hotel is a third-rate tourist dump immediately across the street from a complex of go-go bars and burger joints where every western male in Bangkok has gone at least a few times, although most refuse to admit to it.

"Then after that came Project Bojinka," Kate said while I was still trying to calculate the exact distance between the Nana Hotel and my apartment in Chidlom Place.

"I don't know anything about that either."

"You don't know much about what's been going on in Asia, do you?" Kate gave me a sharp look. "Where in the world have you been, Jack?"

"In Washington," I answered reflexively, then laughed in spite of myself at what I had just said.

"Yousef built up a terrorist cell in Manila," Kate went on without smiling. "They rented an apartment there in late 1994 and planned to assassinate the Pope when he came to Manila in early 1995.

When Yousef was preparing the explosives, he made a mistake and started a fire. He and the others fled the apartment, leaving behind a laptop computer containing his plans to hijack eleven American commercial aircraft flying over the Pacific on a single day."

"It's a lousy excuse, I know, Kate, but no one in Washington pays much attention to what happens in Southeast Asia these days. After China and maybe Japan, the rest of Asia just isn't on anyone's radar anymore."

Kate just sat and shook her head slowly for a moment. When she continued, her voice was tinged with exasperation.

"The files on the laptop made it clear that Yousef was planning to crash the planes into high-profile targets in the United States, including CIA headquarters in Washington."

I blinked at that, but I didn't say anything.

"Ramzi Yousef was an Iraqi intelligence agent," Kate said, watching my eyes as she spoke. "We know it and so does your CIA. They just won't admit it publicly."

"Are you trying to tell me the Iraqis were responsible for September 11? That Dick Chaney was right?"

"I don't know that. Anyway, that's not the point I'm making now."

"Then I guess you're going to have to spell it out for me, Kate. What *is* your point?"

"Look, Jack, all those big Iraqi operations during the nineties had their roots in Southeast Asia. The reason for that was the Iraqis were developing a deeply entrenched, anti-western terrorist network in Asia that would survive no matter what happened anywhere else. They may have succeeded at precious little otherwise, but they succeeded at that."

"That's pretty hard for me to believe."

"Is it? Think about this. Yousef's operation to hijack the eleven American planes was financed by a Malaysian company called

Konsojaya that was fronted by a shareholder list drawn from the highest levels of Malaysian business and government. If Yousef was an Iraqi intelligence officer, then almost certainly Konsojaya was actually a cover for Iraqi intelligence and it was deeply tied into the political and military power structures in Malaysia."

"Even if that's true, so what? That was a long time ago."

"Was it?" Kate asked. "In January 2000, Malaysian intelligence monitored a meeting in Kuala Lumpur between two of the directors of Konsojaya and two of the men who flew the planes into your World Trade Center on September 11 of the following year."

"Then you *are* saying the Iraqis were behind the attack on the World Trade Center. That this company in Malaysia had something to do with it."

"It might well be true, but that's not what I'm telling you."

"Then for Christ's sakes, what *are* you telling me, Kate?" Now I was the one with the exasperation in my voice. "What had all this cloak-and-dagger Iraqi terrorist stuff got to do with Plato Karsarkis? The Iraqi intelligence service is dead and buried now. Nobody cares anymore even if once upon a time they might have had some connection with the September 11 hijackers."

"Plato Karsarkis sold smuggled oil for the Iraqis. Sedco, the Panamanian company brokering the sales, sold oil to Konsojaya. Then Konsojaya resold the oil to the Malaysian National Oil Company at a handsome profit and accumulated a lot of cash. Think about that carefully, Jack. Directors of the same company that was buying Iraqi oil from Plato Karsarkis and reselling it at a huge profit were meeting with the terrorists who flew planes into the World Trade Center on September 11. Do you think that was just a coincidence?"

Suddenly it seemed very quiet. I could hear the waters of the gulf scrapping the pilings twenty feet below and I listened to a seagull calling from somewhere very far away.

"What we don't know," Kate went on, "is exactly *why* that oil went through Konsojaya. Karsarkis claims he was working under instructions from the White House, but if he was, why would he have been arranging for a company linked to Iraqi intelligence to accumulate cash in Malaysia?"

"Because his story is bullshit?"

"Maybe, but then it might also be true. We know anti-western terrorists now have significant financial and banking operations in this region, so who knows what was really going on?"

"Perhaps—" I began, but Kate cut me off.

"Along the way Karsarkis could well have acquired an intimate knowledge of at least the financial aspects of terrorist operations in this region, possibly even some indications of what future operation plans may exist."

Then I saw where this was all going.

"You think those are the people who are after Karsarkis, don't you?" I said. "Not the marshals. You think someone killed Mike O'Connell because he knew what Karsarkis knows about terrorist operations in Asia, and now these same people are going after Karsarkis himself."

Kate said nothing. She didn't have to.

"But what about those email intercepts you gave me?" I asked. "Those weren't intercepts of some terrorist cell. They were emails originating from the United States marshals and they seemed clear enough to me. Somebody was talking about killing Karsarkis, even if they were being very subtle about it."

"Yes," Kate admitted, "I don't understand that either."

"So what are you telling me here? That the poor bastard has both a band of Asian terrorists and the US marshals gunning for him at the same time?"

"That could be."

"Is Karsarkis aware of any of this?" I asked.

Kate gave a little shrug, but she didn't say anything.

"Does he at least know what the marshals might be up to?"

"I don't think so," she said

"I don't see how he could be. He'd hardly be so keen on going back to Washington if he knew the friendly feds were out to punch his ticket."

"Maybe they aren't," Kate said. "At least not all of them. I think the protection of the United States government is the only chance Plato Karsarkis has to survive. If you don't take him in, if you can't find a safe haven for him in the US, he's lost."

I started to object to the *you* thing, but I decided it wasn't worth the effort and let it go.

"You said you would consider helping Plato after you read our files, Jack. I've let you read them, and now I've told you more than I should about some things that aren't in them. I need to know what you're going to do. I need to know now."

"What do you want me to do?"

"The same thing Plato wants you to do."

I noticed that Kate had begun calling the man Plato, just like Anita had begun doing on very short acquaintance. The old bastard was a real babe magnet. No doubt about that.

"Plato has asked you to file an application for a presidential pardon on his behalf, Jack, and he wants you to use your White House contacts to push it through. He's not going back to the United States any other way."

"Except dead."

"There's that."

"And you want him alive."

"We want him in safe hands. We want him willing to tell what he knows. We want to hear from him exactly how much danger we are in here in Asia, and we think he knows."

"Then why not just ask him?"

"He's not going to give up whatever he knows for nothing, Jack. You know better than that."

"Then arrest him and send him back. Problem solved. Right?"

Kate tried to keep her face expressionless and mostly she succeeded, but for just an instant I could see the embarrassment as it passed behind her eyes.

"That's not an option," she said. "You of all people ought to understand that."

I did understand that. I didn't like it, but I understood it.

Corruption ran deep in Thailand and there were too many people eating off Karsarkis' table for an arrest to be in the cards. I rubbed my hands over my face and thought about what Kate was asking me to do.

"This is all a hell of a mess," I said after a while.

"Yes," she agreed. "It is."

"Even if I was inclined to try and get the White House to pardon Karsarkis, I don't think I could pull it off. Nobody has that many favors to call in."

"Plato thinks you do. So do I."

I let that pass without comment. There was something else I needed to ask Kate about. I didn't really want to ask, but I knew eventually I was going to have to, so I took a deep breath and just plunged it.

"Do you have any personal reason for caring whether or not Karsarkis gets a pardon?"

I had to know if Kate was acting solely out of conviction or if there was another reason. Karsarkis obviously owned a lot of powerful politicians and other public figures in Thailand and there were many ways to own people. The crude way was to buy them, but there were other subtler ways and even the possibility of webs of personal loyalties that I could never hope to understand.

Kate looked at me for a long time in complete silence. I just looked back. I didn't bat an eye. I had been in Asia far too long to be ashamed of asking that kind of question.

"First, Jack, please understand this: I have never taken anything from Karsarkis or from anyone else. There are still a few honest people in government here and I'm one of them. Second, I'm not sleeping with Plato now and I'm not going to be in the future. Whether you help Karsarkis or not, I want you to know both of those things are true."

I nodded. I wanted to believe Kate and I did. I saw no reason not to.

"There is a lot at stake here," she continued. "Karsarkis may know a great deal about terrorist operations in Asia that threaten all of us. If your people get him back in one piece and he gives them what he has, that would be a good thing for all of us. We need to know what he knows."

"I guess they could always make it a condition of the pardon that he come clean."

"You already know they can't. Under your Constitution a presidential pardon is unconditional. Karsarkis can promise them anything he wants in order to get it, but if he doesn't deliver, they can't take it back. His help has got to come from genuine good will. If he promises to tell you what he knows just to get his pardon and then you give him one and he laughs at you and says he's changed his mind, what are you going to do about it?"

"Have the marshals kill him?" I suggested.

Kate didn't smile at that. Perhaps she didn't think it was all that funny.

"Giving Plato Karsarkis a pardon would be difficult for your president politically," she said. "That's why Karsarkis needs you. The White House owes you, Jack. You delivered big for them not very long ago. You even made you friend Mr. Redwine quite the hero. He's the White House counsel. Pardon applications are filed with his office. And he owes you now."

"You're assuming an awful lot."

"I don't think so."

I took a deep breath and looked away. The thunderclouds were coming closer and I heard the first rumbling in the distance. After a minute or two, my eyes drifted back to Kate.

"If I'm going to represent Karsarkis," I said, "I need to know everything."

"All you need to know is what I've just told you."

"That's not enough."

"It ought to be. Mike O'Connell probably knew everything and look what happened to him."

"No, there's something else," I said. "Something specific."

"What is it?"

"Did Karsarkis kill that girl? Did he cut Cynthia Kim's throat in that hotel room in Washington?"

Kate sat back and folded her arms. "I don't know," she said quietly. "I really don't know. He may have."

We sat for a while in silence after that, both of us watching the storm build. There was still food on my plate, but I had pretty much lost my appetite.

Kate's story about Karsarkis' shadowy connections and his knowledge of terrorist operations in Asia might well have been nothing but a lot of horseshit, something she had concocted to make me feel okay about helping a traitor and a murderer. Still, I had no doubt she really did want me to help Karsarkis get his presidential pardon and the reasons she was giving me for that were no doubt at least partially true.

I took my time about finishing my beer and tried to appear thoughtful, although looking back, I'm not sure why I even bothered. I had known what I would eventually say almost from the moment Kate had started spinning her tales of spies and terrorists and secret money trails leading to Asia. I had always been a complete sucker for stuff like that.

"Look," I finally told Kate, "let me talk to Karsarkis again. If I'm satisfied he deserves a pardon, maybe I'll take him on."

Men are, on the whole, foolish and predictable creatures. I'd had no problem at all looking Karsarkis right in the eye and telling him to shove off when he asked me to get the president to pardon him. Then Kate had asked me to do exactly the same thing and I had gone all goo-goo and said, 'Oh, sure, whatever you want.'

Kate flashed me one of those smiles Thai women keep in reserve, but she didn't say another word. She knew she didn't have to.

Smart woman, I thought to myself. Quitting when she was ahead.

Was I ever going to learn to do that?

Probably not.

THE END

PHUKET

"*The greatest trick the Devil ever pulled was convincing the world he didn't exist.*"

— Roger 'Verbal' Kint,
The Usual Suspects

Thirty Six

THE MORNING AFTER my lunch with Kate I woke up early. Way too early.

After making some coffee I stood at the window and watched the air glowing purple with a false dawn. When the sun finally appeared at the horizon, it turned the whole world the color of freshly spun cotton candy. I drank coffee for a while and watched the city ooze to life. Then I ate a bowl of raisin bran, shoved a few things into a duffle bag, and took a cab to the airport.

I hadn't bothered to call for a reservation. There were flights from Bangkok to Phuket almost every hour and getting a seat was never much of a problem. Sure enough, the nine-o'clock flight had plenty of room and I was in Phuket just after ten. By ten-thirty I was pulling onto the highway for the drive to Patong Beach in a black Jeep Cherokee I had rented from Avis.

When CW and I met at the Paradise Bar—back in a time that now felt at least a century ago although it had really been just a couple of weeks—he told me he was staying at the Holiday Inn. If CW was in Phuket now, and I had no doubt he was, I would bet my last dollar he was still there. Besides, the Holiday Inn was always the first place you looked for Americans in Phuket.

I had barely driven up the hotel's circular driveway and climbed out of the Cherokee when I heard his voice.

"Goddamn, Slick," he bellowed. "What the fuck you doing here?"

I followed the sound across the open-air lobby and found CW nursing what looked like a cup of coffee in an otherwise empty bar. When I walked over and sat down across from him I saw he was puffy and drawn. He looked like he had aged ten years since I had seen him last.

"What's wrong, CW? You look like somebody shot your dog."

"I ain't got a dog."

I nodded at that, waiting, but CW didn't say anything else.

"No progress on Karsarkis?" I prompted.

"Ah, son of a bitch," he muttered. "I am so damned tired of that little pissant I'd like to go in and just string him up on a palm tree. Then at least I could get home to Dallas."

I raised my eyebrows at the implication, but CW was staring into his coffee cup and didn't notice. Besides, I doubted irony was a big part of his conversational repertoire.

"Forget about Karsarkis for a couple of hours then," I said. "You like barbeque?"

CW looked at me as if I had just begun speaking in tongues.

"What are you talking about, boy?"

"Don't call me boy, you redneck motherfucker. Now do you want to eat barbeque with me or don't you?"

CW grinned and spread his palms. "Shoot," he said. "Why not?"

The Cherokee was still in the hotel driveway exactly where I had left it. CW and I got in and I went back to the highway and headed south.

DON'S BARBEQUE WAS at the far south end of the island, almost all the way down to the yacht harbor at Chalong Bay. The building itself looked as if it might once have been a gas station and it sat in solitary splendor alongside the potholed asphalt of an uninspiring rural highway. Its nearest neighbor was a mosque. I seriously doubted very many barbeque joints in the entire world could make a similar claim.

A tile-roofed pavilion open on three sides fronted the building. It was furnished with poured-concrete picnic tables with matching concrete benches. In a modest nod to graciousness, blue plastic tablecloths covered at least parts of some of the concrete tables. Several electric fans hung from the ceiling struggling valiantly against the heat and humidity, but about all they succeeded in doing was pushing the heavy air around a little.

"Well, goddamn it all to hell," CW said as we sat down. "Looks just like home."

I wasn't absolutely sure whether CW was joking or not.

A young girl came over to the table carrying two thick plastic folders. CW ordered a beer and I asked for an iced tea. When the girl went off to get our drinks, we leafed through the folders.

"They really got all this shit?" CW asked.

"They do," I assured him.

"Enchiladas, tacos, tamales, barbequed chicken, rack of ribs. Man, oh man, Slick. This is better than getting laid."

The girl brought our drinks and I ordered. Then I looked around while CW made up his mind. The place was fairly crowded. Although there were a couple of women who appeared to be local girlfriends or maybe even wives, most of the customers were middle-aged Caucasian males. At one table were four men I had no doubt were Americans. They were big men: big arms, big legs, big shoulders, and big wristwatches. They had sunny, open faces with deep tan lines, and wore faded golf shirts with jeans or khakis and scuffed boots. All of their arms seemed unnaturally hairy and, deeply bleached by the sun, the hair enveloped their forearms like loosely woven blankets. They looked like oil-field workers on R&R, or maybe military or cops. I hoped they were oil-field workers.

When the girl had taken our orders and left, CW folded his arms on the edge of the table and leaned toward me.

"So what have you got to tell me, Slick?"

I looked around Don's in mock surprise. "You mean I give you all this and you want more?"

"Don't try my patience, boy."

"I thought I told you not to call me boy."

We stared at each other a while after that and I could feel the testosterone levels climbing. Then we both laughed a little and everything settled down.

"You enjoying yourself here in Thailand, CW?"

"Yeah, I like Thais. They're primitive as hell. They talk to spirits and dead chickens, shit like that, but they're okay."

"You ever make it back up to Soi Katoey again?"

I thought I saw a touch of caution in CW's eyes. "Why would you ask that?"

"Just making conversation."

"Well then, Slick, you better watch out how you go about doing that, you hear me?"

There was a pause as two motorbikes passed on the highway, both in need of muffler jobs.

"I wasn't questioning your manhood, CW, I was just asking what you'd been up to since I saw you last."

CW looked at me for a while, and then he sighed heavily in what seemed to me to be a genuine mixture of disgust and exasperation.

"Ah, I wouldn't know where to start. I've been running around like a two-dicked rooster with a key to the henhouse."

I laughed in spite of myself, but CW didn't even smile.

"Nobody seems to know jack shit about what they really want us to do with Karsarkis," he continued. "They run me one way and then they run me another. I just wished they'd make up their damned minds and we could get on with it."

I let a moment pass, and then because it seemed as good a time as any to do it I laid out the question I had brought CW here to ask in the first place.

"Did your men kill Mike O'Connell?"

CW looked at me without answering. I tried to read his eyes, looking for surprise, but they had gone flat.

"Well, did they?" I asked again.

"Son, you watch your mouth or I'm gonna kick your goddamned ass."

"Somebody shot him, CW, somebody who knew exactly what they were doing. Local hitters don't use silenced sniper rifles. A couple of wild shots off the back of a motorcycle with a handgun is the best they can manage."

"And that's why you think it was my boys who killed O'Connell?"

"Marcus York was in Bangkok the day O'Connell was shot. Do you want me to believe that was just a coincidence?"

"I don't give two shits what you believe. You can go fuck yourself right up your sorry ass with a garden rake for all I care."

The air was so heavy it felt almost solid. I could probably have reached right out with my hand and ripped away a piece of it. Sweat ran in tiny rivulets behind my ears and down my back.

"I know what's going down here, CW. I have friends at the NIA. They laid it all out for me."

"What the hell is the NIA?"

"The National Intelligence Agency. The Thai CIA."

"Well, whoopee do."

"They showed me transcripts of the intercepts they've been running of your email."

"Intercepts of my *email?*"

"Not your personal email; the communications between your

operational headquarters here and Washington."

"Are you pulling my pecker, son?"

"Nope, they got it all, CW. They know what your instructions are."

"Well then, son, maybe you better tell me, because I ain't all that clear what those instructions are myself."

"You're going to make me say it, aren't you?"

"Say whatever you want. Don't make no difference to me."

"You're not here to take Plato Karsarkis back," I said, "because the Thais aren't going to extradite him."

CW's eyes shifted onto mine and stayed there. He stared at me like a fish gazing out of a tank.

"You're here to kill him."

"*What?*" CW reared back away from the table. "We're here to do *what?*"

"I saw the intercepts, CW."

"I don't know what you saw, you sorry motherfucker, but whatever it was, it was a crock of shit."

CW reached in his shirt pocket and pulled out a telephone that looked like an Ericsson. He slammed it down on the table so hard that for a moment I thought he had broken it.

"*That's* what I use to talk to Washington, dickweed. I don't even use email."

"You're not using email to communicate with Washington?" Now it was my turn to feel ambushed. "Not at all?"

CW shook his head. "If what your Thai spy buddies showed you were real intercepts rather than something they just made up, they weren't intercepts from the United States Marshals Service. We ain't hired killers, Slick. We're just here to haul this asshole back to Washington and then he's somebody else's problem."

"But then why not get the Thais to agree to extradition? Surely Washington could do that if they really wanted to."

CW consulted a spot somewhere over my shoulder and seemed to think for a while before he answered. "We'd like to do it all nice and legal, Slick, but you're a smart guy and you know how things work out here. The government of the United States of America isn't gonna be pushed around by a bunch of third-world peckerwoods who've been bought and paid for."

"So you're going to kidnap Karsarkis. Is that about the size of it?"

"What do you expect us to do? Just stand around here with our dicks in our hands?"

"Certainly not in Phuket. Not when there are so many people willing to hold them for you."

CW didn't laugh and he didn't smile. He just pointed his forefinger at me.

"We'll do what we have to do," he said. "And don't you forget it."

Two guys came in and sat at a table not far away. They glanced over at us briefly but without any obvious interest. I made them for Irish. It's hard for Irish guys to be inconspicuous at a beach resort, regardless of how hard they try. They were slim and hard-looking with reddish hair cut very short and skin so pale they both glowed like a pair of Japanese lanterns. I wondered if the men were part of Karsarkis' IRA bodyguard or if they were just a couple of Paddy sex tourists recouping their strength for another run at the massage parlors.

"You think that's right?" I asked CW. "You happy with that?"

"With what?'

"Kidnapping a man. Putting him in chains and dragging him out of the country with a gun to his head no matter what the Thais might have to say about it."

CW shook his head very slowly at me while his eyes watched the Irishmen. "We don't use chains."

I noticed he didn't mention anything about the gun-to-the-head part.

"I was exaggerating," I said. "For effect. But I'd still like an answer to the question. Do you think it's right?"

"Ah, put a sock in it, you little shit. Who the fuck do you think you are, sitting there all high and mighty and passing judgment on me? Do you have the slightest idea who we're dealing with here? Do you know who Plato Karsarkis *is*, Slick?"

"I think so."

"I *don't* think so. He funnels his hot oil deals through all kinds of companies—"

"I know all about that," I said.

"Oh, do you now?" CW looked at me with what seemed to be genuine curiosity. "Then where do you think the money from those deals actually goes, Slick? What do you think it pays for? When some bastards plant another nail bomb at an embassy or blow up another discothèque, you just remember you had a nice civilized dinner one night with the man who gave them the money they needed to do it. You think about that and you tell me how you feel when you see kids lying on the ground with their arms and their legs blown off. You tell me then you know who Plato Karsarkis really is."

I said nothing.

"Karsarkis is the motherfucking devil, Slick. I shit you not. He does business with arms dealers and terrorists; he launders money and passes it to people who shouldn't have it; he bribes some people and kills the ones he can't bribe. He's everywhere, and he's nowhere. He is a wisp of smoke, and when things go wrong, he's gone."

CW stuck his hand in front of my face and snapped his fingers.

"Like that."

I almost slapped his hand away, but I didn't.

"Did he kill Cynthia Kim?" I asked instead.

"I don't care." CW's voice crackled like dry leaves. "If he didn't, he killed a thousand others."

I gazed out at the road and watched a middle-aged man roar by on a motorbike, two little children wedged on the seat between him and the handlebars.

"I'm taking Karsarkis back however I have to do it," CW went on when I didn't say anything. "I'm gonna jack that fucker up and then haul his ass back. After that somebody else can decide what to do with him."

I said nothing.

"And as for you, my little friend, you better stay the hell out of my way. I can put your dick in the dirt anytime I want to. You got that, *boy*?"

I looked back at CW and caught him full in the eyes. Very slowly he turned his head away from me, moving it carefully, like a man with a bad headache who didn't want to make it any worse.

"You don't frighten me, CW."

"Why not?" He sounded genuinely curious.

"Because you're a little man in a big game," I said. "And you don't even know what the game *is*. I like you, but the truth is you don't matter here. You're just an extra in somebody else's big scene."

A tired-looking old woman with a leathery face shuffled over to the table carrying two slabs of barbequed ribs and dishes of coleslaw and beans. The edges of the slabs were crusty with blackened fat and the meat was deep red and moist-looking. CW and I sat in silence as the woman put the plates in front of us, then shuffled away again and returned a moment later with a bowl of sauce. It was deep mahogany in color with chunks of green jalapeños floating in it. She also brought a glass jar filled with toothpicks and two hand towels in plastic packets.

The ribs were so tender I didn't even need a knife to separate them. I pulled the smallest one off the end of the rack and dipped it into the sauce, then chewed away the meat. I dropped the bone on the plate and glanced up at CW. He seemed to be concentrating on his food.

Neither of us talked much while we ate and the subject of Plato Karsarkis didn't come up again. When we were finished, I paid the check.

After that, I drove CW back to Patong and left him at the Holiday Inn.

Thirty Seven

I SPENT THE night at Panwaburi, the same hotel where Anita and I had stayed the last time we had been in Phuket. Maybe that wasn't a good idea, but I did it anyway. The next morning I had coffee and toast from room service, then I got in the Cherokee and headed for Plato Karsarkis' house. Karsarkis wasn't expecting me—at least not as far as I knew—but there wasn't anybody else left for me to annoy.

The day was so bright the air seemed almost white. The world was a cloud of light veined with streaks of blue. I couldn't remember ever experiencing light that intense before. Although my sunglasses were as dark as pitch, the day scratched at my eyes like sandpaper.

Once through Phuket Town I punched it and made the turnoff from the main highway to Karsarkis' estate in less than half an hour. Driving west on the two-lane asphalt I passed through the eerie, symmetrical ranks of rubber trees that had been my main landmark on my previous trip and a couple of miles later I turned onto the loose-packed gravel of the narrow track that led to Karsarkis' gate.

As I took a curve around a grove of palm trees I was surprised to find a dark gray minivan blocking the road. I slowed to a crawl to slip by it and had just registered that the van looked to be American, perhaps a Chevrolet, when a man stepped out from in front of it and raised his right hand at me, palm out like a traffic cop.

Ordinarily I wouldn't have pulled over, but the man was a westerner who looked vaguely familiar. He was dressed in some kind of khaki uniform. There were no insignia on it, at least none that I could see, but he had a holstered sidearm on his hip.

I lowered my window and the man walked slowly toward me with one hand resting casually on the butt of his pistol. He reminded me of a highway patrolman making a traffic stop, and that was when I realized why he looked so familiar. He was the man who had been with Marcus York at the Blue Lotus Pub in Patong the night CW and I had watched the *katoeys* boogieing down on Soi Crocodile.

He looked me over carefully. "You're Jack Shepherd, aren't you?"

"Yes."

"I'm—"

"I know who you are. I just don't remember your name."

"Chuck Parker," he said. "Deputy United States Marshal."

"Right."

"Could you step out of the vehicle, sir?"

"What?"

"I asked if you'd step out of the vehicle, sir. We just need to have a quick word with you, and then you can be on your way."

"I'm fine here," I said. "Say whatever you want."

Chuck Parker first looked surprised and then confused. He didn't seem accustomed to having people say they weren't going to do whatever he told them to do. Now that someone had, he wasn't all that certain what to do about it. His head swiveled back and forth on his fleshy neck as if he was searching for help. When I heard the open-handed slap against the Cherokee's passenger door, I knew he had found it.

"Move it, asshole." Marcus York slammed the door with his palm one more time for good measure. "Get out of the fucking car."

From the first moment I had met York something made me wonder about him. I didn't actually have the slightest idea what he was if he wasn't really a marshal, but right at that moment it didn't really matter. Playing with Chuck Parker was one think, but looking into Marcus York's hard black eyes right then left me with no doubt that playing with him would be quite another, regardless of who he might be. I opened the door and got out of the Cherokee.

"A rental?" Parker asked, looking it over.

"What?"

"I asked you if this was a rental, sir." Parker gestured unnecessarily at the Cherokee.

"Yes," I said, "it is. But why do you care one way or another?"

Parker didn't answer. Instead he pointed to the gray minivan.

"Would you step over there please?"

I nodded my head and followed Parker. When he opened the van's sliding door I saw the interior was bigger than I would have expected and was fitted out with all kinds of things. There were two upholstered benches at right angles and in front of them was a low table with storage space underneath. At the very rear of the minivan was a floor-to-ceiling rack of electronic equipment. I didn't know what it actually was, but I doubted it was a stereo system.

Parker gestured for me to get inside and I did. I took the bench facing forward and Parker took the other one.

"You are on your way to see Plato Karsarkis, are you not?"

"I am," I said.

"Are you armed, sir?"

"I'm sorry?"

"It's a simple enough question. Are you armed?"

"Only with my sly wit."

Parker nodded as gravely as if I'd given him a perfectly sensible answer. Since York hadn't joined us in the minivan, I was just starting to wonder where he had gone when the obvious answer occurred to me. York was searching my Cherokee.

"Look," I said to Parker, "when are you two Brylcreem buckaroos going to tell me what this is all about?"

"You think you're a real funny guy, don't you, sir? With the wisecracks and all that stuff?"

"People either love it or hate it. I'd say it's about fifty-fifty. How about you, marshal? What's your vote?"

Parker looked at me without expression. I thought he was about to say something, but then he seemed to think better of it. Instead he reached under the table, lifted up a metal case about the size of a cigar box, and unsnapped the top. Nested inside surrounded by a thick lining of white Styrofoam was something that looked like a tie clip.

"This is the transmitter we'd like you to wear while you're up at Karsarkis' place, sir. It has an effective range of about two miles and we think that—"

"Hang on," I said holding up one hand. "Is this is some kind of a joke?"

Parker looked genuinely puzzled. "No, sir. It's not a joke."

"Then what on God's green earth ever put it in your head that I might be willing to do anything remotely like that?"

Parker's eyes shifted back and forth in confusion and his head wobbled slightly on his thick neck.

"CW said you'd be willing to cooperate. That you'd help us out, you being an American and all."

"He did, did he?"

"Yes, sir. He did."

"And what do you think, Parker? Do I seem to you to be a cooperative kind of guy?"

My question caused a momentary look of panic to slide across Parker's face. Evidentially thinking wasn't a big part of his job description.

Parker had produced the case from beneath the low table between us. While he wrestled with my question, I ran my eyes over the other storage compartments.

"What else you got down here?" I asked, yanking on the handle nearest my ankles.

A drawer glided smoothly out on silent rollers and inside in foam-rubber padded mounts were two M-16s with laser sights and built-in noise suppressors. I slid one of them out and worked the action. It was Teflon-coated to reduce noise. Very spiffy.

"Just imagine," I said looking at Parker, "I'd always thought US Marshals carried six-shooters."

York appeared in the minivan's open doorway before Parker could say anything. He stood looking at me for a moment and then he reached out and jerked the M-16 out of my hands.

"Get out," he said, gesturing with his head toward the ground next to him.

"My pleasure."

I got up from the bench. In a half crouch to keep from hitting my head, I pushed myself out of the minivan.

"Find anything interesting in the Cherokee?" I asked York as I shouldered past him.

He turned, following me with his eyes.

I still couldn't see York as a marshal. He had an air about him that was entirely different, a sense of knowing something I didn't know, something that maybe *nobody* else knew; and knowing whatever it was gave him a pass from the rules that applied to the rest of us. But then that meant York must be…what? FBI? Secret Service? Military? CIA? None of those seemed exactly right to me either, but what else *was* there?

I wasn't sure what I was supposed to do next. Still, this was York and Parker's party, so I figured I'd let them tell me.

"You know what Karsarkis has done," York said eventually. "Why are you protecting him?"

"Why are you going to kill him?"

That wiped the smirk off York's face, but I didn't much like the look that replaced it.

"I don't know what you're talking about."

"I think you do. I also think you killed Mike O'Connell, but I don't understand why."

That made York smile for some reason.

"Get the fuck out of here," he said, after he got tired of smiling. Then he turned away, climbed into the minivan, and slammed the sliding door.

THE REST OF the way up to Karsarkis' house the road ran through a massive mangrove forest. Tree branches scraped at the sides of the Cherokee as I crunched slowly over the hard-packed gravel.

Just past Karsarkis' driveway another gray minivan sat across the road and blocked it entirely to anyone coming from the opposite direction. Two men leaned against the side of the van, arms folded, watching me. I didn't recognize either of them, but they were both westerners and both wearing the same khaki uniforms and carrying the same sort of sidearms Parker and York had been carrying.

After turning into the driveway the road became much smoother and I followed a thorny hedge until I got to the green metal gate. The Thai guards who had been there on my previous visit were nowhere in sight this time. Instead, a slim, fair-haired man in jeans and a plaid shirt stood smoking and talking to another equally Irish-looking guy who had what appeared to be an AK-47 hanging off his shoulder. They glanced at me as I got out of the Cherokee and the man in the plaid shirt stopped talking. They spread apart slightly as I approached, but neither man seemed particularly concerned.

"Can I help you?" Plaid Shirt called out when I was still twenty feet away.

An Irish accent. No doubt about it.

"I'm here to see Plato Karsarkis," I answered, stopping about halfway between the Cherokee and the metal gate.

"And who would you be, mister?"

"Jack Shepherd."

"Are you expected?"

"Not unless somebody is clairvoyant."

Plaid Shirt gave me a look I couldn't read, but it didn't appear to contain a great deal of admiration for my sense of humor. Then he said something to the other man too softly for me to catch and the second man unclipped a walkie-talkie from his belt. He lifted it to his lips and turned his back to me.

"Look," I said, figuring I probably ought to be playing this one straight. "Tell Karsarkis that Jack Shepherd wants to talk to him. I'm sure he'll be happy to see me."

Plaid Shirt dropped his cigarette onto the crushed rock of the driveway and ground it out with the heel of his boot. Then his hand went behind his back and produced a large-caliber automatic. He held it dangling at his side rather than pointing it at me, but the distinction didn't seem particularly important under the circumstances.

"Just stand where you are, mister."

The other man turned back around and returned the walkie-talkie to his belt. Slipping the automatic rifle off his shoulder, he racked the cocking lever and walked past me to the Cherokee. He made one circuit of the vehicle peering through the windows from a slight distance, then he got much closer and made another. He opened both the front and rear passenger doors and inspected the Cherokee's interior carefully, stepping up into the doorframe and leaning over the backseat to get a clear view into the rear cargo area. When he was apparently satisfied, he stepped down again and nodded to Plaid Shirt who looked up over my head toward a tree where I assumed a security camera was located. He lifted one hand, gave a little rolling motion with his index finger, and the metal gate began to slide open.

"I'll be riding up with you, mister," Plaid Shirt said.

I nodded and got back behind the wheel of the Cherokee while Plaid Shirt climbed into the front passenger seat. He cradled the automatic casually in his hand, but he kept the barrel pointed more or less at my chest all the same.

Beyond the gate the roadway was asphalt. Neither Plaid Shirt nor I spoke as I drove uphill though a vividly green jungle of mangroves, rubber trees, and coconut palms with bright red lashings of bougainvillea here and there. When I reached the clearing where Karsarkis' house surveyed the sea from atop a rise, Plaid Shirt pointed with his free hand toward where I thought the swimming pool and tennis court were.

"Park back there, mister."

I drove across the grass and stone courtyard, circled the fountain, and followed the driveway off to the left. When it ended at the small parking area next to the tennis court, I nosed the Cherokee toward the fence next to a silver Jaguar that was the only other car there and cut the engine.

"The boss is by the pool. You walk around—"

"I know where it is," I interrupted.

"Oh, do you now?" The man sounded amused, although I couldn't see at exactly what.

I got out and closed the door, but Plaid Shirt didn't move. He stayed in the Cherokee, slouched down in his seat, and leaned against the passenger door as if he was preparing himself for a long wait. He could sit there forever as far as I cared. I jammed my hands in my pockets and walked toward the swimming pool.

Thirty Eight

THE SWIMMING POOL in Plato Karsarkis' courtyard where he and I had sat and smoked cigars after dinner about a hundred years ago was an aquarium compared to the immense, no-nonsense pool halfway between the tennis court and the main house where I found him now. Set in a vast expanse of polished teakwood decking, it offered an unobstructed view west into the cobalt blue distances of the Andaman Sea. Not a lot of people I knew had two swimming pools. Actually, not a lot of people I knew had one.

Karsarkis was sitting alone at the end of the pool furthest away from the house. He was at a round glass table shaded by a canvas umbrella and was barefooted, wearing a black T-shirt and white tennis shorts. I walked out, pulled up a chair, and sat down.

Karsarkis didn't offer to shake hands, but he inclined his head toward the silver pot on the table.

"Coffee?" he asked.

"No thanks."

I took in the plate of sliced mango in front of Karsarkis and what appeared to be a half-eaten basket of toast.

"Breakfast," Karsarkis said before I was able to make one of my characteristically sly and witty observations. "Got up a little late."

"Having a hard time sleeping?" I asked.

"No."

Karsarkis seemed to think about it.

"No," he repeated. "I'm not."

Karsarkis picked up a knife and fork, cut one of the mango slivers in half, and popped it into his mouth. I noticed he held the knife in his right hand and the fork in his left, eating the mango as a European might rather than like an American.

"Who killed Mike O'Connell?" I asked him.

"I don't know."

"But you can guess."

"Anyone can guess. *You* can guess."

"Actually," I said, "I can't."

Karsarkis nodded slowly at that and ate another sliver of mango.

"Are you sure I can't get you some coffee?" he asked again when he had finished it.

"Okay, fine," I said this time. "I'll have some fucking coffee. Let's sit here and drink fucking coffee together in the morning sun like a couple of old fucking pals and just see what happens."

The mobile phone was so small I hadn't noticed it until Karsarkis picked it up and pressed a button. When someone answered, he murmured, "*Gafair*." Then he pushed another button on the telephone and put it down again.

"Maybe we could try it another way," I said. "*Why* was Mike O'Connell killed?"

"I expect somebody thought he was me."

It seemed to me Karsarkis made the observation rather dispassionately, at least dispassionately for someone saying one of his employees had taken a bullet for him.

"I don't think so," I said. "And neither do you."

"I don't?"

"Nope. O'Connell was twenty years younger than you are, one or two inches taller, and probably twenty pounds lighter. A professional hitter lying in wait with a silenced sniper rifle wouldn't make a mistake like that."

Karsarkis examined the toast basket and selected a piece. He buttered it, took a bite, and chewed reflectively.

"That part about the twenty pounds lighter…you said that just to hurt me, didn't you?"

"And O'Connell being shot through the head? His brains splattering all over the front of your apartment building? That didn't hurt you?"

Karsarkis' mood changed abruptly.

"You self-righteous little shit," he snapped. "Who the hell do you think you are? That boy was like a son to me. I'll miss him every single day for the rest of my life and I'll blame myself that he's dead. You can go fuck yourself!"

A maid came out carrying a silver tray and I watched her walk toward us across the teak decking, her heels clicking on the polished boards. She was young and pretty, and I wondered if Karsarkis cared or had even noticed. She set out two china cups and saucers, a box of cigars, matches, and a cutter, and then she poured coffee from a big pot that matched the tray. She exchanged the pot for the one that had been on the table when I arrived, then walked away. Karsarkis never even glanced at her.

Karsarkis poured a little milk into his coffee and stirred it absentmindedly. He sipped from the cup, staying silent, waiting me out. I waited longer, and eventually he spoke, his voice tight and controlled again.

"Why did you come here this morning, Jack?"

"I want to know what this is all about."

"Do you?"

"Yes."

"Why?" he asked.

"Does it matter to you?"

Karsarkis seemed to think about that.

"No," he said after a moment. "No, it doesn't. Not if you're willing to go to bat for me with your friends in the White House. Not if you're willing to file a pardon application for me and twist arms until the bastards grant it. Not if that's true."

"It's not," I said. "At least, not yet."

Karsarkis raised one eyebrow at that.

"Let's just see how it goes," I said. "I'll ask you some questions. You'll give me some answers. We'll drink some more coffee, and then we'll figure out where we are."

"Okay," Karsarkis said. "Let's do that."

I watched two pure-white seagulls swoop in on the ocean breeze and glide to a silent stop on the grass just over Karsarkis' left shoulder. They examined the two of us curiously for a while, their heads swiveling back and forth as they focused on us first with one big yellow eye and then the other. Soon, apparently losing interest and sensing no threat, the two gulls bent slightly toward each other and hoisted their wings. With a few quick beats, they plunged over the cliff, glided across the beach, and skimmed away together just above the ocean waves. It was the kind of sight I needed on that clear early summer's morning to remind me of what a grand and graceful place the world actually is and how its design, vouchsafed beyond the understandings of man, would no doubt survive even the worst we can do to it.

"How are your children?" I asked Karsarkis after the seagulls had disappeared.

He rubbed at his cheek with one hand, then leaned forward and folded his arms on the table. "Frank's okay. Columbia's the right place for him as far as I can tell. As for Zoe ...well, she's not good."

"I'm sorry," I said.

He nodded slowly and ran his index finger around the rim of his coffee cup.

"And what about your family?" he eventually asked. "Okay?"

"Yes," I said, but I had hesitated for just a fraction of a second and I could tell Karsarkis caught it. "Great, thanks."

Karsarkis' eyes caught mine and for a second I saw something so soft and melancholy in them that I had to look away.

"I know what happened, Jack."

I cleared my throat, but I didn't move or look back at him. "What do you mean?"

"I know Anita left you, and I know why."

I felt sucker-punched. I cleared my throat again and did my best to cover it.

"How do you know?" I asked, my voice sounding smaller than I would have liked.

"Back when I first asked you to help me, Mike put some discreet surveillance in place. I'm sorry if that offends you, Jack. Really, I am. I apologize if it does. But my life is on the line here and I needed to be certain what you were doing with the confidences I shared with you. I didn't know you that well then."

"And you think you do now?"

"Yes," he nodded. "I think I do."

"Then the bug I found in my apartment was yours?" I asked.

"There were several. We didn't leave them in very long, if you care."

"Just long enough to find out about Anita."

"I'm sorry. I truly am."

I started on an inventory of all the things I was feeling right then, trying to decide whether there was any point in getting angry. I had not gotten very far into it before it got too complicated and I just gave up.

"You said you know why Anita left," I said. "What do you mean by that?"

Karsarkis seemed genuinely embarrassed now. He shifted his

weight in the chair causing it to scrape slightly against the teak decking. Then he poured more coffee into his cup, although I noticed he didn't drink any of it.

"Can I tell you something as a friend, Jack?"

"You're not my friend."

Karsarkis took a deep breath, then he let it out.

"There are things you don't need to know about this life. They take you nowhere you really want to go."

I was beginning to feel cold. I folded my arms and leaned back.

"What are you talking about?"

"You really don't know?"

"Apparently not."

"Then leave it, Jack. Take my advice. Just leave it."

"Don't do this, Karsarkis."

Karsarkis looked straight at me for a long time. I just stared at him until he looked away. Finally he exhaled heavily and picked up the mobile phone again.

He punched a button and waited. Then he spoke quietly to someone in English. "There's an envelope in the bottom left-hand drawer of my desk. It's…" Karsarkis paused, listening. "No, not that one. The one on the bottom, in front. Get it and send it out to the pool."

After he had hung up, we sat quietly saying nothing for what was probably only a few minutes, but looking back it seems to me to have been hours.

I did not know the man who walked out from the house and handed Karsarkis a flat letter-sized envelope, manila in color, and I do not remember now what he looked like. All I can recall was watching the envelope he was carrying and being relieved beyond all reason it was so thin as to appear almost empty.

Thirty Nine

I HAD BEEN expecting the worst, but for a moment my hopes soared. It wasn't transcripts of conversations that had taken place when I was out of the apartment. That was what I had feared at first, but the envelope was too thin for that. But then what was it?

Karsarkis held the envelope in his right hand until the man who had brought it was gone. Then he shifted it to his left hand, absently tapping it against the edge of the table.

"This is not something I want to do, Jack," he said, watching my eyes as he spoke.

I said nothing. Just held out my hand.

It was whatever it was. Waiting to look at it wasn't going to change it into something else.

Karsarkis pushed the envelope across the table. I picked it up and opened it.

It contained a single photograph.

It was hard to tell where the photograph had been taken, but I did not think it was Bangkok. Anita was standing next to a dark blue Mercedes. She was wearing a short green dress I had never seen before, one which suited her perfectly. She had on yellow pumps and a big yellow belt with a silver buckle. She looked absolutely breathtaking.

There was a man with Anita, of course, but I didn't know him.

He was a few inches taller than she was and I thought they looked to be about the same age. His hair was long and he was dressed in what seemed to be an expensive, well-tailored suit with a white shirt and dark tie. He was unquestionably a handsome man, and he looked poised and confident.

His left arm held Anita around the waist with what was obvious familiarity and her right rested on his back. Her head was bent to his shoulder, her cheek pressed against it.

All of that I could have survived. All of that I could possibly have even one day forgotten. But it was the look on Anita's face that took everything out of me. Even I could see the grace of love written on her features, the deep familiarity and indisputable devotion to the man at her side. And it broke my fucking heart.

I returned the photograph to the envelope, tucked in the flap, and slid it back across the table to Karsarkis. He left it where it was.

A yellow long-tail boat tracked across the cove below us, scoring it with a line as straight and as white as if it had been drawn with a ruler. Then after a few minutes the boat passed out of sight and the mark faded away and everything was exactly as it had been before. I wondered briefly if I had ever seen the boat at all. Perhaps I had only imagined it.

But I had not imagined the photograph of Anita and her… well, what? I supposed I had to decide what word to use, if only in my most private thoughts. I would be thinking about this a lot, of course, swimming back and forth between hatred and hurt, and thoughts that came without words were hard to get a grip on.

Her lover perhaps? Obviously true, but not an expression I would be able to bring myself to use. Her boyfriend? That sounded juvenile, dismissive, and this was a pain I could not dismiss with ridicule. Her friend? Christ, I couldn't call him that. That hurt more than calling him her lover. The word would have to wait. It was too soon. Too soon for a word.

I sighed deeply and laced my fingers together behind my neck. Here I was, sitting in the bright sunshine of a beautiful Phuket morning, watching the sea capping gently in a light breeze, sharing coffee with the world's most wanted fugitive, and trying to absorb the simple fact that my beautiful wife, the woman I had been devoted to beyond measure and loyal to without exception, had found someone else to love.

So drawing on the sum total of the wisdom I had gleaned from well over forty years of living, what was I going to do now? Was I going to wail and beat my breast? Was I going to fling myself off Karsarkis' cliff and into the sea? Was I going to demand Karsarkis get me a bottle of something and get stinking drunk?

And what would be the point of any of that? I asked myself. *What would be the fucking point?*

I cleared my throat and shifted in my chair until I was facing Karsarkis again.

"Can we get back to business?" I asked him.

"Yes," he said, keeping his expression neutral. "If you like."

Karsarkis watched me carefully, but he didn't say anything else.

"What is it you know that makes so many people want to kill you?" I asked him after a moment or two.

Karsarkis smiled at that, although I didn't immediately see anything amusing about my question.

"It's not so many," he said. "Not really."

"Then exactly who *is* on the list?"

"I would have to guess."

"Go ahead," I said. "Guess."

"I'd rather not."

"Did you know that US marshals have you under surveillance?"

"Of course," Karsarkis said and he shook his head and chuckled slightly. "I've known about the kidnapping plan for a long time. That's not going to happen."

"They're out there right now." I gestured vaguely toward where I thought the road was. "They've got you cut off in both directions."

"Good Lord, Jack, if I really wanted to go anywhere, you don't really think a few glorified rent-a-cops driving a couple of panel vans could stop me, do you?"

I thought about Marcus York's dead black eyes and about the silenced M-16s with laser sights, and I started to tell Karsarkis he probably ought to reconsider that, but I didn't.

"What would you say if I told you it might have been the marshals who killed Mike O'Connell?"

Karsarkis studied my face, although I could read nothing in his eyes as he did. "Why would you think that?"

"I've got friends in Thai intelligence. They gave me a copy of what the NIA claims are intercepts of email between the marshals and somebody in Washington. None of it actually says they have orders to kill you, not in so many words, but that's what it says nevertheless. I'm not even sure the stuff is genuine, but maybe it is. If it is, if the marshals are willing to kill you because of something you know, then maybe O'Connell also knew and…"

I stopped talking and spread my hands, my conclusion having become self-evident.

Karsarkis made little clicking noises with his tongue, thinking sounds, but he remained expressionless.

"Do you really believe the government of the United States goes around killing its own citizens, Jack?"

"Not very often," I said. "But, yes, sometimes."

Karsarkis was watching me carefully. He could see I was thinking about something, but he had to guess what it was.

"You do remember the fee I offered you," he said, keeping his eyes on mine to see if that was it.

He was wrong. That wasn't what I was thinking about. But I kept my face still and he didn't know that.

"Yes, I remember."

Indeed I did. A million dollars just for taking on the case. Four million more if the president ultimately pardoned Karsarkis. It made me think of a crusty old Jesuit priest who had taught me criminal law at Georgetown and of something he never tired of telling us, something he always called the lawyer's prayer. 'Oh, Lord God,' the catechism went, 'I pray for only one reward in this life. Send to me one day a very, very rich man, who is in very, very deep shit.'

In nomine Patris, et Filii, et Spiritus Sancti. Amen.

"Why would the White House even consider pardoning you?" I asked Karsarkis.

Karsarkis offered a mirthless laugh. "Gerald Ford pardoned Richard Nixon. Bill Clinton pardoned Marc Rich. How much worse am I?"

"There's always somebody worse," I said. "Maybe this time it's you."

Karsarkis pulled the box of cigars toward him and flipped up the lid. He studied them for a moment, selected one, and then turned the box and gave it a little push in my direction. I shook my head.

"Was it just about the money?" I asked. "Is that why you sold oil for the Iraqis and laundered the income?"

"You're not thinking big enough, Jack. It wasn't ever about selling oil for the Iraqis. And, for me, it wasn't ever about the money."

"Then what was it?"

"It was about doing the right thing."

"The right thing?"

"Hasn't anyone ever asked you to do the right thing? And then you did it just because it *was* the right thing, even if you harmed yourself by doing it?"

Karsarkis snipped the end of the cigar and lit it with a long wooden match. He drew gently, rotating it in his hand until the tip was glowing evenly. Then he shook out the match and dropped it into a heavy cut-glass ashtray.

"I don't understand," I said when he had finished. "I really don't."

"No, I don't imagine you do. Only a handful of people know the whole truth."

Karsarkis began to snap his index finger rhythmically against his thumbnail. In the silence I could hear the little *click-click-click* it made.

"Go to your friend in the White House, Jack. Tell them the president must give me a full pardon. If he does not, I will tell what I know. And if I do, it will bring them down. It's that simple."

"You want me to threaten the President of the United States for you? Is that what you're asking me to do here?"

"It is not a threat. You are simply delivering a message. I assure you your friend will understand it very clearly. He will also believe the message because it comes from you."

I shook my head and looked away. Maybe the US marshals really were trying to kill Karsarkis. Maybe I was even starting to develop a measure of sympathy for their point of view.

"I don't really understand why you want a pardon," I said, after a minute or two had passed in silence.

"Why wouldn't I?'

"If people in the United States important enough to command loyalty from the US marshals want you killed, why would you even think of going back there? Aren't you safer here?"

"Even if it is the Americans who want to kill me…" Karsarkis stopped talking abruptly and scratched at his ear, then shifted his cigar from one side of his mouth to the other. "If I cannot convince them that killing me is a bigger risk than trusting me, I am a dead man. Next week, maybe, or a month or two perhaps, but eventually I am a dead man for sure. If they really want me, they will get me. Just like I imagine they got Mike."

"And even if the president pardons you, how do you know they won't kill you anyway?" I asked. "You'll still know whatever this is that makes you such a threat. How can you expect them ever to trust you?"

"You will be the proof I can be trusted, Jack. You yourself will be that proof."

My hands rose and rubbed at my face and I closed my eyes. I had heard too much for one day and already had asked too many questions about things I did not really want to know about. But I couldn't stop myself.

"I still don't understand," I said. "What proof am I?"

Karsarkis' voice dropped to a husky, confidential whisper. "The proof that I can be trusted, that I have told *no one* the truth. Even *you* don't know what really happened."

Forty

WHEN I GOT back to the Cherokee, Plaid Shirt was gone. I put the key in the ignition and then just sat there leaning against the steering wheel trying to think clearly. It took only a few minutes for me to abandon the whole concept of thinking clearly as hopelessly unrealistic, at least right then, so I sat up straighter and turned the key.

Nothing happened.

I pulled the key out and stared stupidly at it. Then I pushed it back into the ignition, very deliberately this time, and tried the starter again.

Still nothing.

A grinding sound without the engine firing; an engine that started, then died; even a useless lurch or two from the starter motor. All of these seemed to be within the realm of the comprehension and would have at least provided some clue as to what the problem might be, but… *nothing*? What the hell did *nothing* tell me?

I fumbled under the dashboard. When I found a handle that felt right, I gave it a tug and felt an answering *thunk* as the hood release popped open. Getting out and walking around to the front of the Cherokee, I lifted the hood. That was when it occurred to me I didn't have the slightest idea what I was looking for. Once I had confirmed the engine was indeed still there and pretty much in its accustomed place, my skills as an automotive mechanic were exhausted.

"Car trouble?" a woman's voice asked from behind me.

I turned around and found Karsarkis' wife Mia smiling at me from a dozen feet or so away. Just behind her were Plaid Shirt and another man I didn't recognize. I also noticed they were not smiling.

"It won't start," I said, demonstrating my flair for the obvious.

"Is it a rental?" Mia asked.

Why was it everybody had such a keen interest in my personal relationship with this vehicle?

"Yes," I said. "Avis."

"I could have one of the boys call them for you."

She half turned toward Plaid Shirt, but then she stopped and looked back at me.

"I've got a better idea," she said. "I'm going to Amanpuri to meet a friend for lunch. They have an Avis office there, don't they?"

Amanpuri was the most exclusive resort on Phuket, one of those places where tourists from Europe paid thousands of dollars a night to stay in luxurious villas and avoid mingling with the locals. If they didn't have an Avis office there, it would be the only thing they didn't have.

"They could give you another car now," Mia continued, "and then come get this one later."

Amanpuri was perched on the tip of a heavily forested peninsula on the island's west coast that separated the beaches at Bang Tao from those at Surin. I hadn't had any intention of going in that direction, but sitting around Karsarkis' place for a few hours hoping that a tow truck would eventually turn up was even less appealing.

"Okay, thanks," I said. "I'll take you up on that."

I saw Plaid Shirt and the other man exchange a quick glance, but neither said anything. Plaid Shirt walked over to the silver Jaguar and opened one of the rear passenger doors. Mia got in. Then Plaid Shirt took the front passenger seat and the other man got behind the wheel. Nobody seemed inclined to hold a door for me so I opened the other rear passenger door by myself and got in next to Mia.

All the way down the driveway I wondered about the marshals who were outside blocking the roads with their gray minivans and whether they would try to prevent Mia from passing, but when we drove out through the gate, the minivans were gone. The road was as still and empty as if they had never been there at all.

"You look as if you're about to say something, Mr. Shepherd."

Mia spoke as we passed the place York and Parker had pulled me over on my way in. She was no doubt wondering why I was swiveling my head around like an idiot right then.

"Not really," I said. Then I added lamely, "It's been a bad day."

"Oh, my," Mia laughed, "and it's not even lunchtime yet."

No one spoke again until we had turned onto the main highway and the Jag had settled into a high-speed cruise. The driver seemed skilled and Plaid Shirt sat forward scanning the roadway attentively. Whether these two guys were really IRA I had no earthly idea, but watching them now I had no doubt at all that they were a couple of pros wherever they came from.

"I want to thank you for coming to see Plato today, Mr. Shepherd." Mia spoke suddenly, without looking at me. "Plato needs…he's been a little depressed. Having someone he respects to talk to for a while was probably a great blessing for him."

I wasn't sure what that meant and I said nothing.

"Can you help him?" Mia asked, turning away from the window and examining me, her lips compressed to mask any expression.

"Help him?"

"With a pardon. He says the White House listens to you, that if you will represent him they might grant it."

"If that what he says, Mrs. Karsarkis, I'm afraid your husband has far too high an opinion of me."

Mia nodded absently, letting me off the hook without a fuss, for which I was grateful.

The highway was almost empty and we made good time. The silver Jag's tires sang a steady, high-pitched whine over the asphalt as we passed little houses here and there, mostly simple structures of concrete blocks with a carport occasionally tacked onto one side like an afterthought. For most of the way there was little sign of habitation. The highway ran through thick groves of banana trees, ferns, and elephant ears, their leaves shiny with moisture from the air and flattening slightly in a feeble breeze.

We passed the entrance to the Sheraton Grande and a well-manicured golf course appeared on our right. A conga line of middle-aged Japanese in funny clothes was making its way down a gently rolling fairway with a crowd of young Thai women trailing behind them. Some of the women carried the golfers' heavy bags, while others carried brightly striped umbrellas to shade the Japanese from the sun.

"He misses her more than he would ever admit to you." Mia spoke to the window rather than to me. "Zoe, I mean. His daughter."

I said nothing.

"He wants to go home, Mr. Shepherd." Mia turned from the window and fixed me with a stare so desolate I could not return it. "All he wants to do is to go home."

There were many things I could have said, but none of them seemed worth the hurt they would no doubt inflict on this woman. So I tried to come up with something innocuous.

"Your husband has asked me to lodge a pardon application on his behalf, Mrs. Karsarkis, and I am considering it. But please understand I have not yet made any commitment to him."

That sounded ridiculously tight-assed, and almost as soon as I had spoken I wished I had said nothing at all. Regardless, Mia just nodded as if that was what she had expected me to say, and then she went back to staring out the window.

Forty One

WE LEFT THE main highway, turned directly into the full glare of the midday sun, and followed a narrow, humpbacked road toward the rocky promontory where Amanpuri perched. I watched a column of smoke from a trash fire rise up in ripples so perfectly formed that they looked as if they had been painted on the blue background of the sky. A few hundred feet above the ground unseen air currents bent the smoke and spread it across the highway in front of us, a beige-colored cloud stuck to the earth on an otherwise cloudless day.

A motorcycle roared by. It was a big bike, and noisy, although not knowing one kind of motorcycle from another the model didn't register on me. All I could remember later was that it had been purple with a lot of chrome and that it had a steeply swept-back windshield with two huge rear-view mirrors sticking out from its sides.

The rider, like most motorcycle riders in Thailand, wore a helmet with an opaque visor that entirely obscured his features. He also wore jeans and a dark, nondescript jacket zipped up in front. It was one of those free jackets that companies gave to motorcycle taxi drivers for the advertising. Later, thinking back, I realized I had seen yellow lettering on the back of the jacket that said *The Wall Street Journal Asia*.

After passing us the bike pulled into the lane directly in front of the Jag and almost immediately started slowing down. Our driver tapped his brake and I saw Plaid Shirt's shoulders stiffen as he sat up straighter, his eyes on the motorcycle. I glanced at Mia, but she was still staring out the side window. She was either entirely unaware of the motorcycle or perhaps just disinterested in it.

I bent forward and looked through the gap between Plaid Shirt and the driver. The motorcycle slowed down some more and our driver blipped his horn. The cyclist turned his head back toward us, pointing to the bike's engine and for a moment I saw the leaping chrome Jaguar at the tip of the car's hood reflected in the black mirror of his visor. Our driver lifted both hands from the steering wheel, wheeling them impatiently, a gesture that struck me for some reason as more Italian than Irish.

The motorcycle coughed and choked, then all of a sudden caught again with a loud growl and the cyclist roared away. Barely fifty yards later, it stalled again and the rider turned sharply as if he were trying to get clear of us and off the road to the shoulder. But when he was squarely in front of us, the big bike came to an abrupt halt.

The rider kicked at the starter as we rolled toward him, his helmeted head rotating back and forth between his bike and our Jaguar. Our driver cursed and braked sharply, and he banged the horn again. I saw Plaid Shirt and the driver exchange a look. I couldn't see what kind of a look it was, but I could guess.

I leaned further forward, lowering my head and keeping my voice down in order not to alarm Mia.

"Don't stop," I said.

"Huh?" The driver glanced back at me.

"They use motorcycles here," I said.

"Who does?" Plaid Shirt asked.

"Hired gunmen. Hitters. They do business from bikes. They…"

But my words were lost in the roar of another powerful motorcycle closing on the Jaguar from behind.

At the same instant we heard it coming, the motorcyclist in front of us started his bike and in one smooth movement turned it directly toward us. He jerked a weapon from inside his jacket—I think it was a MAC-10, but I couldn't be sure—and pointed it directly into the windshield. The other bike slid to a stop next to the rear window where Mia sat.

Realizing now what was happening, both Plaid Shirt and the driver produced handguns from somewhere. Before they could bring them into play, the motorcyclist in front of us fired two brief bursts from his rifle. The first blew out the Jaguar's windscreen. The second caught both Plaid Shirt and the driver in the faces, shattering their skulls like two eggshells. A fine mist of blood and tissue filled the car, swirling through it as if a tiny storm of pink rain had just passed over us.

In his death convulsions, the driver must have pushed the Jaguar's accelerator to the floor because the car leaped forward, smashing straight into the surprised motorcyclist in front of us. The heavy car plowed over the man and his bike, grinding them both into the road. In a shower of sparks, the gunman, his motorcycle, and the heavy Jaguar grated along the asphalt until the whole mass crashed off the road and down into a narrow drainage ditch, pinning the gunman and his wildly roaring bike underneath the weight of the engine block. The impact dislodged the driver's foot from the accelerator and the pile of wreckage stopped there, tilting nose-down into the ditch.

The force of smashing into the shooter and then toppling down into the drainage ditch threw me forward and to the left, leaving me more in the front seat than the back. I could feel a sting as if a knife had slashed my cheek and the unmistakable warm wetness of blood. I knew I hadn't been hit. I must have caught a ricochet from somewhere.

The front passenger door hung open and instinctively I hauled myself further forward to get to it. Twisting around to pull my legs under me, I looked back at Mia who was strangely silent. Then I saw why. The second motorcyclist must have fired, too, although I didn't remember hearing any gunfire other than from the front.

Mia sat almost straight upright in spite of the list of the car, but there was a neat crescent of entry wounds stitched high into her chest. Her mouth hung open and her eyes stared through the empty space where the car's side window had been not so very long before.

Struggling for purchase in the blood soaking Plaid Shirt's body, I grunted as something dug into my stomach. Pushing my hand under me, I felt a heavy automatic, a .45 that either Plaid Shirt or the driver had dropped. I wrapped my hand around its grip.

I slid downward and toward the open door, skidding through the blood as if I were belly down on ice. My elbow hit the ground first, then my shoulder, but I held onto the .45 and rolled, pulling my legs free of the car and curling them under me.

The Jaguar's sudden lurch forward had caught the second motorcyclist by surprise, but now he roared up on the side of the car opposite me and raked it efficiently with short bursts. Glass shattered and popped and bullets pinged into the metal skin of the car with a sound like bells gone mad. When the shooter's magazine was empty, a silence fell that was more terrible than the noise of the crash, worse even than the glass and metal of the Jaguar ripping open in a storm of bullets.

And in that silence I knew with absolute certainty the other shooter would be coming. He was in no hurry. He would not leave until he had examined each body to make certain we were all dead.

From near the rear of the car I heard the characteristic *clack-clack* of a magazine being replaced and I went prone as silently as I could, my arms extended out in front of me.

Twisting my hand to examine the pistol in it, I saw the safety was off and it was cocked. I said a silent thank you to whichever of the security men had been quick enough to get me at least that far before he died. The rest was up to me.

I took a deep breath, willed my fingers of my right hand to relax on the grip, and nestled the butt into the palm of my left hand for stability.

There was a sudden movement just in front of me followed by a crash. I almost fired, but I didn't. The shooter had thrown a hubcap out from behind the car and it had caught the rear tire and ricocheted off some rocks before rolling into the drainage ditch. Whoever he was, he was a professional and he was cautiously probing for any sign of survivors before he ventured closer to the wreckage.

A few moments later there was another sudden explosion of noise and a dozen jets of dirt shot into the air from the bank of the ditch behind me. The gunman was firing over the top of the car, still probing around for survivors.

I held my fire. I didn't move.

Move? I could barely breathe. I was damned near petrified with terror. I probably couldn't have moved if I had wanted to.

Then, all at once, there was a sudden flash of black right in front of me, like a dark curtain closing across the landscape.

It was the gunman, diving out from behind the car, tumbling toward the cover of the ditch.

Time seemed to slow for me. I always thought time slowing was just something that happened in the movies; but it isn't, and it did.

Somewhere inside my head I heard my old instructor speaking to me in calm, clear voice and I followed his directions. With the front sight of the .45, I tracked just ahead of the black mass. I raised the back sight until the blade nestled perfectly into the notch in the front sight. I squeezed the trigger, twice, in rapid succession.

The noise of the big .45 exploded all around me. I had no idea it would be so loud. The sound reached right down deep into my chest, grabbed me by the heart, and squeezed until I thought it would stop beating.

The gunman hit the ground with a thud that vibrated through

the earth all the way to where I lay a dozen feet away. For several long minutes after that he did not move. Nor did I.

When finally I started to crawl cautiously toward him, his black helmet lifted all at once and he twisted toward me.

I fired twice more.

The man's body shuddered with the impacts. The helmet bent unnaturally to one side and then fell back against the ground. He did not move again.

Keeping the .45 centered on the man's helmet, I reached out slowly with my free hand. When my fingers touched the curving magazine of his rifle, I wrapped them around it and jerked the gun away. His limp hand gave it up without a struggle and flopped against the ground.

Pulling myself around until I was half sitting and half leaning on my left hand, I put down the .45 and unsnapped the strap of the man's helmet. Then I slipped my hand underneath the visor and wrenched it off his head.

Blood was coming from the man's nose and one of his ears, but his eyes were frozen and open. The hard black pupils stared at me in death with the same emptiness they had stared at me in life.

I examined Marcus York's bloody face for a moment or two.

Then I passed out.

Forty Two

WHEN I OPENED my eyes the world looked dim and watery. It was as if I were diving and a long, long way beneath the surface.

I tried to move my head, but my neck muscles ignored me and nothing happened. Before long, I gave up. Using only my eyes, I scouted my surroundings as well as I could.

Everywhere I seemed to be looking through water. Down at the far edge of my vision I could see bits of what appeared to be yellow seaweed streaming upward from the sea bottom, long slender tentacles of plant life waved gracefully in the unseen currents like those Nebraska wheat fields they show on television when they play "America the Beautiful" before a football game. I could hear nothing at all except for a slight rushing in my ears. That seemed more or less consistent with being underwater, too, so cautiously I focused my consciousness on my chest and took stock of how the breathing process was going for me.

My lungs seemed to be working just fine. I could feel my chest rising and falling as they went about their work of pumping the air reliably in and out with what seemed to be their usual efficiency. Still, I thought they might be doing it somewhat more slowly than they had before…

Before?

Before *what?*

I couldn't remember.

All of a sudden a face loomed in front of mine, a woman's face, watery and wavering, but still real and so close I could touch her. I tried to touch her, but my arm muscles were working no better than my neck muscles had been and I couldn't.

Anita? I called out to the face. *Is that you, Anita?* But the face didn't answer.

Of course, it had to be Anita, but…

I fought my hazy memory, skirmishing with it in slow motion, and I felt myself moving toward something. I willed my eyes to focus on the face. I struggled to capture a clear image of it, one that I could lay next to the picture of Anita's face that I carried always in my mind.

I could not do it. The face started to move away.

Wait! I shouted. *Come back!*

But the face slid beyond the edge of my vision and disappeared.

I thought about it for a moment and then I realized that I should hardly be surprised.

She couldn't hear you, I told myself. *You can't shout underwater.*

Underwater?

There it was again. The only idea I seemed to be able to grasp clearly. The only thought I could hold onto. I was underwater and yet I was still breathing just as if I were on dry land.

Abruptly there was a flash of motion off in the corner of my vision and I had a sensation of a brilliant golden light being born. Emergent and intensifying, it seemed to be pushing straight toward me. Frantically, I twisted my eyes as far as I could, searching desperately for the source. I found it and focused on it, and saw a fish coming directly toward me. A giant goldfish.

A fish? A goldfish?

Ah, shit, I thought, *you're not underwater.*

You're dead, man.

You're dead and you've gone to the place where people go when they die, and this is it.

But I was so tired, I could only hold a single thought clearly. And it was this.

If that were true, if I *was* dead, then there was nothing I could do about it anyway.

So I closed my eyes and waited for whatever came next.

THE NEXT TIME I woke up and opened my eyes, the world looked different. A lot different.

I was in a darkened hospital room and in the gray dimness a faint glow of artificial light came from somewhere. This time when I tried to move, I found my neck muscles worked pretty well. I rolled my head in the direction of the light, then waited for my eyes to focus.

When they did I found myself looking into a softly lighted aquarium with tiny plantings of yellow sea grass lining its sandy bottom. I could hear the aquarium's air pump humming in the background and a goldfish that seemed to me to be the size of a housecat was bumping against the glass side of the tank.

"Are you awake, Jack?" The woman's voice came from the other side of my bed, the one opposite the aquarium. "Can you hear me?"

Slowly I rolled my head back. The woman had a nice face, but it was not Anita's face. An Asian face instead. Dark hair, dark eyes, and skin that made me think of looking into a cup of *café au lait*.

At first I couldn't put a name to the face, although I was sure I knew it. I swam upward through memory, groping for it.

Then I could put a name to it.

Kate.

It was Kate's face.

"Where am I?" I asked her.

"The hospital," she said. "You've been shot, but you'll be fine."

I kept gazing at Kate's face.

"What are you staring at?" she eventually asked.

"You look so Thai, but you sound…so English."

Kate laughed and it was a lovely laugh, throaty and warm. "Does that bother you?" she asked.

"No," I said. "I was only thinking that…well, thank God it's not the other way around."

Kate thought about that for a second and then started laughing again, this time sticking her tongue into the corner of her mouth in mock disapproval. "I gather your sense of humor has survived pretty much intact," she said.

I started to say something smooth and witty, then all at once everything that had happened to me came back. In a single fast-forwarding rush, it all came back.

"How long have I been out?" I asked.

"A little over twelve hours," Kate said. "We were worried about you there for a while."

"It was just a scratch on the cheek," I said.

"Hardly," Kate said. "You were shot twice. Once in the left side just below your heart and once in the left arm. The arm was only a flesh wound, but the other shot did some damage. You lost a lot of blood. You might have bled to death if we hadn't found you when we did."

I tried to take all that in, but I couldn't get my arms around it. It didn't really make any sense to me.

"It was just a scratch," I repeated doggedly.

"As soon as you came in, they got the bleeding stopped and the bullet out of your abdomen. I know the surgeon. He's a good man and he says there is no major damage to any organs."

"I don't remember anything like that."

"When you feel like it, I'd very much like to hear what you *do* remember."

I took a deep breath, pushed hard against the bottom, and rose all the way up until I broke through the surface.

"Now is okay," I said.

Forty Three

I THOUGHT FOR a moment and did my best to clear my head. Then I told Kate about the motorcycle pulling in front of us and the other bike coming up from behind. I told her about the Jaguar jerking forward and smashing over the first gunman, and I told her about killing the second shooter with the .45 before I passed out. Something told me not to mention pulling off the man's helmet and recognizing Marcus York's face, at least not quite yet, so I left that part out.

"Where did you learn to shoot like that?" Kate asked.

"I used to play tennis with some DEA agents in Washington. They took me to ranges sometimes. Just screwing around. They said I had a knack for it."

A short silence fell after that. I was pretty badly muddled, but I was lucid enough to probe Kate gently, just to see where it might go.

"Who were those guys anyway?" I asked her.

"We don't know yet. No ID on either of them, of course. They might have been local hitters, but probably not. More than likely imported. Malaysian, would be my guess."

"Why would you think that?"

"Well...they looked more Malaysian than Thai to me, but I'm just guessing."

That stopped me.

"You saw the bodies?" I asked.

"Yes."

"And they were both Asians?"

"That's right. So if you're wondering whether the marshals had anything to do with this, I think the answer is no. I doubt they would have trusted a couple of local hired guns."

There was no way in hell Kate could have mistaken Marcus York for a Malaysian. If she was telling me the truth, somebody removed York's body and substituted another one before she got there. On the other hand, maybe Kate was lying to me. Maybe she *had* seen York's corpse and she thought I hadn't, so she didn't want me to know.

I tried to work out where each of those possibilities left me, but I couldn't. Before I could even decide whether or not to tell Kate the truth, to tell her I already knew who was behind the attack, she changed the subject

"Is there anybody you'd like me to call for you, Jack? To tell them you're going to be all right?'

"Yes," I said automatically, "Anita will be worried if she hears…"

But then all that came back to me, too, and I trailed off.

"No," I said. "No one."

The finality of it caused me to groan audibly. I turned my head away and Kate leaned closer.

"Shall I get a nurse?'

"No," I said, "just give me a minute."

I felt myself plunge into a cavern of coldness and my ears filled with sound that had no source. Kate moved slightly. The gray light in the room shifted and I caught a glimpse of the green luminous numerals of a clock face. My hands trembled against the bedsheets. Then, as abruptly as I had entered it, I was through the cavern and rising again into warmth. My hands stopped trembling and the sound in my ears faded away.

"What about the others?" I asked Kate.

"Dead," she said. "All of them."

I had known that already, of course.

"Has anyone told Karsarkis?" I asked. "About Mia, I mean."

"I sent people out there as soon as we found the wreck. The estate appeared to be secure, but the guards wouldn't let us in. There's been no reply to the message we left."

My eyes searched the room for the clock face I had glimpsed before. I found it on a table.

Just after one o'clock, it said. Was that afternoon? Or night? I struggled to work it out.

Night, I decided. It had to be night. It must be after one a.m.

"What are you doing here?" I asked Kate. "Where did you come from?"

"When Mia didn't arrive, I called her cell phone and there was no answer. We followed the road back to see if there had been an accident and we found you"

"Didn't arrive? What do you mean?"

"We were having lunch together at Amanpuri. You didn't know?"

"She told me she was having lunch with someone. She didn't say who."

Kate showed a half smile. "It was me," she said.

I lay quietly and turned my new discovery over in my mind. It didn't fit with anything else and I didn't know how to try to make it fit, so after a while I let it go.

"Who would want to kill Mia?" I asked.

Kate looked at me for a long time.

"What?" I asked.

"Why do you think they were after Mia?"

"Are you trying to tell me it was another mistake? Like Mike O'Connell. Another botched attempt on Karsarkis?"

"That's possible, I guess. Karsarkis' car. Mia on one side. A man on the other. Maybe they thought you were Karsarkis."

"Except I don't look anything like Karsarkis."

"Then maybe there's another explanation, Jack."

I looked sideways for a moment and then shifted my eyes back to Kate. Her face was professionally empty, but I had no doubt what she meant.

"You're shitting me," I said.

Kate shook her head.

"Jesus Christ," I said. "Why in God's name would they have been trying to kill *me*?"

"If you're working with Plato, there are people who assume you know what he knows."

"But I'm not working with Karsarkis."

"There're people who probably assume you are."

"And he hasn't told me anything."

"They would probably assume he had."

"And you think whoever is doing all of this goddamn assuming would send two goddamned gunmen to ambush Mia's car and kill everybody in it just to get me? Just in case I actually *do* know whatever it is I'm supposed to know?"

"You can put it together that way."

I stared at Kate. "Oh, man," I sighed, "You have *got* to be kidding me."

"I feel like I got you into this, Jack," Kate said.

I noticed Kate's voice had turned businesslike. So much, apparently, for the personal warmth part of our program.

"Until I figure out how to get you out of it, a team of my best people will be with you around the clock. You can trust them absolutely."

"With my life?"

"That's about the size of it."

"Gee, then I guess my worries are over."

"They can't get set up until morning, but I've got local police all around this hospital until then. Don't worry. We're not going to give them a second chance."

"Give *who* a second chance?"

Kate glanced briefly out the window, which there was very little point in doing since it was pitch black out there. Then she put her hand on my shoulder and gave it a little squeeze.

"I don't know. The truth is I just don't know for sure."

But of course *I* did. I knew. For sure.

"And you think the marshals had nothing to do with this?" I probed again.

"No."

This time I was watching Kate's eyes when she answered and I decided she believed what she was saying. She didn't know about Marcus York, I was certain of that now, but something still kept me from telling her.

"What about the email intercepts?" I asked, trying to make up my mind how to play it from there. "They had to mean something."

"I don't know what you're talking about, Jack."

"Kate, I'm talking about the email intercepts, those transcripts you gave me…"

"I never gave you anything."

I was a little slow-witted right then, I realized, but not *that* slow-witted.

"Okay," I said. "I see."

"I'm glad."

Kate may not have known specifically about Marcus York trying to kill me, but she knew there was something out there. She also knew it was something ugly and something neither of us understood. She wanted to get as far away from it as she possibly could. I could hardly say I blamed her.

"So," I said after mulling that over for a bit, "if I told anyone you had given me copies of the NIA email intercepts from the US

Marshals that implied they were actually here to kill Karsarkis rather than return him for trial…"

"I imagine most people would have a hard time believing that. Without copies of the intercepts, of course, which you don't have."

"Which I *do* have," I said.

Kate went completely still.

"You couldn't have gotten past the security routine in that file," she said after a moment.

"You're right," I said. "I couldn't have."

"I didn't think so."

"But I know people who could. Did, in fact."

Kate measured me with a long look. As she did, she bit unconsciously at her lip. One tooth made a little white mark there and I looked at it until it had faded away.

"All right," she said after a time had passed in silence. "So what are you going to do?"

I blew out a breath and popped my lips.

"Maybe I'll just go back to sleep," I said, "and think about everything again tomorrow."

"That's probably the best thing for you to do."

Kate smiled and started to turn away, but then to my surprise, and possibly to hers as well, she reached out and stroked my hair with the tips of her fingers. Her cool hand lingered on my forehead as she might let it linger on the face of an injured child. I could see a thought come into her eyes like a dark bird, stay a moment, and then fly away.

"I'll be back in the morning," she said after a moment or two had passed that way.

I was about to say something in reply, something that would tell Kate how happy I was she was there right then and that she would be coming back, but before the thought could shape itself into words, the drugs took me and I was gone.

Forty Four

WHEN I WOKE again Kate was gone. All the lights in my hospital room were off. Even the glow of the aquarium had been extinguished by some thoughtful soul who must have feared it would disturb my sleep.

My eyes searched the room for the clock. They did not find the clock, but what they did find made me lose all interest in the time.

Plato Karsarkis was sitting on a chair at the end of my bed. He was wearing jeans, a black golf shirt, and black loafers without socks. One leg was draped casually over an arm of the chair and he was facing away from me as if he was studying the heavy draperies that covered the windows.

"What are you doing here?" I asked.

Karsarkis tilted his head back and turned it toward me without moving his body.

"I would think first you'd want to know how I got in. Your girlfriend is supposed to have this place locked down tighter than a gnat's asshole."

I let Karsarkis' characterization of Kate pass. I was hardly in any state to engage in a pointless debate.

"Apparently not," I said instead. "I gather you walked right in."

"Ah, well…" Karsarkis made a little movement with his hands he probably thought was self-deprecating. "People like me do pretty much what we want to do. You said as much once yourself, didn't you?"

I didn't take the bait.

"So," I repeated instead, "what *are* you doing here?"

"I wanted to tell you I'm sorry for what's happened. I wish now I hadn't gotten you involved in this."

"Mia's the one who's dead," I said, "not me."

"Yes, well…"

Karsarkis swung his legs to floor and pushed himself out of the chair. Its springs squeaked in the stillness. He took a few steps toward me and put both hands on the rail at the foot of my bed.

"Now we've both lost people we loved," he said.

For a moment, I didn't see what Karsarkis was talking about, then Anita's face faded into my consciousness like a transparency projected on a screen.

I said, "It's not the same thing."

"It is, in a way," Karsarkis said. "There are all kinds of losses."

"Your wife was cut to pieces by rifle fire and left to bleed to death. Mine just found somebody she liked better."

"Either way there was no way for either of us to avoid the final outcome," Karsarkis said. "How such things happen is less important than that they have."

"Do you ever think about anything except yourself?"

"Actually, I was thinking mostly about you, Jack. About what you've lost."

"I'll bet you were."

Karsarkis took a deep breath and glanced away, but when he looked back at me his face showed such weariness and resignation that for a moment I was almost embarrassed at the way I was treating him.

"You're right, of course," he said. "It's just…well, I guess we all have our own ways of dealing with things."

"Some of which aren't very attractive," I said.

Karsarkis nodded slightly as if he hardly cared one way or the other, then he folded his arms and stood silently for a while, looking at the wall over my head.

"First Mike O'Connell, then Mia," I said. "They're getting closer."

"They are, aren't they?"

"You know who it is." I didn't bother to make a question out of it. There was no reason to.

Karsarkis seemed to weigh the idea for a while as if he were genuinely considering its nuances and implications.

"Yes," he finally nodded. "I do."

"Why didn't you just tell me at the beginning?"

"I assumed it would scare you off, that you wouldn't be willing to help me if you knew."

He had me there. He was probably right.

"Some very bad things have happened, Jack. Some things no one wants anyone to know about, ever. Your country has a greater interest in keeping them buried than anyone."

"My country? Not your country?"

To that, Karsarkis offered the smallest smile I had ever seen.

"I don't have a country," he said.

"Maybe you should get one. A little loyalty to something might be just the ticket for you."

"Oh, I had a country once, and I was loyal as hell. I risked everything for it. Then they fucked me. Flat out fucked me. That's why I don't have one anymore."

I remained silent, waiting for the rest of it. I did not have to wait very long.

"They came to *me*, Jack. They came to me and asked me to do a dirty job because they thought I was a hard enough man to do it. There are always a lot of those jobs around, but most of them go begging because there aren't a hell of a lot of people to do them. I agreed, of course. Agreed without conditions. My adopted country was asking for my help. And besides, I thought it was *right*."

"Agreed to do what?"

"I put my ass right out there and risked everything," Karsarkis continued, ignoring my question. "I asked other people to do the same thing, and then the bastards walked away and left me twisting in the wind when they decided I didn't matter any longer. I learned a real lesson there, I did. I could teach a course on loyalty. Maybe I could lecture to some of your classes on the subject. What do you think?"

A minute or two passed in silence after Karsarkis' outburst. I studied the pattern in the vinyl upholstery on the chair at the foot of my bed. It wasn't a very interesting pattern.

"You still haven't told me why you're here," I said after a while. "I don't believe you came just to say how sorry you are that you got me involved."

Karsarkis straightened slightly, shifting his weight back onto his heels.

"No," he said, "you're right. I didn't."

Karsarkis unfolded his arms, then folded them back again and fixed his eyes on mine.

"I'm leaving Thailand."

"When?"

"This morning." Karsarkis glanced at his watch. "I have a plane waiting at the airport," he said. "I'll be gone in an hour."

"To where?"

"Paris."

"Paris? Why Paris?"

Karsarkis shrugged slightly. "At least maybe I can get a decent meal before they shoot me."

Abruptly Karsarkis turned away and strode to the windows.

Putting his hands on the drapes he paused and then, as if in an afterthought, he glanced back at me.

"Do you mind?" he asked.

I shook my head. He pushed the drapes open and shoved them as far apart as they would go.

It was almost sunrise. I could see the faded disk of a three-quarter moon fighting an unpromising battle against the rising light. Moisture glowing with an otherworldly intensity ringed the moon in a halo. I knew Phuket would be wet with rain before the morning was out.

"They're going to get me, Jack. The bastards can get anybody they want, even me. Once I thought I was bigger than they are. But I'm not. And they can."

Karsarkis spoke without turning around. He just kept staring out the window, his eyes seeing visions I could not even imagine.

"What are you going to do?" I asked.

When Karsarkis turned back toward me his face was perfectly still. Then he put both his hands in his pockets and tilted his head slightly to one side.

"An hour before I land in Paris, the press will be told where I am and what I'm about to do. Half the fucking television cameras in the world will show up to meet me. I'll walk off the plane and—"

"They'll grab you and turn you over to the FBI. Even the French don't have the balls to let you just wander around loose. You can't buy them like you did the Thais."

"Yes, I can," Karsarkis smiled tightly. "They just cost a lot more."

"What I'm trying to say," I began, "is that if you—"

"Look, it doesn't matter," Karsarkis interrupted. "The French Minister of Justice has agreed to let me have my say to the press when I arrive. He assumes I'm going to stick a big one up some American asses and the little froggie bastard is wetting himself waiting for that."

"And then what?"

"After that they can arrest me if they want to, but my guess is they won't bother. Not after I've already told everything I know."

"What *do* you know?"

"Ah, well. That's always the problem isn't it, Jack. Yes, *what* do I know indeed?"

I struggled to sit upright on the bed. The bandages pulled at my side and pinched my skin and I winced.

"You're right, of course," Karsarkis said when I was still again. "I didn't come here this morning just to tell you I was sorry. I came here for a far more important reason."

"Look, I'm not sure—"

"You are close to something very big, Jack. Closer than you know. Before I leave, I want to tell you what it is."

Well, here we are, I thought to myself.

Plato Karsarkis is about to tell me whatever it is that he knows, whatever it is that somebody wants to kill him for knowing.

I closed my eyes and tilted my head back against the pillow. I should have stopped Karsarkis right then without hearing anymore. I should have just told him to get the hell out and leave me alone and that would have been that.

But, of course, I didn't.

Sometimes the desire to know—just to *know*—turns into a feeling like the one you get when a beautiful woman catches your eye and doesn't look away. You see her, and you want her, and you know perfectly well that you shouldn't chase after her, that it will cost you, but you do it anyway. In the end, you chase after her anyway.

And then you pay for it, exactly the way you knew you would.

Forty Five

PLATO KARSARKIS STOOD quietly in front of the windows, his hands in his pockets. It seemed to me that he stood that way for a very long time. Finally he turned around and examined my small hospital room as if he were seeing it for the first time.

I said nothing. I just waited.

"Let's start at the beginning, Jack," Karsarkis said after a few moments passed like that. "Eventually maybe we'll even come to the end."

"It's your story," I shrugged, at least I shrugged as well as a guy lying in a hospital bed wrapped in bandages can shrug. "I'm hardly in any position to throw you out."

Karsarkis walked over to the couch and sat down, slouching back as if he was settling in comfortably for a long chat. Outside the windows, the dawn looked as if it was further away than I had thought it was a few minutes before, but probably that was only my imagination.

"About eight years ago, a man I knew very well…" Karsarkis paused and cleared his throat. "His name doesn't really matter. Anyway, I had just bought control of a Hong Kong company that had shipping interests in the South Pacific and he asked me to allow some American intelligence officers to operate a small freighter under the cover of this company. He told me its purpose was to supply some people in the region with whom the Americans had a covert relationship, and he readily admitted the supply process would include weapons. I didn't really understand what was going on, but I gathered it was a CIA operation and they probably wouldn't tell me the truth even if I asked. So I kept things simple. I agreed. I didn't ask for the truth."

"What were you getting out of it?"

"Ah, well…" Karsarkis laced his fingers behind his head and studied the ceiling with what seemed to me to be unnecessary care. "There was a matter of an SEC investigation and some claims of securities fraud—pure horseshit, you understand—and my friend promised they would be dealt with. But I would have been delighted to help my adopted country regardless, Jack. Absolutely delighted."

"Of course you would have."

Karsarkis looked at me, but he said nothing else.

"So the CIA used your shipping company as a commercial cover in return for killing off an SEC investigation of you," I said. "Am I supposed to be shocked? Maybe even morally outraged? I've heard worse."

"That was just the beginning, my friend. The thin end of the wedge. There was another favor after that, and then another and another."

"And more favors for you in return?"

"Naturally," Karsarkis nodded without any apparent embarrassment. "When I set up Icon and shifted our group operations to Luxembourg, they suggested I form an entirely separate division to work with them. Technically, it was only another Hong Kong trading company called Global Resources that was controlled by Icon, but it was a lot more than that in reality. You have no idea, Jack, how much of American intelligence operates through perfectly ordinary looking companies like Global Resources. They use commodity brokers, air freight forwarders, oil drillers, all sorts of companies."

"All part of the vast right-wing conspiracy, huh?"

"I doubt you have any understanding at all of the real scope of it, my friend. Any understanding at all."

Karsarkis drew a deep breath and stood up. He stretched slightly and walked over to my bed, resting his hands on the rail at its foot.

"I never knew the whole story. Only pieces here and there. Companies operating through Global Resources were used for secret construction projects, selling and shipping arms, money laundering, bribery, extortion, blackmail, disinformation, and plain old espionage. They acquired high-resistance steel and sold it to Pakistan for nuclear weapons research; they traded weapons for information with Abu Nidal; they built the Al Shifa chemical plant in the Sudan; they founded an executive jet service in Switzerland that made planes available to anyone anywhere with no questions asked. You get the idea, Jack. It was nothing less than the administrative apparatus of covert action on a grand scale. And it was all being done in my name."

"So you're saying …what? That you're really a spy?"

"No, nothing so grand. Or nearly so clear. I was…" Karsarkis stopped and thought, searching for the right word, "a facilitator. I used my commercial resources to facilitate various operations by American intelligence about which I knew very little."

"In return for what? A get-out-of-jail-free card from the SEC? An agreement by the IRS to look the other way? You played 'Let's Make a Deal' and ended up in over your head. That's about the size of it, isn't it?"

Karsarkis smiled, once again without the slightest appearance of any embarrassment.

"Let me tell you how the Iraqi oil sales worked," he said. "It's a good example of the way these things were usually done."

I said nothing.

"After the Vietnam War ended," Karsarkis continued, "America lost interest in Asia. Americans largely turned their back on half the world for nearly two decades. In the period just before the first Gulf War broke out, at least some Americans started to realize they might be in trouble because of that."

I listened, but still I said nothing.

"In the early nineties, I was told a significant quantity of crude oil was being smuggled out of Iraq in spite of the economic embargo. I was also told I could obtain access to this oil through a certain Jordanian intermediary and no objection would be raised by the Americans if I brokered this oil to a very specific list of companies. As it turned out, all of these companies were controlled by politicians in Thailand, Indonesia, and Malaysia."

"Why would anyone in the US want to help the Iraqis sell embargoed oil?"

"Just think about it, Jack. It was really a very clever play. The Americans knew the Iraqis were going to sell the oil anyway, so if they secretly helped do it, they would at least have some measure of control over how much got sold and where it went. They would even know how the Iraqis were being paid and could keep track of what they did with the money. Best of all, they could use the sale of the oil itself to funnel money to people in Asia who they wanted to influence, a part of the world where they needed some new friends. It was a sweet deal all around."

"For you, too, I imagine."

"Well…yes, it was. I wasn't doing all this for intellectual stimulation. I made money at it. That's the way business works."

"Did you make a lot of money?"

"Yes," Karsarkis said, "I made a lot of money."

His tone had an edge of challenge to it, but I didn't argue the point. If Karsarkis was telling the truth and if his oil sales had been officially sanctioned, then there wasn't very much of an argument to be made. Companies were in business to make money, weren't they?

I could hardly object to Karsarkis doing it, particularly if his deal carried the stamp of approval of the United States of America.

"That was when things started to go bad." Karsarkis looked at me and hesitated. "I was asked to take on Cynthia Kim," he said, "to give her cover as my assistant."

He paused again, but I made an impatient gesture and he went on.

"I was told she was involved in tracking the money the Iraqis received from the oil sales and I assumed Cynthia was CIA. But she wasn't CIA after all it turned out, and she had a rather more ambitious agenda than accounting for a little oil money. Eventually I found out Cynthia was sent to me straight from the White House."

"Are you saying you were in direct contact with the president?" I asked carefully.

"That was always implied, of course, but…well, if not directly with him, then with the boys in the basement. That's more or less the same thing."

"The boys in the basement?"

"The National Security Council. Their operations center is in the basement of the Executive Office Building next door to the White House. The President's staff calls them the boys in the basement. Very colorful, huh? Full of implications."

"But the NSC is just—"

"Yeah, that's what everybody else thinks, too. Nothing but a bunch of paper pushers and professors on leave." Karsarkis shot me a quick look. "No offense, Jack."

I ignored both Karsarkis' insult and his apology. "Maybe I'm really not with you here. The NSC doesn't handle covert operations."

"Really?"

Karsarkis seemed amused.

"You mean covert operations like the guns for hostages deal with Iran Ollie North ran out of the Reagan White House? Or maybe you mean covert operations like the hit squads the NSC funded in Nicaragua to murder the left-wing priests and other threats to their friends there. Or maybe, if you want an example a little closer to home, you mean covert operations like using the Asian Bank of Commerce for large-scale money laundering and then murdering people to cover it up when Jack Shepherd discovered what was going on and—"

"Okay," I interrupted, "you've made your point."

"Good."

I sighed and waved to Karsarkis to continue.

"Cynthia's mission was focused on Indonesia," he said. "Indonesia is the fourth largest country in the world and it has the largest Muslim population on earth. Historically, Southeast Asian Muslims have been far more moderate than Arab Muslims, but that was changing, partly because of a determined effort by Arab Muslims to create instability there and partly because of the homegrown efforts of some Indonesians. The country seemed ripe to blow. If it did, Afghanistan would look like the good old days."

"I don't see anything odd about the NSC being interested in Indonesia. That's what they do. They track hot spots and advise the president on how to respond before a full-blown crisis develops."

Karsarkis leaned back and crossed his legs at the knee. He seemed to think for a moment about what I said, but I doubted that. My guess was that he was thinking about something else altogether, something I probably could never even begin to imagine.

Forty Six

"CYNTHIA'S JOB WAS to build a close relationship with a group of presumably moderate Indonesian Muslims," he said. "The idea was to cultivate a manageable force as buffer between the military and the worst of the Islamic radicals."

"That sounds familiar."

"Yes, it does, doesn't it? It's the formula you Americans always use, and it just keeps blowing up in your faces. Good God, you can see the same thing happening over and over. Americans try to make friends with some revolutionary movement that seems less dangerous than the rest of them, starts supplying resources, even weapons, then eventually these people turn the very weapons you gave them against you and the cycle starts all over again with someone new."

Karsarkis uncrossed his legs and leaned toward me.

"Cynthia was in contact with an Indonesian known to her as Jabir. He convinced her if his group was to maintain its credibility with Indonesian Muslims, it had to show the ability and the will to engage in violence. Eventually Cynthia bought the argument—actually, it did make sense—and agreed to provide weapons as well as some explosives and detonators to Jabir. I agreed to allow her to use ships owned by Icon to do it. For his part, Jabir promised he would only engage in small operations that caused limited damage, undertaking them just for the effect of it but…" Karsarkis rolled his shoulders in a sort of shrug, "things didn't work out quite that way."

"What happened?"

"Some of the explosives we delivered to him were used for the Christmas Eve bombing campaign in 2000. Thirty Christian churches in Indonesia were bombed almost simultaneously, but most of the devices were so badly made they only managed to kill about a dozen people. Some more of the stuff turned up in Singapore five years later when the Singaporeans broke up a plot to bomb the American and Australian embassies there."

"And the rest of it?" I asked. "What happened to the rest of it?"

I thought I could guess where this was going, but I hoped I was wrong.

"Yes, well…" Karsarkis looked away.

"Bali?" I asked.

Karsarkis nodded slowly. "When the bombings took place in Bali, some of the explosives and one of the detonators were traced back to the original lot Cynthia acquired for Jabir, the stuff Icon delivered to him."

"Oh, Christ," I said, shaking my head slowly. "And Jabir? What happened to him?"

"I don't know. He just faded away. Maybe we were manipulated from the beginning. Maybe he never even existed." Karsarkis spoke so softly I had to strain to hear him. "Nearly two hundred people dead, most of them Australian kids, and the stuff that killed them traceable to an NSC operation gone wrong and a man who may never have existed."

"And you, of course. Those explosives were also traceable to you."

"Yes," Karsarkis nodded. "With your usual quickness, Jack, you seem to have grasped the first part of my problem."

"Was that when they indicted you for the oil sales?"

"It was a neat move, I have to admit. Painting me as a traitor for selling embargoed Iraqi oil pretty well gutted any claim I might make that I'd been nothing but a delivery boy for the NSC in Indonesia. Cynthia was the only person who knew the truth of it, at least the only person I had any contact with who knew, and she had always been straight with me. Without her, the NSC could pin the weapons and explosives shipped to Indonesia solely on me whenever they wanted to."

"And Cynthia was dead."

"I see you have now grasped the second part of my problem. Cynthia would have told the truth," he said. "Cynthia would have saved me."

At first, what Karsarkis was saying came to me only fleetingly, like a sudden draft through an empty room. Then suddenly I understood it all. The truth broke over me like a cold ocean wave.

"You're saying someone working for the NSC killed Cynthia Kim?"

"Yes."

"They killed her because she knew the NSC was behind the shipments, not you?"

"Yes."

"They killed her because she was going to testify to that?"

"Yes."

"And then they killed Mike and Mia, and they tried to kill me to warn you to keep your mouth shut?"

"The others, yes. But I'm not sure about you. Maybe it was just a coincidence you were in the car with Mia that day."

Karsarkis looked like he was about to say something else, but instead he walked back over to the green vinyl chair where he had been sitting when I first saw him. His back was to me and I couldn't see what he was doing, but when he turned around again he was holding a white, letter-sized envelope. He gave me a half-smile, rueful and cheerless, and tossed it onto my bed.

"Fortunately for me, however, all is not entirely lost."

I eyed the envelope. It wasn't flat like it would have been if it had folded paper in it. It was slightly lumpy.

"After the Bali bombing there was a panicked debriefing of Cynthia by some NSA and White House people," he said. "They conducted the debriefing in Singapore. Because they didn't want Cynthia anywhere near the embassy, they used the Four Seasons Hotel for it, but they were in such a hurry they ignored even the most basic security precautions."

Karsarkis looked at me as if he wondered whether I caught the importance of that. I said nothing.

"Cynthia was scared," he went on. "She wasn't sure whether they would try to hang Bali on me or on her, but she knew damned well they weren't going to let it be tied back to the White House. She asked me to arrange to bug the suite at the Four Seasons where the debriefing took place. Mike took care of it. Cynthia's questioners never suspected a thing."

I glanced at the envelope again. I had no doubt now what was in it.

"I have the original tapes myself, and those…" Karsarkis inclined his head toward the white envelope, "are the only copies."

"What's on them?"

"Two NSC people and a very senior White House official discussing damage limitation with respect to the Bali bombing. They wanted to make sure there was no way to connect it to their screwed-up operation."

Karsarkis watched me with a slight smile when he said that and I felt the pieces of his story beginning to come together in my mind.

"A senior White House official?"

"Uh-huh," Karsarkis said, his expression neutral.

"That wouldn't happen to be anyone I know, would it?"

"It's a funny old world sometimes, Jack."

Things that never made any sense before were beginning to click together like pieces of an animated jigsaw puzzle that had all of a sudden lurched into motion and started to assemble itself.

"Does the NSC know about the tapes?"

"When the rumors started about Cynthia testifying for me, they guessed we had something, but they couldn't be sure what it was."

"This was behind the pardon all the time, wasn't it?" I watched Karsarkis carefully. "If I had gone to the White House with a pardon application, they would have known you really *did* have something."

"Yes, I think they would have looked at it that way."

"Even you wouldn't have had the balls to ask for a pardon if you didn't have something pretty good to trade for it."

"As always, Jack, you seem to have cut straight to the heart of things."

"And that was why you needed me all along. I have a personal connection to the man whose voice is on these tapes. You wanted me to blackmail him, to blackmail the White House. That was how you intended to get your pardon."

"Yes, that's all true."

"You used me."

"Of course. What are friends for?"

I couldn't look at Karsarkis any longer, so I let my head fall back against the pillow and stared at the ceiling.

"It was all just a game of pin the tail on the donkey," I said after a while. "And I was the goddamned ass."

After that, neither one of us said anything else for what felt like a very long time.

"They might still get to you," I said after a while, breaking the silence.

"I doubt it. After I spill everything in Paris, I'll have too much light on me. They won't dare touch me then."

"And if you're wrong, or you don't make it to Paris?"

"That's the reason I came here this morning, Jack. That's why I'm leaving the copies of the tapes with you."

"Now wait a minute, if you think—"

"I commit the truth into your hands, Jack. If they get me, you will be the only one left alive who knows what really happened. Be careful what you do with that knowledge."

Karsarkis let his eyes linger on me for a moment and then he walked around from the foot of the bed and extended his right hand. Automatically I took it and we shook, but even as we did I wondered why I was shaking hands with this man.

"What do you expect me to do?" I asked.

"I really don't know, Jack. I don't know what I would do if I were in your place."

Karsarkis raised a hand to his forehead in a mock salute. "Regardless, I'm off now. Wish me luck."

Then, with a half-dozen strides, Karsarkis crossed the room and disappeared through the door. It swung shut behind him and closed with a snap that sounded harsh and final.

THROUGH THE WINDOWS I watched the palm fronds lift and churn in a rising wind. A carpet of trees stretched to where the dim edge of the Andaman Sea lay like a smudge on the far horizon. The sky was strung with rain clouds and the dawn mushroomed through them. The horizon was etched into the sky with a pure white light as finely grained as bone.

I picked up the envelope and I held it for a long time. Now that I knew what was in it, I could feel the tapes. Three microcassettes lying in a neat row.

After a while I pushed a finger under the flap and tore the envelope open. I dumped the cassettes out into my palm. They didn't look like much. Just three ordinary Sony microcassettes with silver and red labels. No other markings. None at all.

Perhaps there was nothing on them, I mused, wishing for just a moment that would turn out to be true. But I knew it wasn't going to be that easy.

There was a drawer in my bedside table, and I opened it and dumped the cassettes inside. Maybe, I thought, someone would save me a lot of trouble and just steal them.

Forty Seven

IT WAS NOT long after Karsarkis left before the drugs took me again. This time I fell into a sleep so fitful and shallow that I drifted in and out of it with every blink. I dreamed in disconnected bursts, like a man flipping through cable television channels with which he was unfamiliar.

Around nine a young girl in a nurse's uniform woke me with a cup of very weak tea. Smiling, she pointed to a plastic tumbler of water on the table next to my bed, placed a small paper cup half full of pills next to it, and then slipped quietly out of my room. I sipped the tea and swallowed the pills and looked out the window.

For a while I wondered if my early morning conversation with Plato Karsarkis had been just another episode in my parade of pharmaceutically enhanced visions, or if it was something that had actually happened. Then I put my hand on the drawer in my bedside table and pulled it open. The three microcassettes with the silver and red labels lay inside exactly where I had put them. That seemed to settle that.

I leaned back against the pillows and was thinking about what Karsarkis had told me when I felt rather than heard the door to my room opening.

"Man, you look like you been rode hard and put up wet," CW

bellowed. He walked over to the bed and patted me awkwardly on the shoulder. "How you feelin'?"

"Fine," I replied automatically, then thought about it. "Actually, I feel like shit to tell you the truth."

CW nodded slowly as if he was thinking about that, then suddenly he thrust a hand toward me and held out a stack of magazines. "This was all they had downstairs," he said. "Couldn't find a Playboy."

Taking the stack from him, I put it down on my bedside table.

"Who is Marcus York?" I asked him.

My question caught CW off balance and he tried for a moment to look vague, but he was the worst actor I've ever seen, except of course for Sylvester Stallone.

"What do you mean?" he finally mumbled when I said nothing to take him off the hook.

"It's a simple enough question. Who the hell is Marcus York? And don't bother claiming that he's a United States marshal. We're way past that now."

CW hitched up his pants and coughed unnecessarily, then he threw me a baleful stare. "He's one sorry-assed motherfucker who thinks he's slicker 'en owl shit."

"But *whose* sorry-assed motherfucker, exactly, is he?"

CW looked down and kicked at the floor with the toe of his boot like he was playing with gravel in the dirt.

"You may not believe me, Slick, but I got no goddamned idea. None. When this operation started, they told me I had to take this sorry sack of shit along and give him cover as a marshal. The bastard might be…"

CW stopped talking and his head bobbed around as if it had momentarily become detached from his shoulders.

"What?"

"Maybe CIA," CW said. "I just don't know."

"It was York's email the NIA gave me, wasn't it?"

CW consulted a spot on the floor. "Yeah, I think it probably was."

"Do you know where York is now?"

CW said nothing.

"You don't know what's happened to him?"

"I got no idea."

"I do," I said.

That got CW's attention. "You do?"

"Yeah," I said, "I killed him."

"What the fuck you talking about?"

"He was one of the two hitters who attacked the car. York was the one I shot."

"Ah, stop pulling my pecker, Slick." CW cocked his head at me and I saw something like a half-smile on his face. "I saw those two myself. They was just local boys. Shit, I thought you were serious there for a minute."

"I *was* serious. I pulled the helmet off the man I shot and I saw his face. It was Marcus York. There's no doubt about it. Somebody switched the bodies."

CW opened and closed his mouth. He looked as if he was experiencing a change of cabin pressure in an airplane. But he didn't say anything.

It started to rain just then. CW and I watched in silence as fat drops slapped against the windows, joined together into little streams, and ran down the glass. Even from inside the room I felt like I could smell the dense aroma of wet trees and damp earth that always accompanied rainfall in the tropics. I remembered the ring I'd seen around the moon at dawn and I wondered how long the rain would last.

When the door from the hallway opened again, CW and I looked around at the same time. Kate took a step into the room and stopped. She obviously knew CW and she didn't seem particularly happy to find him in my hospital room.

But then I caught something else in her expression, too, and I knew she had something to tell me, something that was about to change everything.

I raised my eyebrows, waiting.

"He's dead," she said.

I said nothing. I didn't even need to ask Kate who she was talking about.

"He was leaving Phuket this morning," she went on. "His plane exploded just after takeoff."

While I thought about that, CW walked over to the windows and peered out as if he might be able to see the crash site just by looking hard enough through the rain.

"Now ain't that a hell of a thing?" he said after a few moments, his voice subdued.

After a few moments of silence, I pushed myself into a sitting position and swung my feet over the side of the bed.

"What do you think you're doing?" Kate asked.

"I want to have a look at the crash site."

"What on earth for, Jack?"

"I don't see why I have to have a reason."

"They just took two bullets out of you. You can't go anywhere."

"How are you planning on stopping me?" I asked.

I stood up and started toward the closet, my hospital gown flapping open over my bare ass. As my feet hit the floor, each impact traveled straight to the stitches in my side. I tried not to wince.

"I could always steal your pants," Kate smiled.

"You could."

"But that isn't really necessary."

When I opened the closet, I saw what Kate meant. It was completely empty.

"Would somebody get me some goddamned clothes?" I asked.

Kate said nothing. She just looked at me.

"Please?" I asked.

"Are you sure about this?" Kate asked.

"Absolutely sure," I said.

A few minutes later I was wearing a blue scrub suit and a dirty pair of green flip-flops Kate had scrounged from somewhere. We were all out in the hallway before I remembered the cassette tapes lying in the drawer in my bedside table. My previous desire to have someone steal them had evaporated.

"Wait a minute," I said. "I forgot my watch."

Back in the room I walked around the bed and opened the drawer in the sidetable. I stood for a moment, looking down at the three cassettes lying there, willing them to speak or move or do some damn thing, but of course they didn't. They just lay there.

The scrub suit had two deep pockets and I scooped up the cassettes and shoved them down into the left-hand one. Then I slipped on my watch, buckled the band, and walked out to where CW and Kate were waiting for me in the hallway.

Forty Eight

IF YOU HAVE never been at the scene of a plane crash, I can tell you now your first encounter with one will be the most horrifying and unsettling experience of your lifetime.

The world never lacks for terrible images: a subway car reduced to a smoking skeleton by a suicide bomber; bodies piled one on another in a shallow ditch alongside a nameless road; the rubble of a village bombed into oblivion by mistake, or perhaps on purpose. Still, there is some particular revulsion that comes with contemplating the destruction brought about by a plane crash. Perhaps it is because the impact is always so violent; perhaps it is because the bodies of the human beings who were on the aircraft are so grotesquely mutilated; or perhaps it is just because the dead are so easy for us to identify with.

People who die in plane crashes are generally healthy and prosperous people with no notion their lives are about to end in sudden terror. When the corpses are found, they have usually been torn to pieces by the massive impact and the body parts scattered over the ground with the most mundane sort of litter: books, newspapers, bits of fabric, pieces of wire, and shoes. There are always so many shoes. It always adds up to the same picture. Right up until the moment of impact, these were people very much like us, people living altogether normal lives, lives not unlike our own.

It may be the smell that gets to you first rather than the sight. The combination of burning jet fuel, melted plastic, singed fabric, and charred flesh is like nothing else you have ever smelled. Or it may be a recognizable piece of the aircraft or even the sight of pieces of human bodies that causes your stomach to begin churning, but churn it will. You will feel dizzy and faint, and you will fight back nausea. I know all this is true for the simplest of reasons: that was exactly how it was for me when we reached the wreckage of Plato Karsarkis' plane.

It had stopped raining and the morning had turned bright blue and nearly cloudless. Kate took barely twenty minutes to race north on the main road from the hospital to the airport. We were opposite the east end of Phuket's only runway when I spoke the first words any of us had spoken since we got into Kate's car.

"Where the hell is it?" I asked, looking around at a scene that appeared so utterly normal it was almost disconcerting.

Kate pointed vaguely ahead of us and continued driving north. CW was in the back and he leaned forward, pushing his head up between our seats. "What kind of plane was it?"

"Plato had a Gulfstream in Bangkok," Kate said. "His pilots brought it to Phuket to pick him up."

There it was again, I thought to myself. Not Karsarkis. Not even Plato Karsarkis. Kate referred to him simply as Plato. It probably meant nothing, but I noticed it nevertheless.

"He boarded and the plane took off to the east, over the island," Kate continued. "There was an explosion of some kind."

"Were there any survivors?" I asked.

Kate glanced briefly at me without expression.

We continued northward on what I knew was the main highway leading to the twin bridges that were Phuket's only connection to the mainland. Just where the highway made a sharp bend to the west, I saw a large sign set in the median strip between the lanes. In white lettering on a blue background, it said, *Have a Nice Trip!*

Kate pulled out her mobile phone and pushed at a button. The conversation was short and I missed what she said, but right after that she slowed the car and turned off at an open wooden shed that was painted bright green. We bumped over a rough dirt track in the general direction of the airport, but I still saw no sign of anything unusual. No fire, no smoke. There was no noise either. The world around us seemed almost unnaturally quiet.

We came to a junction where the track we were driving on intersected another, but there was a closed gate to our left so clearly no one had gone that way. People racing to the site of an airplane crash do not stop to close gates behind themselves. Kate paused briefly, but then she continued straight on.

After another mile or two, I saw it.

Off to our left a grove of rubber trees was hacked and mangled as if a giant lawnmower had sliced through them. Chunks of metal, brightly-colored wiring, scattered papers, pieces of cloth, and lumps of beige plastic were everywhere.

Kate pulled the car to the side of the road. The blue pickup truck and the clutch of motorcycles parked there looked as if they had been abandoned in haste. We all got out without saying a word.

There was a scar through the trees about five hundred yards long and at least thirty or forty yards across. It ran away from the road and between two low hills, bisecting a narrow gully that still had a shallow layer of water in the bottom from the morning rain. On the other side of the gully the trees were more severely hacked and the concentration of debris was greater.

All along the scar a gruesome mixture of wreckage and human remains coated the landscape. Apart from the plane's engines that were indestructible masses of hardened steel, there were few pieces of wreckage of any size at all. But worse by far was what I could plainly see entangled in the orange life jackets, fragments of metal, and endless loops of colored wire. Half-buried here and there in the sandy ground, even hanging from the limbs of trees, were what had unmistakably once been parts of human beings.

There were a half-dozen brown-uniformed police down near the main body of debris, but they seemed to be in shock and were hardly moving at all. Two other men in short-sleeved white shirts and nondescript dark pants appeared from somewhere and Kate walked over to meet them. The three of them stood in a tight little knot, just out of earshot, and they murmured in low voices. Otherwise, the whole panorama was oddly silent.

When I could bear looking at the wreckage no more, I glanced away and looked down at my feet. A red toothbrush lay in the dirt just in front of my left foot. I hesitated a moment, then bent down and picked it up. It was an Oral B, the same brand I used.

"Goddamn, Slick," CW breathed out. "I ain't never seen nothing like this before in my whole fucking life."

I turned the red toothbrush over and over in my hands and nodded to CW. But I said nothing at all.

"It was Plato's Gulfstream," Kate said when she returned from talking to the two men. "No doubt about it. The explosion occurred while the aircraft was climbing away from the airport. It wasn't a big enough explosion to destroy the plane. Just big enough to cripple and crash it."

"Could it have been an accident?" I asked, knowing of course that it wasn't.

Kate glanced at me. "You don't think so and neither do I."

"I don't get it," CW said. "If somebody wanted to kill Karsarkis, why a small explosion? Why not just blast him right out of the sky?"

"My guess is they were trying to do just enough damage to make certain the plane went down more or less intact," Kate said. "Normally planes take off from Phuket out over the sea. That's deep water out there. If the plane went down there, and it went down intact, we would have never found any wreckage."

"But it didn't go down at sea," I said. "Because the pilot took off in the opposite direction."

Kate nodded.

"Why would anyone…" I started to ask, but then I trailed off.

I realized the answer was pretty obvious. The only reason somebody would want the wreckage intact and at the bottom of the sea was because they didn't want the wreckage found, and the reason they wouldn't want the wreckage found was they expected something to be *in* the wreckage that they didn't want found.

Kate had obviously figured it out, too. "What was Plato carrying, Jack?" she asked me right on cue. "What did he have with him that somebody wanted lost forever?"

"Got me," I shrugged.

Kate watched me, her face as flat as a dinner plate. "From the moment I walked into your hospital room and told you what happened," she said, "you never expressed the slightest surprise Plato was leaving Phuket today."

I thought about it, eyes half closed. "Okay," I said after a moment, "so I knew Karsarkis was leaving. He came to the hospital this morning and told me."

"Why did he do that?" Kate asked.

"He said he wanted me to know he was sorry he had gotten me into all this."

"Where was he going?"

"I don't know."

"You weren't curious enough to ask?"

"I wasn't."

Kate didn't even try to be polite about it. "I don't believe you, Jack."

"Hey, I understand," I said, spreading my hands in the universal gesture of innocence. "Sometimes I have a little trouble believing me, too."

Kate shook her head and looked away. We all fell silent.

"The American ambassador called the prime minister about the time the first reports of the crash came in," Kate said after a few moments. "How do you suppose he found out about it so fast?"

"Beats me," I said.

"He demanded the crash site be completely locked down until American personnel could get here. I figure in about another hour the FBI, the CIA, the Secret Service, the DEA, the military spooks, and God only knows who else will be crawling all over this place and carting away everything you see. After they're done, we probably won't even have to clean up."

"Probably not," I agreed.

"Jack, if there might be anything out there…" Kate waved her arms vaguely over the devastation, "anything at all that it might be better for us—or you—your fellow countrymen don't find when they take over the site, this is the only chance you're going to have to tell me about it."

"If I knew of anything like that, I would tell you, Kate, but I don't."

"Why don't I believe you?"

"Because you're a deeply cynical woman with a suspicious nature who is professionally paranoid about nearly everything?"

Kate said nothing. She just walked away, picking a cautious path forward through the field of wreckage. Not really knowing what else to do, CW and I followed.

After about twenty yards, Kate stopped and pointed at the mangled rubber trees lining both sides of the swath the dying aircraft had dug through the landscape. "When there is a crash right after take-off," she said, "there's generally a large fire because the plane is fully loaded with fuel."

I could see most of the rubber trees were scorched and blackened although not really burned. A number of them were still damp from the morning rain and looked to be wholly untouched.

"There was no fire here," Kate said. "Plato's Gulfstream would have had thirty thousand pounds of jet fuel in its tanks when it hit, but there was no fire."

She looked at me to see if I understood the significance of that.

"You're saying the impact was so great the fuel vaporized before it could catch fire," I said.

She nodded.

"Then the explosion was probably just large enough to shear off the tail section and cut the control cables," I said. "Most of the plane would have been left intact. Those poor bastards rode it all the way down, didn't they?"

"Yes," Kate said. "I think they did."

"Son of a bitch," CW muttered to himself.

The three of us continued to walk slowly south, picking our way through things I did not want to examine too closely. After another fifty or sixty yards, we reached what appeared to be the center of the horror.

"Do you know exactly who was on the plane?" I asked Kate.

"Just Plato," she said, "and two pilots and two cabin attendants. No one else we know of."

"But you are absolutely sure Plato Karsarkis was on this airplane?"

"Yes," Kate said. "We had the airport under surveillance. We watched him board, and we watched the plane take off."

"Some people aren't going to believe he's dead, you know."

"Maybe not, but he is."

"There's no doubt in your mind?"

"None at all. Whoever it was, they finally got him."

I nodded at that, but I didn't say anything.

One of the two men in short-sleeved white shirts caught up with

Kate again. He began to murmur into Kate's ear and she turned away from us, listening.

"What do you think, Slick?" CW asked me under his breath.

"I don't know."

"You figure it was foreign terrorists?"

"No."

"Than who the fuck was it?"

I took a deep breath. "I think it was you, C.W, or somebody a lot like you."

"Ah, shit, Slick, you couldn't really think…" CW trailed off. He took a couple of steps away from me and half turned his back. Then he just stood there, his hands jammed in his pockets, shaking his head.

The sightseers were already starting to gather. Men, women, and children had materialized through the trees from nearly every direction and the noise level was rising with each new group of arrivals. Some people picked through the debris looking for things of value, while others shoved and jostled to get a better look at the devastation.

I noticed a whole family pushing eagerly forward. There was a mother, a father, and two little children who couldn't have been more than four or five. The mother had one child, the father had the other, and they held both of them high above the crowd so the children could see as much of the horror as possible.

A few uniformed police moved around the debris making ineffectual efforts to keep sightseers away, but they were overwhelmed and disoriented men and they accomplished nothing. I watched one policeman climb into the lower branches of a badly mangled rubber tree about twenty yards away. He reached up above his head and began pushing with his hands, trying to dislodge something tangled there. Although it took me a few moments, I eventually realized the policeman was heaving at a headless human torso.

The torso had been wedged so tightly into the tree's branches that the policeman couldn't move it regardless of how hard he pushed. Shifting his weight slightly and holding the trunk with one hand, he reached up again and tried tugging at it instead.

Almost immediately the torso disintegrated. A flood of yellow fluid poured down over the policeman's head, followed by strips of gray flesh and coils of pinkish intestines.

The man slid backwards out of the tree, fell to his knees on the ground, and vomited down the front of his shirt.

FIVE MONTHS LATER

NEW YORK CITY
WASHINGTON, D.C.

"America was never innocent. We popped our cherry on the boat over and looked back with no regrets...It's time to embrace bad men and the price they paid to secretly define their time. Here's to them."

— James Ellroy,
American Tabloid

Forty Nine

THE FALL TERM at the university began in September, but it began without me. That was an arrangement agreeable all around. I didn't feel a great deal like teaching and the university didn't feel a great deal like employing a professor whose face had been in half the newspapers in the world after shooting a man to death during the murder of Plato Karsarkis' wife and her security guards.

As one might expect in Thailand the separation was accomplished with massive amounts of face-saving on all sides. I asked the university for a leave of absence based on a detailed account of the injuries I suffered in the attack in Phuket, and the university granted me a leave of absence based on its deeply sympathetic feelings for me and its sincere hope I would return to my post at an early date.

Both statements were, of course, utter crap. After the kind of publicity I'd had, a Thai university wouldn't have touched me with a rubber-insulated cattle prod. And for my part, the bullet wounds had healed completely within a few weeks following my return to Bangkok. It was the invisible wounds that caused all the pain after that.

I thought of Anita constantly: where she was now, and what she was doing. Over and over I summoned up a picture of her, and each time it opened in my mind like an image projected on memory. I would lean toward it, studying the detail, tracing its edges, looking for whatever it was I had not seen there before; but I could not find it. There was nothing that I had not seen there before. That was the part that really frightened me, of course. Even now, even knowing the truth of it now, I still could not see anything I had not seen there before.

It was not until after the school term had actually begun that I started to think about what I was going to do with myself. I had no classes to teach and perhaps I never would again, but at the very least I had none for a while. I had resigned all of my corporate directorships as well and the consulting work I sometimes did had dried up of its own accord. When people hire a lawyer for a matter that they need handled discreetly, on the whole they prefer to hire someone whose public profile is discreet as well. That pretty much ruled me out.

For what was probably the first time in my entire adult life I had no obligations at all. That was when I discovered something that a whole lot of other people no doubt already knew. When you find yourself at loose ends, you spend an inordinate amount of time thinking about lunch. I ended up reading a lot, which I didn't mind, but with Anita gone the apartment was still and depressing and I started spending more and more time every day trying to think of some place to go just to get out of it.

One night in early November, I was at home eating a tuna sandwich and watching CNN when I heard a report that Plato Karsarkis' daughter Zoe had died of leukemia in New York. On impulse, I had thrown a few things into a bag that very night, taken a cab to the airport the next morning, and flown to New York for her funeral.

Even now, I'm not sure exactly why I did that. Maybe it just seemed like a convenient excuse to spend some time under what might be a kinder sky. I could hardly claim I was doing it for Zoe. I had never even met her. And I sure as hell wasn't doing it for Plato Karsarkis.

The plain fact was that I had thought about Karsarkis as little as possible since his plane had smashed into that grove of rubber trees in Phuket, and I had not thought at all about what he had told me in my hospital room that morning before it happened. I hadn't listened to the tapes he had given me. Never even considered it. I had tucked all three of them away in a bottom drawer of my desk together with the transcripts of the email intercepts Kate had given me, and I had not taken them out or even thought about them since I had put them in there. I'm sure a psychiatrist could have come up with a term for how I had managed to bury the whole subject so completely, maybe even why, but I didn't much want to know what it was. I already knew far more than I wanted to know about far too many things.

Karsarkis had claimed that my old Georgetown roommate, Billy Redwine, now counsel to the president, was on those tapes. If he was, and if—as Karsarkis claimed—Billy's voice was recognizable talking to Cynthia Kim about components used in the Bali bombings having originated from a covert National Security Council operation, then the White House would be in very deep shit. At least it would be if the tapes ever became public.

I really had no doubt what Karsarkis had told me about the content of the tapes was true. That was precisely why he had wanted me as his point man in pitching for a pardon in the first place. Pardon applications were filed with the White House counsel's office. If I had filed Karsarkis' pardon application with Billy Redwine, he would have guessed immediately that Karsarkis had, as they say, an ace in the hole—and that his old Georgetown roommate was threatening him with what was nothing short of extortion.

The Thai Airlines flight left Bangkok at dinner time and took me nonstop to Los Angeles. I grabbed a shower and a few hours' sleep at a Hilton on Century Boulevard, then I took the hotel shuttle back to the airport and caught an early morning American Airlines flight to New York.

From thirty-five thousand feet the western half of the United States has always seemed lunar to me: unidentifiable rings that look like craters, ranges of mountains that appear impassable, and a latticework of thin white lines scratched into the reddish-brown earth. I drank black coffee and watched Nevada become Utah, and I thought about the people who two centuries before had worked their way westward over that very landscape on horseback or even on foot. If they had realized what they were getting into, if they could have seen the place whole from thirty-five thousand feet like I could now, I was willing to bet they would have said *to hell with this* and just stayed home.

But they couldn't see what they were getting into, of course, so they just kept going. Like the rest of us did when we were digging a hole for ourselves, they moved forward step by step, no single step seeming all that important, but the sum of all those steps propelling them into the heart of a wasteland so terrifying that surely they would have turned and fled if they could have seen it for what it really was.

I was still trying to decide what to make of that dazzling insight when jet lag took me and I fell into a deep if short-lived sleep.

Fifty

ZOE'S FUNERAL WAS at a Catholic church on Eighty-Third Street near Park. Predictably it drew a crowd of television and newspaper photographers, but there were actually fewer lenses poking at Zoe's small, rose-covered coffin than I had expected. I gathered, in death, Plato Karsarkis was already on the inevitable slide to becoming nothing more than yesterday's news. Another year and he would be in somebody's whatever-happened-to column.

Karsarkis' ex-wife, Zoe's mother, was both younger and more striking than I had expected. She was tall and very thin, and her blonde hair was twisted up into what I think women call a French braid. A black Chanel suit set off her pale skin and her blue eyes looked both warm and guarded at the same time.

When the brief ceremony ended, she stood and crossed herself, and then while we all waited respectfully in silence she left the church alone by the center aisle. Strangely, just as she passed me she turned her head slightly and caught my eye. Normally I would have looked away, but she didn't, so I didn't either.

For a moment it seemed almost as if she was going to stop and say something to me, although I couldn't imagine what it would be. She didn't stop, of course, but stranger still, she tilted her head slightly in my direction as she moved past and appeared to mouth something that looked to me exactly like *thank you*. Then she continued out of the church onto Eighty-Third Street. By the time I had made my own way outside, she was gone.

I had no idea at all what that could have been about, or even if I might have imagined the whole thing. No idea at all.

Back at the hotel that night I ordered a burger and a beer from room service and I watched Monday Night Football until I realized I didn't give a damn about American football anymore. After that, I went down to the bar mostly just to have something to do. Pleased to find the place nearly deserted, I took a stool and sipped a Bushmills and water in silence.

The television set at the end of the bar was tuned to New York One, a twenty-four-hour cable news channel that featured mostly local news. I didn't pay much attention to it until I happened to glance up and see the church where Zoe's funeral had been held that afternoon.

"Could you turn that up?" I called out to the bartender.

The ferret-faced man who looked like Al Pacino with bad hair was washing glasses in a sink at the other end of the bar. He dried his hands on the towel hanging over his shoulder, then picked up a remote control and raised the television's volume.

As I listened to a woman reporter deliver a rambling and unnecessarily detailed description of Zoe's funeral, the bartender eased over, tilted his head up, and watched along with me. The reporter wrapped her story with a brief account of Plato Karsarkis' own death in a plane crash and then summarized some of the more outrageous stories that had swirled around him in life.

"Good riddance," the bartender mumbled in a thick Eastern European accent of some kind. "The bastard."

"I'm sorry?" I asked automatically, not entirely certain I'd heard the man correctly.

"I said the bastard got what he deserved," the bartender repeated, gesturing with his towel toward the TV set. "Plato Karsarkis getting killed like that, I meant. Not the little girl dying, God bless her."

I said nothing.

"That scumbag was a piece-of-shit criminal and everybody treated him like a movie star," the bartender snorted in disgust. "Made a fortune helping the rag heads kill people. Got what he deserved, if you ask me."

"There was never a trial," I said. "Plato Karsarkis might not have been convicted of anything if one had taken place."

The man snorted again. "I expect you got that right, pal. Make the crime big enough and nobody ever did it. Notice how that always works?"

The bartender tossed his towel up in the air, caught it smartly, and scrubbed a spot off the bar. Then he turned the television set back down and returned to washing his glasses.

I let him, finishing my whiskey in silence.

The next morning, wrapped in a hotel bathrobe and trying to read the *New York Times* over toast and coffee, I found I couldn't stop thinking about what the bartender had said.

He was right about one thing, of course. The really big crimes had little or nothing to do with justice. What they had to do with was power. I didn't like it, but I understood it. What I didn't understand, at least not yet, was exactly what the really big crime had really been in this case.

Was it Plato Karsarkis' deal to peddle smuggled oil and launder the profits? Was it corrupt Asian politicians taking payoffs when their countries bought the oil? Was it some cockamamie National Security Council scheme to subvert Indonesia? Was it the secret diversion of American weapons to terrorists who then used them to kill hundreds of kids? Was it somebody, maybe even the Americans in the White House who had set the whole scheme into motion in the first place, murdering people in an effort to retrieve tape recordings implicating them in the plot?

Or was it something worse? Something even worse than that.

Was it that a few powerful men knew exactly what they had done; that their scheming and plotting had set in motion events that they could no longer control; that innocents had been killed as a consequence; and that they were all going to get away with it?

When I thought about it that way, a hard knot of anger began to form deep within me. If they did get away with it, wouldn't I be responsible now? Didn't I possess both the means and the ability to see they *didn't* get away with it?

I knew I had to forget all about abstract concepts like good and evil, fairness and injustice, honor and shame. What I had to focus on now was power. Who had it, how they used it, and where it was.

I knew where it was.

The White House was just at the other end of the Delta Shuttle, hardly more than an hour from New York.

In the bottom of my bag there was a flat manila envelope and inside that envelope was the printout of the NIA files Kate had given me together with the three microcassettes Plato Karsarkis had committed into my care. When I had packed in Bangkok, I had put them into my suitcase without really understanding why I was doing it.

But now I understood completely.

What Karsarkis had wanted me to do all along was to carry a message to the White House, to my old roommate Billy Redwine in particular. The message was to have been that Plato Karsarkis wanted off the hook for everything he had done or he would make them pay. He would tell the world what they had done, what the White House had done, and he would bring them down with him. He would bring them all down.

Plato Karsarkis might be dead, but the soul of his message still lived on the three little cassettes I had in my possession. The time had come for people to start doing the right thing, not because Karsarkis would expose them if they didn't, but just because it was right.

I tossed the *New York Times* onto the couch and got dressed. Then I packed and took a cab to LaGuardia, where I caught the Delta Shuttle to Washington.

Fifty One

BILLY REDWINE AND I hadn't actually spoken since the time a year or so ago when he had flown all the way to Phuket to hear my tale about the Asian Bank of Commerce and the string of dead bodies somebody in Washington had been leaving across Asia to hush up the real story behind its collapse.

I was at National Airport waiting for my bag and trying to decide what to do now that I was in Washington when I noticed a big Hertz sign at baggage claim. That sounded like as good a start as any, so I went out to the curb, caught the yellow and black Hertz bus, and about half an hour later was tooling up the George Washington Parkway in a shiny red Mustang that smelled of new vinyl and old tobacco.

I pushed the radio buttons and found an oldies station and all at once I remembered how much I missed cruising the streets of a city listening to music on a car radio. In Bangkok or Hong Kong or Singapore, they didn't get the idea at all. Driving just for the sheer hell of it was such an American thing to do. It wasn't a concept that translated very well.

The disk jockey started playing the original Rolling Stones version of *Honky Tonk Woman* and I slapped out the rhythm on the steering wheel with my palms.

Damn, that felt good.

When I got to Key Bridge, I turned off the Parkway and crossed over the Potomac into Georgetown. A brisk wind slashed at the city from the east, bringing with it a damp chill off the water and leaving piles of yellow leaves splotched with crimson banked like snowdrifts against the hubcaps of parked cars. The wind spun the dry leaves into miniature tornadoes and lifted scraps of paper and sailed them over the car like tiny squadrons of paper airplanes. The Four Seasons was full, but the Georgetown Inn had a room, so I left the car with the doorman, got my bag out of the trunk, and checked in.

Then I picked up the telephone and called the White House switchboard.

I left a message with a woman who identified herself as Billy Redwine's administrative assistant. I think that meant she was his secretary. She was cool and correct, and her voice contained no suggestion she expected my call ever to be returned by anyone at all, let alone by Billy Redwine.

It was less than twenty minutes before the telephone in my room rang.

"Mr. Shepherd?" It was the voice of a different woman, her tone professional but with subtle hints of deference and warmth. "Mr. Redwine wonders if you are free for dinner."

"That would be fine."

"Do you know the Old Ebbit Grill?"

"I do."

"Could you meet Mr. Redwine there tonight at eight?"

I told her I could.

"If you will give Mr. Redwine's name to the hostess, they will seat you at his usual table."

THE OLD EBBIT Grill is right across Fifteenth Street from the Treasury Building, barely a five-minute walk from the White House.

I left the Mustang with the valet, then lingered out front for a few minutes examining the place's Greek Revival façade. At exactly eight o'clock, I took a deep breath and pushed through the revolving glass door.

Naturally Billy hadn't turned up yet. I declined the hostess' invitation to go to Billy's table and instead went into the bar to wait.

Down one wall of the bar was a line of booths with tufted, rust-colored velvet benches and forest-green tops. Each booth had a little table lamp with a yellow-cream shade that threw a dim but appealing glow. A huge, gilt-framed oil portrait of a woman with impossibly ivory-colored skin and an outsized rump hung just above the long mahogany bar and there were some stuffed deer heads scattered around together with one wild boar and something else I took to be a walrus. Heavy brass chandeliers, vaguely art deco in appearance, hung from a very high tin ceiling, undoubtedly fake. The tiny bulbs flickering inside frosted glass cylinders made them look almost like gaslights.

I slid into an empty booth, laid down the large manila envelope I had brought with me, and ordered a Bushmills and water. Somewhere far in the background I heard Frank Sinatra sing the first notes of "Nancy with the Laughing Face."

When my drink came I slipped at it slowly and watched a television set tuned to CNBC that was hanging over the bar. It was discreet and silent, captions flickering over the bottom of the picture, and nobody but me seemed to be paying the slightest attention to it. The music changed to "Can't We Be Friends," then "That Old Feeling," and finally, "I Can't Get Started with You."

Billy was an actor at heart, and when I saw him walking across the bar toward me about fifteen minutes later he looked every inch of one. He moved at a stately pace, rhythmically slapping a rolled-up copy of *The Wall Street Journal* against his thigh, nodding perfunctorily at the occupants of some tables and pointedly ignoring others. There were a couple of what I assumed to be Secret Service types trailing him and they sized me up professionally as he approached the booth. Since they didn't shoot me, I guess I passed whatever test they were using.

"This fucking town," Billy sighed as he sat down. "This goddamned motherfucking town."

Then suddenly he straightened up and looked around as if he had just realized where he was.

"What the fuck are you doing in the bar?" Billy asked. "Didn't they offer to take you to my table?"

"I like bars. All kinds of interesting things happen in bars."

Billy shook his head and slid back out of the booth. He nodded toward the main dining room and shortly afterward we settled in at a table in a far back corner of the restaurant. There was no one else within earshot and Billy's escorts took another table strategically placed near the main entrance.

Almost immediately an elderly waiter in a long apron materialized and placed a drink at Billy's elbow, a martini containing two olives impaled on a red plastic sword.

"Evening, Mr. Redwine."

"Evening, Paul."

I had brought my Bushmills from the bar so I lifted it and tilted the glass toward Billy in a half-assed toast. He lifted the martini glass in turn, tilted it at me, then took a long, slow pull.

"Man," he said when he put it down, "that is so good."

After that, Billy folded his arms and leaned back a little. He tilted his head slightly to one side and studied me with a half-smile on his face.

"So what kind of outrageous horseshit have you gotten yourself into this time, Jack, my boy?"

I reached across the table and put the brown envelope I had brought with me in front of Billy. Inside was the copy of the email intercepts Darcy had printed off Kate's disk. I kept the cassettes in my pocket.

Billy eyed the envelope as warily as if I had just laid a rattlesnake down in front of him, which in a manner of speaking I guess I had.

"What?" he asked, looking back and forth from me to the envelope.

"It's some stuff you ought to see."

"Stuff?"

"You going to look at it?" I asked. "Or are we going to dance around a little first?"

Billy laughed at that, then he extracted a pair of half-glasses from his breast pocket and slipped them on. I watched his face as he flipped quickly through the pages, although he remained mostly expressionless. Taking a sip of his martini, he went back to the beginning and read carefully through everything, then slid the pages back into the envelope and returned his reading glasses to his jacket pocket.

"So," I asked, "what do you think?"

"I think you've got some pretty good contacts in Thailand."

"Is what I read there true?" I pointed to the envelope. "Were the marshals in Phuket with instructions to kill Karsarkis?"

"Ah, Jack…" Billy shifted his weight slightly and ran his fingers up and down the stem of the martini glass. "Everything around here is a little true and nothing is completely true. You ought to know that."

"Don't bullshit me, Billy. Why were the marshals really in Phuket? To bring Karsarkis back, or to kill him?"

"It's not that simple, Jack."

"Yes, it *is* that simple."

"Look, Jack, there were different people there. They had… different responsibilities."

Billy flicked a glance at his minders, then he cleared his throat and tapped at the table with his forefinger.

"We were hoping Karsarkis would see the wisdom of coming back on his own. On the other hand, if we could have found a way to snatch him, we would have done it. I don't mind telling you that. But nobody really wanted to kill him."

"Which means you might have. If you thought you had to."

"Yeah, we might have if we thought somebody else was going to snatch him first."

"God *damn*, Billy—" I started in, but he interrupted me before I could get started.

"What else could we have done, Jack? Just sat there with our thumbs up our butts while Karsarkis became Exhibit A in the great hit parade of American fuck-ups? Hell, Karsarkis would probably *rather* we'd shot him than let the crazies get him."

"Look, Billy, there's something important here that you don't know anything about."

Billy nodded slowly. "That wouldn't surprise me."

"Karsarkis was going to spill it all," I said. "He thought if he just told the world everything he knew, that would protect him. Then no one would want to kill him anymore to shut him up."

"How do you know that?"

"Before Karsarkis got on that plane, he came to see me. He told me he was going to go public."

"Huh," Billy said. "How about that?"

"There's more."

Billy said nothing.

"He told me exactly what it was he was going to spill."

Billy blinked then, twice in rapid succession, but otherwise his eyes gave nothing away.

Fifty Two

"PLATO KARSARKIS SPILLED the beans to me before he got on his plane, Billy. He spilled the fucking beans to me about everything he had been doing and all the rest of it as well."

"And by the rest of it you would be referring to…"

"Cynthia Kim, the NSC operation in Indonesia, and the explosives and detonators used in the Bali bombing."

Billy didn't say anything right away. He just scratched the back of his neck and examined the ceiling, which kept me from seeing his face clearly. I assumed that was the whole idea.

"And there's one other thing you ought to know, too, pal," I went on before he could regroup. "Karsarkis bugged your debriefing of Cynthia Kim in Singapore. He had tapes of the whole thing, tapes with your voice on them."

Billy stopped pretending to study the ceiling and shifted his eyes back to mine. "Have you heard them?" he asked.

"No," I answered truthfully. "I haven't."

"But you're sure he had them."

"Yes," I said. "Absolutely sure."

"How can you be so sure if you didn't hear them?"

"You've known me for over twenty years, Billy. Would I tell you I was sure if I wasn't?"

Billy's expression never changed. He was a cool one. Whatever else he might be, I had to give him that at least.

"Well, *damn*," he sighed, flicking his eyes around the room and then back to mine before taking a deep breath. "Don't that beat all?"

Looking back it was probably only a minute or two before Billy spoke again, but at the time the silence had seemed to stretch on for much longer than that.

"Do you know if he had the tapes with him when his plane blew up?" Billy asked.

"Not for sure."

"But you think he did."

I nodded.

"What about copies?" Billy asked. "Were there any copies?"

"There may have been," I said, avoiding Billy's eyes. I wondered if Billy noticed me avoid his eyes, but he just nodded slowly a few times, giving no indication of it if he had.

"I could always have those guys," he inclined his head toward his security men, "come over here and torture you."

"You could," I said, "but you probably won't."

"No." Billy made a little popping sound with his lips. "I probably won't."

The waiter returned unbidden and replaced Billy's empty glass with a fresh martini. I noticed he didn't offer to do anything along similar lines with my nearly empty glass of Bushmills.

"So what happens now?" Billy asked after he had taken a sip.

"I don't know," I admitted. "I guess I was hoping…"

I stopped talking and stared for a minute at a spot on the tablecloth.

"I really don't know," I said again.

Billy nodded as if that all somehow made perfect sense.

"Look, Jack…"

Billy paused. He look as if he was trying to make up his mind about something and I waited for him to decide on whatever it was.

"A lot of things are more complicated than they seem," he said after a moment.

"Did your people blow up that plane, Billy?"

"*My* people?" Billy smiled slightly at that, although I thought he looked tired and a little sad when he did. "No, not my people."

"But somebody's people?"

Billy put his glass down again and adjusted its position slightly. He didn't say anything.

"Then let me put this plainly just to make sure there's no misunderstanding between us," I said. "You're willing to let me think it is at least possible *someone* in the government of the United States blew up a plane in order to kill Plato Karsarkis and keep him from telling the world what he knew about White House involvement in covert operations that turned sour."

Billy leaned across the table. Lowering his voice he tapped me on the back of the wrist with one finger.

"You do not have the first fucking idea how much is possible, Jack. Governments do things all the time that in your wildest imagination you would never begin to believe. We do what we do because—"

"Oh, please," I interrupted. "Spare me the for-the-sake-of-the-greater-good speech. Could you just do that for me?"

"Sure," Billy said. "I can do that for you. If you want me to."

We sat for a while in silence again after that, me looking at the wall behind Billy and him watching the room over my shoulder.

"Who was it, Billy?" I asked him finally. "Who sent those guys to kill Karsarkis?"

Billy shook his head, but he didn't say anything.

"How about me then? I asked. "Who send those guys who tried to kill *me*?

"You may not believe this, Jack, but nobody wanted to kill you."

"You're right. I don't believe that."

"They thought it was Karsarkis in that car," Billy said. "It was just a coincidence that you were there instead."

"Nothing about any of this shit *ever* turns out to be a coincidence," I said. "Besides, Karsarkis told me it was you who was behind it."

"*Me?*"

"Not you personally. The White House. The National Security Council. The boys in the basement. You were the ones who wanted to keep Karsarkis from talking because you were afraid of what he was going to say. You were the ones who wanted to shut him up."

Billy Redwine nodded, but he didn't say anything.

"Was it you, Billy? Did you send those guys to Phuket?"

"No."

"Then who?"

"I…don't…fucking…know." Billy waved his hand quickly back and forth through the air as if that would brush it all away. "What part of that don't you understand?"

"If you wanted to know, you would."

"Listen to me for a second here, Jack. Just listen to me." Billy spoke in the kind of soothing tone normally reserved for dealing with animals that were dangerous and unpredictable. "You're playing in the big leagues now. Be careful."

"Is that some kind of a threat, Billy?"

He pushed his tongue into one cheek and held it there a while, and I thought I saw in his eyes the look of a decision being made.

"You know more about international money and banking than anybody I've ever met, Jack, and that's where the action is these days. We could use somebody like you."

"What are you talking about?"

"Come work with us."

"*Us?* Who's us? The White House? NSC? The CIA?"

"Ah, Jack…" Billy shook his head slowly, "things aren't that simple anymore."

"What the fuck does *that* mean? Sometimes you play your cards so close to the vest I'm not sure you're holding any. Anyway, you can't be serious."

"Oh, but I am. Dead fucking serious. You haven't put a foot wrong so far. I'm very impressed."

"Exactly what was it I did that was so damned impressive?"

"You didn't do anything, Jack. There you are, handed one of the really ugly secrets of our time, and you didn't do a damned thing. You stayed calm and unruffled, and eventually you came to me, which is exactly what you should have done."

"Then I wonder why I'm really not all that proud of myself right now?"

"I need you with me, Jack," Billy pressed.

"What would you have done if I'd gone public?" I asked.

"What do you mean?"

"I didn't have to come to you. I could have gone straight to the Senate Intelligence Committee. They would have probably been pretty interested. Held big public hearings. That kind of thing."

Billy gave a little half-shrug. "We would have blown you right out of the water."

"You mean you would have had me killed."

I didn't make a question out of it.

"Well…" Billy looked as if he was thinking about it. "Not unless we really had to."

After that he snorted in a way he apparently thought amounted to an ironic laugh.

"I'm joking, Jack."

"No," I said, "you're not."

"Yeah, I am…mostly."

After that we slipped off into a silence in which we avoided looking at each other. When it became obvious Billy was prepared to wait me out all night if he had to, I took a deep breath and slugged back the rest of my whiskey. Then I leaned forward and folded my arms on the table.

"You're going to have to convince me all this was really okay, Billy. You really are going to have to convince me, or…"

"Or what?" he asked when I hesitated.

"I don't know, Billy. I can't tell you yet."

Billy nodded slowly at that. He lifted his martini glass, but when he realized it was empty he put it down again. Then he leaned forward and folded his own arms on the table.

"Regardless of what Plato Karsarkis may have told you, Jack, and in spite of what you may think you've guessed on your own, there's a lot more going here than you know about."

"Guys like you always say things like that, Billy, but—"

He waved me impatiently into silence.

"It's smelly shit. Stuff you would never believe. The only way anything is *ever* going to be okay is if some hero steps up and hammers a stake right through the bad guys' fucking hearts." Billy cocked his thumb and tapped himself in the chest with it. "That would be me."

I said nothing.

"But to pull that off," he went on, "I've got to have somebody I can trust to do a little business for me from time to time." He squinted slightly, then reversed his hand and reached out and jabbed me in the chest with his forefinger. "That would be you."

I pushed away his extended finger and folded my arms again.

"You're a paper shuffler, Billy, just like I am. What do you think you're going to do? Throw your laptop at the villains? Besides, you've got to find them first."

"I can do that."

"How?"

"It's called reconnaissance by fire, my friend. You shoot at the trees. If somebody shoots back, they're there."

"Look, Billy, I don't—"

"And there's one other thing you need to know."

I waited.

"Two weeks from tomorrow, the president is going to announce a little reshuffle in the White House staff."

"You're leaving?"

"Hardly."

I watched Billy carefully and I could have sworn I saw him sit up a little straighter.

"The president is going to announce my appointment as his new National Security Advisor," he said. Then he leaned back and cut me a major wink. "I'm going to be running the NSC."

For a moment I was too flabbergasted to say anything, but Billy was plainly expecting me to so I did my best.

"Well, congratulations…" I fumbled.

"Thank you, Jack."

"I mean…well, that's great…but, Billy, after what I've told you tonight, how in the world could you even think about—"

"Just shut the fuck up, Jack. Let's order some red meat and a lot of booze and you can hear me out. Then if you want to tell me to stick my offer straight up my ass, go ahead. But listen to me first. You owe your old roommate that much at least."

Dinner went on for over an hour after that. Billy did all of the talking. I chewed at my food without tasting it, and I nodded and said uh-huh a lot, but looking back, I can't remember what I ate or even very much about what Billy Redwine said to me.

When we exchanged goodnights on Fifteenth Street just outside the Old Ebbit Grill, Billy insisted I meet him at his office the following afternoon at four. At first I refused. I was tried and a little angry, and I hadn't decided what I was going to do next, or if I was going to do anything at all. But I knew Billy wasn't going to take no for an answer so eventually I gave up arguing with him and just nodded.

After that I stood for a long time on the sidewalk and watched as Billy and his minders crossed Fifteenth Street and walked back toward the White House. I followed them with my eyes until they were lost to sight behind the line of marble columns marking the north portico of the Treasury Building.

I have no idea at all why I did.

Fifty Three

I DIDN'T LEAVE a wake-up call so the next morning I slept late.

When I finally got up I ordered coffee and toast from room service, then pulled on a hotel bathrobe and retrieved the *Washington Post* from outside my door. I skimmed the paper while I was waiting for my breakfast and, after the waiter had come and gone, I turned on CNN. With half an ear, I listened to the weather while I drank two cups of coffee, then spread marmalade on a slice of toast and ate it.

I went to the bathroom and was coming out again when I heard Billy Redwine's name mentioned. The main news had just begun and I sat down on the couch and watched while a smooth-skinned black woman with short hair and round glasses read the lead story.

"...according to Vernon Jackson, the Park Service patrol officer who discovered the body just after seven this morning. Ft. Macy Park is a little-visited civil war monument on the Potomac River in Northern Virginia and the presence of Redwine's Mercedes in the parking lot just off the George Washington Parkway at such an early hour had attracted the attention of the patrol officer. Upon investigation, he found Redwine's body on a grassy slope about two hundred yards into the park. At this hour details remain sketchy, but sources tell CNN the cause of death appears to have been a single gunshot wound to the head. Redwine's death is being investigated as a suicide. There has not yet been any comment from the White House although the President is expected to issue a full statement this morning. In other news at this hour…"

I pushed the mute button on the remote and sat without moving for a long while as I watched the woman's lips flap silently. Once she reached up and pushed her glasses back against the bridge of her nose with her forefinger, but the gesture was quick and absent-minded and I imagined she did all the time without really noticing it.

A little later I stood up and walked over to my breakfast tray and poured another cup of coffee.

The coffee was cold, but I drank it anyway.

THREE DAYS AFTER that, late in the afternoon, I took the Mustang and drove out the George Washington Parkway to look for Ft. Macy Park. The day was overcast and bloodless and the Potomac River oozed lazily toward the Atlantic under a distant pewter sky.

The entrance to the park was marked by nothing but a small highway sign half hidden by a curve. I almost missed it.

A narrow asphalt road ran slightly uphill from the Parkway through a thick forest of oak and birch trees and it ended in a small parking area surrounded by a low, grassy bank. A deep coating of dead brown leaves covered the asphalt. They crunched under my tires as I parked the car.

Ft. Macy had been part of Washington's defensive perimeter during the civil war, but there was little recognizable left of it now, just a few forlorn-looking cannons and some earthwork mounds heavily overgrown with weeds. As I stood in the parking area looking around, I couldn't see any obvious pathways or jogging trails leading into the interior of the park, but I had brought a copy of *TIME* magazine that had a detailed story about Billy's death, so I took it out and folded it back to the page with a map of the park that illustrated where his body had been found.

The climb up the bank surrounding the parking area was harder than it looked and my loafers slipped and slid on the decaying leaves. Eventually I hauled myself up to the top by pulling on a dead branch that was hanging off a birch tree. On the other side of the bank was an undulating beige and yellow ocean of leaves that stretched all the way to the Potomac River broken only by clumps of tall, spindly trees mostly bared of their leaves, a few rusted iron cannon supported by wooden wagon wheels, and one lonely-looking picnic table.

I consulted the map in *TIME* again, turning it to match the contours of the land, and I traced a course with my eyes toward the spot where Billy's body had been found. Starting down the back of the slope in that direction, I slipped on the leaves and fell, but I caught myself with my hands before I was completely down and kept going. My feet made crackling noises in the dead grass and far in the distance I could hear the sound of the Potomac River where it squeezed through a rocky narrows just below the park.

According to the magazine, Billy was stretched out on his back on a grassy slope about two hundred yards into the park, so neatly placed he might have already been embalmed and laid out for viewing. He looked as if he had shot himself once in the roof of the mouth with a .38-caliber revolver. The bullet went straight into his brain and he died almost instantly. There had been very little blood.

The slope wasn't very hard to find. It was near the river, just past the one lonely picnic table, but it was covered with tall weeds rather than grass and it was more like three hundred yards away from the parking area, not two.

On the whole, it was a strange place for a suicide. If you intended to kill yourself, why would you work so hard to get to a place that had so little to recommend it? Why would you stumble hundreds of yards in the dark through rotting leaves and up and down pathless slopes before you sat down in a patch of weeds, put the gun barrel in your mouth, tasted the sour metal and your own fear, and pulled the trigger?

I stood on that slope for a long time looking down at the place where Billy's body had been. There was a fresh coating of leaves over everything now and no suggestion at all that anything out of the ordinary had ever happened there. Still, I had no difficultly picturing it. I could imagine Billy's body laid out right there, neatly dressed in a white shirt and dark suit, stark in its contrast against the yellow and tan leaves.

I took the cassettes Plato Karsarkis had given me out of my pocket and juggled them back and forth, shuffling them from one hand to another. Just three little plastic boxes capable of doing more damage to the White House than the biggest truck bomb.

But now that Billy was dead, what were the tapes? Proof that someone close to the president had gone too far? That someone with the president's ear may have been behind some slick and shadowy operation and then tried to cover it up when it spun out of control? That someone so racked with guilt over what he had done had gone out in the dead of night and shot himself through the head?

That would be that, wouldn't it? Mystery solved, blame assigned, case closed.

You deserve a better epitaph than that, Billy, my friend. You really do.

I began unspooling each of the cassettes with my fingers. As I worked I watched the narrow brown tape slide through my hands and snake to the ground. Curling into the rotting leaves right on the spot where Billy's body had been found, it fell in masses of loops and whirls almost invisible against the russet-colored compost.

Just as I finished it started to snow. The flakes were big and wet and turned to water as soon as they hit. I pulled up the collar of my jacket and wiped the wet snow off my face.

I would like to say it was over then, that it ended there.

But it wasn't, and it didn't.

Billy Redwine hadn't committed suicide, of course. He was murdered, shot in the head and dumped in a rundown park because somebody bigger than he was thought it would be better that way.

There was always somebody bigger, wasn't there? There was always one more rung on the ladder.

It was never over. It never ended.

I jammed my hands in my pockets and started the long walk back to the car.

THE END

About the Author

JAKE NEEDHAM is an American screen and television writer who began writing crime novels when he realized he really didn't like movies and television very much.

Mr. Needham has lived and worked in Hong Kong, Singapore, and Thailand for over twenty years. He is a lawyer by education and has held a number of significant positions in both the public and private sectors where he participated in a lengthy list of international operations he has no intention of telling you about. He, his wife, and their two sons now divide their time between homes in Thailand and the United States.

Please visit Jake Needham's website at www.JakeNeedham.com for excerpts from his other books or to join his mailing list and keep up to date on his new novels. Read his 'Letters from Asia' at www.JakeNeedham.com/blog for more about the places, the people, and the things that make up Jack Shepherd's world.

OTHER BOOKS IN THE JACK SHEPHERD SERIES

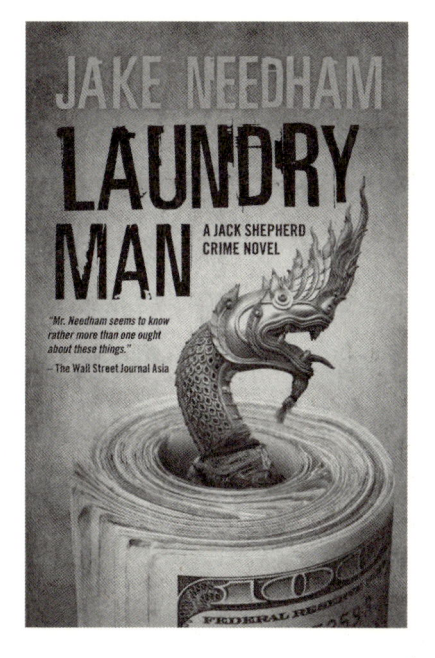

LAUNDRY MAN
ISBN: 978 981 4361 27 9

Once a high-flying international lawyer, part of the inner circle of government power, Jack Shepherd has abandoned the savage politics of Washington for the backwater of Bangkok. Now he is just an unremarkable professor at an unimportant university in an insignificant city. Or is he?

A secretive Asian bank collapses under dubious circumstances. A former law partner Shepherd thought was murdered reveals himself as the force behind the disgraced bank and coerces Shepherd into tracking the money that disappeared in the collapse. A twisting trail of deceit leads Shepherd from Bangkok to Hong Kong and eventually to an isolated villa on the island of Phuket where Shepherd confronts the evil at the heart of a monstrous game of international treachery.

A lawyer among people who laugh at the law, a friend in a land where today's allies are tomorrow's fugitives, Jack Shepherd battles a global tide of corruption, extortion and murder that threatens to engulf both him and the new life he has worked so hard to build.

OTHER BOOKS IN THE JACK SHEPHERD SERIES

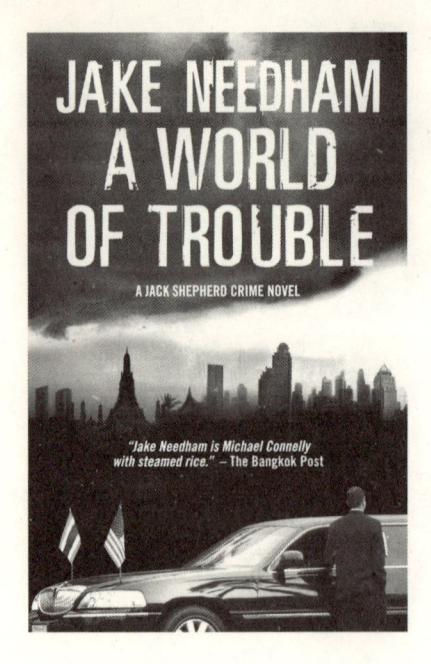

A WORLD OF TROUBLE
(Spring 2012)
ISBN: 978 981 4361 51 4

Jack Shepherd is sick of Washington politics, sick of corporate law, and even a little sick of himself. So he hits the road looking for a new start, makes a couple of wrong turns, and somehow winds up in Hong Kong. Now he needs a job, and being General Chalerm Kitnarok's lawyer is a job, so he takes it.

He could do worse. Charlie Kitnarok is the world's 98th richest man and controls billions in assets. But he's also a former prime minister of Thailand living in exile in Dubai where he's plotting his return to power. For Shepherd, that could be a real problem. The new Thai prime minister is Kathleeya Srisophon, a woman with whom Shepherd was once involved.

Then Shepherd discovers Charlie is smuggling arms to his supporters in Thailand. Is he going to assassinate Kate and use the Thai army to seize control of the country?

Thailand is hurtling closer and closer to a bloody civil war. And as unlikely as it sounds, Jack Shepherd may be the only person on earth who can stop it.